The World of Evendaar

Book Three

The Demon Revealed

⚖

A. R. Winterstaar

Cover Illustration by Anastasia Ward (akward13@live.com)

First Published 2016

Second Edition May 2018

ISBN: 0991479440

ISBN-13: 978-0991479443

Evendaar Publishing

www.evendaar.com

More books in the

World of Evendaar Series:

Book One:

The Child Revealed

Book Two:

The Queen Revealed

Book Four:

The Warrior Revealed

Discover more by visiting

www.evendaar.com

DEDICATION

L.J.W.

A warrior. A gentleman. A whiskey-drinker.

CONTENTS

THE PROPHECY OF THE END OF THE WORLD

"A child born into the Golden Age shall be stolen from the Light and hidden from the eyes of the world…

…Only the Hidden Child shall defend the Throne from the Favored and cast the Shadows into the Light to restore the Glory of my Chosen Ones on the Throne of my Kingdom.

Beware and rejoice for only in the greatest darkness does the brightest light shine."

"The Empress of a Dark God will want to burn the blood of the Lost Child Hidden.

The Child must sacrifice a fear of the Dark and go without a Magek to save the World from an evil pestilence that will destroy all Life in its path.

All who defy the Child shall burn to ashes, and those ashes shall feed the North Wind."

Excerpts taken from "The Prophecy of the End of the World" and printed by Pere Manus and dictated by the Child Prophet Celestina and Voice of the Goddess Serena. Translated from the old tongue by Pere Raindor Marchant.

PROLOGUE

The young man stood at the window of his small chamber and looked out over the gardens of the Golden Palace. He pursed his lips, thinking hard.

This Unisian Queen was proving stronger and wilier than he had anticipated. Looking down, he ran his hands over the heavy, wooden frame of the Magic Glass, and willed an image of Queen Adelena to appear but all he saw was green static. Again. He ground his teeth and cursed. The witch had covered herself completely in the dark magic of her Marchant blood, and now she was invisible to him. Though he hadn't expected to be able to see her at the Belvoir Estate, with its curse on magic, he had since discovered that only days ago the queen had left Belvoir Estate for the Grey Palace in the company of the Marchant prince, taking her children, the Queen's Guard and Charlie with her.

When the court of the Golden Palace discovers that their precious queen has aligned herself with the wicked Marchant prince there will be chaos, the young man thought. *But what is she planning to do, and what does she need Prince Rainere for?*

The young man couldn't help but think the very worst of people. It was how he had managed to control the snake pit that was the court of the Golden Palace for so long. Yet there was nothing he hated more than chaos, because chaos presented opportunities to the underserving when they were clever enough to seek power in disorder. If the false Queen Adelena thought that she could bring that kind of unrest to the kingdom of Unisia, then she was very much mistaken.

But what to do about her? The young man had already started to undermine the queen's reputation in the smaller towns outside of Concordis, but perhaps now was the time to really saturate the powerful Guild Class with anti-queen propaganda in the city center. Then, hopefully, it would be the people themselves who would drag the queen off her throne.

In his role as the Boss in the criminal underworld of Concordis, there was much he could do to create dissent and feed the rumor mill. *Yet perhaps nasty propaganda won't be enough to destroy the reputation of the queen when she arrives with the Fire Orchid stamens,* the young man thought. *Maybe actions instead of words are needed to really make the people actually rise up out of their comfortable lives and demand her head on a pike.*

The young man's mind spun with all the twisted possibilities until, suddenly, he knew what he needed to do. Moving to the rosewood desk in the corner of his chamber, he opened a drawer and took out a small gilt box no bigger than a book. Holding his breath, the young man opened the box and looked upon the three tiny glass vials on their velvet cushion. He picked up two of the vials. The metal stoppers clinked together in his hand as the motion stirred up the contents, suspended in a clear fluid.

It had taken him decades to collect this poison and he couldn't help but feel a spark of pride. He was the only wizard in Unisia who knew the true cause of the Summer Influenza, and where to find it. He smiled as it churned about in the vials, the black particles glittering in the sunlight. So pretty, yet so very wicked - he called it God Dust.

The young man placed the vials in the inside pocket of his jacket and felt their weight against his chest. Even through the Sticking Glass, the magic made the hairs on the back of his neck stand up. Shaking off his discomfort, he quickly replaced the box with the last glass vial back in its little drawer and grabbed his cloak and silk scarf from the chair. There was really no time to waste now that he had made the decision, yet he hesitated. The fuzzy green static had cleared from the surface of the mirror, and the young man's face appeared, a frown pulling his brow down over bright blue eyes. *Should I really be the cause of such devastation to our own people? The Guild Class are mostly St Lucidis descendants even if they are only commoners now.*

The Influenza season had started out milder than expected this year, but with his help it would spread like wildfire through the middle-class neighborhoods of the Guild Quarter. Born with less and less magic in their blood, the children of the middle-classes grew weaker with every generation. With no claim to the strength or favor of the goddess Serena's magic, these children marred the glory of the St

Lucidis line. Their deaths would serve two purposes: angering both the magical and non-magical population and cleansing the city of their common blood. This economy should be celebrated, not feared.

The pain will be short-lived, the young man promised himself. *The Summer Influenza is fast-acting and those who suffer will die quickly. Once the funerals are over, the people will be angry and aggrieved, looking for someone to blame for the deaths of their non-magic kin. Then the queen will come dancing back from the Belvoir Carnival, looking like a callous bitch, feting the Marchant prince as her own people die in droves. The people will rise up against her, and all my problems will be solved.*

With a quick step, the young man made his way to the portal next to the unlit fireplace and jabbed a finger into the invisible door to ignite the magic. He knew for sure now that only he could do what needed to be done. His resolve strengthened, the young man stepped through the swirling green portal.

CHAPTER ONE

"The Journey Home"

It was at the end of a long afternoon when Adelena finally untangled herself from a sleepy Stella and climbed out of the carriage. After so long in the dim interior, the late afternoon sun was blinding. Adele stumbled on the uneven cobblestones of the courtyard, swallowing a curse. The royal party had pulled into an inn on the outskirts of Pettington, a highway town halfway between the Belvoir Estate and the Golden Palace. She pulled at her sweaty clothes, all too aware that she looked and smelled like she had been sitting in a carriage for five hours with three small children and their over-grown puppies.

Adele squinted across the dusty courtyard of the inn and saw that General Ohrig was speaking to a man in the doorway. By his plain, well-cut clothing, she guessed he was the proprietor. An older blonde woman peeked out from behind the proprietor and Adele caught her eye. The woman squealed in either fright or excitement and ducked back inside only to appear a moment later without her work apron on. She almost skipped over to Adele and then dropped into a deep curtsy.

"Your Majesty, welcome to our humble abode." The woman's voice was shrill and caught in a lisp. "My name is Mrs. Beverly Byers and that over there is my husband, Mr. Joseph Byers." When she stood up again, Mrs. Byers pale blue eyes were cold, though a smile stretched across her thin lips. "To be considered worthy of your royal-ness is just the highest honor, we are overjoyed that you would bless our humble lodging with your royal presence. Though those bigger inns in town might have more luxuries, we know you will find that we humble folk make up for all of that with our warmth and hospitality."

Adele let the woman gush at her, more because she had no idea how to stop the river of words than from any desire to accept such an awkward welcome. General Ohrig had picked this modest inn because it was so out of the way, and because low suburban buildings surrounded it, making it easier to defend than a hotel in town would be in case an emergency might arise, like if an angry wizard came looking for her. Adele would have preferred to ride into the night and camp, but Ohrig had pointed out that would expose the children to other hazards. Poor little Stella was still ill with the virus she'd picked up two days ago and needed a night of rest in a proper bed. At only two years old, she couldn't be expected to tolerate camping while she was so unwell.

Adele lent a hand to Seraphina, the young redheaded nanny who was carrying Stella out of the carriage, and then helped Natalie and Aaron leap to freedom. The puppies poured out in a stream of ears and tails, and immediately relieved themselves in front of the women and children. At only six and four, respectively, Natalie and Aaron found their puppies hysterically funny, but Adele caught the glare of Mrs. Byers as she eyed the wet mess on her cobblestones.

Aaron was laughing so hard he had tears in his little hazel eyes. "Hero said he…was going to…drink his own pee." Aaron's laughter stopped suddenly and he frowned in concern for his pet. "Seriously though, he said he is very very thirsty."

"What sweet little children!" trilled Mrs. Byers, whose chest and throat were now covered with blotchy, red hives, as Adele picked up that the anxiousness in Mrs. Byers manner couldn't be explained away as excitement. "Well, now, I just have to think where I'm going to put you all."

Mrs. Byers flapped a hand, and a young serving girl came bolting over from the stables where she'd been gawping, open-mouthed, at the royal party.

"Julie, see that the best rooms are aired and fresh for the royal family, and that our other guests move to the ground floor rooms." Mrs. Byers turned to Adele, her smile decidedly strained. "Nothing is too good for our queen."

"Please, there is no need to disturb the other guests," Adele protested. "We'll only be here for the night, and I will share a room with the children."

"Nonsense!" cried Mrs. Byers. "It is our pleasure to have you here, Your Majesty." She gestured for her husband to approach, as she pushed the serving girl off to her duties. The man shambled over, his face creased as if there was a bad smell in the air.

"Your Majesty, welcome." He nodded curtly. "I was just explaining to your general that we won't be able to accommodate your party tonight. We are only a poor inn. You would be better suited to a hotel in town." Mr. Byers spoke in short clipped sentences as if he was restraining himself from saying even less pleasant things. His large hands were wringing a saddlecloth so tightly that his knuckles were white. Adele noticed the way Mr. Byers' eyes darted to the each of the men of her Queen's Guard, as if he was counting them, or sizing them up.

"Mr. Byers!" shrieked his wife in horror and gave Adele another deep curtsy. "Forgive my husband, Your Majesty, he has been working in the sun all day and it's addled his senses."

"But Mrs. Byers, what about the meeting tonight?" Mr. Byers interjected. "Cancel it," snapped Mrs. Byers, sending her husband a warning glare. "We are now hosting *Her Majesty*, and the dear royal children, the meeting can wait."

Mrs. Byers turned back to her guests and Adele could see that the red flush had crept up from her throat to stain her cheeks as well. "Your Majesty, let me take you inside out of the sun. I can prepare an early dinner for you and serve it immediately, if you would like? Please, come with me."

Adele gathered up the children and made to follow Mrs. Byers, but she gestured to Ohrig to hang back a little so she could have a private word with him. "Ohrig, I don't like this at all. These people are clearly unhappy to have us here. Don't you think we should go somewhere else?"

Ohrig shook his head. "Your Majesty, I understand your concern, but I've stayed here before and know the layout of this place inside and out, and it's the last inn on the road to the Golden Palace that can hold us all. We'll just have to stay tonight and head out early tomorrow morning."

Still unsure, Adele nevertheless knew to trust her general and followed him inside. The common room of the inn was ordinary enough. Long, straight trestle tables stood in two rows of three, lined on each side by plank benches. There was a small stage set up in one corner of the room, its deck covered by a few plain wooden chairs and an antique-looking megaphone. The serving girl, Julie, was hurriedly taking down gold and white paper decorations and posters from the walls and shoving them into a sack. Adele led the children over to a large empty fireplace where two well-used armchairs stood, the leather covered in beer stains and a strong smell of urine and tobacco. She didn't let the children sit down.

"I've got the men checking every room and interviewing the other guests, Your Majesty," said Ohrig in a low voice, as they both watched Mrs. Byers who kept darting them nervous glances as she dashed in and out of the swinging kitchen doors. "According to Mr. Byers, there are only two other guests, both farmers in town for trade. Byers wouldn't tell me what that meeting was about but it sounded like they expected a big crowd, and he's mightily annoyed to cancel it."

Just then, Captain Lucky came in from the front door of the inn, looking furious. He had a rolled-up paper in his hand and made straight for Adele and the general.

"General, we have cleared the area. Both of the guests have decided to leave so as not to 'get in the way'. Their words." Lucky lowered his voice and his bright blue eyes were clouded with anger. "But QG Leith found this on the notice board outside the front gate. Mr. Byers claims he doesn't know who put it there because the notice board is owned by the local community, not the inn."

Lucky unrolled the poster and presented it to Adele. On it was one of the images used to advertise her coronation just weeks ago, but black crosses had been drawn over her eyes and the lettering had been replaced with the words: 'The Queen is Dead', and under that 'Long live the Regent Orgustus'.

Adele looked up at the white and gold bunting that was being pulled down off the walls by Mr. Byers and young Julie, and it all fell into place. "They must have planned some kind of political rally here tonight, and they are probably Lord Orgustus' supporters."

She gazed down at the poster and tried not to feel hurt that someone hated her enough to claim she was dead. Logically, Adele knew that she was a figurehead who had been foisted upon the population of Unisia by the High Wizard Ohren at the Golden Palace, yet it stung, if only because Lord Orgustus was such a horrible man.

The way Lord Orgustus saw it, Adele had stolen his power as regent in the court and he had attempted to undermine her at every turn, desperate to scrape it back. Lord Orgustus had been left in charge of the Golden Palace when Adele had taken her family to the nation of Sandar, just over a month ago, and she would not put it past him to launch a smear campaign against her, intending to discredit her to the people of Unisia before she had had a chance to prove herself.

"Your Majesty, this is treason." Lost in her thoughts, Adele hadn't sensed Ohrig's anger but it was clear that her general was as furious as Captain Lucky. His pale blue eyes were buried deep under his brow as he glared down at the poster in her hands. "We have laws against this kind of agitation."

"Which is why I imagine our hosts are so anxious, Ohrig," Adele agreed. "But you were right, we'll pass this one night here, and we'll be on our way tomorrow as early as we can. The Byers are new owners, and if they are Lord Orgustus's supporters they won't want to advertise our presence here anymore than we do."

"I'll turn them on a spit if they should dare," Ohrig blustered, but stopped when Adele raised her hand for him to lower his voice. "If Lord Orgustus is inciting the people of Unisia to rise up against you, Your Majesty, then it could mean that he is planning to take back his position as regent. The man is a blustering braggart, but he is very smart and very cunning. You would be wise to get his measure as soon as we return to the palace. That is of course, after you've confronted High Wizard Ohren about his lies."

Adele grimaced. She knew, beyond the shadow of a doubt, that she was not the golden St Lucidis queen that the high wizard had once called her. She was something much more complex, and much more dangerous. She was also sure that the high wizard was probably the only man in Unisia who could tell her what she really was.

Tonight, Adele needed to concentrate on what was in front of her, and that was her family and the Queen's Guard. They had all gone to hell and back in the last twenty-four hours and General Ohrig looked exhausted. In fact, all the men looked exhausted, which was only natural after the night that they'd had fighting in the Spiders' Nest.

"General, it is important we rest and regain our strength tonight because tomorrow we will face High Wizard Ohren, and for that I will need you all to be fighting fit. Take the night off. That's an order, so no arguments, alright?"

Ohrig gave a reluctant nod. He knew she had a point. "Of course, Your Majesty, but the rest of the QG's will sleep in shifts, so you and the children will always have some of us close at all times.

There was nothing more to say as Mrs. Byers had chosen that moment to announce dinner, and despite knowing they were resented by their hosts, Adele couldn't resist a hot meal.

CHAPTER TWO

"Once a Thief"

After dinner at the inn, Charlie followed the rest of the Queen's Guard into the dormitory room the men had been given for sleeping quarters. He stood in the doorway and grinned. *A full belly, now a bed to sleep in, and it hadn't cost me a coin of my own money,* he thought. *Life was pretty sweet when you lived in the light of a queen's gratitude.* For Charlie, this inn was like a palace.

"This place is a shithole," complained QG Bear as he threw his kit on the closest bed, and then dropped his considerable bulk after it. The bed frame creaked ominously. "I wouldn't let my dog sleep here."

QG Owens also took one of the single beds lined up, three against each wall, in the narrow room. "Sorry it's not to your liking, Princess, but I'll take this over camping on the side of the road. I heard the queen suggest it to the general, but he managed to talk her out of it."

Owens stretched out on the bed and tried to plump up the thin pillow, to no avail. He reached over and grabbed another off the bed next to him, propping the two of them behind his head. "Ah, that's all you need," he groaned appreciatively.

QG Pepper had just dropped his kit bag at the foot of the bed next to Owens, so it was his pillow that had been stolen. Charlie was interested to see how the young carrot-top would react. Pepper was about the same size as the older guard, Owens, if a little less broad in the shoulders, but he said nothing. Charlie wasn't the only one watching the interaction though. Soon enough, Captain 'Too-Good-Looking' Lucky swooped in and claimed the bed for himself, demanding the pillow back from Owens with a sharp word and moving Pepper's kit to the bed on the other side of his. Pepper didn't seem grateful at the interference. Instead, he hunched even smaller at being rescued by his captain over such a minor issue. Charlie thought that was interesting.

Young QG Leith was having a good look out of the only window in the room. The yard was lit by lanterns against the evening dark and their horses were being groomed in the courtyard as there wasn't enough room for them all in the stables. "Bear's right. This place is a shithole," Leith agreed. "Why didn't the general want us to stay somewhere fancier in town?"

"For safety's sake." Lucky produced the vandalized poster and showed the others. Their light mood evaporated at the sight of the nasty image.

"Long live the Regent, eh? Must be Orgustus's supporters here then," remarked Leith as he took his own bed and started undoing his boots.

"Yes, thank you, General Obvious." Captain Lucky rolled his eyes and threw the poster at Leith's head.

"*General* Obvious," Leith replied with a grin, "is that actually a rank? 'Cause I'll take that over QG any day of the week."

Charlie gave the poster a disparaging glance as he made his way through the room and went to sit on the last free bed but Leith stuck out his long leg to bar the way. "That bed's for the general."

Fair enough. Charlie looked about the room for another sleeping option and spied a low cot shoved in the corner, piled with spare blankets and sheets. *That'll do nicely.*

Then General 'Beefy' Ohrig came in and everyone jumped to their feet. "I have the roster for guard duty tonight, fellas," said Ohrig and his voice was as croaky as hell. "Captain Lucky, you take Pepper for the first shift. Owens and Bear take the next, and then Leith and Charlie will take the dawn watch. I'll be getting my beauty sleep all night long on the queen's orders, so don't even think about waking me."

QG Leith groaned but Charlie felt a warm glow heat his chest. *They want me to help guard Queen Adelena?* Of course, Charlie had worked in a team before. As a kid living rough on the streets of Concordis, teamwork had been essential, but he had never been so proud to be included. He wouldn't ever let them know it, but he admired these men and their honorable life serving a woman like Queen Adelena.

At the thought of her, Charlie felt his chest grow almost unbearably hot. *Queen Adelena was amazing. Beautiful yet intense, kind yet fierce and all with a gorgeous arse that he could just...*

"Don't know what you're grinning about," grumbled QG Leith when he caught Charlie's eye. "Dawn watch is the worst."

"Stop whining, you two." Owens threw his filthy boots at both of them. Leith cursed, but Charlie was just relieved to know that it was the dawn watch Leith resented and not the fact that he was paired with Charlie.

"Enough," growled Ohrig. He gave Charlie a hard look and Charlie saw the old man's eyes flicker over his ramshackle bed. "That going to be alright for you, kid?" General Beefy didn't miss a trick.

Charlie grinned wider. "The ladies were nice enough to give me the best bed in the room, General, and I'm more than happy with it."

"How's that?" sniggered QG Bear.

Captain Lucky had opened his mouth to speak, and Charlie was instantly afraid that he would do something chivalrous and stupid like offering to swap with him, and that would be embarrassing.

"It's nice and low for a start," Charlie answered quickly. "Backed right into the corner here, so I can't get snuck up on." - He pointed to the door. - "That's if an intruder would even see me from that angle, giving me plenty of time to hide. Plus it's furthest from the door and the window, so I won't be the first with my throat slit if someone did get in. Yet again more chances to escape with my life."

General Ohrig raised an eyebrow at Charlie's little speech, and there was a twitch at the corner of his mouth. "Your shift starts at two in the early morning. Don't make me wake you twice."

High praise indeed.

"Now, to the showers! You lot stink worse that a horse's arse," shouted General Beefy.

Charlie watched as all the QG's pulled out neat little canvas satchels of toiletries from their kit bags. He didn't have anything like that. The only things he had were the clothes on his back, which he had stolen from the Belvoir laundry just this morning.

"Hey, Pepper?" Charlie risked poking the tall QG in the back as they all filed out and down the hall to the communal washroom. "Mind if I borrow a bit of soap?"

QG Pepper had a nice open face, with rusty freckles across his nose that contrasted well with his wide blue eyes, and his mouth seemed made for smiling. Before last night in the Spiders' Nest, Charlie remembered Pepper as a happy, chatty kind of guy. The downturned mouth and serious expression didn't suit the young QG at all.

"Sure, Charlie, just don't touch my razor," murmured Pepper.

"No need of one anyway, mate." Charlie rubbed his hairless chin, giving Pepper an opening to tease him about his age but Pepper had already turned away. At first, Charlie was embarrassed - *wasn't he even good enough to be made fun of?* But then he realized that he was acting just like Captain Lucky. He was trying to be nice to Pepper because any fool could see there was something wrong with him. Charlie had known young men like Pepper on the streets, most often runaways from comfortable homes, who came for the fun of it. Then the streets took each of them and broke pieces off their spirits until nothing much was left. They never lasted too long after that.

A cold voice in Charlie's head wondered idly, *if Pepper dropped out of the Guard, maybe I could take his place?* Charlie shook his head to dislodge the selfish thought. The Queen's Guard was small enough as it was, and the queen needed them all working together to defend her from her enemies.

Even you? Interrupted the cold voice. *Aren't you supposed to be stealing something precious from her for the Boss? By working against her, wouldn't that make you her enemy too?*

The warmth of pride and belonging dissipated, leaving Charlie feeling cold in the steamy shower room. He couldn't deny the original reason he had attached himself to Queen Adelena was to steal from her. He had yet to find the small box that the Boss had sent him to take only a week ago. Getting caught and becoming a messenger between Queen Adelena and Prince Rainere hadn't been part of Charlie's plan; and neither had staying with the queen to help her rescue Princess Natalie from a filthy nest of spiders.

Charlie had been told by the Boss that the queen was an evil witch, but over a very short time he had come to see her differently. Kind and doting, she had given Charlie the sort of respect and attention he'd never had before. Sure, she was scary as hell when someone betrayed her but...*but, nothing*. Charlie dreaded the idea of Queen Adelena ever looking at him the way she had looked at Prince Rainere last night: when her face was wreathed in shadows, her eyes sparkled with odd gold and silver lights, and she had seemed like Rage itself had come to life.

Charlie felt there was no way he could tell the queen the truth about himself. *After knowing I'd lied to her from the very beginning she won't ever believe another word I say.* In his sixteen years of life, Charlie had known pain, hunger, anger and humiliation, but he had never truly known forgiveness. After all, the queen had been in love with the Marchant prince, but when he betrayed her, Adelena's revenge had been swift and brutal. *If that's what she did to the man she loved, what would she do to a street kid she'd known only a week?*

Charlie stepped under the hot water when a shower became free. He heard the ribald jokes of the men around him as they washed away the road grime but couldn't join in. Charlie didn't cry, he was too hard for that, but he did let the water run over his head for the longest time before he felt he could face the world again.

When Charlie made it back to the bunk room he saw that someone had left him a clean, cotton shirt on his bed. By its starched and spotless appearance, it probably belonged to Captain Lucky. Charlie's heart dropped further into his pit of shame. As he climbed into his little bed, Charlie pulled the blanket up over his shoulders and listened to all the night noises of the Queen's Guard settling down to sleep, and QG Pepper and Captain Lucky leaving to go on duty. It was only just after seven in the evening by Charlie's reckoning, but it wasn't long before he heard snoring.

General Ohrig's dark figure appeared in the doorway not long after. He walked softly for such a big man and brought the smell of soap and tobacco with him. Charlie closed his eyes quickly as he saw the general approach his own bed, close to Charlie's. There was a soft groan as the old man settled himself and the mattress coils pinged against his weight. Charlie let his breathing deepen and steady. He feigned a sigh and shifted about but couldn't bring himself to turn his back on the room. Old habits died hard. He heard a low chuckle in the dark.

"Go to sleep, Charlie," growled General Ohrig. "I can spot a con job a mile away, and you, kid, are no con artist."

Charlie squeezed his eyes shut tighter and prayed hard to the Goddess Serena that Ohrig was wrong.

CHAPTER THREE

"Sleep Eludes Her"

Adele heard the door of her bedroom open and then close again.

"Her Majesty is asleep." QG Pepper's voice was gravelly with fatigue. Adele had asked Ohrig to let the men rest, but he wouldn't hear of it. They both knew that she could take better care of herself than a couple of tired QG's, but to keep the peace Adele feigned sleep and let the men think she needed them.

Adele was uncomfortable with the three hot bodies of her children pressed against her under the blankets. Stella's fever had cooled after dinner and a bath, but she still whimpered in her sleep, making Adele's heart clench with every tiny noise.

Finally, the long day of travel had ended and now there was no defense from the memories that clamored at the edges of her mind. Adele allowed herself to feel the aftershocks of fear and fury shudder through her in sudden jerky waves while horrible staccato images of the night before flashed through her head.

Down in the nest, spiders had been everywhere, their long hairy legs in her hair and on her skin; the piercing shrieks of the dying creatures as they exploded into clouds of black dust; a wall of blue flame roaring towards her; Schiss's face disappearing under the filthy water; Rainere carrying Natalie, limp in his arms, as he screamed at Adele to run; Rainere lying on his back in the dirt, his mouth wide in a silent cry, his eyes begging her to forgive him; and the music, always the music, wild and crashing, it had driven her onwards and it infused every memory like a wicked soundtrack, ringing in her ears.

Adele had left Rainere for dead on the forest floor, Grotto screaming curses at her. She burned at the memory of her lover's betrayal. *How could Rainere have given Natalie away? Why would he think that I could ever value my own life over my daughter's?*

Adele closed her eyes against the horror and waited for the grief and guilt to overwhelm her. It didn't come. Instead, something else waited in the dark of her mind. The Chime Voices murmured a comforting melody, and Adele stopped ignoring the presence of magic. It was time for her to accept that something inside of her had broken free.

When Adele had killed the Mage in Sandar, the power of her Marchant magic had exploded forth with deadly strength to protect her. This time Adele's anger, as horrific as Rainere's betrayal, had released a potent new magic that had guided her hand to plan the attack on the nest carefully. Adele felt the first stirrings of pride, despite her fear. Intuitively, she knew that this new force was entirely different and separate from both the Chime Voices and her Marchant power.

Adele had the sensation of holding the unfamiliar magic at the back of her neck, right where the skull met the spine. Cautiously, she laid a psychic hand on it, and the energy felt warm and hard, but when she poked it with a tendril of her green magic, it suddenly growled and a flash of gold sparked behind her eyes. Adele almost gasped in surprise.

Instinctively, Adele reached down for the green magic coiled under her heart and felt the stirrings of the cold power shift and slide over itself. The Chime Voices hummed in happiness and Adele listened, letting their delight with her new strength suffuse her thoughts.

The Chime Voices had been a near-constant song in her head since the Marchant magic had awakened. Always alert, they gave her words of command, chimed warnings and sang to Adele about all the ways she could protect herself. The Chime Voices were wonderful but they also made her pause to think about how they had taught her to penetrate Rainere's body, seeking to steal his power to feed her own green magic. This newly-awakened magic could well be the golden St Lucidis magic that High Wizard Ohren had told her she possessed at the very beginning. Adele couldn't help but wonder, what price would this new power ask of her? *Just because this magic is gold doesn't make it right, and just because the other magic is green doesn't make it evil,* thought Adele with a shiver.

As if in response to Adele's unwelcome fear, the green magic inside of her began to stir again, coils sliding over coils as it roused itself, sending thin tendrils out into her limbs and up the back of her neck. The gold magic growled and lashed out again with warm, shiny sparks that flashed behind her closed eyes. Its message was clear: this gold magic would not be controlled by the green.

The confrontation of the two magics caused a powerful surge of energy to race through her, igniting the magic in her blood. Unable to keep still, Adele climbed out of bed, doing her best not to disturb the children. She made her way to the single window in the stuffy room and opened the shutters, trying to breathe as her heart hammered at a break-neck pace. The waning moon shone down on the rooftops and courtyard below. Nothing stirred. Adele took another deep breath and fought to control the two magics as they continued to race through her veins, demanding action, as if looking for a fight.

Adele slapped a hand over her mouth to cover the sob that choked her. *Sweet Christ, I can't handle this power,* she thought, giving a voice to her deepest fear. Since arriving in Evendaar, Adele had trusted the wrong person, risked her children's lives and a nation into the bargain. She was the worst mother in the world, and probably the worst queen Unisia had ever seen.

As if insulted by Adele's self-recriminations, the tendrils of the magics inside her began to retract, pulling back under her ribcage, or retreating to the back of her head. Adele felt colder without the warmth of their energy, instinctively seeking to feel them again. Her touch soothed them both, and Adele felt her panic recede. The hard truth was that Adele did not have the luxury of giving into her usual anxiety. There was still so much to be done in the coming days and she would need to trust in herself and learn to use every bit of her magic just to keep her family and her Queen's Guard alive. Those brave men were the only physical line of defense between her children and this bizarre world.

When we get back to the Golden Palace, I will tell the Queen's Guard everything, Adele promised herself. *I cannot keep any secrets from the men if I want to them keep them safe.*

A noise behind her made Adele turn. She saw her eldest daughter sitting up in bed, long dark hair tangled in a cloud about her heart-shaped face. "Mummy, is it time to get up?"

Adele came back to the bed and tucked herself in beside Natalie, pulling her daughter close as they lay side by side. "No darling girl, it's still night. I'll wake you when it's time."

"In the morning we are going back to the Golden Palace, aren't we?" asked Natalie sleepily.

"That's right, darling," replied Adele and stroked her daughter's arm, feeling the fragile bones beneath the skin. She tried not to remember Natalie lying unconscious on the cold stone table, her little limbs limp as the hideous Spider Empress lurched towards her.

"Will Prince Rainere be at the Golden Palace too, Mummy?" murmured Natalie, close to sleep again. "I want to show him our home."

Adele's breath caught in her throat. Natalie adored Rainere, and she would be devastated not to be able to see him again. So Adele gave the stock answer that every mother had to stave off an argument. "Of course, darling. Not now, but definitely sometime soon."

It worked as always and Natalie cuddled into her mother's shoulder, placated. All was quiet in the inn, and Natalie's breath was like a warm breeze on her neck. Yet Adele still couldn't sleep. When she closed her eyes, all she could see was Rainere's face begging for her to come back and love him again. The Chime Voices crooned sympathetically. They missed him too.

With aching eyes, Adele watched as the moonlight moved across the floor of the room and ever so slowly, morphed into the first light of dawn.

Chapter Four

"The Defeated Prince"

Prince Rainere stood naked before the mirror in his bedchamber. His dark eyes travelled down the length of his body, then back up again to meet his own hooded gaze. Goosebumps prickled his pale flesh, making the skin tighten over the hard lines of his well-defined muscles. His hands hung by his sides looking as limp and impotent as the member between his legs.

The North Wind blew in through the open window, splattering the floor with raindrops, blowing papers about the room and whispering nonsense in his ears. As if moved by the breeze, Rainere swayed this way and that. His eyes were searching for that invisible aspect of his body that had fired such passion in his beloved and made her pant with lust for him. Adelena had always praised his beauty and had taken such delight in his nakedness. Rainere raised a hand and lightly traced the muscles of his stomach, outlining each of the eight pillows where Adelena had kissed him so often.

How could it be that her worship of this body had filled me with such strength, when now I feel so very weak without her? Rainere rested his hand on his chest and felt the dull vibration of his heart, still beating though it should have been ripped out by Adelena's delicate hands; ripped out and crushed into a pulp, until only the pain remained. The pain, and her Mark.

Twisting in front of the mirror, Rainere angled himself to examine his right side. He pulled his long hair out of the way, its silky, black lengths still matted with sticks and mud from the Dark Forest. Caught between two tails of the black tattoo that covered his entire back and licked out and over his lower ribs, the royal insignia of Queen Adelena St Lucidis could be seen, grey and soft, like an old scar stamped on his body, forever marking him as hers.

Rainere winced as the Mark undulated and pulled tight. An answering jolt of adrenaline raced through him, making his hands shake with the desperation to return its call and go to her. She must be thinking of him now. The magical bond that linked them was a spell that he had never encountered before. Its power was intense and consuming. Even after she rejected him, and even after her violence in the Dark Forest, he still couldn't resent this connection between them. It was all he had left of his love: only the Mark and the memories of their too-short nights of passion together. Those things at least, remained with him.

Rainere looked deeply into his own eyes. The circle of silver surrounding his pupils spun slowly, still tarnished and fragile after Adelena's attack. Even then, he had failed her. Instead of giving her the comfort of his death, the cursed immortality spell had forced the air back into his lungs and strength into his limbs, giving him back the life that had been Adelena's to take. Rainere watched numbly as a sparkling green tear traced its way down his cheek. After over a century of nothing, suddenly his eyes wouldn't stop crying.

The chamber door opened and Rainere didn't have to look to see that the quiet tread belonged to his manservant, Grottonski, nor did he bother to cover his nakedness. Grotto had held the prince on the day he was born and had been by his side every day since.

Grotto appeared in the mirror behind Rainere, his almost-iridescent green eyes meeting Rainere's deep, forest green gaze. Grotto looked old tonight. The thin black hair on his head was plastered down with a slick of grease and his tattered black suit hung on thin shoulders. Though almost as tall as his master, Grotto stood hunched under the burdens of his responsibilities.

"What do we do now, Grotto?" asked Rainere, his voice only a dry rasp. "What do we do now that your precious Prophecy of the End of the World was broken apart by Adelena? Alone she brought the Shadows into the Light, and alone she rules from the throne of Unisia with the blood of Marchants, and something stronger, flowing in her veins. She has no need of me, and she never did. So I ask you, what do we do now?"

In the closest he ever came to embracing the prince, Grotto rested his hand lightly on Rainere's shoulder. "Master, the Prophecy continues, despite our disappointments. There is a future for you with the queen, but we must look now to the past for the answers. Your father..."

"My father is dead," interrupted Rainere. "He cannot help any of us."

"Your father," persisted Grotto, "was a terrible prince but he was a very great wizard. Although it is his fault the Marchant family lies in ruin, it is also he who can help us heal."

"You speak in riddles, Grotto," sighed Rainere and turned from the mirror's reflections to face the open window. The North Wind blew his hair into his eyes, as if teasing him.

Grotto shook his head, a sly smile dancing across his lips. "Queen Adelena is aware that the St Lucidis wizards have lied to her about her heritage, yes? She knows now that more than gold magic flows through her veins, she fears that she has the blood of another and thinks it is Marchant?" He paused to enjoy his moment. "Let me remind you, master, of the Prophecy; it says the Lost Child was stolen *'from'* the Light but it doesn't say that the Child is *'of'* the Light. You see, the High Wizard, Ohren, had been tricked into hiding another child away from Evendaar, the daughter of your step-mother, Princess Rainestra after her affair with the St Lucidis king, Octavius."

"But that's ridiculous," replied Rainere, turning to Grotto and rising to the bait. "If she is my step-mother's daughter then that would make Adelena my younger sister-by-marriage."

"And by right of the Laws of Marchant, everything your sister has belongs to you." Grotto's smile was triumphant. "As your younger sister in the descendency, and with both of you being orphans, then you are the senior heir and the crown of Unisia is yours, master!"

Rainere was shocked. Wanting to get out of Grotto's reach, he walked to the window, staring sightlessly as the dark rain lashed at him. It was summertime in the rest of the Unisia, but the Grey Palace lived in an eternal winter of Rainere's own making. Weather magic could be powerful, but he had only ever used it to reflect his moods, wreathing the palace turrets in gloomy, grey clouds and constant rain. Only when Adelena had stepped foot in the palace had the sun shone. *Adelena, his lover, was his stepsister? Impossible!* Though they were not bound by blood, this was still a legal tie almost as binding. Rainere spun to face Grotto again.

"In the nest of the Spider People, Empress Ka-kik called Adelena an abomination after she tasted her blood," Rainere's glare was accusing. "Is that what she meant? That Adelena has damaged herself by being with me, the way she did, using magic and going so deep inside me? Did I hurt her by letting her do that when we are" - Rainere almost couldn't bring himself to say the word – "related."

Grotto hid his impatience badly. "The false queen's damage is not your concern, master, you did nothing wrong. It is her own wickedness that has brought about…"

"No!" Rainere's hoarse shout silenced Grotto. "This is *your* fault, Grotto. Adelena endangered herself to be with me, and now you would have us tell the world that I am brother to the queen I lay with? They will destroy her in the court of the Golden Palace, and she will be dead within a day. I will have to kill anyone who even suspects…"

"*Could* you kill High Wizard Ohren?" Grotto's gaze was crafty. "It was he, after all, who took the child away as a favor to your father when Prince Rainold couldn't bear to see his wife's bastard killed by the Eldars like she ought to have been. The High Wizard knew she was your half-sister when he brought her back from Earth and presented her to the court as the child of the King Octavius and his own sister, Queen Olivia. He knew she was a false queen, a bastard with Marchant blood in her veins, and yet he still crowned her and had the gall to invite you to the coronation!"

Spittle flew from Grotto's mouth as he became more and more livid. "He thought you would be too weak and addled by the Blue Tonic to protest. He thought that you would never know that the crown he gave that wretched demon was yours as soon as it touched her head and by Marchant law, you now have every right to swoop in and take it. He thought I would never tell you the truth about Princess Rainestra as it negates your…"

"It negates my what?" Rainere's eyes narrowed at his manservant as Grotto's mouth snapped shut. "If Adelena is technically no closer relation to me than a step sibling, once removed, I have no claim to her kingdom, just as she has no claim to mine."

Grotto dropped to his knees and clasped his hands in front of his chest, beseeching Rainere, "Master, please, you must stay focused on the crown. The High Wizard doesn't suspect you know about the queen's heritage, and he knows nothing of your relationship with her. The queen has no interest in marrying you after the…*incident*…with Princess Natalie, so you must go to the Golden Palace and steal that crown off her head."

Grotto climbed to his feet, mistaking Rainere's silence for assent. "I will pack immediately. We should move into the Marchant townhouse in Concordis to prepare for our assault on the palace. We will need the most dangerous magical weapons we can find. I will ask my contacts in the city for supplies and men."

Turning away from Grotto's insanity, Rainere looked out again at the black night. Rainere hadn't thought it possible to feel any worse about what he had done to Adelena, but Grotto was trying to destroy the last beautiful thing about their shattered relationship by saying that their love had been cursed from the very beginning. Yet, Rainere's heart fought to deny it. Grotto only spoke like this because his sanity had finally cracked. To speak of the long-dead Prince Rainold as some sort of phantom savior in Rainere's hour of need was worse than ridiculous. Grotto was insane and nothing that he said could be believed any longer. Rainere didn't say a word when Grotto gently laid a blanket over his shoulders, and Rainere saw the determination in his old servant's face.

"Shall I pack the carriages and follow you, master?" - Rainere remained silent – "Yes of course, you travel faster through the portals anyway, and then I will come later with the baggage, as is right. I'll pack everything we need, don't you worry, Master. You can be in

Concordis by tomorrow, me the day after that, and we can plan our attack when the demon queen least expects it of us. I have friends who can help us. Strong friends." Grotto became incoherent as he continued muttering of all that needed to be done and left the room.

A sigh welled up in Rainere's chest, but when he exhaled all he felt was a deeper hollow in his being. There was nothing left for him in this world. Everyone he loved had left him, either by walking away or retreating into madness. There was no way that Rainere would be going to Concordis to steal Adelena's crown. He didn't want to rule Unisia, he had just wanted to be part of her life, and that was impossible now.

Stepping away from the window, Rainere made his way to the bed to see that Grotto had already laid out his clothes and grooming kit on the coverlet. Rainere spied the long narrow blade of the razor and picked it up, twirling it in his hands and watching the candlelight flash on its keen edge.

Rainere caught sight of himself in the mirror again, his wretched eyes had filled with tears and they glittered greenly against the whites. Rainere held the razor to his throat and pressed lightly. The cold blade felt good against his skin, but he could cut a thousand times, and bleed from a thousand wounds, and it would not end his life. His immortality would keep him here in this world, a prisoner of his own misery.

Did the Eldars not think of this when they dragged their own unwilling descendants into this living hell? Rainere wondered. Rainere's only hope of an early death had been the Dragon Fire, but he had given it to Adelena when she needed it to kill the spider empress.

A gust of wind rattled hard at the window and the shutter flapped, crashing against the wall and sprinkling glass on the stone floor of his chamber. The North Wind came shrieking into the chamber once more, scattering fat drops of rain over everything. Rainere's long hair tangled and got into his eyes, he grabbed a handful and pulled it away.

"What do you want?" he whispered to the gusts blowing about him.

"*Go to the Eldars,*" chortled the North Wind and its many voices chilled Rainere to his core. "*They are waiting for you. Go to them. The Eldars know what you want. They want you. Go, go, go!*" The North Wind howled in glee, pulling at Rainere's blanket and picking up all the tiny things in the room only to dash them on the floor again. It often spoke in riddles, but tonight its message was oddly clear.

Of course, the Eldars can take what I do not want to have any longer, thought Rainere with a flash of dark joy. *Only they can flay this immortality curse off my back and take away the Mark Adelena gave me.* Rainere had come to the end of his patience with this world and the loveless, lonely life he had pursued for over a hundred years. *I will go to the Eldars. I will make them take back this cursed tattoo, and I will be Marchant no longer.*

His hair blew about like the branches of a tree as the North Wind plucked and pulled at it. Rainere felt a sudden urge to strip away every aspect of his Marchant heritage. Dropping his blanket on the floor, Rainere grabbed a thick hank of his hair and gripped the razor tightly. The strands pattered to the ground and Rainere didn't stop until he had cut it all off.

The blade scraped across stubble and revealed the undulations of his skull. Staring at his handiwork, Rainere was almost relieved that he couldn't recognize himself in the haunted visage that stared back at him. Without long hair to frame his face, his features seemed larger and uglier. His nose was now too beak-like and his brow was too hooded and low over his red-rimmed eyes; his scalp gleamed, as pale and naked as the rest of his skin. Rainere twisted to see the enormous black tattoo that covered his back and the Marchant family crest stamped on the back of his neck. His eyes lingered on Adele's Mark as he watched it twitch and pulse. Rainere gave a hoarse yelp at a savage pull that yanked at his heart. Adelena was thinking of him and hating him.

Soon he would be free of this agony.

Not wanting to waste another moment, Rainere took the clothes from the bed and pulled on his leather trousers, snapping the studs at the front as he shrugged on a simple shirt and his heavy tailored jacket. The rain wouldn't bother him but it would be cold where he was going, so Rainere pulled on his winter cloak. Grabbing an old leather duffel bag, he looked about the room for the things he would need. It wouldn't be much. He shoved in an extra shirt and the blanket from the floor, shaking off the mess of cut hair, then made his way to the mantelpiece above the fireplace.

Rainere's expression softened when he picked up a piece of parchment covered in a penciled image of two smiling stick figures holding hands and wearing crowns. He carefully folded the paper and put it in his pocket. He slipped a tiny wooden box into the same pocket as it had been a gift from the artist who had drawn the endearing portrait. Rainere spied the portrait of his father, Prince Rainold, in its tiny pewter frame, but he only let his eyes rest on it for a moment before he gently placed it face down. Rainere gave the room one last glance. He already felt disconnected from the chamber where he had slept every night for the past one hundred and forty years. In his heart, he had already left.

The prince walked to the door and checked the hallway for Grotto. There was no point in saying good-bye to his old servant. The words would never be enough. Better just to leave. The door clicked shut behind Rainere and a pale green glow pulsed briefly as the protective wards re-aligned themselves.

CHAPTER FIVE

"Dark Plots"

High Wizard Ohren slammed the book shut and threw it across the library desk, startling Orestes and making him drop his piece of cake onto the floor.

"Hey, that was my last one!" Orestes complained to his twin before picking up the crumbs from the rug.

"I don't know how you can eat, its only just gone three in the morning," snapped Ohren and flipped open another book. "You should be panicking, not eating. Tilburn's letter said that Queen Adelena and Princess Natalie have been missing since before the steeplechase and we have no idea where she is."

"Well, we do have some idea," corrected Gorrik as he stretched out a liver-spotted hand to take another slug of Firewhiskey from his glass. "She was last seen at the Grey Palace with Prince Rainere. The real mystery is why she sent her two younger children back to Belvoir without her. I can't imagine what has happened that would make her split up her family like that?"

Ohren tossed the book he had just read back onto the table, jostling the others in their teetering pile and cursing roundly.

"Stop it, Ohren," admonished his brother. "We're all worried about the queen but it is no good having her come home when we don't even know how to camouflage her heritage from the court of the Golden Palace. All of that exposure to the Marchant prince and his dark magic might have brought out her Marchant blood by now. The rings in her eyes will probably be bright silver when we see her again, and the magical population of the court will know straight away what she really is." Ohren looked like he would snap something rude in response but Orestes held up his hand for peace. "So all the more reason we work to find something in light magic to help her now."

"I should go to the Grey Palace myself," said Ohren, starting back on an old argument. "The queen has no capability with magic. That Marchant prince has probably put her under some sort of glamour and is manipulating her as we speak. He is a danger to us all, and I'm cursing myself that I didn't deal with him when I had the chance."

"When did you have the chance to deal with him?" asked Orestes sharply, and raised a disapproving eyebrow at his twin. "You have no legal right to approach the prince-in-residence at the Grey Palace, you know that."

Ohren grumbled something incoherent into his beard and then changed the subject. "Gorrik, any luck with that text?"

The ancient historian sighed and rubbed at his milky eyes, as he rolled another scroll away. "No luck, my lad. I still think our only option will be to pray that her magic still rests dormant and then cast an illusion on her, just the eyes of course. The magic won't have to be too dark to do that - just a bit grey." He gave a throaty chuckle at his own joke. "We can bind the spell to a piece of jewelry, or maybe even to the crown she left behind, and give it to her as soon as she enters the Palace."

"You cannot cast a dark illusion spell with the crown of Unisia," replied Orestes, aghast. "I can't even begin to tell you how many laws of the constitution that would contravene."

"Alright, alright, calm down, High Magistrar," grumbled Gorrik. "Just something small and tidy she can keep about her person then. Maybe a gift from you commemorating her return from Sandar, Ohren? A High Wizard would do that for his queen, yes? She wouldn't suspect anything out of order."

"Or I could tell her it used to be her mother's," added Ohren, warming to the idea.

"Not *her* mother's, but Queen Olivia's," corrected Orestes. His acid tone caught Ohren's attention.

"Orestes, I'm so sorry about all this, you know I am." Ohren could never stop apologizing to his brother for what he had done so many years ago, betraying their St Lucidis family and the crown, and causing the royal mess they were in now. "I never meant to cast our sister's child away, but Olivia's boy would never have survived the civil war anyway. I really believe that this queen is the Hidden Child and her role in the Prophecy of the End of the World will save Unisia. I know she isn't who I said she was at first, but even without being a pure St Lucidis queen, she is still the strongest link we have to the old blood and to the magic in her father's line. Adelena *will* follow the prophecy and she *will* guide us in the Days of Darkness ahead, even if I have to hold her hand the whole way to do it!"

Ohren pretended not to hear all the contradictions in his own words and looked plaintively at his brother for forgiveness. He needed Orestes's help to hide the queen's true heritage from the court. Ohren could do much with magic, but High Magistrar Orestes controlled the law in Unisia, making him Ohren's most useful ally.

Orestes held his brother's gaze for a long moment before a smile finally ticked up at the corner of his mouth. Orestes could never stay mad at Ohren. "Well, I've never known you to be so keen on a woman before. If you really think she is *special* then I guess I can go along with this feeble plan," he teased.

Ohren rolled his eyes at the taunt but didn't respond as he still needed his twin's favor. "When I cast the spell, could you not perhaps just add an addendum to one of the laws preventing dark magic in the Golden Palace? For example, unless it is performed by a high wizard for reasons of national security?"

Orestes frowned, all traces of humor gone. What Ohren was asking him was not just illegal but also morally wrong. "So we are choosing the path of despot now? Changing the laws to suit our graces while the rest of the nation must follow them to the letter. Ohren, you are playing with fire now…green fire," he added sternly.

"But you'll do it?" Ohren insisted, more as a statement than a question. "Meanwhile, I promise that Gorrik will search tirelessly for a better way to perform the spell. I still think I should go to the Grey

Palace tomorrow. We really don't know what that Marchant prince is capable of, and Adelena might need my help."

A loud knock at the door to the library interrupted the high wizard. All three men looked at each other, surprised. They were in a quiet room tucked away in the 'Ancient and Protected' section of the Accadaemia Library, no one should have known where they were, especially not in the wee hours of the morning. There was another knock before the door opened and a young man stepped through the doorway, his curious gaze searching the room until he found the three men, frozen in their chairs.

Gorrik was the first to recover. "Hello, it's a Belvoir messenger!"

The messenger smoothed down his bright green and brown tunic with nervous hands, and bowed, his hat falling off and dark curls sprung out over his forehead. "High Wizard, I bring a message from Prince Bertrand II." The messenger stood up again and held out a glass tube with two wolf heads carved into either end. *Sticking Glass,* Ohren thought, *so this message is important enough to protect with magic.* The messenger looked from one identical twin to the next, unsure which of them was High Wizard Ohren. Ohren saved the young man from further embarrassment and took the message, searching for a knife on his belt with which to cut his finger and open the tube. Though he had no intention of reading the message aloud, he looked up to see the young man shifting from foot to foot, desperate to have his leave to speak again.

"What's your name, son?" asked Ohren kindly enough.

"Benjamin, sir, High Wizard, sir," stammered Benjamin and pushed back the curls from his sea-green eyes. "I also have a verbal message for you. As soon as Queen Adelena left the Belvoir Estate, Prince Bertrand sent me here to inform you of her return, but I should tell you that I saw Queen Adelena on the road, though I didn't stop to hail her. She's spending tonight in Pettington with the Queen's Guard, and will no doubt arrive later this afternoon."

"Yet, you made it here now, almost a day ahead of her?" Ohren was suspicious of this boy's coloring already, he was obviously of a long-diluted Marchant strain with his raven black hair and pale green eyes. "How?"

 The messenger straightened and his chest puffed out a little. "Prince Bertrand bade me take the Marchant prince's horse, Titor, to the Golden Palace, High Wizard. He is the stallion who won the grand race at the carnival, as you might have heard? I would have let him stop for the night but he never once faltered. We made the entire trip here in only fifteen hours. I'm sure that's some kind of record," Benjamin added with a proud grin.

Ohren's heart quailed in his chest and he heard Orestes's sigh at the news just delivered by this enthusiastic boy. "That is a great run," agreed Ohren and hated that his voice shook just a little. "Take the horse back to the Golden Palace now and find a room to rest with the Household Guard. I'll ask you to stay until I have a letter for you to take back to Prince Bertrand."

Benjamin bowed again and then made for the door, turning just as he reached the handle. "Oh, and just so you know, gentlemen. I was told by a cook that you would be here but I saw someone following me from the palace. The gentleman was close on my heels until Titor took off, but he shouldn't be far away." The messenger gave another grin and a nod before shutting the door behind himself, leaving only the smell of sweat and bad news.

"You told your *cook* where to find you." Ohren turned to Orestes, incredulous. "Like our work isn't any kind of secret that the kitchen staff can't know about!"

"I didn't think that anyone would bother to ask my cook," protested Orestes.

"Boys, boys!" Gorrik said, interrupting the twins, "this is not the time for your arguing. Read the letter, Ohren, and put us all out of our misery."

Ohren opened the tube and a scroll fell out. As the wizard read silently, his cheeks became ashen, and his expression was puzzled. "Bertie says the queen returned suddenly yesterday morning from the

Grey Palace with her daughter Natalie, but without Prince Rainere or Bertie's priest, Pere Raven, but I don't know who that man is, or why it matters?" From their non-plussed expressions, Ohren guessed Orestes and Gorrik didn't know the priest either. "He says that the queen re-entered the estate through the forest and not the portal he had shown them."

"Goddess be damned," swore Orestes. "That portal is completely illegal."

Ohren continued, "he says the queen was in a terrible state, as were her men, and that she only stopped to change her clothes before she packed up her children and one nanny with her. She took a single carriage, led by her Queen's Guard, and she is heading to the Golden Palace in all haste. He notes that she didn't speak to anyone but her men, and her ladies-in-waiting could not give any reason for her behavior. The rest of the St Lucidis party, hot with scandal, is preparing to return to the Golden Palace, ready to spread any number of vicious rumors. *Be careful, dear Ohren, they are gunning for your Queen Adelena.*" Ohren drifted off and looked up at his twin and oldest friend. "She is coming home. Adelena's alive and she's coming home." He couldn't hide the relief in his voice. "Thank the Goddess, she is alright."

"It doesn't sound like she is alright, boy," said Gorrik, who reached over to take the letter and read it for himself. "The queen has caused a terrible scandal going off to the Grey Palace like that, and the court will be watching her with steel in their eyes now, so she'll have nowhere to hide here in the Golden Palace." He gave the letter back to Ohren with a heavy frown.

Ohren looked to his brother, silently pleading. Orestes swore and finally gave in. "Give her the illusion spell, and damn us all with it. I'll find a way to change the law, but I will not forgive you for asking me, Ohren."

"It's for the kingdom, Orestes," said Ohren, rescued yet again by his brother's help. "I promise you, I will never use that power for dark purposes, on my oath as the high wizard."

Orestes's mumbled reply was covered by the sound of the door crashing open, startling the three men for the second time that night.

"Lord Orgustus, what is the meaning of this?" asked Ohren, too shocked to be angry.

Lord Orgustus filled the doorway, his blond head almost brushing the architrave. The Lord surveyed the room like a predator finally finding its prey. His glare was ferocious and his deep blue eyes were icy. Ohren dropped his gaze from the young man's face and noticed that the usually-impeccable Lord Orgustus was covered in dirt, his trouser leg ripped and the smell of cooking fires hung about him in a cloud. Even his fine, chiseled features were covered in grime.

"High Wizard Ohren, please forgive my intrusion," began Lord Orgustus with a shallow bow that somehow still managed to convey disrespect. "But tucked up here in this office you have missed the catastrophe that has struck Concordis." His glare became accusatory. "A fresh outbreak of the Summer Influenza has struck at the heart of the Guild Quarter. Hundreds are sick, and many have already died. The hospices tried to contain the spread of the disease but it managed to evade all their efforts. Every doctor and magician on the ground is trying to stem the tide of death, but we have exhausted all supplies of the Influenza tonics. The very same tonics that you said the queen would provide for us when she returned from Sandar with the Fire Orchid stamens. But instead, she is dancing at a fete with the Marchant prince while her people die." Orgustus deep voice carried enough force to silence the room.

"I have been in the city all day, tending the fires as the people burn their dead." The lord's glare scorched them each in turn. "Have you ever seen the pain on a child's face as he turns green and dies, High Wizard? Have you ever heard a mother's screams when she knows the disease has come to take her little one, High Magistrar? Have you ever held a father back from leaping onto a funeral pyre to touch his dead son one last time? Well, gentlemen, have you?" Orgustus's voice cracked. "Because that is what I have been doing this night."

"What do you need?" Ohren croaked in shock.

Lord Orgustus immediately became business-like. "Mrs. Ollenby has the key to the emergency stores of the tonic in the Golden Palace, I need your permission to allow her to release every one of those tonics to me. I will take them into the city this morning and save as many lives as I can. Though inoculations are too late, the tonics will still heal those who have only just contracted the disease and help ease the pain of those who are too late to save."

Ohren nodded and scribbled a note for Mrs. Ollenby on the back of the closest piece of paper to hand, then thrust it at the young lord. "Take it, and go, now."

Lord Orgustus took the note and shoved it in his pocket. As always, he still had more to say. "High Wizard Ohren, you and I have always had a civil accord between us, but I have to address the fact that this new queen of ours has caused nothing but trouble since she arrived. If it hadn't been for Queen Adelena's coronation, then the Empress Sandaha'ni would have sent the stocks of Fire Orchid stamens as usual. This terrible outbreak would have been prevented by the regular inoculation of the non-magical citizens affected, and the status quo would have remained. You cannot honestly tell me now that she had been good for the nation of Unisia, even as she dances at a horse carnival at the Belvoir Estate."

Ohren coughed. "Queen Adelena returns this very day, Lord Orgustus, she will aid her people in any way she can, rest assured."

Lord Orgustus's sneer reflected his own thoughts on the matter. "Be that as it may, I shall return to the dying people on the streets of Concordis, High Wizard, with your permission, of course." Again, the lord only gave his superior a shallow bow and a hard glare.

Ohren nodded and watched as Lord Orgustus stalked from the room and slammed the door so hard it rattled the light fittings in the ceiling.

"Shit." The expletive sounded young and desperate coming out of Ohren's mouth, but his expression had aged him another hundred years.

"Don't look for me for the rest of the day," said Orestes and stood up. He made his way to the door. "I had better make this plan of yours legal before the queen returns. At least let's get one thing right, eh brother?" He gave Ohren a sad grin before closing the door.

Ohren turned to his old friend and saw that Gorrik looked as miserable as he felt. "Shit," he repeated.

"You got it, boy," agreed Gorrik. "Your queen better come back from Belvoir trailing gold dust and roses out of her arse or this court is going to kill her, and then you."

"Shit," Ohren whispered, as the truth of Gorrik's words crushed him down into his chair.

"Yep," nodded Gorrik, and poured himself another shot of golden Firewhiskey. "And, of course, you do realize that you just gave Orgustus the letter from old Bertie on the back of that note you wrote him?"

Ohren closed his eyes and let his head drop to the table with a bang. "Shit."

CHAPTER SIX

"Home, But Not Sweet"

Adelena stood at the bottom of the steps and stared up at the Golden Palace. She swallowed hard and wiped sweaty hands down her suede riding pants, marking them with damp streaks. The moment she had been dreading was finally here.

The Golden Palace was enormous. Taller and much grander than the somber Grey Palace, it absolutely dwarfed the manor house of the Belvoir estate. The white-stone that gave the Golden Palace its name was embedded with shards of crystals that glinted brightly in the late afternoon sunlight. Along each floor of the palace, hundreds of windows glimmered in shiny rows and the great terraces of the upper floors hung like floating gardens draped with vines and flowers.

Just a moment ago, the huge gilt front doors had been opened wide, and Adele watched in dismay as a long golden carpet was pushed out and quickly unrolled down the steps to where she stood at the bottom. Stewards and heralds rushed down, ribbons and jacket tails flying as they arranged a hasty welcome salute to the royal family on their unexpected arrival. The formality of it all made her stomach drop, and Adele found herself clinging to the baby in her arms as tightly as Stella clung to her. She pulled Natalie and Aaron closer to her legs, smoothing their hair and patting down their collars. Adele felt the sweat dripping down her temple mix with the road dust caked on her skin. She had never felt so frumpy and ill-equipped to deal with the glamour of the Golden Palace than right now.

"Apologies, Your Majesty," said General Ohrig with a rueful grimace. "We should have followed your request to go in through the stable yard door. I know you hate this kind of fuss, but I honestly didn't think anyone would be expecting us so soon. We should have beaten any messenger back from Belvoir."

Adele had never voiced her discomfort with the ridiculous pomp of the Golden Palace to Ohrig but it didn't surprise her that the general knew her well enough to read her every expression. "Well, we're home now, and like you said, I need to start acting like a queen if I want to be treated like one," Adele said.

"Bit of rough paraphrasing there, Your Majesty," coughed Ohrig. "I'm sure I was more polite this morning."

The queen and her general exchanged a smile. General Ohrig had never been famous for his tact, and Adele had heard him correctly when he had attempted to coach her on their return to the Golden Palace and on strategies for dealing with High Wizard Ohren.

Almost two weeks ago, on her return from Sandar, Adele had received a letter from the high wizard telling her not to come home, but not for how long. If Ohren was angry with her for coming back now, she needed some way to deal with him without resorting to violence. Although Adele had proven to herself that she could take down an immortal wizard, she wasn't ready to fight an entire nation - nor did she want to. General Ohrig hadn't been able to offer much specific advice. While he knew 'of' the high wizard, Ohrig had no relationship with Ohren to speak of, as the two men had moved in different political circles. However, High Wizard Ohren did have a reputation as a political pacifist, so that spoke in his favor with Adele. She could only hope it was true.

"Who's this joker in the wig?" asked Charlie, popping up from behind and peering over Adele's shoulder. Everyone watched the steward with the tall blond curls approach and bow deeply to Adele.

"Your Majesty, our good Queen Adelena, you are welcomed home to the Golden Palace by the High Wizard Council, the former Regent Lord Orgustus, and the court of the Golden Palace. May the Goddess Serena bless your arrival and that of the royal children, Princess Natalie, Prince Aaron and..."

Stella let out a perfunctory wail of boredom and buried her hot little head in Adele's neck. The toddler was still miserable with her cold, and she had suffered on the long carriage ride.

"Thank you so much for your kind welcome." Adele had to shout over the booming steward. "But we would really much prefer to go inside if it's all the same to you? It's very hot out here for the children, you see?"

The steward looked mortified, but he acquiesced to the queen's wishes with a bow. He turned and rushed up the stairs ahead of them, waving away the musicians and courtiers who had assembled to greet their returning queen. Adele walked past the whispering crowd and gave them an apologetic wave. She didn't even know who these people were. They lived in the Golden Palace too, and there was no doubt that they were very curious about her.

Adele wasn't at all familiar with the front entrance of the Golden Palace, never having had a chance to explore the enormous place much further than the royal apartments and a few meeting rooms. So she was relieved when the steward took her immediately to the large apartment that she had come to think of as 'home'.

Natalie and Aaron didn't try to contain their excitement at being back in the palace, and despite Adele's anxiety, she smiled as the children whooped and ran down the corridors and skidded about on the polished floors. Adele avoided looking at the walls lined with mirrors. She saw all she needed to in the faces of the courtiers who moved aside for her, their lace fans raised to not-so-subtly disguise their shock and horror at such a bedraggled queen.

Adele wished again that she had taken the time to clean up a bit before entering these halls. The women of the Golden Palace were normally preened within an inch of their lives. Adele's dusty pants and riding jacket ensemble fell very short of the fashion standards she was expected to maintain as queen. The Chime Voices in her head tinkled, annoyed at such foolish thoughts when she should be preparing herself to come face to face with an angry high wizard. Adele felt for her two magics resting at her back and under her heart, giving her strength.

"Mrs. Ollenby!" Natalie and Aaron shrieked at the welcome sight of Mrs. Dolores Ollenby standing outside the door to their apartment. Mrs. Ollenby's blonde curls were arranged in a high bun and her pink tulle dress sparkled in the light, making her look so much like a fairy godmother from the stories of Adele's childhood. The children streaked down the hallway and threw themselves into the older lady's arms.

"Mrs. Ollenby," echoed Adele. She didn't stop walking but crushed the woman in a giant hug that squashed a giggling Stella between them. Natalie and Aaron both joined in the hug, laughing with joy at seeing one of their favorite people in the Golden Palace.

"Well, what a warm welcome!" Mrs. Ollenby's smile made her dimples dip, and happy tears flooded her bright lavender blue eyes. "I cannot tell you how much I have missed my royal family. Thank the Goddess you are all back safe and sound with me!" Mrs. Ollenby kept her hands on all of them, rubbing backs and squeezing shoulders as she ushered them through the antechamber and into the living room of their large, bright apartment. The table had been set up for an elegant afternoon tea with towers of cakes and sandwiches, and the air in the room was perfumed with the smell of the summer roses that had been squashed into vases everywhere. For a moment, the rainbow patterns of silks and velvets overwhelmed Adele. She had forgotten just how sumptuous and rich the palace was, but then she blinked, and chose to revel in the beauty of the familiar instead of picking out the differences between here and the Grey Palace. That, at least, was a place she would never see again.

Natalie and Aaron had a thousand questions about their things, and if their bedroom had been left in the same condition as they remembered. They scampered off straight away, with their nanny Seraphina hustling to follow, and Mrs. Ollenby calling for them to wash their hands for afternoon tea.

"Oh, they are just the dearest little children, Your Majesty, and I am so very glad to have you all back." Mrs. Ollenby wiped the tears out of the corner of her eyes with a bejeweled finger, and gently pulled Stella out of Adele's tired arms, to hold the baby against her shoulder. "But where is the rest of your entourage? And why did I only just hear an hour ago from the high wizard that you had reached the city limits of Concordis? I'm sure Tilburn would be furious that there was not a proper welcome waiting for you. I'm very surprised that he would have let you travel without all your staff, especially after the hardships you have suffered traveling with such a spare crew from Sandar." Mrs. Ollenby rocked Stella against her shoulder with a professional hand while simultaneously signaling for a servant to serve refreshments to the waiting Queen's Guard.

"It couldn't be avoided, Mrs. Ollenby," said Adele. "I need to see the high wizard immediately and I couldn't wait for the entire St Lucidis court to decamp from Belvoir Estate and come back with me."

Mrs. Ollenby registered Adele's tone and her gaze flitted to each of the Queen's Guard and over Charlie before settling on General Ohrig for a beat, taking in their dusty clothes and stink of horse sweat. Her smile faltered and she stepped closer to Adele, lowering her voice. "What can I do to help, Your Majesty?"

Adele was speechless with gratitude at the lady's quick assessment of the situation. Dolores Ollenby was the first person Adele had met when she had woken up on that first fateful morning in Evendaar. Like a baby bird just out of the shell, Adele felt that she had imprinted on Mrs. Ollenby as her mentor and friend in the tumult that had become her life as Queen of Unisia. Mrs. Ollenby was so much more than just her Head of Household and Matron to the Royal Nursery; she was one of the rare people whom Adele actually trusted with the safety of her children, recognizing Mrs. Ollenby's genuine affection for her kids. It helped that, despite her sweet and pretty appearance, Adele knew that Mrs. Ollenby was a force to be reckoned with in her own right, and she ran the Golden Palace like a benevolent dictator.

"I need a meeting with Ohren, right now," said Adele. "And it's imperative that we have a room where we cannot be disturbed or overheard."

Mrs. Ollenby reached out and squeezed Adele's hand. "Have General Ohrig take you to the Lavender Chamber, the walls and windows are properly protected by insulating spells, only those within will hear what's discussed."

Adele nodded. "Yes, I remember it, we had a Meeting of the Families there once. That'll be perfect. Can you tell High Wizard Ohren to meet us there, please?" Adele turned to her men but Stella let out a little whimper thinking her mother was leaving her.

"The baby feels a little feverish, You Majesty," said Mrs. Ollenby, feeling Stella's forehead with her cheek. "And she is not as happy as she normally is."

Adele leaned across to kiss Stella's sticky cheek. "She has been trying to shake this little cold since the Grey Palace, but she ate well this morning so she can't be too bad. Could you call a doctor for me though, just to check?"

Mrs. Ollenby jiggled Stella to jolly her along. "Of course, Your Majesty. We'll have a little bath, a bit of lunch then a nap after the doctor. You'll be right as rain in no time, my poppet." Mrs. Ollenby kissed Stella's head and cuddled her close. "You go along, Your Majesty, the high wizard will be coming from the Accadaemia so he might be half an hour or so, but the children will be fine with me here."

Adele watched as Stella lay her head back down on Mrs. Ollenby's pillowy shoulder. *Maybe Stella was a bit paler than she had been this morning?*

"Your Majesty?" General Ohrig interrupted Adele's train of thought. "The men will need a briefing before our meeting with the high wizard."

Adele nodded and was swamped with insecurity again. She tried to squash the thought that this might be the last time she would see her children if High Wizard Ohren took it into his head that she was his enemy.

Not knowing what else to do, Adele ran to kiss her children good-bye as they played in their bedroom. In her own chamber, Adele splashed some water on her face before peeling off her dusty blouse and swapping it for a fresh one. By the time she re-entered the living room, her Queen's Guard had taken the opportunity to devour most of the buffet laid out in the dining area and had drunk every jug of water on the table. They had been riding all day in the hot sun, and they were probably close to dehydration. Adele berated herself for not taking better care of her team and let them load up on the food a little more before gesturing that she was ready to leave again.

General Ohrig led the way down the hallway and Adele followed, Charlie almost bumping her shoulder as he raced to keep step and eat at the same time.

"Why is all this food so bloody tiny?" the teenager asked as he squashed another couple of sandwiches in his mouth from the collection in his hand.

"Because the more fancy something is, the less they give you," replied Adele quickly, she had to send Charlie on his way right now before too many people saw them together. "Remember, you are going to be my eyes and ears in the palace today, Charlie. If anyone tries to talk to you, just play dumb and tell them that you are on loan to me from Belvoir Estate, but feel free to wander wherever you can go, and gather as much information as you can."

Charlie nodded and shoved the rest of the sandwiches in his mouth, his hazel eyes alight with curiosity and excitement. His job was to keep a low profile and get the feel of the mood in the Golden Palace when the news spread that the queen had returned. Ohrig had thought it wise for Adele to have her own intelligence, and Adele wholeheartedly agreed with him on this. She watched Charlie for a moment as he tried to take in the luxury of his new surroundings. This was just an ordinary corridor in the Golden Palace, but with the beautiful china vases on plinths and the gold gilt frames of the portraits, not to mention the plush, red silk carpet beneath their dusty boots, this was a paradise of wealth to a street kid like Charlie. From humble beginnings herself, Adele knew how he felt. She didn't even see when Charlie disappeared at the next corner of the hallway.

CHAPTER SEVEN

"A Meeting of Minds"

The Lavender Chamber was as beautiful as Adele remembered. Lilac-colored, silk fabric covered the walls and gave the room its name. Violet lace curtains hung at the balcony doors and a long, oval-shaped rosewood table stood in the center of the room, with twelve chairs surrounding it. Adele immediately took the head charger and waited for the men to sit, General Ohrig to her right, Captain Lucky to her left and the other men, sitting two to each side of them. Six pairs of blue eyes turned to her in rapt attention. Adele cleared her throat and looked to General Ohrig for reassurance.

The general gave her a respectful nod. It was time to tell her Queen's Guard everything.

"Men, we have been through hell these last few weeks but despite your loyalty there are important things about myself that I have kept from you all." Adele saw the general stiffen in his seat and the men cast him sideways looks. She hoped she wasn't undermining his authority, but she just didn't want him to be blamed for any of the things she had done without his knowledge. "What you hear today will be the truth about everything that has happened to me since I arrived in Evendaar seven weeks ago. High Wizard Ohren knows none of it, but it is essential that he believes you already have been privy to my actions, so we will present the wizard with a united front."

Adele took a deep breath and cast her gaze around the table. "I promise I will answer your questions after the meeting, but for now just know that everything I did was to protect my children in an alien world. Whatever happens today with the High Wizard…"

"We stand at your back, Your Majesty," said General Ohrig firmly. "We are outside the law of the court and the constitution, and we answer to no higher power than our queen. Long live the queen!"

"Long live the queen!" The voices of the Queen's Guard were strong and loud in the closed room.

Adele was deeply touched. "Thank you all. That means the world to me."

The doors of the chamber flew open and there in the doorway stood High Wizard Ohren. Surprised that he had travelled to the palace so fast, Adele shot to her feet and felt her magic uncoil in response. Grasping at its strength, she held herself firm. Ohren seemed taller than she remembered, but his grey beard was just as long. His familiar purple and grey robes were billowing about his lanky frame, and his eyes glowed with the same intense, magnetic blue, capturing her gaze and pinning her where she stood. Adele flinched when Ohren strode across the room, ignoring her men, who had all reached for their swords, and came to stand in front of her.

Adele almost choked on her nerves. "High Wizard Ohren, I…"

But Ohren had folded Adele into his arms, hugging her hard to his chest. Adele stood stiffly as she felt Ohren's heart hammering against her cheek. His arms were like two wire bands holding her tight. The high wizard smelled of something toasty and delicious. "Thanks be to the Goddess, you have returned," Ohren whispered and Adele felt his lips press soft and quick against her forehead.

Adele could not be more baffled by this outpouring of affection from the high wizard. The last time she had seen Ohren he had dismissed her coldly and refused to come with her on the journey to Sandar. If he had been there, she might have been able to avoid all the awful trouble that she had gotten into. The thought made Adele angry enough to pull out of Ohren's hug.

But Ohren didn't let go so easily. Holding her shoulders in his hands, he stared down at Adele, and she felt the familiar sensation of falling into his electric blue gaze. The high wizard seemed to stare through her and down into her very soul. The Chime Voices tinkled prettily in the back of her head, singing a flirty little song, and Adele could feel them being charmed. She hadn't known how to recognize it before now, but Ohren had magic in his gaze, and he was using it on her. She blinked hard and the spell was broken.

"What has happened to you, my dear queen?" Ohren voice was heavy with sympathy. "You have changed so much."

Adele frowned and stepped out of Ohren's reach. She wasn't '*his* queen' any longer. She turned her attention back to the table where her men stood, swords half drawn from their scabbards, just awaiting her word to leap into action. Their support warmed her. She gestured for them to relax.

"Ohren, if you could take a seat, please." Adele was relieved that her voice stayed firm. "There is much to discuss and we should get started so I can return to my family."

Ohren was clearly taken aback by her coldness, but he obediently circled back around the table and found a seat at the end. "I take it you wish for the Queen's Guard to remain during the meeting, Your Majesty?" The disapproval in Ohren's tone was loud and clear, though he kept his expression neutral.

Adele nodded and hoped Ohren didn't notice her shaking hands as she folded them together on the table top. "They will not hear anything they don't already know," she said.

Ohren's face creased into a concerned frown and Adele had a sudden urge to again become the young woman who trusted the high wizard and believed him to be one of the good guys in this strange world of Evendaar. Ohren had always acted like her friend and confidante when she had first arrived. He had promised to help her be the best queen that she could be and guide her through his Prophecy of the End of the World. Then he had sent her to Sandar where she had almost died, and now she couldn't be sure if he had arranged it. She needed to know the truth before she could either move forward as queen or get the hell out of the Golden Palace.

Adele cleared her throat and set her shoulders straight. "Let me start at the very beginning. Our journey to Sandar had been uneventful, and my meeting with Empress Sanda'hani was amicable enough. The empress was intent on my going with her mage into the Holy Caves of Sandar alone to perform the Ceremony of the Blood to prove that I was a St Lucidis queen. I did as she demanded, accompanied only by the Sandarian ambassador, Ripenzo Shale, and the Mage."

The light in the room dimmed as clouds passed over the sun, and Adele felt as if the world had stopped turning to hear her story. The Chime Voices sang wordlessly in her mind, like a soundtrack behind the memories that clouded Adele's vision until they were all she could see.

The golden white, sand of the beach at Sandar... The green, aqua blue of the sparkling ocean, so calm under the hot midday sun... The candy-colored tents lined up on the shore like a tranquil wedding party... Empress Sanda'hani, tall, beautiful and voluptuous, with her pale green eyes that saw so much but never the truth about Adele... And then the Mage of Sandar, his mohawk bobbing and weaving as he hopped across the lava field, then flashes of the knife raised high in his hand, his grotesque penis erect, a leering, covetous grin on his face.

"I went into the Holy Caves with the Mage and he had already set up the sacred fire for the Blood Ceremony. I was nervous, but I let him cut my wrist and the blood dripped into the bowl. There was a heavy scent in the air, like roasting herbs and the tang of raw meat. I wanted the Mage to let me go when he had enough blood to cover the bottom of the bowl.

"I tried to pull away but when I looked up, the Mage had a knife in his hand. He raised it above my heart and slashed." Adele swallowed and tasted burnt herbs on her tongue. "I don't know how it happened, but a word came into my mind, it was a command, and when I touched the Mage he... he couldn't move or fight me anymore."

The Chime Voices whispered the fatal command in her head and it made Adele shudder. The command was a word that represented a void, bottomless and cold. "He was dead when the command had finished with him."

Adele rubbed a hand over her eyes to wipe away the memories. "I screamed loudly, and Ripenzo Shale came running into the cave and saw the dead mage. He said the empress would want revenge for the Mage's death, so he helped me hide the body in a chasm at the back of caves. I didn't see where the body landed, but Ripenzo assured me it was gone."

The guilt and terror washed through her at the memory of the little lights of the scorpions dancing across the roof. Evil. It had all been so evil, but Adele had been helpless to choose another path. Kill or be killed....

"After Ripenzo and I left the Holy Caves, he came up with the idea to tell Empress Sanda'hani that the Mage had been called by their Volcano God to go on a vision quest, which was why he didn't return with us. When we got back to the Sandarian court on the beach, Ripenzo started acting oddly. I became unsure of trusting him. If he betrayed me to the empress, my children would be taken from me, and we would certainly all die." This time Adele's conscience pinched her hard.

"I lied to the empress and said that Ripenzo had tried to force himself on me sexually. She offered to kill him for me but I claimed that I wanted to have it done in Unisia and encouraged the empress to give me Ripenzo, so he couldn't tell her the truth about what I had done in the Holy Caves, without looking like he was trying to make excuses. Shale was an ambassador, but he was also a slave at the Sandarian court and his word wouldn't count for much if it was a queen who accused him of something so awful.

"I was planning to bring Shale back to the Golden Palace with me, but I couldn't abide keeping a slave, so I freed him as soon as we left Sandar. Stupidly, I thought he understood that he would be rewarded for all the trouble I had caused him when we returned to Unisia, but he disappeared the night he was freed, and I couldn't afford to waste time looking for him when we had to get the Fire Orchid stamens back to the Golden Palace. While we were on the road, we received your letter telling us to ride for the Belvoir Estate." Adele looked up at Ohren for the first time since beginning her speech. His cheeks were pink above his grey beard and his eyes almost danced with emotion. She couldn't tell if that was good or bad.

"We were trying to get to Belvoir Estate when a massive snow storm hit us in the Dark Forest and we got lost in the woods. Eventually we found ourselves at the gates of the Grey Palace and asked the Marchant prince for shelter while the storm died down. Two days later, we continued to the Belvoir Estate, but then Prince Rainere appeared at the carnival and offered me the chance to return to the Grey Palace to recuperate from an awful illness I had caught while at Belvoir. I accepted and the children and I went to the Grey Palace."

Adele voice petered out. Talking about Rainere, even saying his name, was almost excruciating. Their love had been so beautiful at the beginning. Perfect and passionate, Rainere had given her hope for a real life in this alien world. His betrayal had destroyed that dream, along with so many others. Yet, Adele didn't want to show that weakness to Ohren before she was sure she could trust him.

"I loved Rainere," Adele said, simple and the truth. "Ever since I saw him at my coronation, I was in love with the Marchant prince. He was familiar to me, you see. I had dreamed of him for years back on Earth, and again after I came to Evendaar. I finally knew why our love had stretched across the stars and two different dimensions. Finally, here in Evendaar, we could be together. He knew it too." Adele paused as Ohren made a weird, strangled sound but he didn't try to talk so she continued.

"But I wasn't stupid. I could see that he was on the dangerous side of politics, and though he begged me, I refused his offer of marriage. It hurt him, and us both, so much. You see, he too believed in your Prophecy of the End of the World, Ohren, and he thought he could save me from it. He was beholden to the Spider Empress and she had requested he deliver me to her. Rainere gave her my daughter, Natalie, in my place. As soon as I discovered what he had done, the men and I rescued Natalie from the underground nest and destroyed all the spiders in order to escape again." Adele felt her expression turn haunted, she could almost smell the burnt smoke of the blue Dragon Fire.

"Everything died in that evil hole, and then I punished Rainere for kidnapping Natalie." The silence in the room was deafening. "The end."

Adelena tried to smile but it caught at the side of her mouth and felt ugly.

Ohren sat forward in his chair and suddenly his expression made him so much less like the kindly old man she knew and so much more like the immortal wizard that he was. General Ohrig had told her that Ohren was the most powerful man in the kingdom of Unisia, and that she should never underestimate him. This was also the reason that she needed him as an ally.

"How did you kill an entire race of dark entities?" asked Ohren, his white eyebrows twisted high on his forehead.

Adele thought it was an oddly scientific question considering all she had just told him. "With Dragon Fire," she replied. "The prince had a small spark and he gave it to us. It was the only thing we could use." She didn't mention Charlie yet, wanting to keep his presence in the adventure a secret from the high wizard for now.

Ohren sat back in his chair and continued to stare at Adele, making her feel even more nervous. She slipped a mental hand over her magic and felt it tense, though the Chime Voices tinkled calmly enough, she looked down at her clasped hands.

"Ohren, I'm telling you all of this not because I want your pardon, or because I am declaring myself your enemy. I'm telling you all of this to let you know that the prophecy that you were following is finished. I killed the Empress of a dark god, because she was going to eat my daughter, and I killed her people because they were going to rise up and take over Unisia, and their first target was the Golden Palace. Rainere was supposed to marry me, then take my crown away and pass a law to allow the dark entities to live in the light again, or something. He didn't want to do it. It wasn't his idea to steal my crown from me even though he believed it was in the prophecy." Adele fell silent. Defending Rainere was not part of her plan right now.

Adele looked back at Ohren and tried to gauge his reaction. There was nothing else to say. The story had been told and she didn't know if he would believe her. If he did, what exactly would he do with a queen he didn't need anymore, now that the prophecy had been resolved? Unisia had gotten along just fine without her, and no doubt it would again soon, if Lord Orgustus had his way.

Adele carefully watched the high wizard. *What the hell is he thinking?* She wondered.

CHAPTER EIGHT

"Judgement From On High"

Ohren tried to gather his reeling thoughts together as he stared at Adelena and searched for the frightened, young woman whom he had sent away only three weeks ago to fulfill her part in the prophecy, but the woman staring back at him was another creature altogether. Rings of power glittered around Adelena's pupils now, shining with a weird mix of silver and gold. These were the eyes he desperately needed to disguise. Ohren thought of the little ring he had enchanted for Adelena and wondered if he had made the spell strong enough.

Breaking away from Adelena's hazel gaze, Ohren regarded the men surrounding the table. This motley bunch of misfits and troublemakers were once rejects of the Unisian Ordinary Army, but behind their powerful queen they had graduated into a force to be reckoned with. Ohren cast a quick glance at the general - of course he had Ohrig to thank for all this. *Damn me, that man was always too smart for his own good,* Ohren thought, beginning to rue the day he had so casually handed over the safety of the new queen to one of the smartest, and most contrary tacticians the Army had lost to royal politics.

Ohren had always trusted in his talent for being able to read people and their intentions, and he hated the fact that he had gotten it so wrong with Adelena. The look of defiant trepidation she was giving him meant that she still cared what he thought of her, but he could almost smell the power that clung to her like a haze. Politics and prophecy aside, Ohren had to admit that, as a wizard, Adelena's power excited him, making his blood race just from sitting in the same room as her. Adelena had discovered her magic, and it was even more beautiful and frightening than he could have predicted, and that made her the queen that Unisia needed her to be. But first, he had to help her clean up this awful mess she had created. He began with the betrayal, which troubled him most.

"So you began your affair with Prince Rainere even though you knew he was dangerous?" Ohren couldn't keep the judgment out of his tone. "Even after I warned you about him?"

"Imagine yourself in my shoes, Ohren," replied Adelena, and he could see by the flush in her cheeks and the way her eyes skittered around the room that she didn't want to talk about Rainere. "I was pulled out of my world and given a throne that I didn't want in this alien land. You told me I could never return home but Rainere promised he could help me get back to Earth again. Who was I supposed to trust? You said the prophecy was controlling my life, and you spoke of Dark Days I had to lead you through, but I had dreamed of Rainere for years back on Earth, so when I got here, I thought that he was the true reason that I had been brought to Unisia."

Ohren frowned. "Where is Prince Rainere now?"

"He was lying in the dirt in the Dark Forest when I left him." And Ohren saw the dark flicker of anger in her gaze before she dropped her eyes. "I had hurt him badly and he wasn't far from death, but I know I didn't kill him."

Ohren raised a brow and tried not to look as impressed as he felt. He, of all people, knew how hard it was to take down an immortal wizard, and a Marchant prince at that. "How do you know?"

Adele looked uncomfortable. "I accidentally put a Mark on him. Now we have this sort of connection between us that allows me to feel his presence."

"No, that is impossible," Ohren shook his head firmly. "You could not *Mark* a Marchant prince because he would never allow it. Marks were used in older times to bind slaves into servitude, the bound one could never be free of their Marker, not even in death. I know that Marchant kings would sometimes enslave their wives in such a way, to ensure the purity of their bloodlines, but no prince would endure such a humiliation."

"If it helps, High Wizard, we were witnesses to the Mark on the prince," General Ohrig spoke up from his place at Adelena's right hand. "Queen Adelena had drawn her royal insignia on the prince's ribcage."

Ohren's tight smile was condescending as this conversation was becoming frustrating for him. "But the prince is an immortal! The immortality spell makes it impossible to change a single hair on his body, let alone imprint a *Mark* onto one of the most powerful spells in dark magic. Do you understand me? It. Is. Impossible."

Adele and Ohrig exchanged a glance and their familiarity made Ohren feel an odd jealousy. Adelena should be looking at *him* like that and depending on *his* advice. She was *his* queen, goddess bedamned! Ohren felt the need to reassert his authority over Adelena and bring her to understand fully just how bad this situation actually was. He held up a hand and counted off her mistakes on each finger.

"Let us look at the facts, shall we? One, whatever you did to Prince Rainere is beside the point, because right now you have left him wounded and rejected, yet fully cognizant of the fact that you are not a full-blood St Lucidis queen. Two, you have left a witness to your murder of the Sandarian Mage free to roam around Unisia. Three, you have killed an entire race of magical creatures, be they dark entities or no, you committed genocide on behalf of the Unisian crown, which is forbidden."

"They aren't all dead, High Wizard," interrupted Captain Lucky. "There were a few spider people left in the Dark Forest, and the queen made one of the folk an emperor of those who like to live above ground. That was well done, I believe." The young captain gave his queen a proud nod.

"Ah!" Ohren felt his earlier shock growing into anger. "And now you are holding coronations in the Dark Forest without any authority to do so."

"Look, Ohren," Adele leaned forward in her chair and nailed Ohren with her glittering eyes. "I know I have made mistakes but you are the one who sent me out into this world with no help or knowledge.

I never meant to hurt anyone. Everything I did was only to protect my children and try to get us home again."

"Forgive me if I find that a little hard to believe, Your Majesty," Ohren replied and could feel his own eyes flash with anger. "Your actions do not appear to be the actions of someone who doesn't want to *hurt* anyone. By killing everyone and destroying everything in your path, you have left Unisia in a much more dangerous position than ever before. If any of your enemies get hold of this Ripenzo Shale, the scandal could take down the entire court, and start a war we can ill-afford with Sandar. If the Marchant prince should decide to take his revenge on you after your little romance, he could burn down half this kingdom before breakfast. You have no idea how psychotic these Marchant princes can be."

"Oh, I think I know all about psychotic princes," snapped Adelena, infuriating Ohren further by refusing to be cowed. "I took Rainere down once, and I'll do it again, but you have to know I couldn't care less about these political games."

"These aren't games, Adelena." Ohren's temper snapped and he smashed his hands down on the table top and gold sparks flew from his fingers making the Queen's Guards jump to their feet. "You stupid girl! I *gave* you a crown. I *gave* you the kingdom on a platter. All you had to do was follow the bloody prophecy and bring yourself back alive…"

"How dare you!" Adelena was just as incensed as the high wizard and she jabbed at the air in front of her as if she could reach him. "You should have left well enough alone, High Wizard, and you *should* have left me on Earth."

"Your Majesty!" QG Bear's shout made Ohren and Adele both turn to the door, where the QG was holding the young nanny, Seraphina, around her shoulders. Bear's cheeks were grey. "You have to hear this."

"What is it?" asked Adele, alarmed and began walking to the door.

"Mrs. Ollenby told me to fetch you, Your Majesty." The pretty redhead bobbed into a curtsy. "It's the baby, Princess Stella, she - Seraphina gulped a sob - the doctor thinks it's the Summer Influenza, Your Majesty."

Ohren met Adelena's gaze and the wizard almost heard her heart stop beating. He saw the fear in her eyes and felt it reflected in his own. In an instant, they were united by the same terror.

"Take me to her!" Ohren's order was echoed by Adelena, as they both dashed to the door and down the hall to the royal apartments without another word.

CHAPTER NINE

"The Innocent Fall"

Adele flew through the long corridors of the Golden Palace to get back to the royal apartments. She was vaguely surprised that Ohren could keep up with her as the men of her Queen's Guard fell further and further behind. Ohren was the first to push open the door of the royal nursery, and Adele leapt to her baby's bedside.

Stella lay on her little bed wearing only a cotton chemise. Her head was in Mrs. Ollenby's lap as cloths were dabbed against her forehead and limbs by the nannies. Adele stifled a cry. Since leaving her little girl just a few hours ago, Stella's mild virus had deteriorated into a full-blown flu. The two-year-old had an almost greenish tinge to her skin and was limp and sweating. Stella whimpered when she saw her mother and reached out a tiny hand.

"My poor baby," whispered Adele as she pressed her lips to Stella's fingers. "What has this world done to you?" Adele stroked the damp blonde curls from Stella's forehead and felt the heat of the fever so hot it almost burned her.

Adele looked up at Ohren. "Do something, please!"

The high wizard gently moved Adele out of the way so he could examine the baby. He checked her pulse and felt the fever with the back of his hand, before checking the whites of her eyes. He sat back on his heels wearing a puzzled expression.

"I don't know how it is possible," he murmured. "The Summer Influenza only affects those with little or no magic in their system. For one of your children to be born without power - it's impossible."

"This is my fault?" Adele asked, instantly sure that it was.

High Wizard Ohren gave Adele a look deep with pity and squeezed her hand. "Every year it gets worse, Your Majesty," he said gently. "Every year, more children are born with no magic and then die because of this dreadful influenza. Rest assured I will do everything in my power to try to save Stella, I promise." A green spark passed between their clenched hands that made Ohren flinch, but he quickly turned away to speak with the man next to him. The man was dressed in the simple cotton robe of a priest, so Adele presumed that he was also a doctor, like Pere Raven.

"Fetch the tonic immediately," Ohren ordered the doctor. "And bring two doses, the princess is in an advanced stage of the virus."

Adele mopped Stella's brow with one of the cold cloths and tried to croon a lullaby but her mouth was too dry. She only began paying attention to the murmured conversation when Ohren's voice rose in agitation.

"Well then find the last of the emergency reserves," the wizard shouted. "There should be something left."

Yet still the doctor hesitated. He was pulling at the collar of his robe and casting Adele increasingly furtive looks while he continued to whisper at Ohren. When Ohren's angry expression became anguished, Adele began to panic.

"What is it?" she asked. "Why won't he get Stella the tonic?"

The high wizard turned to Adele, his cheeks ashen. "Your Majesty, I-" But he was silenced by the crash of someone trying to push their way through her Queen's Guard where they stood at the nursery door.

"Let me through. I will see her! Get out of my way, you fools!"

"Lord Orgustus!" Ohren's voice thundered through the room making the lord freeze in the doorway. Then Ohren quickly corrected himself, "You are just the man we need now, QG's let him in."

Adele waved for her men to release the lord and stood to face him as he came into the room, bearing down on her and using his six-foot-four height to full effect. "Your Majesty." Lord Orgustus gave a shallow bow. "Finally, you have returned from the carnival to run your kingdom again. I hope High Wizard Ohren has informed you of the grave…"

"Lord Orgustus, do you still have the key to the tonic stores?" Ohren interrupted. "I will need it back."

Lord Orgustus's cold gaze flickered from the wizard to the queen and then to the limp toddler splayed on her bed. His sneer disappeared, replaced by incredulity.

"The princess has the Summer Influenza?" Lord Orgustus rounded on the high wizard, pointing his finger accusingly. "You let a child with the virus be brought into the Golden Palace, are you mad? It will sweep these corridors like wildfire."

"Not if you have done your job and inoculated everyone properly," Ohren snapped back and held out his hand for the key.

Lord Orgustus bristled at the insult. "I can only do what I can with the limited powers I am given, High Wizard," he replied acidly. "At the very least the child should be quarantined."

"Stella needs the tonic!" Adele forced herself between the two glaring men. "Lord Orgustus, either give Ohren the key or get it for her yourself."

Lord Orgustus kept his eyes firmly on Ohren as he answered Adele. "The high wizard gave me the key to the stocks and permission to give every last one to the sick people of Concordis, Your Majesty. The stocks are empty."

Adele heard Orgustus's words, and turned to Ohren, who could only close his eyes and nod. "May the Goddess strike me down, yes I did."

"But my baby is dying," Adele shrieked, searching the room for an answer from any of the silent people around her. "Somebody do something!"

Finally, Lord Orgustus looked at her and Adele could see that his anger too masked a terrible desperation in his own heart. "All the babies are dying, Your Majesty," he whispered. "All of the young children on the streets of Concordis are dying, and all the children in the villages and neighboring towns. All over Unisia, our babies are dying."

Lord Orgustus's voice petered out in a dry rasp and his blue eyes became wet with unshed tears. He coughed and shuddered as if to shake off the indignity of the emotions that claimed him. "I will mourn your daughter, Queen Adelena, but you too must mourn for the nation of Unisia. There weren't enough tonics left to inoculate the non-magic population. We could have saved hundreds of lives if you'd just come home when you were told to."

Adele gasped, as if she had been punched in the stomach. She spun to face Ohren. "You! You told me not to come home, when I could have been here."

"Your Majesty, that is not important now," and Ohren spoke loudly enough to cover the rest of Adele's damning words. "Time is of the essence if I am to concoct a tonic quickly enough to save Princess Stella. Please, give me the Fire Orchid stamens now!"

Adele only had to think for a moment. "The box is in my traveling cloak, right in the deepest pocket at the back. I packed the cloak in the bottom of the little purple trunk."

"I know the one," Charlie piped up from the doorway. He was already dressed as a St Lucidis squire and had followed Lord Orgustus into the room. "I'll fetch it for you." He ran off to her bedroom.

"Ohren, how soon can you get the tonic made?" asked Adele.

"It might take as little as four hours, but as much as six to work, Your Majesty." Adele felt Ohren's hand on her shoulder as she sank back to her knees beside Stella.

"And how long has my baby got?" whispered Adele as the tears coursed down her face and dripped onto Stella's hand as she held it in her own.

"I think she has another day's life in her, Queen Adelena," said Ohren, and his voice was gentle as if to soften the horror. "But that is all we can hope for."

CHAPTER TEN

"Sugar and Spice and All Things…"

Natalie hated the hollow place that was back in her chest again. It had been there ever since she had woken up in Mummy's arms in the middle of a field at the Belvoir Estate. The Queen's Guard had all been so serious and quiet, and no one would tell her why they had left Prince Rainere behind, or why they weren't at the Grey Palace anymore. Prince Rainere had made the hollow place go away whenever he had hugged her and told her interesting things and smiled. Natalie missed him now.

Natalie was only sort-of-happy to be back in the Golden Palace again. She had missed her bed and toys, and Mrs. Ollenby, but there were too many people here, and they were always trying to get in between her and her mother. Like this morning when the apartment was full of people standing about in groups but no one would tell her where her mother had gone. Natalie knew something bad had happened to Stella, and that she was very sick. The hollow place in her chest seemed to grow whenever she thought about her baby sister, until it felt like there might not be anything left of her but the empty feeling.

"Are you alright, my poppet?" Mrs. Ollenby interrupted Natalie's morose thoughts by putting another scone with jam on her plate. Mummy would have wanted Natalie to finish her fruit salad first, but she ate the scone anyway.

"Can we go and visit Stella in the hospital today?" Natalie asked through a mouthful of crumbs.

"Stella is sleeping," remarked Aaron mildly, licking jam off his fingers.

Natalie wasn't sure why Aaron's happy face made her angry so quickly, but it did. "I know that, Aaron," she shouted. "I meant after, when she is awake."

Mrs. Ollenby didn't scold Natalie for yelling at Aaron, which made Natalie feel even worse about doing it. "We might leave Stella to sleep quietly today, my lovely," smiled Mrs. Ollenby and gave Natalie's shoulder a pat. "She is quite ill, you see, and needs her rest."

"Hero Boy said that Stella will be dead soon," said Aaron and made Mrs. Ollenby gasp in shock. Everyone looked down at the overgrown puppy at Aaron's feet.

"Then Hero Boy is stupid, just like you," insisted Natalie and gave her brother's arm a pinch, making him yelp. "Stella can't die, because Mummy won't let her."

Natalie really liked Mrs. Ollenby, but she didn't like it when Mrs. Ollenby moved to scoop Aaron up onto her lap and said, "The Goddess Serena has a plan for all of us, my poppet."

That didn't mean anything. Natalie thought, then narrowed her eyes at Mrs. Ollenby. Normally, the older lady was so beautiful with her silvery blonde curls, pretty puffy dresses and the way she always smelled of peaches. It was so nice to cuddle up on her lap and she always had time for a hug. But Natalie wasn't stupid, and now that she was really looking beyond the lady's warm smile, she could see the tell-tale signs of crying in Mrs. Ollenby's sad eyes and the tip of her red nose.

Natalie was startled when her Mummy suddenly came back into the room, making all the servants freeze and bow. Her Mummy looked tired as she made her way over to the dining table but Natalie was relieved to see that she didn't look as though she had been crying. *That should mean everything is alright and Stella is going to be okay,* Natalie told herself.

Mummy's hands were cold when she hugged Natalie and pulled her into her arms, sitting down at the table with Natalie on her lap.

"Is Stella happy in the hospital?" Natalie asked her mother. "She doesn't really like sleeping alone, you know."

Mummy kissed Natalie on her forehead. "She is comfortable, darling. That is all we can do for her right now."

Natalie leaned into her mother's arms and watched the Queen's Guard hover around the dining table. Everyone looked so tense and angry. Only Charlie sat down to eat a plate of scones and jam, even though QG Owens cuffed him on the back of the head, making Natalie giggle at Charlie's comical expression.

Natalie had a question. "Why can't High Wizard Ohren make Stella feel better? Doesn't he have something magic from his labora-tormy that he could use as medicine? Also, I bet that Prince Rai-"

"No, darling," Mummy sighed, her breath making a warm spot on Natalie's hair. "High Wizard Ohren needs a special ingredient for a magic potion that comes from Sandar. If he hasn't got this ingredient, then he can't make the potion and he can't help Stella get better."

"Mummy, Hero Dog says…" Aaron began, but Mrs. Ollenby quickly shushed him and said, "Are we quite sure your rooms at the Belvoir Estate were checked thoroughly before you left, Your Majesty?"

Natalie heard Mummy sigh again as she was gently pushed off her lap and popped back on another chair. "Mrs. Ollenby, it was a small wooden box covered in engravings and filled with something incredibly valuable to the kingdom, it should not have had a chance to fall out of my cloak. It should never have left my hands. Its loss is all my fault. If only I hadn't…"

But Natalie couldn't hear anything else her mother said as the blood had started pounding loudly in her ears, and her stomach dropped away.

Natalie remembered the little wooden box. She remembered getting her hand slapped away from it and being told it was more precious than gold. She remembered her mother hiding it in her big traveling cloak and putting it up high in the wardrobe in their bedroom at the Grey Palace when she thought Natalie had left the room. It hadn't been hard to push a chair up to the wardrobe, and put a tall box on it, and climb right up, stretching out a hand to catch the heavy fabric in her fingers.

Frozen with fright, Natalie's gaze fell on Charlie. He had visibly paled at the bad news and even pushed away the last scone on his plate. Natalie didn't like to see his normally-smiling mouth pressed into such a hard line.

"I will go and ask Ohren if maybe he had a tracing spell, or something we could use to contact Bertie without having to travel there and back for an answer. Perhaps he has some of the magic sand that Charlie used at Belvoir," Mummy said as she kissed both Natalie and Aaron on their heads and prepared to leave. "What do you say, Charlie, do you think that would work?"

Natalie saw Charlie flinch at her mother's words, and he only shrugged in response.

"Well, anything is better than doing nothing." Mummy's voice caught like she was going to cry but when Natalie looked at her all she saw was her eyes glittering with tiny sparkles. Then Mummy left again and took all the Queen's Guard with her. Charlie stayed seated, staring at the table.

Mrs. Ollenby picked up Aaron and took him off to the bathroom with Hero Dog following on their heels. Natalie's own Tra La La was asleep under the table, curled up with Stella's dog, Bunny. Natalie felt the empty place in her chest ache like a big hot stone had been plunked down into the middle of it. It was so hard and heavy it made her eyes burn and she almost couldn't breathe. This was the most frightened that Natalie had ever felt in her life. She had to tell someone and Charlie was the only one left at the table.

"Charlie?" Natalie's voice quavered. "What should you do if you took something that didn't belong to you, but gave it to someone else to make them happy?"

Charlie looked startled at Natalie's question, his hazel-green eyes widening. "I didn't take anything," he snapped.

She had always liked Charlie but he was being weird when she needed him to be nice. Natalie stared at the teenager and hoped he could help her. "No, I mean, I took something, but he'll look after it carefully, I'm really sure he will."

Natalie didn't like the way Charlie's eyes suddenly went all sharp and cold. "Who will? What are you talking about?"

Natalie shook in her seat and gulped. "I know where Mummy put that little box with the pictures on it, because I got it down…"

In a flash, Charlie was in front of her, his hands holding her arms. "Tell me," he ordered. "But think very carefully, Princess: what did you do with the box from your mother's cloak after you saw it? Can you remember who you gave it to?"

Natalie nodded and was too scared even to squirm in Charlie's tight grip. She could see the thin rings of silver around his pupils start to turn and flash, but for all his anger, he looked as frightened as she felt. He shook her a little, but it was so hard to say the words out loud.

"Natalie, you have to tell me! Where is that box?"

"The prince," whispered Natalie. "I gave the box to Prince Rainere."

CHAPTER ELEVEN

"A Boy to Do a Woman's Work"

Adele, General Ohrig, and Orestes were helping Ohren search his cramped attic office hoping to find the hand mirror that Ohren claimed might be able to help him communicate with Prince Bertie at the Belvoir Estate, when Charlie burst in with the news that Natalie had given the Fire Orchid stamens to Rainere.

Adele blinked at Charlie. "You can't be serious?"

Charlie nodded, looking pale and terrified. "The princess admitted it to me just now, Your Majesty."

"But when could she have – Oh!" Adele suddenly remembered the teary farewell on the steps of the Grey Palace when Natalie had handed the prince a clumsy little parcel. Adele had been too distraught at leaving Rainere to be cautious. She had been too much in love to fear anything he might do.

She should have checked Natalie's gift. She should have hidden the Fire Orchid stamens better. Now, because of her negligence, Rainere held the fate of another one of her children in his hands.

"The prince has the Fire Orchid stamens," repeated Ohren to Orestes, his hands still full of papers from the drawer he was emptying. The twins stared at each other with the exact same expression of horror.

General Ohrig turned on his queen in whirl of anger and frustration. "I warned you, didn't I? I told you to be careful with the prince, but did you listen to me?"

Adele dropped into a chair as her legs collapsed under her. She felt like she was going to be sick. "But it's not like the prince took them. Natalie gave them to him." *Why am I defending Rainere?* Perhaps she was just too determined to claim all the blame for herself. Either way it only made General Ohrig more furious.

"This is unbelievable," he spluttered, choking on his anger. "You think he doesn't know what he was given? You think he doesn't understand the value of those Fire Orchid stamens to the kingdom of Unisia? He wanted to be your king, and your hero, and if you married him he would have given them back, but now he's got you right where he wants you, doesn't he?"

Adele shook her head to clear the shock away and pulled at the magic inside of her. It hissed in irritation at Ohrig's presumptuous scolding, and the Chime Voices sang a command that would soon shut him up but Adele knew that Ohrig was right to be angry. He *had* warned her and she hadn't listened to him. Guilt held her heart in a tight grip but Adele refused to give in to its crushing weight.

Just days ago, Adele had fought an impossible war with a mythical foe when everyone about her had given up hope. She would be damned before she forgot those hard-won lessons.

"I will go to the Grey Palace," she announced. "I will ask the prince for the Fire Orchid stamens back, or I will take them from him by force."

High Wizard Ohren's laugh was loud and hollow. "Did it never cross your mind, my queen, that it was the prince who made your child so ill? She caught the fever first at the Grey Palace, didn't she? And now we find out that it is the prince who holds the last Fire Orchid stamens hostage. Do you really think that is a coincidence?" Ohren looked miserable despite his cruel words. "He is probably lying in wait for you at the Grey Palace now, just hoping to spring his trap when you come calling to beg for the stamens back to save your daughter."

"The high wizard makes a good point, Your Majesty," agreed Ohrig. "It would be worse than foolish to allow you to cross the threshold of the Grey Palace ever again. It would surely mean your death."

"So I should let Stella die?" Adele glared at her general. "Ohrig, you should know me better than that by now. I will tear this world apart to help one of my children, and if that means giving my life I will do that too."

Ohrig held Adele's gaze. His pale blue eyes all but disappeared beneath his heavy brows, but she could see the grief there too. "I would give my own life to save the princess, Your Majesty, all of your men would, but we can't lose you to a useless battle when there must be a better way to win the war. All Marchant princes are wicked, and have been since the beginning of time…"

"Wait!" Adelena interrupted Ohrig before he could continue with the history lesson that she had heard before, but the memory of it gave her an idea. "Ohren, the Golden Palace used to belong to the Marchant family hundreds of years ago, right? Well, that means there must be a portal linking the two palaces somewhere in these halls, or maybe underneath the palace in the basement. Rainere wouldn't be expecting me to come through a portal, but I know I would come out in the Portal Station under the palace. From there, I'm sure I could find my way to his room."

Ohren shot an alarmed look at his brother and then at the door of his office. "Your Majesty, to cross a portal is impossible without proper training. I know your blood is - he coughed - different, but portals require those of *the* Blood, which is pure Marchant blood."

Adele raised a brow at the High Wizard and almost rolled her eyes. "I think we can both admit that my blood runs a little greener than you told me, Ohren. While that is something you are going to explain to me later, right now I can tell you that I have travelled a portal by myself before and I came out the other end just fine. I will risk it again."

"I will not risk you," began Ohren. "The throne of Unisia…"

"Does not matter to me," argued Adelena. "The only thing that matters to me is keeping my family safe, and alive."

Charlie's cough made all heads turn to him. He was sixteen but he looked younger than that as he stood up, pulling his sleeves down over his hands and flicking the fringe out of his eyes with a sharp toss. "I have an idea."

Charlie looked to Adelena, and she saw something strong in his hazel-green gaze. "Why don't you send me to the Grey Palace, Your Majesty? I can travel the portal because my Marchant blood is pure enough, you know that, and I also know my way around the Grey Palace from my time there."

Adele appreciated the offer, but she couldn't send a boy to do a woman's job. "Charlie, the Grey Palace is huge, and it is protected by dangerous magic. If you don't ask the prince where they are, how would you even know where to look for the stamens?"

"Because, I know where the prince is keeping that little box, Your Majesty." Charlie's words almost echoed in the shocked silence. "I saw the box you described in his bedroom, on the mantlepiece above the fireplace. It's the same place he kept the Dragon Fire. I didn't know the box was special before today, if I had known I would have stolen it already... for you, I mean." Charlie's eyes pleaded with her to believe him.

"Look, no one has even told me who this kid is," Ohren said. He directed his irritation at Charlie. "Young man, I don't know what you think you can do, but the Marchant prince will snap you like a twig if he caught you trying to steal from him in the Grey Palace."

Charlie stood taller, pushing his thin shoulders back, and his dark eyes flashed angrily at the High Wizard. "Listen, *old man*, I probably know more about that palace than anyone else here. I broke into it once and almost died, but I won't make that mistake again. I know how to get past the Sleeping Guards lining his hallways and I know how to hide. So I'm the best hope we've got if you are not going to go yourself."

The High Wizard's eyes narrowed at the insult. "Now, you listen here you little gutter-cat..."

"Ohren!" Orestes raised a hand to silence his brother. "Young Charlie makes a good point. If we send him to retrieve the stamens now we could have them in our hands before morning, and if he isn't as good as his word then we have lost nothing for trying."

"But the prince would be alerted to our need for the stamens if the boy fails," protested Ohren. "Any element of surprise would be lost."

"I will take a solid effort over a lot of waiting and doing nothing, Ohren," said Adele, joining the debate. "Charlie will go."

Adele gave her young spy a tight smile. "There is no Plan B, Charlie. I need you to steal those stamens and be back here with your life intact before morning. Do you really think you can do it?"

Charlie's chest swelled with pride and his eyes lit up with excitement. "It'll be a doddle, Your Majesty." He gave Adele a cheeky wink, making Ohren groan and drop his head into his hands.

"What you are asking this boy to do is highly illegal, Your Majesty," interrupted Orestes and adjusted his gold chain of the High Magistrar's office. "You are willingly and knowingly sending a thief to illegally enter a fellow sovereign's palace and advocating that a gift freely given to Prince Rainere by Princess Natalie be stolen back, and you do not plan to offer restitution to the prince after the fact."

"I'll give him restitution," replied Adele darkly. "But he will get more than he bargained for if he should ever dare ask."

"You misunderstand me, Your Majesty." Orestes' eyes were the exact same electric blue as his twin's though they didn't have the same sparkle. "As the high magistrar, and a witness to this crime, I am ultimately culpable for what is discussed here, but I am also the only one here who can channel the blame to myself and not have it touch anyone else in this room should Charlie be discovered. Let me do this for you, please? I will take Charlie down to the portal and see him through myself, then wait for him to come back. *If* he returns, I will bring you the stamens. Your hands will touch no part of this crime except to accept stolen goods, but then we can argue that you had no knowledge of how I obtained the stamens. Your hands will remain clean."

Adele didn't care about the laws of the constitution of the Golden Palace but she knew that what Orestes offered was his way of helping her. "That is very good of you, Orestes. I thank you."

There was a knock at the door, interrupting their conversation. Mrs. Ollenby poked her head into the room. "I didn't want to disturb you at work, Your Majesty." Mrs. Ollenby's sweet face was crumpled with the effort of holding back tears. "But it's Princess Stella, she is awake and wants her mama."

Adele was on her feet in an instant, making her way to the door. The time for discussion was over.

"Charlie, you will leave immediately. Ohren, maybe you could give Charlie a weapon of some kind so he has some way of defending himself if he encounters the prince. Orestes, I trust you will not leave that portal entrance until Charlie has returned to us. General, please let the men go to bed and sleep, I know none of you have slept properly for over a week. I will need you all rested and ready for what tonight may bring."

Adele made her way over to Charlie, the boy who had helped her save Natalie, selflessly battling the Spider Empress by her side, and now he was again putting himself in harm's way to try to save her baby.

"I am depending on you, Charlie." Adele enclosed him in a tight hug. "I want to save my baby, but I want you to come back safe to me too. If you cannot find the stamens, come home. I'm sure it's what Stella would want if she knew the sacrifice you were making for her." She gave Charlie another quick hug before letting him go. "Your place is with me, your queen, never forget that." Adele turned away, missing the look of adoration lighting Charlie's face at her words.

"Gentlemen, I will be in with my daughter if anyone needs me." Adele said as she made her way back to the door. "Ohren, please join me when you can." Then she left the room.

High Wizard Ohren lingered a moment, watching Ohrig give Charlie advice for his dangerous mission. General Ohrig clapped the boy on the back, called him a 'miniature Queen's Guard', and promised him a white and gold uniform when he returned from the Grey Palace.

"I'll be alright," Charlie said, smiling despite his pale cheeks. "You let those QG boys get some rest and leave all the work to a real man. I'll see you all tomorrow over tea and scones."

General Ohrig caught the high wizard's eye. Ohren could clearly see the worry and fear in his expression, though the old general tried to hide it behind a stern facade.

Ohren knew of General Ohrig by reputation, though he had rarely spoken to him much before today. Still, if General Ohrig was going to be such an important influence on Queen Adelena perhaps it was time to befriend him.

Ohren gestured for the general to join him, away from the others. "General Ohrig, from your outburst today, I get the sense that the queen has been somewhat difficult to deal with." Ohren smiled to soften his words and invite confidence. "She seemed like such a sweet little thing, before I sent her off to Sandar."

"Queen Adelena was a sweet little thing before Sandar, High Wizard," agreed Ohrig but his look was accusing. "It's our world that has brought out the darkness in her. Despite her mistakes, she is only trying to do what's best for her family. If she had been given more information about her situation, or a reason to trust someone, this mess we are in might have all been avoided."

Ohren stepped back from the general's poorly suppressed rage. The man was as tactless as he was loyal. No wonder he had failed in the political fishbowl that was the Unisian Ordinary Army. Though it was true that Adelena would need all the friends she could get in the coming days, Ohren was suddenly unsure that having a soldier like Ohrig around was the best thing for her. He decided he would look into finding others more qualified to provide her with political support, and to be more conducive to suggesting she listen to her elders.

Despite his own grief, Ohren couldn't help but start thinking about life after Princess Stella died. So much needed to be done to shore up Adelena on the throne and getting the Fire Orchid stamens back from the Marchant prince wasn't the only problem he needed to deal with. Ohren felt for the small ring in his pocket. It had been enchanted with an illusion charm that would hide Adelena's ever-changing eyes, but with all the chaos since she had come home he had yet to find a moment to give it to her. He would have to tread carefully with this particular gift as he could tell she didn't trust him as she had before. *She has discovered her power but how much does she really know about her blood? What can I still keep hidden from her?* Ohren thought, before he was distracted by Charlie waving at him.

"So, High Wizard," smiled the boy. "What've you got for me that can take down a Marchant prince?"

Ohren regarded Charlie seriously for the first time, and noted the boy had a strong ring of silver around his pupils. It was almost a shame the kid was about to embark on a suicide mission as Ohren could sense a lot of potential magic in him. He decided to be kind to Charlie.

"Come to my laboratory with me," he said. "I'll give you everything I can to get past those Sleeping Guards, but when it comes to Prince Rainere, I suggest you avoid him. That is a battle you could never win."

"Yes, be careful Charlie," agreed the general. "We want you back here as soon as you can. May the luck of the Goddess go with you, kid."

Ohren led the way to the door of his office and opened it. "After you, Charlie."

CHAPTER TWELVE

"Fire Burns All"

Prince Rainere pulled up his collar against the rain that was dripping down his neck and shivered. A chill wind blew through the clearing in the Dark Forest, ruffling the leaves in the trees and filling the glade with the sound of scratchy applause. It was a gloomy, mocking sound and Rainere sought to banish it by building a bigger fire. He picked up another piece of wet wood from his small collection of fuel, muttering a charm to make sure the damp had steamed away before throwing it on the fire. It didn't help much.

Exhausted from a long night of travel, Rainere's strength was spent. He had been building and taking apart portals for hours to make it this far into the Dark Forest. Now he had come right to the foot of the Black Mountains where the dark magic had fought even his manipulations, and his portals were disintegrating as quickly as he could build them. It was clear that he would now have to travel on foot. The prince wrapped his arms around his knees and stared into the orange flames. He had just drunk a dose of the Gift of Life and waited for the rush of healing energy that it would bring him. Yet, even that powerful potion would not be enough to restore the shredded ruins of his heart.

Of all the gifts Adelena had given him, Rainere hated this new desire for company the most. Loneliness had been his constant companion since his father had died. No one had come into his life since, and he had become accustomed to only ever hearing his own thoughts and attending to his own needs. But now, ridiculously, Rainere craved noise, laughter, and the company of people.

In his more adventurous youth, well before he had become immortal, Rainere had ventured into the Portal Station beneath the Grey Palace and found the portal that led directly to the Royal Unisian Accadaemia. He had risked visits whenever Grotto was distracted, and his very few memories of adolescent happiness had come from that time.

Like a shadow, the young Prince Rainere had crept about the grounds of the Accadaemia, sneaking into lectures and hiding in corners to watch the groups of young wizards-in-training, eating their picnic lunches and chatting in the sunshine of the quadrangle. Rainere had longed to join them, and to be as happy as they seemed, discussing their schoolwork and their professors.

There had been one teacher whom everyone had loved. Standing in the courtyard, his hands clasped behind his back, as he held court amongst the admiring crowds of students, Wizard Ohren had impressed and thrilled Rainere. He even remembered the man visiting his father when Rainere had been very little. He remembered the sound of his booming laugh and those blue, blue eyes. Just once, Rainere had been consumed with the urge to approach Ohren to talk to someone who had actually known his father. But Wizard Ohren had been too shocked by Rainere's appearance to speak, and the young prince had run away from the horrified expression and belated shout, "Stop!"

It was only a day later that Grotto discovered Rainere's trips through the portal to the outside world and he had dismantled the portal doorway, warning Rainere yet again of all those who would kill him should they ever see him beyond the boundary of the Grey Palace.

Shortly afterwards, Grotto started putting the women in his bed. Rainere shuddered to remember them all. So many women: the mewling, virgin girls, who were always terrified of him, and then the older women, brazen and painted, mocking his inexperience in giving pleasure. As soon as he knew that he could, Rainere forbade Grotto from bringing him anymore miserable bedmates, vowing to remain celibate until death. It was Adelena who had made him break that vow.

The first time he had gone to Adelena's bedchamber she had trembled in his arms. He had thought it was fear, not excitement that shook her and his disappointment was bitter. On that fateful night, Rainere had tried to do his duty as quickly as possible, but Adelena had surprised him and unleashed a magic that had pinned him to the bed and stolen all his control. Rainere had fought her but Adelena had matched his strength with her own and shown him what love really was.

Never before had Rainere known the euphoria that Adelena's powerful magic had fired in him. The symphony of sensations that intertwined the physical with the magical was indescribable. However, it was her very human sweetness and affection to which Rainere clung time and again, as he realized that he was deeply and irrevocably in love with Adelena.

With her, I could have been someone, Rainere thought morosely. *I could have been a husband by her side, a father to her beautiful children, and a king who treasured his people as Adelena treasured me. She opened the world up to me and welcomed me into her family. The Goddess Serena told me we were meant to be together. How could I have destroyed our destiny? It's just too cruel that by trying to save Adelena's life I cursed myself by losing her love.*

Suddenly, Rainere's mind was flooded with endless images of his *cara mia*.

Adelena naked on his bed, laughing her smoky little laugh, ready for him…

Adelena pressed tight against him, begging for his touch on her skin…

Adelena's magic, her whispered charms that made his bones melt as she invaded his core and possessed him so fully that he could only hear the voice of the Goddess in her moans…such sex…such magic…

But the memories dissolved as the wicked truth revealed itself - Adelena was not his any longer.

Rainere wiped away the hot tears leaking from his eyes with the back of his hand and sniffed. Self-loathing rolled through him in a sickening wave. He was a sad and pathetic thing, and he would not allow himself to remain so any longer. He would find the Marchant Eldars up in their Eeyrie in the Black Mountains and his torment would end. *I cannot deny that the world of Evendaar will be better off without my kind in it,* Rainere thought bitterly. *There will be no one here to mourn me.*

The small fire hissed and spat and Rainere looked about the forest glade for more fuel. Seeing nothing, he tucked his hands in his pockets and found the piece of parchment and the little box together. He pulled out the paper and unfolded it.

Little Princess Natalie had her mother's eyes, and the same dark brown hair, the same beautiful heart-shaped face, and the same willingness to trust a stranger. Rainere held the parchment out over the flames and watched the smiles of the stick figures blacken and turn to ash. *I was a fool to think that I could ever have belonged to their family,* he thought.

Rainere took the little box from his pocket. He didn't look at it too closely, but when he held his hand over the fire and was about to drop it in, a flash of green caught his eye. This box was protected by dark magic. Pulling it back from the flames, Rainere made short work of the rudimentary lock charm and opened the box. As the rain pattered about him, he studied the tiny pile of thin black filaments. He took a pinch and sniffed at them. The scent of sulphur was unmistakable - Fire Orchid stamens.

Rainere stared down at the queen's ransom he held in his hand. A blinding pain suddenly shot up from the Mark in his side, and Rainere could only gasp as it radiated out over his whole body before slowly receding and letting him breathe again. Nausea spiked and he had to spit sour water through his teeth. *Adelena is thinking of me,* he knew instantly. Rainere felt the echoes of her distress and anger directed at him, and his hand shook around the little box almost spilling its contents on the ground. This box was meant for a woman who no longer loved him to help save a people who had always hated him.

Rainere felt bitterness pull up the corner of his mouth in a smile at the realization that Adelena had let her own daughter steal the Fire Orchid stamens from her and give them to the most despised man in the kingdom. He wondered how long Adelena would last on her throne when High Wizard Ohren discovered that his precious queen had failed to bring back the prize her kingdom depended on for its very existence. The Mark in his side pulsed again, pulling at his dignity and igniting his temper. *She still thinks that I am a plaything to be sent away and called back to torture. If she hates me so very much then I will do us both the service of destroying myself. She could not ask more of me than that!*

Rainere let the rain drip onto the open box of Fire Orchid stamens. It was odd to him that such light magic was grown in such a dark place like Sandar. He pinched out a single stamen and examined it closely. The Mark tugged at him again, disturbing his thoughts. With a curse, Rainere snapped the box shut and climbed to his feet. Though he was consumed with dread at the thought of it, he still had a journey to make and he would not let these distractions keep him from it. The time had come, and he was determined to take back control of his destiny once again.

CHAPTER THIRTEEN

"The Scent of Madness"

Charlie stepped out of the portal like a cat climbing out of a bucket of water. He'd been strong enough to pass through on his own, but only just. The magic of the portal had pulled and pushed at him, trying to force him off the path to the Grey Palace. It was only by imagining Queen Adelena's face that he'd had the strength to get through at all.

Charlie looked up at the sign, 'Portal Station One'. *Good.* He had come out right at the top of the Portal Station, and he wouldn't have to take a ride in one of those creepy horseless carriages. Charlie kept all his senses on high alert as he made his way through the chamber, and over to the dark hall which would take him into the palace proper. He didn't spare a glance for the hundreds of stone ravens lining the passage, glaring down at him with jeweled eyes. Instead, he kept a wary eye out for the prince and his manservant, Grottonski.

As he crept and picked his way down hallways and up staircases, Charlie reflected on this new predicament he had volunteered himself into. Charlie wasn't stupid, not by a long shot, and he had put together the pieces of the puzzle pretty quickly.

The small box the Boss had wanted him to steal had been taken by the princess long before the queen had even come to the Belvoir Estate. That was why the spell in the magic sand had failed him. It drove Charlie crazy to think that he had actually put his hand on the box itself when he was in the prince's bedchamber and then had let go of it, thinking it just another ornament. If only he had palmed it then, he could have handed it off to the Boss and avoided the anger he knew he would face when the lord of the underworld finally caught up with him again. Charlie dodged a tiny thread of magic running crossways in the hall. The gold powder that High Wizard Ohren had given him to reveal invisible spells was working a treat.

Charlie returned to his musings. *But what in the hell does the Boss want with Fire Orchid stamens?*

Charlie ducked as he narrowly avoided a web spell that might have blinded him. None of these thoughts mattered anyway. He was going to give the Fire Orchid stamens to the queen when he found them and she was going to save her daughter and the rest of Unisia from the Summer Influenza.

He tried to ignore the dark voice in his head, but its muttering was too loud. *There is a chance to be clever instead of good here,* said the voice. *Everyone in the Golden Palace thinks the Black Prince, Rainere, has the Fire Orchid stamens, and if you actually manage to steal them from him, what is stopping you from fulfilling your obligation to the Boss by giving him the stamens instead? No one would have to know it was you who gave them away, and all the blame would fall on the Marchant prince who they hate anyway. If you betray the Boss, he will definitely torture and kill you, but if you betray the queen she will never know. Princess Stella would die, but you would live.*

Neat. Tidy. Charlie would be home free, without a street price on his head and with his relationship with the queen intact.

It was just a pity that he would rather sacrifice himself for one more hug from Queen Adelena, than protect his own arse. That hug had truly been something else. He shivered as he remembered the psychic zap that went from his brain to his groin in less than a second. Queen Adelena's body had vibrated with power, and his own magic had responded, hot and hard, to her proximity. Charlie swore quietly and tried to pour mental cold water on the lust that had his pants tightening already. The queen was a woman and though she only thought him a boy now, he would rescue these stamens for her, to prove that he could be a man that she could respect, and maybe even come to love in return. Charlie's lightning reflexes saved him from a translucent green arrow that shot at him through a doorway. *Shit, man, focus!*

It took longer than he thought to get to the prince's bedchamber. Directing magic to his five senses, Charlie discovered that the palace was almost entirely empty, no people-noises anywhere, raising his hopes that he could get this job done quickly, but when he got to the prince's door he was dismayed to hear that someone was most definitely inside. He ducked low into the shadows and planned to wait until whoever it was left the room. His heart was hammering so loudly in his ears that he had to hold his breath to hear any other sounds. He tensed when he realized the door handle glowed greenly and the door swung open.

"I can hear you waiting out there," Grottonski's gravelly voice called from inside the room. "But he's not here, you filthy spy."

Screwing up all his courage into a hard little ball, Charlie straightened and stepped into the light of the doorway, but what he saw made him stop on the threshold. The prince's manservant had stripped down to his shirtsleeves and was on his hands and knees scrubbing at the fireplace with a hand brush. All the furniture and carpets in the room had been piled on top of the large four-poster bed, and the wind blew in the open window, swirling wildly about the room and bringing in the cold rain.

"Mr. Grottonski?" Grotto only grunted as the chill wind blew his stringy bits of hair about and his shirt flapped in the breeze. Charlie could see Grotto's naked back with its white skin stretched too tightly over bony knobs of spine. It made Charlie think of a scorpion shedding its armor. Without its hard shell or a spike to attack, the creature was just a wet, jelly-like worm: disgusting, but helpless. That is what Mr. Grottonski looked like now, without his dignity.

"Mr. Grottonski?" Charlie began again. "I'm looking for Prince Rainere, sir. I have a message for him from Queen Adelena."

"*Queen* Adelena, hmph!" grunted Grotto and scrubbed harder at the hearthstone. "Don't mention that abomination's name to me again. What was that?" Grotto's head snapped up and he sat back on his heels, listening.

Charlie recoiled from the madness in Grotto's fluorescent green eyes. "I said…"

But Grotto's head had swiveled to the window. "Yes, I said it!" He shouted at the open window. "I told you before, North Wind, she is an abomination and nothing better." The manservant cocked his head to the side, a look of intense concentration on his face as he listened to the wind blowing about the room. "No, stop saying that!" Grotto shouted, as a violent gust of wind almost knocked the man over. The hairs on the back of Charlie's neck tingled.

"If my master has gone to the Eldars, then it is to get their help in killing that demon woman," grumbled Grotto when the wind had died down again, and he got back to his scrubbing. "She is an abomination and she's no queen of Marchant blood, you know that as well as I do. Queen of the Demons, maybe. Hah! Just like her mother she is, just like her mother. They will thank my master when he gets that demon off the throne."

Charlie had seen a lot in his young life, but the deranged manservant and the sentient wind was thoroughly creeping him out. He needed to get out of this place as fast as he could. Edging closer to the fireplace, he scanned the mantlepiece and saw that it was empty. Looking over at the mess of furniture and knick-knacks on the bed, he groaned as the realization hit him that the box could be anywhere in there. Charlie saw something out of the corner of his eye, and again his lightening reflexes saved him from getting hit in the head by the flying brush let loose from Grottonski's fingers. "What are you staring at, you filthy cat?"

"Mr. Grottonski, where are his things?" asked Charlie, panic giving him the strength to advance on the kneeling manservant. "The prince had something that belonged to the queen sitting right there on the mantel."

"Gone! All gone!" shrieked Grotto. "He took everything she had touched and he is going to get his crown off her head too. I know it." Grotto's face was screwed up with uncertainty. "I told him that crown was his, and he always listens to his old Grotto. He knows I only want the best for him. The North Wind says he's gone to the Eldars, foolish wind. My prince will be back soon enough, you'll see. You'll all see."

Charlie didn't waste another moment before turning and bolting out of the room and back down the corridor, trying not to let panic

confuse him as he re-traced his steps down into the bowels of the
Grey Palace and back to the Portal Station One. His hands were
shaking hard as he fumbled for the two hand mirrors in his pocket.
He took a deep breath and thanked the Goddess that the mirror that
Orestes had given him was markedly different from the one the Boss
had given him which had a black enamel cover. Life would get a lot
more complicated if he told the Boss that not only had he failed again
to get the stamens but that they were actually in the hands of Prince
Rainere. Charlie took another deep breath and called to the High
Magistrar. He almost cried with relief when the face of Orestes
immediately began to coalesce across the surface of the little mirror.

"Charlie, did you get the box?" Orestes voice was as close as if he
spoke directly into Charlie's ear.

"No." Charlie shook his head and gave the old man a grimace. "Bad
news. The prince has left the palace, and he took the box with him.
At least that is what Grottonski said, and I'm not sure he can be
trusted, but that's what he told me." Charlie didn't want to reveal all
of Grottonski's ramblings about the North Wind and the Eldars to
the High Magistrar. He would save that information for the queen
herself.

"Of course he is." Orestes voice was more analytical than upset.
"The prince will want to bargain, and we must be ready for him."

"Please tell the queen that I'm sorry," Charlie blurted, his young heart
unable to contain all the guilt he felt. "Please tell her that I'm sorry I
was too late."

"I know, Charlie," snapped Orestes. "We are *all* going to be very
sorry, very soon. Head to the portal right now, and we can tell the
queen of your failure together." The solemn face of the high
magistrar winked out.

Charlie gulped. In his heart, he knew Queen Adelena wouldn't blame
him for not getting the stamens in time but her forgiveness would
make her grief so much harder to bear. Without the stamens, her
daughter would die and the queen's heart with her. Dread settled
over Charlie like a heavy cloak.

So don't go back to the Golden Palace. The cold voice inside Charlie's head was loud tonight. *You screwed the job, so why do you think you will be of any more use to those St Lucidis pricks? And what if the prince does get himself to the Golden Palace before you, how lucky do you think you will be when the queen finally works out that you were never his messenger when she met you?*

Looking about near the dark archways of the portal station, Charlie thought he caught a movement out of the corner of his eye. This place was so creepy even a cat wouldn't live here. He walked towards the portal that would lead him straight into the Golden Palace. Of all the stupid things he could do right now, going back to the people he had betrayed was probably the worst. After all, the high magistrar could break the news of Charlie's failure without him.

The image of Queen Adelena stuck fast in Charlie's mind, as did the ghostly feel of her arms around him as she whispered in his ear. He would go back to her; he couldn't help it. *Damn it!* That woman had marked him, as sure as she had marked the prince, Charlie's was just an invisible scar.

Charlie took a deep breath and stared into the swirling depths of the green portal, feeling his own magic respond. He hesitated for just a moment when a shadow appeared, hovering in the green sparkles. Charlie backed up a step and didn't even think to look behind himself. The blow that struck him made his ears ring so loud he didn't hear the crack of his knees hitting the stone floor. His head followed just a moment later, and then the darkness had him.

CHAPTER FOURTEEN
"The Midnight Watch"

The small hospital room was dark and windowless, lit only by a few candles. Princess Stella slept fitfully, dozing for a few minutes and then whimpering until she awoke. Her breath was hitching in plaintive little cries that broke Ohren's heart as he sat next to Adelena by the bedside, their shoulders close enough to touch as they mourned together.

Ohren placed his hand on Adelena's back as she rocked beside him, tears coursing down her face. She whispered prayers to the god of her Earth world to save her baby Stella, but Ohren knew that her god would be no help now. Here in Evendaar, she needed magic to heal Stella, and it had to be old and powerful magic at that. He noted that the green tinge had spread from the baby's face to her throat and reached under the thin cotton chemise to mottle the skin of her chest. Even the blonde curls over Stella's ears were turning white as the Summer Influenza leached the life and color from her tiny body. Yet the baby still breathed, and Ohren was very surprised she hadn't died already. *Maybe her mother's prayers were helping?*

The wizard didn't want to admit to himself that he was actually afraid of what Adelena's reaction would be when her child died, and he didn't have the heart to even suggest that the Fire Orchid tonic wouldn't be enough to save her daughter now but would merely ease Stella's suffering as she passed away.

Stella yelped in pain as her body convulsed then settled again. Ohren felt Adelena tremble as she stifled her sobs and pressed her tear-soaked hands over her unconscious baby's cheeks.

Despite his anger with her in the Lavender Room, Ohren could only feel sympathy for this young mother fighting with everything she could to save her daughter. Adelena's magic was strong now, he had seen it in her eyes, but he had seen something else too, something *other.* He could feel it pulse within her as he rubbed her back in large comforting circles. In Adelena, Ohren sensed an aura of power with a sharp edge that confused him. Holding the queen close like this, he felt as if he was sitting next to a giant, as if her power loomed over the both of them. He wanted to believe that the darkness he sensed in her was just a result of the Blood that her mother had given her, but there was something magnetic about Adelena that simply hadn't been there before. He felt sure the secret lay in her eyes. *The rare mix of silver and gold glitter could mean that she had not one, but two different powers within her body,* Ohren thought, *but which magic was more dominant?*

In the guise of giving her comfort, his hand rose to touch the bare skin of her shoulder and Ohren almost gasped at the sensation that followed the contact. He quickly removed his hand. He had definitely felt that type of power before, but his shocked mind could hardly believe he was near it again.

"Once an addict, always an addict," he thought ruefully and let the shame burn away his desire. After all this time, the taste of dark magic could still rock him, and make him pine for more.

He had told Adelena there was nothing he could do for Stella, but there were at least ten spells that would help the princess with her pain resting heavily on the tip of his tongue. Each of those spells contained dark magic, and so to cast them he would need to steal energy from those living around Stella. He would be compromising the health of others to give the child a short-lived comfort, and that was not the moral thing to do.

They could do nothing but wait for the Fire Orchid stamens to be returned. Though inside his own heart, Ohren was sure that there was no chance that skinny kid, Charlie, could steal anything from the prince's own chamber in the Grey Palace.

As if sensing his pessimistic thoughts, Adelena leaned away from the High Wizard and over her baby, crooning a lullaby and kissing her little one repeatedly. Magic or no magic, this is what every mother did to communicate her love to a child. Guilt deepened the crack in Ohren's breaking heart.

Ohren patted Adelena's shoulder and tried not to enjoy the sensation it gave him. "It will be alright, Adelena," he lied. "Charlie will return soon and everything will be alright."

"Stella will come back to me," murmured Adelena, her voice heavy with tears. "She will be healthy again. She has to be."

"Of course, my dear." Ohren patted Adelena again when a flash of gold caught his eye. The baby's cheeks were covered in wet sparkles that caught the lamp light. Adelena's tears had carried the gold magic of her blood. Ohren was stunned. He didn't even want to think how that was possible, but it was impossible to ignore that Stella was now breathing better and had turned her little body towards her mother's crooning voice.

"Adelena, my Queen?" Ohren shook her shoulder a little. "You are crying gold magic."

"I know," sniffed Adelena. "I can feel it coming out of me. I just don't know how it's going to help her."

Ohren was nonplussed. "Neither do I," he admitted. "I've never seen that before. Yet your St Lucidis magic has awoken and is giving her comfort."

Adelena gave the high wizard a smile that wasn't a smile. "It's a bit late now," she said. "Ohren, I have so much inside of me, so much magic pulling and pushing at me, and I have no idea what to do with it. Please can you tell me, what am I?"

Ohren pulled Adelena into a one-armed hug. "You will always be you, Adelena. Magic isn't all you are, and you need to remember that. All that matters is that you are home here and I will always be by your side. Come what may after Stella…"

Adelena turned away from Ohren and towards her baby. She brushed the tears from her cheeks and wiped them onto her daughter's. "Stella will come back to me," Adelena repeated. "I won't let her die here in Evendaar, Ohren. I won't."

Ohren had nothing else to say. He sat next to his queen, unable to give her any comfort.

CHAPTER FIFTEEN

"A Knight in Soot and Grime"

It was midnight in Stella's hospital room. Ohren had already been replaced by Mrs. Ollenby without Adele even noticing. Adele only looked up from her baby when she heard the commotion in the hallway outside. At the sound of men shouting, both women started in surprise and made for the door.

Adele's heart clutched in her chest when she stepped out into the hall and approached the knot of people. She could see her majordomo Tilburn, dressed only in trousers and a striped nightshirt. Tilburn had obviously just been roused from bed and he was berating the group of Golden Palace Guardsmen for not informing him of events sooner. High Wizard Ohren was standing in Adele's way, and she had to touch him on the arm before he moved, and to Adele's shock revealed that the figure standing before him was none other than Prince Rainere.

"Your Majesty," huffed Tilburn, completely put out by the affront to the queen's dignity to receive any visitors right now, and the Marchant prince most of all. "May I present His Royal Highness..." But Adele held up her hand for silence. This was not the time for protocol.

Rainere stood before her. His bearing was straight, although palace guards were on either side of him, holding his arms behind his back. His chin was held high and one of his eyebrows was raised in an imperial arch. Rainere looked so strange without his beautiful long hair to frame his face. His normally immaculate clothes were dirty and he smelled like a campfire. Yet he still stole her breath away.

"It's Stella," said Adele and her voice was just above a whisper. "She has the Summer Influenza I can't... no one can heal her. We need the Fire Orchid stamens that Natalie gave you to make a tonic."

Rainere paled beneath his soot-smudged cheeks. "But Stella is your daughter, how could she not have the magic to fight this?"

Adele suppressed a sob and felt herself lean towards Rainere, as if gravity pulled them together. "I don't know how she was born without magic, but now she is dying and no one can help her without the tonic."

The prince looked to the high wizard and Adele didn't recognize his expression "Why would you tell her that?" Rainere asked. Ohren did not reply but only turned his face away.

"Please," said Adele, desperation making her voice hoarse. "Rainere please, give me back the stamens."

Rainere easily shook off the guards and took a tiny box from his jacket pocket. He held it out on his palm. "Queen Adelena, I return to you the gift that was given freely to me. I would not have kept it from you had I known what it was." Rainere's dark green eyes drilled into her own. "You have to believe that, Adelena. I will never steal anything from you ever again."

Adele could only stare at Rainere as his words washed over her. Her bruised and battered brain tried to absorb the reality of the stamens appearing before her. Adele swayed on her feet. She felt Mrs. Ollenby at her side and leaned into her safe embrace. *Sweet Christ*, Adele thought, *Stella is saved.*

But when Adele reached for the box, Ohren put his hand over hers and stared suspiciously at Rainere's outstretched palm, as if it was dangerous. "You would give the most precious treasure in all of Unisia back to her," - he gestured at Adele – "just like that?"

Rainere turned his hollow gaze to the high wizard. "Would you prefer to fight me for them?"

Ohren took a moment too long to answer and Adele was suddenly afraid the wizard might agree to something just that stupid. She snatched the box out of Rainere's palm and pressed it into Ohren's hand. "Make the tonic. Now," she ordered.

The wizard finally closed his fingers over the box and gave the prince one last glare before pushing through the group of guards and taking off down the hall at a sprint that sent his long robes billowing behind him. Adele sighed in relief.

Tilburn bowed in front of her, his hair all askew and his expression anxious, "Your Majesty, I had arrived just a few hours ago to hear the dreadful news of the baby princess's illness. My thoughts," - he reached for her hands – "and my love are with her. Please instruct me on anything I can do for you during this dreadful time."

Adele nodded and gave Tilburn's hand a squeeze in appreciation of the offer. The responsibilities of the kingdom still needed to be dealt with. "Do what you can for the people in the city where children are still dying, Tilburn," she said. "I will stay with Stella until the tonic is made and she is well again." Tilburn bowed and let go of her hands to dash off down the hallway, taking the Household Guard with him.

Adele turned to return to Stella's room.

"Adelena," Rainere's voice was a rasp.

Adele looked back over her shoulder at Rainere. Across the few yards of plush carpet between them, lay everything they had been to each other - all the happiness and all of the terror they had caused each other. Adele didn't think it possible but her lips formed a smile, and she could see the relief it gave Rainere as his own expression softened under her gaze.

"Stella." He nodded at the hospital door. "Can I see her?"

Adele looked into Rainere's beautiful damaged face and saw the hope in his eyes.

"No," she said. "You can't." Adele disappeared into the hospital room once again, closing the door behind her with a solid click.

CHAPTER SIXTEEN

"An Unexpected Kindness"

Rainere stared at the door for a long moment, trying to control a wild urge to knock it down. He wanted to demand to be allowed to see Stella and to grieve by Adelena's side too. He wanted to insist that Adelena allow him to console and care for her as she suffered. Rainere knew she needed him now, even if she wouldn't let herself acknowledge it.

Rainere considered causing a scene. *For spite, I could reduce this palace to rubble and leave Adelena with nothing but her pain and the knowledge that she had caused this tragedy by denying me such a simple request,* he thought.

Rainere sagged against the wall and cradled his head in his hands. Sunk deep in his misery, he didn't realize anyone had remained with him until he felt a light touch on his arm. Embarrassed, Rainere pulled himself up to his full height and glared down at the woman standing before him. She looked harmless enough, wearing a soft pink dress that puffed out from her waist and a diamond necklace glittering on her ample chest. A smile scrunched up the corners of her lavender blue eyes and gold curls framed a gentle face. Rainere tried to assess the threat she posed him as she dropped into a curtsy, but he could see no reason for the lady's presence.

"Your Highness, my name is Dolores Ollenby. I am the Head Keeper of the Royal Household and Matron of the Royal Nursery," Mrs. Ollenby said, smiling warmly. "We met briefly once before, when you were here for the queen's coronation. I would like to offer you a much more hospitable welcome to the Golden Palace than you have so far received."

Nonplussed, Rainere could only stare.

"May I take you to the Marchant family quarters to give you time to refresh and rest a while?" she asked.

"I have no need of it," said Rainere and his voice grated painfully over the words. He suddenly became aware of how filthy and strange he must seem to this decorous lady of the Golden Palace. "I shall leave immediately. I don't believe the queen will want…"

"Nonsense!" Mrs. Ollenby scoffed, and surprised Rainere by taking his arm and leading him down the corridor. "If the queen wasn't so distracted by the illness of Princess Stella she would insist on it herself, I am sure."

Though she only came to his shoulder, Mrs. Ollenby's pulled Rainere along the halls in the direction of the guest apartments with a firm grip. He had to be careful to match his long stride to her quick little steps.

Rainere had been made to study the layout of each of the old Marchant properties, the Golden Palace included, though it now belonged to the St Lucidis family, and he knew that Mrs. Ollenby was taking him down the quieter corridors, far from the main thoroughfares. He couldn't decide if this was to be sensitive to his reluctance to be here, or because she was hiding him from the eyes of the aristocrats who lived there. His irritation surprised him. He had no love for the court, after all, but it still rankled to be treated like the queen's dirty secret.

The corridors, though empty of courtiers, were busy with the palace staff running errands or standing in small groups. Mrs. Ollenby knew everyone by name and the chores they were supposed to be performing, and she corrected more than one gawking maid who stared, open-mouthed, at the frightening figure of the Marchant prince in the quiet halls.

When they reached the right door, it was Mrs. Ollenby herself who opened it, and then lit the lanterns in the small suite of rooms. She inquired politely if he would like someone sent to run a bath, and what he would like for dinner, and offered many apologies for the impeccable room being coated in a light layer of dust. Mrs. Ollenby didn't seem to mind Rainere's monosyllabic answers and kept sending him beaming smiles as if they were two old friends. Rainere found Mrs. Ollenby's familiarity disconcerting, yet also comforting.

So when Mrs. Ollenby came to stand before him and took his long white hands in her own, Rainere didn't pull away. Instead, he looked deeply into her eyes, where he could see two thick bands of pale gold almost melted into the lavender blue. Her emotions swam in happy tears and Rainere had a strange compulsion to wrap this little woman in his arms and hug her. Naturally, he resisted the urge.

Mrs. Ollenby's twinkling eyes scrunched up at the edges again as she gave his hands a squeeze. "You did a noble and selfless thing, bringing those Fire Orchid stamens back, Your Highness," she said. "You know that our queen doesn't understand our world yet. She couldn't realize what you risked to help her tonight. But I do, and I thank you for it from the bottom of my heart."

Rainere shied away from the compliment and pulled his hands out of hers. Mrs. Ollenby had snuck under his emotional armor. "I only did what was right," he muttered, and dropped his gaze to see his muddy boots dirtying the carpet.

"You saved the princess and all of the other non-magic folk of Unisia," insisted Mrs. Ollenby gently. "And for that I will always be grateful to you. Whether or not you want it said, you are the hero of the day, Your Highness."

Rainere could only watch silently as Mrs. Ollenby made her way to the door, shutting it behind her. He took a deep breath and for one beautiful moment he could imagine himself as the champion that Mrs. Ollenby had just described. Then he breathed out and the moment passed.

I am nothing but a craven supplicant, risking everything for the grace of a queen who hates me. Rainere recoiled in horror from the truth in his own mind, and his trembling legs sunk down to land him on the bed. He would rest now but he would be gone before morning, and he knew that no one would miss him.

CHAPTER SEVENTEEN

"The Goddess Loves All Her Children"

Charlie woke to the smell of burning. The smoke stung his throat and lanced his eyes when he tried to open them. He coughed and moaned as a splitting headache hammered the inside of his skull and jumbled his thoughts.

"Easy, boy, easy," a deep voice soothed him. "You've had a nasty knock, don't try and sit up yet."

Charlie tried again to open his eyes. Through the blue smoke of the fire he could just make out a chubby man with a bald head, dressed in a rough brown robe. "Pere Raven?"

Pere Raven chuckled. "The one and only. I'm sorry, I've forgotten your name, kid."

Charlie groaned as he tried to sit up, making the pain in his head bite back. "Charlie," he replied through gritted teeth. "The queen's envoy. Remember?"

"Oh, that's right, Charlie! You came across with us to the Grey Palace with the queen, didn't you?" The priest sounded more pleased than was probably warranted under the circumstances and handed Charlie a clay bottle filled with something that sloshed thickly inside. "Drink this and you'll feel better in no time. Just a bit though."

Charlie took a swig of the liquid and tasted the sweet burn of Firewhiskey, which was there to disguise the earthy taste of Skag root. He took another sip for good measure before handing the bottle back. "Thanks." He had questions to ask, but he couldn't remember what they were. His brain sloshed around like the medicine in the bottle. For a start, Charlie wanted to ask how he was outside the Grey Palace, but then the pain of his head injury nailed him again and he could only grit his teeth and wait for it to recede and the Skag root to work its magic.

Pere Raven's face became clearer as Charlie's eyes started to focus better. The priest had set up his camp on the edge of the Dark Forest, not far from the stables of the Grey Palace. In the light of the waning moon, Charlie could still see the outline of the palace turrets looming against the clear night sky.

"It stopped raining a few hours ago," noted Pere Raven. "So the prince can't be at home."

Charlie only just stopped himself from shaking his pounding head, and instead shuffled to sit on his behind, holding his hands out to the fire. He remembered one of the questions he wanted to ask. "Where did you find me?"

Pere Raven pointed to where Charlie was sitting and gave him a grin. "Right there, kiddo. I noticed the knock on the back of your head and I didn't want to leave you, so I set up camp here. You've been out of it for a couple of hours, but you mumbled a fair bit in your sleep though: something about a message for the queen."

Charlie could only grunt in response. *I am a bloody terrible spy*, he admonished himself as he searched his pockets for the two hand mirrors and was sick to realize neither of them was still on him. He cursed inwardly. Whoever had dumped him out here had cleaned him out before they did. That bastard Grotto was his first suspect. Charlie hoped that Orestes hadn't waited to tell the queen that Prince Rainere had the Fire Orchid stamens.

"Did you have a message for the queen?" Pere Raven's tone was jolly as he interrupted Charlie's anxious musings. "I lost track of you folks when I went in search of the Marchant chapel library. For no reason I could tell, Grottonski locked me in there, then just yesterday he finally let me out and told me to go home. Very odd behavior, even for a Marchant servant, if you ask me."

Charlie gave the priest an incredulous look. *How could he be so calm about being Grottonski's prisoner?* "You should go and complain to the queen! That Grotto is as mad as a bag of cats, and she wouldn't like that he locked you up while she was there."

Pere Raven just shrugged and threw another couple of sticks on the fire. They hissed and crackled, the wet wood almost useless at feeding the flames. Charlie was feeling chilled but he wished he could tell the priest to stop making the smoke worse. "I'm sure the queen has more to worry about than a silly old bugger like me," Pere Raven said with a smile. "Besides no one hurt me, and I got a bit of wine and food to keep me going, so no harm done really. But I won't lie to you, Charlie, I was *very* pleased to get out of there."

"I bet," agreed Charlie. "So why are you still here? Thought you would have legged it back to the Belvoir Estate by now." He shivered in his thin summer coat. "Even just for the warm bed."

"Well, a good priest's work is never done, my son," said Pere Raven, somewhat ruefully. "I thought I would take the opportunity to tend to the flock of good people in the Marchant villages nearby while I was here. I hardly ever get near to this area, you know, because the Dark Forest makes it tricky to travel here from Belvoir Estate." He raised a hairless brow at Charlie. "Tell me, what happened after I left you folks? I tried to get the story from one of the Grey Palace servants, but the man was no help at all."

Charlie lifted his head off his knees and looked directly at the priest. The man's eyes were wide and his expression seemed like genuine innocence, but Charlie wasn't sure that he should say anything at all. What had happened was the queen's business and no one else's, so he cobbled together a story as best he could to fill the priest in. "The prince got a bit familiar with the queen and she didn't like it," he replied. "She took off really fast for the Golden Palace once the carnival had finished, and she is there now."

"Did she now?" Pere Raven rubbed his clean-shaven chin and looked at Charlie curiously. "So why are you here then?"

"You were right, I had a message for the prince from the queen," Charlie answered shortly. *Who was this guy to be so chatty? Weren't all priests supposed to be humble and discreet followers of the Goddess Serena?* "But the prince wasn't in his palace, so I guess I'll head back in the morning if you don't mind sharing your fire with me tonight?"

Pere Raven chuckled, the cheery sound coming from deep within his chest. "You are welcome to share that which I have made badly, Charlie. I confess I generally prefer to sleep inside a barn than out here under the stars, but the villagers didn't seem keen to give a bed to a nosy priest so here I am, terrible fire and all."

Charlie's heart softened a bit towards the old guy. He seemed a happy sort, and he was man enough to admit he didn't know how to build a proper fire. "You just need to dry out the wood, that's all," said Charlie, and picked up a broken branch, hefting it for weight before muttering a charm and letting the steam evaporate. He threw it on the fire and watched in delight as the sparks turned blue and green as the wood, and the spell, burned away.

"My goodness, look at your magic," laughed Pere Raven. "My, goodness me. You seem like you could be a Special, Charlie. Really special."

The priest's voice was dropping in and out strangely and Charlie couldn't quite catch what he was saying. Then Charlie caught sight of his hand backlit by red flames and was momentarily stunned by the sheer beauty of the firelight as it made his skin glow. *It is so pretty.* Something was wrong with his head. *The fire is so warm, and so pretty.*

Dropping deep under the haze of drugs, Charlie fought the warm feeling, but his head soon grew light and fluffy as the world melted away. Charlie heard Pere Raven's voice, but not his words, as he curled up on the damp ground and slept like a baby.

CHAPTER EIGHTEEN

"Cures and Opiates"

Adele looked up as the timepiece on the mantel chimed three o'clock in the morning. She was watching over Stella again, as if she could keep death at bay by holding her maternal vigil. Mrs. Ollenby had been with Adele all night to keep company with her but eventually Adele had sent the lady to her bed to get some proper rest. Alone, Adele, was left to witness as Stella slipped further and further away from her.

The mottled green rash had spread down to the baby's legs and feet now, and it was deepening to a murky grey on Stella's torso as the virus advanced. Stella didn't wake any more, and her breathing was shallow, as pain spasms occasionally wracked her exhausted little body. Adele didn't need to be told that even the tonic might not be enough to save her daughter now.

There was a sharp rap at the door and Adele got up when she saw that it was Ohren and Rainere who entered. "You have it?" Her voice shook as much as her hands did.

"Is she still breathing?" asked Ohren and rushed to Stella's bedside. His cheeks were pale and he looked exhausted as he dropped a black leather bag on a chair beside the bed and gestured for Prince Rainere to stand on the other side of Stella, nearest to Adelena. Opening the bag, Ohren pulled out a box with two syringes inside, laying them out neatly on the night table. He then took out a tiny glass vial and removed the dropper filled with golden liquid.

"The tonic will negate the opiates in her system when it begins to work," warned Ohren. "But after it's finished I will make her comfortable again." He waved a hand over the needles full of clear liquid, which sparkled with gold particles. They were obviously more drugs. "I hope you don't mind the presence of Prince Rainere here,

Your Majesty, I called him from his bed as I thought I might need him for this procedure."

Adele could only nod. She would invite the whole court inside the room if it would help Stella right now. Checking with a glance that Rainere was ready, High Wizard Ohren leaned over Stella and placed the dropper against the baby's grey lips, carefully emptying it between her teeth. Stella gave no reaction at having swallowed the liquid but Ohren and Rainere both put their hands on her arms and legs.

"Adelena, look." Rainere's voice brought Adele's focus to Stella's feet. A golden light began to shimmer over the baby's skin, lifting the mottled green rash off Stella's body. Within moments, the golden glow had spread up Stella's legs and reached her arms and torso, clearing signs of the Influenza from her body.

"It's working fast, stay with it," murmured Ohren to the prince.

Adele's heart rose in her chest, but Ohren and Rainere were still tense, both wearing grim expressions. Adele had only a moment to wonder about it before she heard Stella moan. She stepped around Rainere to grab Stella's hand and kiss it, but the baby only moaned again. The golden glow had reached the top of her chest before Stella opened her eyes and took in a breath.

Stella's scream was the stuff of nightmares.

Lurching forward, Adele tried to pull her baby up into her arms, hoping instinctively that her touch would calm Stella as the baby struggled and convulsed in a shocking seizure.

"No!" Rainere shouted and had his strong arms around Adele, lifting her up and away from Stella. "You have to leave her." He pressed Adele to his chest and she couldn't fight free, but only watch as Ohren pinned Stella to the bed, easily holding the baby down as the tears coursed down his cheeks.

"Stop it!" shrieked Adele. "You're hurting her!" Adele grabbed at her magic and felt it uncoil but the Chime Voices were strangely calm, only humming softly, and not giving her any words of command she could use to get Ohren off her baby. Angry, Adele pulled harder on the magic and felt it flood her body, ready and willing to fight in all directions. Gold and silver flashes filled her vision

"Adelena, *cara mia*." Rainere's voice was quiet, his breath hot in her ear, and his arms holding her tight. "We need to wait until the rash has lifted. I will take her pain away again, but we have to wait until the virus has been destroyed. Please, darling, let the tonic work."

Adele saw Stella thrashing on the bed and her magic- infused maternal instincts warred with her reason. She knew that the enemy here was the Influenza, but it would be the wizards who she would hurt if Adele lost it now. Adele forced herself to nod, letting Rainere know that she had control of herself again. Rainere slowly loosened his grip on her and returned his gaze to Stella. The golden glow had reached the baby's neck and then, moments later, a bright light burst out from around Stella's head, burning white-hot, and then dissipating in a blinding flash. The virus was destroyed. Stella's screams broke off in a yelp as Ohren plunged a syringe into each of her shoulders and then stepped back. Rainere pulled Adele forward. It was her turn now.

As Adele sat next to Stella on the bed, her convulsions were already slowing. The Chime Voices suddenly spoke up, not with the fierce command that Adele had waited for, but with a gentle and sweet song that spoke of sunshine sparkling on water, cooling breezes and the soft, creeping sleep that warms the back of the neck as it pulls you under. At first, Adele's voice was croaky, but it became clearer as she sang the words and Stella's breathing evened into a natural rhythm. Adele sang on as she wiped the sweat from Stella's brow, and smoothed down her crumpled chemise, setting it right. Adele sang as she watched the color in Stella's cheeks turn from grey to a soft pink. At last, Stella opened her blue eyes and Adele could actually see as Ohren's opiate passed like a cloud through her daughter's vision. "Mummy," whispered Stella, and then closed her eyes again.

CHAPTER NINETEEN

"Blood Will Out"

Adele slapped a hand over her mouth to stop the cry that wanted to escape. Ohren leaned over the bed and checked the baby's pulse, he felt her temperature before gently lifting her eyelids to examine the pupils. "Thank the Goddess, she is asleep," he confirmed with a sigh and sank down into a nearby chair, slumping against the stiff wooden back. The high wizard ran his hands over his face and pulled at his beard as if it annoyed him. His cheeks were pale and the tears had yet to dry.

"Ohren, what now?" asked Adele as she leaned forward to lay gentle kisses on Stella's cheeks. "What happens to her now?"

Ohren heaved a deep sigh. "The virus almost killed her, my queen. When you brought her back to us, I was sure she only had hours left to live. I honestly don't know how she lasted this long without her own magic to battle the virus. But be that as it may, the Influenza will have caused a lot of internal damage to her organs. We must keep her sedated to give her time to heal, but I have never seen anyone come back from such an advanced condition. There is no telling if she will ever return to us as she was before."

"Stella will be brain damaged?" Adele's shell-shocked mind was sent reeling again. "But you said the tonic would heal her. You said it was all she needed."

"I said what you needed to hear, Adelena," replied Ohren sharply but his eyes reddened again. "I know how you deal with people who disappoint you, and there was no telling what you would do if you blamed me for not saving your child."

"She's not saved yet, High Wizard," replied Adele through gritted teeth as her wakened magic began to slip out of her control. She stood up, "Are you telling me that there is nothing else you can do for her?"

"Adelena, perhaps there *is* something else we can do." Rainere's hand brushed hers capturing her attention. "Instead of using an opiate to render the princess unconscious, we could use a stasis coma to hold her frozen while we seek a cure for her condition."

"You berate me for giving the queen false hope with the tonic," growled Ohren. "Yet you will tell her there is a cure for the degeneration?"

The two men glared at each other over Stella's sleeping body and Adele felt that their animosity went so much deeper than this present argument. They genuinely disliked each other. However, that was not her problem and neither would it be Stella's.

"Enough!" said Adele firmly. "I will do whatever it takes to get Stella well again. Anything at all."

"He knew you would," muttered Ohren slumping back in his chair, but he didn't continue the fight.

Rainere pulled out a scrunched piece of paper from his pocket. "I had thought it might be necessary once the tonic was administered so I have already designed the spell," said the prince. He showed Adele a complex diagram of concentric circles, and pentagrams interlinked around a small rectangle with a tiny perfect image of Stella inside it. "The stasis coma will shift Stella out of time. It will be as if she was frozen, and though she will not heal, neither will she deteriorate. We will then have as much time as we need to discover a cure for her while she lies here out of time and pain."

"No!" protested Ohren and sat forward in his chair. "What the prince is suggesting will take powerful dark magic to conjure, and that is the sort of magic that will require other lives to support it. Who would you suggest we should kill to keep the princess alive?"

Adelena was shocked at Ohren's words but Rainere almost snorted in derision. "That only shows how much you know of dark magic," the prince countered. "If you care to look *closely*, you will see that the matrix I designed is based on the energy of lost souls, not the living. I'm sure there are thousands of them floating about the Golden Palace, High Wizard, unused and unwanted."

Ohren shook his head but Adele could see the change in his expression - he was wavering. "Dark magic has not been used in the Golden Palace for hundreds of years and I will not have it polluting these sacred halls now. It will be far too dangerous should something go wrong."

"Adelena, I am a dark wizard." Rainere caught Adele's gaze, his plea clear. "So this is my magic and I know that this spell will protect Stella. While she is frozen, I will work every day and night to find a cure for her, that I vow to you. But for now you need to accept that their light magic can't help her anymore."

"You also have to realize that you will endanger yourself and us all with this sacrilege, Your Majesty," snapped Ohren. "I will not allow myself to be swayed by such insanity."

"Not even for Stella?" Adele was relieved to see Ohren flinch at her words. A shadow passed over his gaze. Adele had noted Ohren's particular affection for her baby daughter. With her bouncing blonde curls and clear, blue eyes, Stella was the perfect St Lucidis princess, and the image of Ohren's own late sister, Queen Olivia.

Adele opened her mouth to speak, but Ohren beat her to it. He already knew her decision. "Your Majesty, what the prince is suggesting is actually a very good idea, but I have neither the knowledge nor the skill to cast such a spell." Ohren leveled his gaze at Rainere, directly challenging him. "Only Prince Rainere can do this for you and once Stella is in the coma, only *he* can get her out again. You will have to completely trust the prince with the life of your child, because while she is under his spell she will be at his mercy, and so will you."

A swirling miasma of blinding fear, grief and fierce hope churned inside of Adele. Rainere stood tall before her, his bald head gleaming dully in the candle light, and the silver rings around his eyes seemed to glow within their dark green depths. Even without his hair, he was beautiful, and even with nothing to hold on to, he still loved her. Adele stepped towards the dark, again.

"The prince will install Stella in the stasis coma," and Adele's voice held firm despite her fear. "High Wizard you will make sure that Rainere has everything that he needs, and then you will help me work on a cure for Stella while she sleeps. I want her frozen for as short a time as possible."

After only a moment, the high wizard gave Adele a resigned nod. "I will do as you ask, Your Majesty, but first let me excuse myself until the morning to make the rest of the tonics for the people of Concordis. The Summer Influenza still rages through the city, and hopefully there is time to save more of them."

A sharp blade of guilt sliced through Adele's heart. *How many other mothers and fathers in Unisia were sitting by the bedsides of their own non-magical children, watching them die of the disease that had taken two powerful wizards to keep her own daughter alive?* "Ohren, please forgive me," said Adele. "You must get to work immediately."

Ohren took his leave without another word, and shut the door behind himself, leaving Adele and Rainere together. It was the first time they had been alone since that awful night in the observatory at the Grey Palace, when they had designed their own cataclysmic ruin. Rainere stepped towards her, almost touching her shoulder. Adele could feel the heat of him, radiating through his silk shirt, and her magic twisted inside her chest because he was so near, the Chime Voices tinkling. "Adelena, I have…"

"No," Adele held up her hand to stop Rainere from speaking. "Please let's just get through this night, and then we can talk. I want to know that Stella is safe from pain before another minute passes."

"I will need to keep Stella away from other people, especially those without strong magic in their blood," said Rainere and looked down at the crumpled paper in his hands. "It is not strictly necessary, but I will be more cautious than I would ordinarily. I'm sure the high wizard has the materials I need, and I have the knowledge already.

The spell will not be simple, but you should not be frightened. Stella will be safe."

Rainere's voice was soft and coaxing, and his nearness was making her head spin. Adele had to concentrate very hard not to give in to the temptation to fall into his arms. "The spell uses dark magic by harnessing the energy of wandering spirits, or lost souls as they are also called. Interlocking their energies around Stella will, in effect, surround her with death. In death, there is no passing of time, and so she will be frozen in that state, not breathing or moving. But she will not be dead, Adelena, and she will not pass over, I promise you."

Adelena's heart lurched as Rainere laid out the bare facts of what he was going to do but, still, she didn't flinch. Stella needed this or she would die when the narcotics failed her, and Adele was determined that would not happen.

"Perhaps I should take Stella to a quieter room now," suggested Rainere. "I can take her along the secret passageways so no one will see us go. I'm sure it would not be wise for the St Lucidis queen to be seen supporting dark magic in the Golden Palace, as the high wizard fears."

"I don't care about their politics, Rainere," Adele sighed.

"Yes, but their politics care very much about you, *cara mia*," replied Rainere gently. "It won't help Stella to have you imprisoned for crimes against the court."

Adele swallowed the truth with some difficulty. "Very well. Mrs. Ollenby will know of somewhere, you can ask her when she wakes up."

Adele finally caught Rainere's eye and instantly regretted it. A half-smile tweaked up the corner of his mouth and she felt an almost savage need to kiss it. While she stared, Rainere's cheeks heated, showing two spots of color that told her he shared her thoughts. He coughed to clear his throat and dropped his eyes. "If it would please you, Adelena, I would like to create a failsafe in the spell that will act like a backdoor." Rainere wiped his palms down his legs and Adele knew he was nervous to ask this next thing of her. "If I included a sample of your blood in the founding matrix of the spell, then should anything happen to me, you will have a way to break it yourself. It would be difficult, of course, but I will write you instructions on how to do it. When you have a cure, you wouldn't need me to bring Stella back."

Adele had no words to say to the man who had stolen her daughter Natalie, now that he was giving her back her Stella. *What was there to say?* Adele thrust out her arm and gestured at the black medical bag that Ohren had left behind. "Do it," she said. "Now."

Adele watched Rainere's long white fingers slip into the bag and pull out a clean syringe. He stepped close to her, so close she could smell his cold spicy scent and feel the magnetic pull of his energy intensify. Adele heard the Chime Voices change their tune as they anticipated Rainere's touch. Ever so slowly, Rainere clicked off the protective cover on the sharp metal needle and slid his hand around Adele's elbow, pulling her arm straight. He squeezed firmly.

"I need to find a vein," he murmured and pressed at the crook of her arm with his index finger. A wet drop splotched down onto the back of his hand, and Rainere looked up in surprise to see her crying.

"Adelena," and Rainere's voice echoed with her own pain. "I'm not going to hurt you."

Adele just squeezed her eyes shut tight as he slid the needle into her vein and drew out a vial of her bright red blood.

CHAPTER TWENTY

"The Lion and The Witch"

It was mid-morning before Adele felt secure enough to venture away from Stella's bed. Disoriented, Adele blinked in the bright light of the corridor outside Stella's room. While she had sat in silence with Rainere by the bedside of her sleeping baby, the world had kept turning and the hospital corridor was full of people heading in all directions, unaware of the tragedy that had nearly happened to her family. Adele wiped the tears off her cheeks and steadied herself for the long walk back to the royal apartments. Rainere had followed Adele out and meant to come back with her to find Mrs. Ollenby, but they hadn't gone more than a few steps when Adele made out a large crowd coming towards them.

General Ohrig led the Queen's Guard, along with Tilburn, who was almost skipping by his side to keep up. Mrs. Ollenby herself was in the mix, holding Natalie's hand while Aaron was getting a piggyback ride from QG Leith. Adele couldn't help but smile when Natalie spotted her and with a shriek broke away from Mrs. Ollenby to run at her, laughing with joy. She had opened her arms wide when Natalie passed right by her mother and instead threw herself at Prince Rainere's legs.

"You're back, you're back!" Natalie hugged Rainere's knees with all of her little-girl-might. "No one would tell me where you went but I'm so glad you are here." Natalie looked up at Rainere, adoration bright in her eyes. "Please don't go again, stay with us. Please!"

Adele noticed her Queen's Guard quickly moved to assemble in a circle around the royal family. Although they could never physically defeat Rainere, it wouldn't stop them from trying to should Adelena give the word. Mrs. Ollenby didn't appear to notice the tension, however, and moved inside the circle to greet the prince in a friendly way, asking after Stella.

"Thanks to Prince Rainere, the Fire Orchid stamens were returned and Stella got the tonic she needed," announced Adele, and caught General Ohrig's eye, trying to tell him more than her words could with the children present. "She is going to be okay for now, and soon she will be even better. She just needs some more magic which Prince Rainere is going to help me find." Adele smiled again. The cheering warmth of her family felt so good after the chill of grief in Stella's dark hospital room.

"Mrs. Ollenby said we could visit Stella today if you say it's okay, Mummy," said Aaron from his perch on QG Leith's back. "Is that okay if we take Prince Rainere with us too?" Aaron smiled at Rainere. "You could come with us if you want?"

Prince Rainere had stood frozen up until that moment, his expression blank as he gauged Adele's reaction to her children's affectionate treatment. She would need to give her permission for him to speak to them, as he would no longer presume that he could.

"The prince is going to be busy today, helping Stella," Adele said, raising her voice over the protests and groans of the children. "But! I was going to say, before you all yelled at me," the children giggled at her deep frown "that if the prince would like then he can spend a little time with you back in our apartment after you have all looked in on Stella, okay?"

Pleased, Natalie finally gave her mother a hug. "Is Stella really better, Mummy?" Natalie's sharp eyes didn't miss a trick, and Adele knew her daughter would notice her tear-stained cheeks and swollen eyes straight away. She forced a smile and dropped to her knees to give Natalie a tight hug, and then big wet kisses that made her giggle.

"Yes, darling, Stella really is better." Adele ran her hand through Natalie's long dark hair, so different to her little sister's soft curls, and smiled. "You can kiss her and talk to her, but she has had some strong medicine which is making her sleep really well, so don't expect her to wake up."

The children whooped and leaped about at the good news, hugging their mother and laughing as Mrs. Ollenby ushered them into Stella's room, and away from the serious adults.

"So that's how it is?" asked General Ohrig, his expression stony as he studied Adele's face as closely as Natalie just had. "The princess is healed?"

Adele shook her head and felt her smile die. She didn't want to say the words aloud in the bright light of day and make it more real. "Stella has been damaged by the virus too badly. The high wizard made her stable, but it's no way for her to live. We have to find a proper cure for her." Adele's voice trailed off into a whisper and she swayed on her feet. "My poor baby girl."

In a flash, Rainere moved to catch her as Adele almost fell over, setting off a chain reaction of drawn swords and General Ohrig all but snatching her out of the prince's arms with a savage curse. Tilburn yelped in surprise and shouted, "Your Majesty, whatever is the matter?"

Adele would have laughed at the chaos but it wasn't quite funny enough. Instead, she pushed herself from the general's rough embrace and stood on her own two feet.

"Gentlemen, there's no need for panic. The Marchant prince came to the palace last night to give me back the Fire Orchid stamens of his own accord. It wasn't his fault that he was too late to stop the advance of Stella's influenza, that fault was mine." Adele closed her eyes, tired even of the self-recrimination that held her heart prisoner. "But even Ohren has admitted we need the prince to help us keep Stella in a coma while we find a definitive cure for her."

"The princess is in a coma?" interrupted Tilburn, and the face of her petite Majordomo crumpled with sadness. "Oh, Your Majesty, I am so very, very sorry this happened. If there is anything you need for Princess Stella, Your Majesty, I am here for you. A queen's man to the end, you understand?"

Adele didn't understand, but she was pleased to see her Queen's Guard give the majordomo respectful nods. QG Bear even gave the little man a thump on the back, so she knew he had made a powerful pledge. "Thank you, Tilburn, I will treasure that oath."

"And now, Your Majesty?" General Ohrig nodded in the direction of the prince without looking at him. "What is your command?"

"The prince will need to see the High Wizard and arrange for Stella's care, then he can join the children in the apartment, but only as long as I am there too." Adele turned to Rainere and it hurt to look at him now they were in the natural light. He looked thinner than before, like he was being eaten away from the inside out, his cheeks so pale they were almost grey. Dark shadows inked the skin beneath his eyes, yet he was still too beautiful for her to stare at for long. "Please, do what you must to prepare another room for Stella. I will send a message to you when I am with the children and you can visit us in the apartment. Afterwards perhaps you can see if Ohren will let you help him make the rest of the tonics. I'm sure he can use all the help he can get."

Rainere bowed but she didn't miss the flash in his eyes at her brusque orders. "As you wish, Your Majesty, I shall just make my request to Mrs. Ollenby for another room. Does the high wizard have one of the grand laboratories on the sixth floor?"

Tilburn gave the affirmative, and Adele watched Rainere slip back into Stella's room to find Mrs. Ollenby.

"Your Majesty, if everything is in order, I have a very important matter for your attention," began Tilburn and encouraged Adele to walk down the corridor with him back to main hallways of the palace.

"Please keep an eye on the prince and the children," Adele said quietly to Captain Lucky, and turned to follow her majordomo, as Tilburn continued speaking.

"I know you have been through a very anxious time these last days, Your Majesty, but the treasury had a meeting in your absence and several irregularities were brought up in regard to purchases you had made." He lowered his voice. "In Sandar."

Adele tried hard to cast her mind back to the four days she had spent in Sandar but was distracted by Captain Lucky rejoining their group and giving her a nod to suggest that nothing untoward had happened with Prince Rainere. "I honestly can't remember buying anything, Tilburn. You were there, do you remember?"

Tilburn looked uncomfortable. "There was the matter of the reduction in silk trade taxes and the road that you promised to build from Concordis to Sandar, Your Majesty, which you traded for the Fire Orchid stamens." He thrust a sheaf of papers into her hand, and she recognized her insignia on the bottom of them all. "The promises you made will cost the kingdom a fortune, Your Majesty, and its money that we can ill afford."

Adele almost tripped on the rich carpet beneath her feet and cast a look askance at her majordomo. "Forgive me if I find that hard to believe, Tilburn. Besides, Unisia needed those Fire Orchid stamens to save the lives of its citizens. I think the human cost outweighed the money I had to spend."

"Unfortunately, as noble as your sentiment is, Your Majesty, those same pundits who would have attacked you for coming home empty-handed are now vilifying you for spending too much of the kingdom's gold to get the stamens." Tilburn paused as they reached a much more populated part of the palace. He looked about as if searching for eavesdroppers. "This is not about ethics, Your Majesty, this is about politics, and your critics are loud and powerful."

"Orgustus." Adele spat the lord's name like a curse.

Tilburn nodded. "Lord Orgustus is not to be trifled with, Your Majesty," he cautioned her. "He was the successful Regent of Unisia long before your arrival, and he has many friends besides. The man is as charming or terrifying as he needs to be, and this is a powerful combination among the courtiers, who only live for scandal and intrigue. Your humble approach is seen as a little primitive, by those who would have you emulate their extravagant lifestyles instead."

"Primitive?" Adele was stunned. "But I only do what I am asked to by the High Wizard."

"Yes, but the courtiers do not know any of that as you keep yourself so quietly and separate from them, Your Majesty," Tilburn said, "like you did at the Belvoir Estate, where they saw you refusing to dance into the night and wearing only the simplest gowns."

Adele could tell by Tilburn's expression that he was reluctant to hurt her feelings, but neither was he going to sugarcoat the facts for her. While she had been fighting for her life and defending her family, first in Sandar and then in the Grey Palace, the court of the Golden Palace had been ridiculing her dress sense and reluctance to stay out and party all night.

Adele turned to Ohrig for his advice but the general looked even angrier than she felt, steam was almost coming out of his ears as he fought to find the words. "Of all the ungrateful and ridiculous shit in the Golden Palace, the queen should not have to put up with *this*," fumed Ohrig. "Why are you bringing this to her now Tilburn, when she has so much else to deal with as it is?"

Tilburn cast Ohrig an angry glare. "Because the Marchant prince is once again in the Golden Palace, and *once again* people are blaming the queen for it," Tilburn hissed, his darting eyes always checking for spies. "Lord Orgustus is going to attack Queen Adelena in the court soon to catch her out in the heat of this new scandal. Even with all of us and High Wizard Ohren backing her, the queen needs to show more strength if she wants the court to follow her lead. It's *politics,* Ohrig, and we all know how you fare in that arena, so why don't you leave this particular battle to me."

The men glared at each other, and Adele was suddenly so tired of their testosterone and anger. She would do whatever Tilburn wanted, as long as it meant she could get back to her children and have a chance to find a cure for her baby. "Where is Lord Orgustus?" asked Adele. "When does he want to have this showdown or whatever it is?"

Their party had reached the busy center of the palace and Adele was suddenly interrupted by a happy shriek as Lady Olivia came gracefully bounding over to the queen in the middle of her tense group of guards.

"Your Majesty, there you are! No one saw you at the welcome breakfast this morning, or would tell me where you were," Lady Olivia said as she clasped Adele in a tight hug, enveloping her in a cloud of perfume and girlish affection. However, it only took the young woman a moment to sense Adele's grim mood. Lady Olivia pulled back out of her hug and studied Adele. "What is it, Your Majesty, what has you looking so sad? Is it the Marchant prince? Oh my goddess, but there are dreadful rumors that he has followed you back to the Golden Palace and means to propose to you! Of course I've been denying it left, right and center. I know you two are friends only in a decorous, platonic way, but the wicked will gossip and it was the talk of Belvoir Estate when we left."

Tilburn gave his eyebrows a meaningful twist, indicating *'This is exactly what I've been trying to say'* over Lady Olivia's shoulder.

Adele shook her head and forced a smile. "Stella was ill, but she is recovering well now. The Marchant prince is just here to help the high wizard make tonics for the sick people in the city, nothing more sinister than that."

Lady Olivia's intelligent gaze lightened at the queen's words and as she linked arms with Adele she whispered, "Lord Orgustus is at the welcome breakfast in the Green Greeting Room, Your Majesty. He seems pretty heated this morning, so if you want to avoid him then, let's go another way back to your apartment."

"Your Majesty, perhaps that is wise advice, today is not the day," agreed Tilburn.

"No, it's fine," said Adele and ran a mental hand over her coiled magic and grabbed at the ruff of the other magic – green and gold combined – and she felt strong. "I think it's time I had a chat with the kingdom's former Regent."

Just let Lord Orgustus try to frighten me now! After the night Adele had just had, his childish whining ranked very low on her anxiety scale.

When Adele entered the Green Greeting Room for the first time, she thought it looked more like a luxurious hallway than an actual room. Then she saw the flock of a hundred lords and ladies, fresh from their leisurely return to the Golden Palace from the Belvoir Estate. Laughter rang through the air and an atmosphere of giddy excitement reigned among the groups of courtiers lounging about or shrieking with delight at seeing each other again. Everyone was impeccably dressed, and the women in particular looked like a radiant flock of birds, quite literally, as multi-colored feathers decorated their hair-styles and featured on their gowns. This was a party, full of fun and frivolity, and so very far from the sick chamber of a dying baby that Adele felt a kind of culture shock fall over her, and she froze.

"Ah!" Adele's sound of reticence said it all.

CHAPTER TWENTY-ONE

"Dancing with the Enemy"

"Maybe I should have got you cleaned up a bit," said Tilburn, running a critical eye over Adele's creased blouse and riding pant ensemble, her hair hanging halfway down her back in a messy ponytail, and no make-up on. "This could be embarrassing."

Adele felt a nudge in her ribs and General Ohrig leaned down to whisper in her ear. "Chin up, Your Majesty, you can eat fools like this for breakfast." He gave her a sidelong grin. "Go show that pompous lord who he is dealing with." Adele returned his smile and pushed her shoulders back.

Adele spotted Lord Orgustus immediately. The man was hard to miss. Lord Orgustus sat on the largest armchair in the room, his back to the terrace so that he was framed by the morning sunshine, which caught the white gems on his collar and made his blonde hair almost glow. The effect was angelic, and Adele couldn't help but think that Orgustus had staged himself perfectly. As she walked through the whispering crowd to where Orgustus sat surrounded by his cronies, Adele held onto her power and reminded herself that this lord hated her and her family, and it was up to Adele to nullify any risk he posed her as fast as possible.

Lord Orgustus got the message that Adele was in the room and she could see him concentrate on *not* noticing her until the very last moment, when she stopped before him. Slowly the lord turned his head and trained his icy blue eyes on her as the crowd fell silent about them, waiting to enjoy the confrontation they had evidently been told was coming. Lord Orgustus sat up straighter, his hands resting on the arms of the throne-like chair he had chosen, but he didn't get up for her and the open show of disrespect had Tilburn hissing in disapproval.

Adele knew right away that this would be a contest of wills, and she realized immediately that she shouldn't be the one to speak first. Instead, she painted her face with an easy smile and prepared to wait. Two months ago, this man had frightened her to tears, but now Adele felt the coils of her power loosen and swell inside her chest. The Chime Voices whispered of the things she could do with a man as tall and young as Lord Orgustus. Even Adele couldn't deny that Orgustus was very handsome, with his chiseled features and broad, muscular body, but it was his personality that ruined the picture and it was irritating that the Chime Voices found Orgustus so attractive when Adele felt nothing but dislike for him.

The silence between Queen Adelena and Lord Orgustus grew, as did the whispers and mutters of the surrounding audience. Lord Orgustus waited until the murmurs grew into chatter before holding up a hand for silence. *As if he were a king to command them all*, Adele thought.

"I have heard that the Princess Stella has been saved from her illness by the Fire Orchid tonic," Orgustus voice was loud enough to carry right to the back of the long room. "May the Goddess bless her and her full recovery, Your Majesty."

Incredibly, applause was given to the lord's insincere words. Adele tried not to show her surprise that Orgustus already knew about Stella but waited until the noise had died down before she nodded. "Thank you, Lord Orgustus."

Lord Orgustus beetled his blonde eyebrows at her and frowned as if in deep concern. "You are welcome, Your Majesty." He paused, theatrically. "And while I am pleased for the good fortune of the crown to be able to call upon High Wizard Ohren to make up a special batch of the tonic for Princess Stella, my heart bleeds for all the other poor mothers of the kingdom who have no such luck." He spread his arms as if to beseech the crowd of onlookers and speared Adele with his icy gaze. "How many more lives could have been saved, I wonder, if only you had returned from Sandar weeks ago, instead of stopping to celebrate the horse carnival at Belvoir Estate?"

Adele only barely managed to keep her mouth shut. Lord Orgustus was the worst kind of politician, always repeating the same rhetoric, all the better for his foolish audience to understand what he stood for. His message was clear: Adele was a terrible queen.

"But that is in the past, Your Majesty," said Orgustus in answer to Adele's silence. "Just like the funerals of your citizens in Concordis, though they mourn their children still." His eyes went sharper and a pink blush bloomed in his cheeks, finally making Adele wonder if his anger with her was actually real and not just political grandstanding? "I know it is not your fault, Your Majesty, I have heard it said that you lost the Fire Orchid stamens on a social visit to the Grey Palace, and that only last night, the Marchant prince had to use his dark magic to transport the flower stamens here himself, when he heard your daughter was ill."

The gasps of shock and horror reverberated around the onlookers and Lord Orgustus's chest seemed to swell even bigger at the reaction. "What good fortune blesses you, Your Majesty, in having high wizards and a Marchant prince to do you every bidding. The magic you wield must be quite extraordinary.

"I hope, as the former Regent of the Court of the Golden Palace, that I have nothing to fear from such overwhelming odds stacked against me. After all, my service is first and foremost to the citizens of Unisia and not to the whims of powerful wizards. Why, anyone would think you were afraid to walk the friendly halls of the Golden Palace the way your Queen's Guard follow your footsteps like faithful hounds." He gave her a tight smile and a dismissive wave, as if she could now have the floor.

A ripple of laughter lifted the crowd, but Adele could hardly hear it over the thudding of the blood in her ears. Her magic stretched itself out and filled her hands, begging to be used against this arrogant, insulting buffoon. She knew she could crush the lord in a heartbeat. She saw the flash of a gold ring around his pupils because despite claiming to be harmless, Adele could see that Lord Orgustus' magic would be no small thing. Then Adele realized that if she could see the color of the ring in his eyes, he could also see hers, and there would be nothing worse than Orgustus learning of her mixed blood heritage. Adele took a breath and tamped down her rage, pushing the magic back under her ribs. She had to be smart, and she had to play Orgustus at his own game, even if she didn't know any of the rules yet. Letting the warm, golden magic at the back of her neck infuse her, Adele decided she would begin by ignoring everything Lord Orgustus had just said, like she had seen her least favorite politicians do in interviews on Earth.

"My Lord Orgustus, you could not know how happy I am to be back in the Golden Palace and home again, after my travels." Adele stepped in close to Orgustus, surprising him enough to sit back in his chair, before turning her back to him. With a wave to her Queen's Guard, Adele arranged the men on either side of her, effectively blocking Lord Orgustus from view, and standing so close to him that he couldn't stand without having to push her out of the way, which she was pretty sure even he would balk at.

"Ladies and gentlemen of the court, the Fire Orchid stamens were indeed lost for a time when they were," - Adele paused for effect – "stolen."

Lady Olivia gasped the loudest of everyone, and Adele could almost kiss her when she shrieked, "Your Majesty, no!"

"Yes, they were." Adele nodded solemnly. "Prince Rainere was a guest at the Belvoir Estate when we realized that the theft had taken place. Wasting no time for official explanations, the prince allowed us to enter his home while we mobilized a search party. Using his special skills, the prince was able to track the culprit while I brought my children home, as Princess Stella was already ill with the Influenza and in need of the tonic herself."

Adele took a deep breath and allowed the moment to build. "I trusted the prince and he came through. Not just for the crown, but also for the people of Unisia as well. Last night, he brought the Fire Orchid stamens to the Golden Palace at great personal risk, and for that I will be eternally grateful to him and his service."

Adele felt Lord Orgustus struggling to get out of his chair behind her, but she didn't move out of his way. Unfortunately, the lord was quite limber for a large man and he managed to climb over the arm of his chair, dropping his dignity in his haste to answer Adele. He pushed her QG's aside and made his way to stand next to her.

"What a fantastical tale, Your Majesty," Lord Orgustus sneered. "One could almost think it was invented."

Orgustus turned back to the crowd, stepping in front of Adele to beat her with her own trick. "If the Marchant prince so gallantly retrieved the stamens for you, then where is the culprit who made off with them?"

Adele almost choked but recovered as quick as she could, stepping around Orgustus's well-muscled bulk. "Not wanting to take the law of Unisia into his own hands, the prince was bringing the thief to justice here in the Golden Palace, when, using the blackest of magic, the thief escaped the prince."

Lord Orgustus turned back to Adele, bearing down on her with his superior height. "The thief *escaped?*"

"Yes," Adele had to shout over the noise of the crowd as it erupted in protest. She held her hand up for silence and felt the sweat trickle down her back as she waited for the room to settle again. "But the Fire Orchid stamens have been returned to us and Prince Rainere is aiding the high wizard in making the tonics for our people."

"Does this culprit have a name?" Lord Orgustus's nostrils flared and his eyes narrowed at Adele. There was no chance he believed a word of what she was saying. She needed to give him a name to garner some sort of credibility but who could carry the burden of guilt for such a terrible crime? Adele desperately tried to invent a name but her mind had gone blank. She saw Orgustus open his mouth to deride her and knew her time had run out.

"Ripenzo Shale," Adele blurted. "It was Ripenzo Shale who stole the stamens."

"The Sandarian Ambassador?" Lord Orgustus didn't like it.

"Yes, he accompanied us back from Sandar and took his chance to steal them when we were on the road home. We followed his trail to the Grey Palace and then on to the Belvoir Estate but we had no hope of finding him until Prince Rainere caught his trail again."

"Oh, Your Majesty, that would explain so much." Lady Olivia's voice managed to travel over the melodrama in the room, and she caught Adele's arm in an embrace. "You were so anxious and worried by the theft there was no way you could pretend to enjoy the entertainments at the carnival." Lady Olivia directed her case to the staring crowd. "The whole court saw how tense and unhappy you were at the carnival, not dancing or taking joy at the parties. Of course, you had the burden of finding the Fire Orchid stamens on your shoulders. While the rest of us drank wine, you were probably counting the days as you knew the Influenza spread through the kingdom, and the thief had still not been found." Lady Olivia dropped into a deep curtsey. "We all owe you a great debt, Your Majesty."

Unbelievably, Tilburn started to clap after Lady Olivia's speech and it caught the crowd, slowly at first, but soon they were all applauding their noble Queen Adelena. Adele almost laughed to see Lord Orgustus's jaw drop at her beautiful, blonde lady-in-waiting who had just stolen his spotlight and shone it directly onto Adelena. Deciding she had said and done enough to save her reputation, Adele waved modestly at the crowd and pulled Lady Olivia into her entourage as, still waving, Adele made her way out of the room. Adele allowed herself to enjoy a moment of triumph before she remembered that she had a far more noble battle to fight today.

"Well done, Your Majesty." Tilburn gave Adele a grin and chuckled. "That should keep Lord lion-face chewing on his own paw for a while."

Adele smiled back and then made the mistake of glancing back to Ohrig to gauge his reaction to her little spectacle but was only met with his worried frown.

"What is it now, Ohrig?" Adele asked quietly, knowing she had probably blundered yet again in his opinion.

"Haven't you already heaped enough on that man?" muttered Ohrig and they both knew he referred to Shale. "You've already named him an attempted rapist, an accomplice to murder and now a thief too. Technically he never did anything wrong, remember?"

Adele scowled but felt guilty all the same. "Ripenzo has disappeared, this won't hurt him."

Ohrig frowned back. "I hope you're right, Your Majesty, because you know they'll put a price on his head for this. Every crime lord and bounty hunter in the country will be looking for him now."

Adele flinched as a nasty idea slipped into her head, *At least then he'll be dead, and I won't have to worry about him turning up anymore.* Her own evil thought frightened her enough to blurt out, "I will offer a reward for his capture," she promised General Ohrig, and herself. "And the reward will only be given for bringing him back to me alive."

"That's not quite how it works, Your Majesty," muttered Ohrig, throwing her a skeptical look.

Thankfully, Adele had no time to debate the point with him as Tilburn interrupted them both. "Your Majesty, I have allocated forty-five minutes for you to wash, change clothes and visit with your children and Prince Rainere before your meeting with the treasury, which will include Lord Orgustus again, just so you know."

"Oh, quick, quick, Your Majesty," trilled Lady Olivia, distracted from her flirting with Captain Lucky by a fashion emergency. "We must get back to your chambers. There is no time to lose."

CHAPTER TWENTY-TWO

"A Storm of Words"

The meeting with the treasury had gone on for hours and Adele was pleased to be done with it as she made her way back to the Lavender Room with Tilburn by her side.

Lord Orgustus had been ferocious and he had worked hard to ensure that the Treasury Council was advised on his sour opinion of Adele's spending of treasury funds in Sandar.

Only one council member had spoken up in Adelena's defense, remarking on the fact that Adelena travelled so simply, with only three carriages and her Queen's Guard, that she had actually managed to save the treasury a fortune in the royal travel budget. Unfortunately, Lord Orgustus managed to crush Adele's short-lived relief at finally doing something helpful when he argued that she was doing the pride of the St Lucidis family a great disservice by acting as a pauper queen.

This, of course, all meant nothing when Adele was made aware of the expenses incurred by the hospices and funeral arrangements in the city. In just a few short weeks, the Summer Influenza had spiked to epidemic proportions in the wealthy suburbs of the Guild Quarter. Somehow, putting a price tag on the tragedy seemed so cold when the human cost was incalculable.

After the treasury meeting had ended, Tilburn had informed Adelena that High Wizard Ohren had organized an emergency meeting to discuss how they were to find a cure for Stella. Adele knew that a cure for Stella would also mean a cure for all the children damaged by the Summer Influenza, and this assuaged her guilt at not accepting Lord Orgustus's invitation to join him at a memorial for the grieving citizens in Concordis later that day. She had no time for memorials when there was still so much to be done to help the survivors.

The servants were still setting up the Lavender Room for their meeting when Adele arrived and Tilburn left her at the door, racing off to attend to other duties. Adele smoothed her hands down the blue chiffon of her skirt, and surreptitiously yanked up the bodice that was dragging a little. Lady Olivia had done her job well this morning and Adele felt more at ease walking about the Golden Palace with her hair braided with pearls, a full face of make-up and a dress that looked like a blue-sky day.

Adele made her way out to the terrace where she could see her Queen's Guard and General Ohrig gathered in a tight knot. A lunch buffet had been set out on the outdoor tables and the men had been enjoying themselves when she heard QG Owen's joke about tiny sandwiches and remembered that her young spy had said the same thing.

"Where's Charlie?" she asked the group of men and filled a plate from the assortment of dishes. "I had expected him back by now. The prince is already here, but we know Rainere didn't come from the Grey Palace. Do you think Charlie is still there, waiting for him?"

There was an awkward silence and Adele didn't miss the glance that Captain Lucky and General Ohrig exchanged. "I have been told that the high magistrar has tried to communicate with Charlie since the prince's arrival here but that he has been unsuccessful in reaching him," Ohrig said.

Adele frowned and a weird frisson of panic ran through her. "That is very strange. Ohren told me that those little magic mirrors never fail. He said they can be used anywhere in Unisia to find someone. If Charlie isn't responding, then something must be wrong."

"Perhaps when Charlie didn't find the prince or the Fire Orchid stamens, he might have been too embarrassed to return to the Golden Palace, Your Majesty?" suggested Lucky. "He was very keen to impress you."

"Or you might have to consider that Charlie didn't want to come back, Your Majesty," added Ohrig. "He got a new set of clothes and a valuable magic device from you. When he failed his mission, maybe he just scampered back to Concordis. To be honest, none of us have known the kid for long and we can't really vouch for his character, not properly."

Adele shook her head. "No, I'm sure he wouldn't do that. Charlie fought by our side in the Spiders' Nest. He wouldn't just leave us like that. Also, if Orestes couldn't tell him the news yet then he wouldn't know that the prince has already given us the stamens, and so he is probably still running around looking for them."

"I'm with the queen on this," agreed QG Bear, with a nod at Adele. "The kid knew the long game. He's already given so much to Her Majesty, I doubt he would be scared to come back now."

Ohrig still looked doubtful. "He is just a boy, though."

"I know," said Adele. "But he is also brave and loyal and I won't abandon him when someone might be keeping him from coming home. I'll ask the prince to have the Grey Palace searched because it could be possible that Grottonski is keeping him prisoner there. Captain Lucky, can you please send someone to ask for him in the city, just in case? Does anyone know Charlie's last name, or where he lived before we met him?"

"Well, even that wouldn't help to find him in Concordis, Your Majesty," replied Ohrig. "Charlie isn't a real name, you see, it's more of a phrase as in 'any old Charlie could do that' meaning any random fellow, if you catch my drift?"

"There are thousands of Charlies in the city," agreed QG Leith. "It's the name you give the law when you don't want to give them a name. If we went looking for a young man with hazel eyes and dark hair who answered to Charlie, we would be describing half the Lower District of Concordis."

Adele huffed at the hard truth and turned her worried frown to the horizon. "I don't like him being out there alone. I have a bad feeling about his disappearance. Something isn't right."

"I'll do my best to find him, Your Majesty," said Captain Lucky reassuringly. "Charlie is a sharp young man, and he knows his way about the world, I'm sure there isn't anything to concern you."

"Your Majesty." Ohrig gestured with the miniature muffin he was eating at the room behind her. "Your guests are arriving, and the Marchant prince and the high wizard are already here. You cannot afford to be distracted with these men just now. They have a shared interest in keeping you happy, but the truce might not last for too long if you aren't careful with them."

The cucumber sandwich turned to sawdust in her mouth and Adele could hardly swallow it. Ohrig was right, she would have to concentrate hard not to let either of these wizards try to fool her again. They had both lied to her for their own ends and they both believed it was in her best interest that they had done so. She would need to play this game very carefully to keep them all on the same side and focused on finding a cure for Stella.

Making sure her Queen's Guard was with her, Adele re-entered the Lavender Room and her gaze immediately fell on Prince Rainere. Rainere was standing near the windows, and Adele knew in an instant that he would have been watching her out on the terrace. His expression was quite blank, but she could see that his shoulders were held in a tense, straight line, and his hands were clasped behind his back as if to stop himself from reaching out to her. Adele had walked halfway to him before she realized what she was doing. The room had gone silent, every man watching her as she approached the prince.

Quick, I had a question for him. Adele tried to think straight, but she was distracted by the stiff black silk of Rainere's shirt collar. The top button had been left undone and revealed the dip at the base of his throat where she had loved to kiss him. Adele's attraction to Rainere felt as familiar and comforting as the Chime Voices chanting in her head, and she almost welcomed their pull.

"Your Majesty, all is well with the princess." Rainere's low voice rasped with suppressed emotion, and it sent shivers down her spine. "She has been moved to a little room close to yours, only accessible by an inner closet in your dressing room, and so therefore, very private. I have contained the stasis spell in as tight a field as I could, and I believe it will not falter for the next hundred years unless disturbed." He raised an eyebrow at her silent stare, and she could see he was proud of the work he had done for her. "The princess will be sleeping with only the sweetest dreams until we find her a cure, Your Majesty."

Adele swallowed hard and stepped away from Rainere. "Thank you, Your Highness, I'm so relieved that Stella is comfortable now, and I am grateful to you for it."

Of course, this was about Stella. Adele shoved her lust away and told herself to stay focused. She took her place at the head of the table. "Gentlemen, it is time we started."

Adele was relieved when Ohrig and Lucky took their chairs on either side of her and the other QG's to the side of them, as she was certain she would need their counsel in this meeting. Rainere settled himself opposite High Wizard Ohren at the other end of the table where another figure already sat but Adele had hardly the time to spare the man a glance before High Wizard Ohren stood up.

"Your Majesty." The high wizard was the first to speak. "May I introduce you to Master Gorrik?" Ohren gestured to the short man by his side. "He is the most esteemed History Master at the Accadaemia and I believe that if anyone can help us find a cure for Stella it will be Gorrik."

"I don't know about most esteemed but I'm definitely the oldest by a couple of hundred years." Gorrik chuckled and waved a liver-spotted hand at Adele with a friendly grin. Adele could believe it. This Gorrik was positively ancient, with sparse white hair and deep wrinkles that pulled heavy jowls off his cheekbones. Gorrik wore a benign expression, and his milky eyes were hooded by hanging skin that gave him a sleepy look, but for some reason Adele had the feeling not much got past this old man. Adele opened her mouth to welcome him when she was startled by a small, black cat jumping up onto her lap. The creature stared at her with sea green eyes and purred loudly.

"Oh, Master, that's not polite," Gorrik said, scolding his cat. "Get over here and leave the queen alone."

"It's quite alright, Master Gorrik." Adele smiled. "I don't mind cats, and he is such a pretty one." As if he understood the compliment, the cat curled up on her lap and squinted his eyes happily at her. She ran her hand over the cat's soft fur and was rewarded with a deeper purring rumble, as well as General Ohrig's disgusted mutterings about 'filthy creatures'.

Orestes took that moment to dash into the room, beating out the steward in closing the door by slamming it behind himself, the cat meowed in surprise and slipped off Adele's lap and disappeared under the table. "Forgive me, Your Majesty," he puffed. "I came as soon as I could."

Ohren waved for his twin to sit, and when Orestes settled himself next to Prince Rainere, the high wizard began the meeting properly.

"I will get right to the situation at hand," said Ohren. "Princess Stella is only two years of age and she contracted the Summer Influenza barely a week ago. We have managed to get the virus out of her system, but the damage it did to her internally has been extensive. The queen has asked us to gather today and come up with a cure for the princess's current condition."

"The opiates won't work for long on such a little child," remarked Orestes, somewhat insensitively. "When they wear off, she will be in incredible pain."

Ohren looked uncomfortable. Obviously, he hadn't informed his brother of Stella's care. "The princess is stable right now, and in a stasis coma constructed by Prince Rainere."

Orestes let out his breath in a hiss. "Dark magic! Every time I turn my back…" He glared at Prince Rainere. "Who authorized you to break at least ten, no, twelve laws of our constitution this time?"

Adele spoke up. "I did, High Magistrar. It was the best treatment for Stella. We have hidden her away in a private room so no one will be able to see her, or the magic, unless they are told where she is."

Orestes forced a smile but his blue eyes had turned hard. "You'll take full responsibility then, Your Majesty, if it gets out to the court that you are using forbidden magic to keep your child artificially alive?"

"No, I will," insisted Ohren. "I will claim that I confused the queen…"

"That won't work," replied Orestes coldly. "No one is going to believe that after everything she has done."

"The point is that the princess is safe," said Gorrik, his creaky voice drowning out the arguing twins. "So we have time to find a cure, and we are going to need it."

The brothers fell silent and Adele was interested to see the respect they both had for an old history teacher. Gorrik continued. "I have searched what ancient texts I could find since Ohren told me of the princess's condition yesterday. As we all know, the Summer Influenza has been a plague on humankind since the time of the gods. A little bit like myself." He grinned at the solemn faces surrounding him, and his cat, now on Gorrik's lap, purred loudly in the quiet. "There are no known cases of a human naturally recovering from the Influenza at such an advanced stage, so that only left the rare cases of *unnatural* recovery to consider."

A fierce hope flared in the center of Adele's heart and made her blurt out, "I will do whatever it takes to cure Stella, dark and light magic be damned!"

Gorrik's face creased in sympathy and his eyes almost disappeared under folds of brow-skin. "I understand your enthusiasm, Queen Adelena, but the 'whatever' might be harder to procure than you think."

Adele took a deep breath to curb her impatience. If the fight to rescue Natalie from the Spider Empress had taught her anything, it was that she needed to keep a cool head during the planning of an assault and loose her anger at the real enemy. This time, the enemy was a hideous virus with no face and no home to burn to ash. She pressed her lips into a tight line, "Go on."

"The only known cure for a complete return to health and spirit in the aftermath of the Influenza or indeed any fatal injury." Gorrik gave her an apologetic shrug, already deeming his answer impossible. "Is a Dragon Tear."

There was an audible groan from General Ohrig and Adele saw Orestes shake his head. Prince Rainere remained still, as if carved from stone, only paler.

"For the love of the Goddess, Gorrik you told me you had an idea for the queen, not this mythical catshit!" Ohren was clearly furious, and it was only at that point that Adele realized he had held the same hope as she did for her daughter's recovery. She took cold comfort from it, but it was comfort all the same.

Gorrik shrugged again. "All history becomes myth eventually, my lad, and we know that one thousand years ago dragons really did walk this world. We know that their powers were documented, along with the gods and goddesses by those who were there at the time."

Adele made a logical leap and looked down the table at Rainere. "You gave us the Dragon Fire, Rainere, was that really from a dragon, or had it been created by wizards?"

Rainere sat forward in his chair, his voice intimate, like it was only the two of them in the room. "The St Lucidis wizards would have you believe that they can do everything, Your Majesty, but they cannot. The Dragon Fire had been a gift from my father before he died. When I was very small, he often told me the story of how he had caught the flame from the mouth of the last living dragon in Evendaar. I was only a child at the time, but I believed every word of it. I searched the things he left behind a thousand times but I never found any other dragon artifacts."

"But are you positive we could not make a synthetic Tear? Surely with the combined knowledge and power around this table there is a chance." Adele gestured to the gathering but the high wizard was already shaking his head at her.

"The Tear is not like an elixir, Your Majesty, it is actually a liquid conduit for a dragon's magic. Only the strongest of creatures can filter pure magic out of their bodies, via tears or blood or breath. Unfortunately, it doesn't matter how strong the magic is inside a human being, one cannot physically extract it in the same way."

"A demon could though," said Gorrik, making everyone at the table swivel towards him. "Demons can even take the magic out of humans and then filter that magic out again in any number of ways."

Adele felt her stomach fall away at Gorrik's words. *Demons could filter their own magic outside their bodies?* Adele thought of her tears glittering with gold magic that she had cried over Stella, praying for her baby to be well again. Before Adele could ask the question on the tip of her tongue, there was a sudden and furious banging on the doors of the Lavender Room, and the sound of shouting could be heard. At a quick word from their general, Bear and Owens sprang to their feet to investigate the disturbance while QG's Leith and Pepper moved to stand behind Adele's chair, swords drawn.

The door swung open to show a chaotic scene in the hallway. Standing up, Adele could see her majordomo struggling to prevent a much taller man from entering the room, while the Household Guard seemed to mill about uselessly, waving their swords and shouting things like "Stand down, Sir!" Adele called out to Tilburn, but when he turned to her with a gasped apology his opponent took the opportunity to stalk passed him, dusting off his jacket and glaring coldly at the table until his eyes clapped on Prince Rainere.

"Mr. Grottonski, what is the meaning of this intrusion?" snapped Ohren but the prince's manservant ignored him, his acid green eyes focused only on his master.

"I heard from the North Wind that you had come to the Golden Palace, Your Highness." Grotto bowed low but when he rose, his eyes speared Adele with pure malice. "I have come to take you and your bride back home."

CHAPTER TWENTY-THREE

"Gather the Lambs"

Charlie woke up. The first thing he noticed was that the pain in his head had receded to a dull ache; the second was the nasty taste in his mouth, like he had been sucking on a swamp-hag's toes. Skag did that to you every time. He climbed unsteadily to his feet and spat out a gob of phlegm onto the ground. *Yeesh, that stuff was hideous.* Charlie wiped the back of his hand across his mouth and looked about the empty campsite. The fire had died hours ago, and it was hard to tell the time, as thick cloud covered the sun, though Charlie got the feeling that it was probably early afternoon.

A chill wind rattled the trees of the Dark Forest, giving Charlie the creeps. He brushed off his coat and decided that the first order of business would be to get back to the Golden Palace. However, he had no horse for the two-day journey back, and he was reluctant to return to the Marchant palace to access the portal that had got him here, if only to avoid his unknown assailant. Charlie knew that the Belvoir Estate was no more than a day's ride through the Dark Forest, but as Pere Raven had mentioned, he had no idea what was waiting for unwary travelers, or even wary ones, when they were on their own. Charlie's stomach growled loudly to remind him that he had other problems, too, like being hungry and badly needing to piss. He automatically felt in his pockets to find the two mirrors that he used to have in his possession. He swore, as he remembered once again that they had been stolen. His thoughts turned to Queen Adelena. *Would she be worried that he hadn't come back yet? Would she even have noticed that he was gone?* With a mental shrug, he repressed his romantic fancies and returned to practicalities.

A quick search of the campsite showed that the priest had only clumsily cleaned up after himself, and certainly had not been able to cook any food on that shitty fire, so he must have moved only recently. Cursing his bad luck, Charlie assessed his situation. *Alone on the edge of the Dark Forest, no mirror to contact the queen, no food and a sore head. I just can't get a break these days.* Addressing his next human need, Charlie pissed in the smoking ashes and wiped his hands on his pants. He was pretty filthy, so the gesture didn't help much. The priest had mentioned a village was nearby and Charlie thought that was probably his best bet to get some food. He had no idea how to forage in the country, and even less inclination to get himself lost in the Dark Forest.

It wasn't hard to spot the dirt road that ran away from the Grey Palace and disappeared over a low hill. Charlie wondered if the priest might know someone who could help him get a horse and food for the road as well. Charlie was praying that he could drop the queen's name in lieu of payment. He was only carrying the few coins he had picked from Pepper's pocket (telling himself that he was just saving them from being lost to QG Bear in the next card game) and they definitely wouldn't buy him what he needed.

As Charlie made his way along, keeping to the center of the cart-rutted track he followed his nose to a rubbish dump on the outskirts of a small, decrepit town. From this fragrant vantage, he could see that here were only a few proper brick houses in the center of the town. The rest were made up of blackened pine boards with paper shutters on the windows leaning together as if for warmth in the grey weather.

Oddly, Charlie didn't see any people on the streets when he entered the town, but there were plenty of mangy cats strolling about as if they owned the place. That wasn't a good sign.

Charlie skirted about the empty houses, peering in windows and trying to shake the uncomfortable feeling he was being watched. He made it to the small central square and surveyed his surroundings, half-hiding behind a pile of barrels. There should have been a market, but today there was only a collection of empty trestle tables and raggedy old canvas umbrellas shielding them from the rain. The square was only partially paved with brick and Charlie could tell that this area had been very busy until as recently as yesterday. In the soft mud, Charlie saw that heavy wagons and lots of horses had been traveling back and forth.

Finding courage in the silence, Charlie wandered about the little town square trying to discern the direction all this traffic had gone, but the tracks were too confusing. A noise in one of the houses on the edge of the square made him leap behind a corner of a brick building. After a long moment listening, Charlie peeked out to see a woman's head appearing out of the window of a nearby house.

"Hey, boy," she called softly and gave Charlie a quick wave. "Hey, boy, you can hide here."

Charlie heard desperation in the woman's pleading tone. She wasn't asking him to hide, she was telling him to. Before Charlie could even decide what to do, he spotted Pere Raven walking down the other end of the street and the woman disappeared back into her house. Charlie watched the portly priest as he strolled down the road, picking up a bit of rubbish here and there and depositing it in an empty water barrel. Pere Raven's expression was as unconcerned as if he were walking through a spring meadow instead of an abandoned town, and he was even humming a jaunty little tune to himself. Taking heart from the priest's nonchalance, Charlie risked coming out of his hiding place and calling out to him, making Pere Raven hurry over to join him on the street corner. He was a cheery fellow, but Charlie still thought the priest seemed inordinately pleased to see him.

"Charlie! There you are." Pere Raven gave Charlie a friendly thump on his arm. "I was looking for you back at the camp but you'd wandered off on me. Thanks be to the Goddess, I am so glad to find you. You seem no worse the wear for your long sleep. I thought you'd be out for the whole day the way you were snoring."

Charlie checked over his shoulder at the house the woman had peeked out from. "Maybe we should lower our voices, eh?" he said. "I think something shady has happened here."

Pere Raven followed Charlie's eyes to the doorway and a funny look came over his face that Charlie didn't quite recognize. "This is a strange little town, and you are right Charlie," Pere Raven said, "something serious did happen here. Just yesterday, in fact." The Priest's face suddenly broke into a wide smile and he clapped a hand firmly down on Charlie's shoulder. "But you know what? I was just coming to fetch you as I've finally made some friends and they have a fire and food. Why don't you come with me to their camp? It's just on the other side of town."

Charlie's stomach growled in response to the idea of hot food, betraying him before he could decline to follow the chuckling priest. He let himself be guided by Pere Raven's meaty hand on his shoulder, as the priest babbled away in his ear about making new friends in this strange Marchant country. Charlie felt his for his magic deep within and concentrated on holding the thin threads in his mind, leading power up to his ears, eyes and nose to try and take in his surroundings more closely. Maybe hunger was making him anxious, but he had a strange feeling that something definitely wasn't right here. The feeling wasn't helped when he arrived at the camp site of Pere Raven's 'new friends'. Maybe the priest had a whole 'every stranger is a friend you haven't met yet' attitude, but to Charlie the four men around the campfire were dead-set villains.

"Another guest for you," Pere Raven sang out, smiling at the men as they climbed to their feet and stared silently at the priest and boy approaching them. Charlie could smell the hot meat and vegetable stew, and camp bread baking, but he could also smell sweat and body odor, and the unmistakable acrid, burning scent of dark magic used for violence, which coated the back of his throat and made his appetite recede as fast as his survival instincts had kicked in.

Pere Raven cheerily dragged Charlie to the fire and pushed him to sit down on a damp log. The Priest parked himself as well and began ladling stew into pottery bowls, handing them around to the grim-faced men. Charlie examined the men as closely as he could without catching anyone's eye. They were all dressed in black, and though it wasn't a uniform they had a military look about them. All the men had black hair cropped close to their heads, and knives and small axes protruded from every belt and shoulder holster that they could wear on their beefy bodies. There was one man who was shorter and much slighter than the others. He didn't carry as many weapons, and the silver epaulets on his shoulders signaled to Charlie that he was the leader. When Charlie accidentally caught the man's silver-ringed eyes, what he saw there made Charlie's blood run cold.

"Thank you, Cedric, for taking us in like this," Pere Raven said through a mouthful of food to the leader. Charlie couldn't even pick up his spoon if it meant he would have to take his eyes of any of these dodgy cat-humpers. "Charlie here had just wandered out of the Grey Palace in a bad way yesterday but even when he was feeling so awful, he chose to help me by drying out my firewood with a strong bit of magic. It's when I saw how valuable his skills were."

The hairs on the back of Charlie's neck stood up. He couldn't believe the priest was talking so openly to this man who looked ready to gut someone. "Worth waiting around for then, are ya?" asked Cedric. Charlie got the sense the man didn't need an answer, he was just letting the priest know he had been inconvenienced. Charlie almost jumped out of his skin when Pere Raven clapped him on the back.

"Worth waiting for? I'll say!" The priest gave Charlie a pleased grin and spooned some more stew into his mouth, nodding at Charlie to do the same. "We're good friends, and friends always help each other."

Charlie's heightened senses were in overdrive and the assault of stimuli on his tired brain was enough to make anyone over-cautious. His nose could smell the violence leaking out of these men, and his eyes could see the myriad scars decorating their hands and forearms. Charlie recognized them as old knife wounds, and everyone knew you didn't get knife wounds from tickling babies. Charlie's ears picked up on the creaking of leather, the spit of the fire and, in the distance, a voice: female, quiet and crying, somewhere down the road that led away from their little camp, further away from the village. Charlie suppressed a shiver. Either the priest was just stupid or too hungry to see the danger they were in, but Charlie decided he had to get the hell out of there and Pere Raven could just bloody well help himself. Charlie recalled the expression of desperation on the face of the woman in the village when she told him to come and hide. These scary gentlemen might be the reason she warned him, and Charlie didn't want to find out for sure.

"Um, thanks for the food." Charlie choked a bit on his fear as he placed the bowl near the fire. "I just need to go and take a piss, I'll be back in a mo'."

"You know what, Charlie?" Pere Raven scraped his bowl clean and licked the spoon. "I've asked Cedric and these gentlemen to help me get through the Dark Forest and back to the Belvoir Estate. Would you be interested in coming with us? Back at Belvoir I can get you a horse, and then you can return to the Golden Palace in no time. It'll only take us a day to get through the Dark Forest with these experienced rangers."

"Rangers, eh?" Charlie looked dubiously at the group. *Well, maybe that would account for their tense demeanor? It couldn't be a life of chuckles guiding people through the Dark Forest.*

Pere Raven nodded. "These gentlemen are on the search for a lost lass, you see. There was an accident with dark magic in the village and they have had teams in yesterday evacuating all the refugees to the Belvoir Estate but there was one little girl who got away. They need to find her before they can take us back through the Dark Forest. I've delayed them already by insisting they wait for me to go and fetch you this morning, and now it's getting late and they are all a bit anxious to be heading back to the Belvoir Estate. Do you think we could help them find this lost little lamb and then go back with them?"

"You men are from Belvoir?" Charlie asked, trying to decide whether he should believe the story he was hearing or what his instincts were telling him.

"Not *from* Belvoir, but they work for Prince Bertie," answered Pere Raven, as his face dropped into a sad frown. "It cuts me up to imagine that poor little girl wandering the woods around here, lost and not knowing what happened to her family. If you would like to stay by the fire, Charlie, you are definitely welcome to it, but I will head off with Cedric now to search for her."

The Priest got up. Cedric and two of the other men followed him, and one stayed behind, not too far from Charlie. The man stretched his hands out to the fire and his knuckles popped and cracked. He didn't spare Charlie a glance, but he didn't need too. His intention was clear. *So, he was the babysitter, was he?* Charlie's rash plan to grab as much food as he could and then scarper turned to ashes. These men had obviously dealt with darker forces than a scared street kid, and they were prepared for it. Charlie realized he would have a better chance of escape if he could agree to help with the search and lose *himself* in the woods.

"Wait up." Charlie stood and quickly joined the priest as he was slowly making his way along the road calling out for the little girl. "I'll help, but then we are going straight to Belvoir, right?"

"Wonderful, thank you, Charlie!" said Pere Raven and clapped Charlie on the back again. "Let's spread out a little, shall we? Cedric told me the girl's name is Leafy, and she is only seven. She's been lost since last night and she'll be very upset so be gentle with her."

Charlie looked over at Cedric to try to ascertain why it was the priest giving directions and not the ranger himself, but Cedric was talking quietly with his men, and nodded at the priest when Pere Raven told him the plan.

Charlie only had to sharpen his hearing a little to catch that the men were talking about taking another wagon through the woods and debating if they could make it to the 'safe haven' by nightfall. Charlie could also hear the crying of the little girl, probably Leafy, which had moved off the road and into some marshy trees deeper in the woods. Charlie guessed it would only take him a few minutes to find her if he really looked, but he needed some time to think. The situation he was in was just too weird. The atmosphere around the fireplace couldn't have been grimmer but Pere Raven was acting as jolly as if they were all at a church picnic, giving away sandwiches to the poor.

Breaking away from the group, Charlie made his way into the woods and made sure to look about, as if he was searching for the little girl. As he went further into the trees, he saw evidence of a struggle. Branches had been broken off trees and the undergrowth had been trampled. Charlie's gooseflesh prickled again when he could see that blood had been spilled, but by bodies that were nowhere to be seen. There was no doubt about it: he had to get out of here.

Following his instincts, Charlie went deeper into the woods, and he had an idea that he was somehow heading back in the direction of the Grey Palace. He hadn't gone very far when black trees began to appear amongst the regular brown and green, and Charlie knew that he was getting a bit too close to the boundary of the Dark Forest. He kept his enhanced senses on high alert and almost jumped out of his skin when he heard a rustle in the bushes, right before a little girl fell out onto the path before him. She was dirty and skinny, wearing only a dark leather tunic and no shoes. Leafy swayed on her feet and gazed up at Charlie, her dark eyes rimmed with silver.

"Can ya 'elp me get awoy?" she whispered and cast a frightened glance over Charlie's shoulder. "The men will take me where they took the others. I can't go 'cause I'm Special and they will hurt me bad, my brother said."

Charlie could barely understand the little girl's words through her thick accent but he didn't need his magic to tell him that this girl had strong power running through her veins. The silver rings shining around her pupils spun and flashed at him in the dim light of the forest. *How could he carry a little girl when he was trying to escape from trouble as well?* She would only slow him down, when he needed to run. Though his conscience was screaming at him to take her with him, Charlie shook his head. "Keep hidden kid, those men are behind me."

The little girl stepped closer to Charlie and slipped her little hand in his. He felt the magic in her touch as if itching ants crawled up his arm. "Please, I'm a Special. Don't let them get me," she whispered and pale green tears filled her eyes. "I dunno how to be on my own, my brother looks after me." The way she said it was "me bruvva loogs afta moy" but Charlie understood well enough.

Cursing his soft heart, Charlie roughly pulled Leafy into step with him and headed off in the same direction he was going before. "I'll take you out of here but I'm only dropping you back in the village," he said. Charlie was so keen to avoid walking in circles that when suddenly he stepped into a clearing, he was very surprised to see Pere Raven sitting on a fallen log with three of the rangers standing about him.

"Ah, Charlie, I knew you could help! Like begets like, you know." Pere Raven said and stood up with a big smile lighting up his face. "Thank the Goddess you found the little lamb. Come here, Leafy." The priest gestured to the little girl in a welcoming hug.

Leafy shook her head and whimpered, trying to hide her slim frame behind Charlie. "Thassa man wonts moy magic," she whispered.

"Look, I don't know what this is about, Pere Raven," said Charlie and tried to back away into the forest, shuffling Leafy behind him as he went. It scared him that he had yet to spot Cedric in the clearing. "I'm going to take this little girl to the queen and tell her what happened here. The queen knows where I am, and she is sure to come looking for me, just as quick as she can."

Pere Raven laughed a big, cheerful booming laugh. "That's why I knew I liked you Charlie. You say such funny things." Pere Raven looked over Charlie's head, and still smiling said, "Catch him, Cedric."

Charlie felt the pain like an unwelcome memory, but instinct forced him to cling to his consciousness and he was rewarded by hearing Pere Raven's voice. "Two offerings for the Goddess today, fate has smiled upon me, boys. She has smiled upon us all!" And his booming laugh echoed around Charlie's head until the darkness stole the light and he passed out.

CHAPTER TWENTY-FOUR

"Mother, Who Art Thou?"

Upon Grottonski's arrival, the meeting in the Lavender Room had devolved into utter chaos.

High Wizard Ohren was shouting so loudly that his voice was making the chandeliers tremble where they hung above the table. Rainere was cursing at Grottonski and telling him to stop what he was doing. Orestes was warning every one of the legal ramifications of what they were yelling. General Ohrig was beside Adele, standing so close that his anger made the hairs on her arms rise. All of her Queen's Guard had gathered about her in a tight knot, ready to defend her from any physical foe.

Grotto himself seemed to be repeating a rehearsed speech, his dry monologue undercutting the shrill protests of Tilburn who was still trying to drag him out of the room again. The Household Guard in their highly decorated purple-and-gold uniforms stood at attention at the door, clearly reluctant to enter the room as it filled with a haze of golden magic.

Overwhelmed, Adele sank back down into her chair and cast her gaze over to Rainere. He quickly looked back at her, as if she had called his name aloud. The silver rings spun about his pupils, flashing at her with tiny sparkles, and two spots of color rouged the edge of his cheekbones. Adele could see that a war waged behind those dark green eyes. Her magic uncoiled in response, raising itself to strike out, and her hands buzzed as if she held handfuls of bees. *Violence would not make this situation right.* The Chime Voices chanted words of stillness and calm, and Adele let the green magic slither back to where is belonged under her heart and encouraged the golden power to come forth.

There was far too much power at play here in the Lavender Room. The air literally crackled with it. Anger had Ohren and Orestes sending showers of magic into the space just above the table, and Adele's gold magic swirled and mixed with the green particles that must have been attracted by Rainere's own rage and her anxiety. Adele dropped her eyes to the table and saw her reflection.

A memory of another world...another shiny table...another time when a man had taken her whole world and ripped it right down the middle...

For a long moment, Adele forgot she was a queen in an alien world, and she forgot that she was powerful. She forgot the magic that sang for her and gave her strength. Just for a moment, she remembered what it was like to be the old Adele, who had given up her own power, burying it deep under a husk of denial and helplessness. The old Adele would have given up already and let all these people tell her what she could do, and more importantly, what she couldn't do.

Adele squared her shoulders and shook off the terror that her memories had laid about her like a sodden blanket.

"Enough." Adele spoke softly but she was echoed by General Ohrig with such a violent shout that the room quietened immediately. She waited until the wizards had all taken their seats and then dismissed a very reluctant Tilburn and the Household Guard from the room. Only Grottonski refused to sit, instead choosing to stand at Rainere's right shoulder and glare down the table at her.

"The issue you are all discussing has already been resolved." Adele took a deep breath and suppressed another flash of terror. Now she was going to have to cut out her own heart and lay it on the table so all these interested men could examine the damage that had been done to it. "The prince did indeed propose to me, and I did accept," - she held up her hand for silence as the protests began again - "But the prince kidnapped my daughter Princess Natalie and I withdrew my acceptance. Let us be clear, I will not ever marry Prince Rainere."

"But the prince himself did not accept your withdrawal, Your Majesty," snarled Grotto. "Insulting his honor does not lawfully excuse you from the obligation to marry him."

Adele felt her gold magic growl and her bones vibrated with the force of it. A warmth coursed through her, and although she knew it was wrong to feed it, the anger felt so much better than fear.

"I will not marry Prince Rainere." Adele's voice held the weight of her convictions. "My decision is final."

"And yet, it is not your decision to make, Your Majesty," retorted Grotto, a triumphant gleam in his eye, as he delivered his blow. "Your Majesty, you did knowingly fornicate with Prince Rainere Marchant on the grounds of the Grey Palace, and thereby in accordance with Marchant law of the Marchant territories, you voluntarily accepted the betrothal offered to you by the prince, and so you are now obliged to marry him."

The room fell silent as everyone stared at Grotto and then one by one turned their eyes to her. Adele swallowed her protest and felt her cheeks flame with humiliation.

"Orestes, is this true?" Ohren asked his twin who was the expert on Unisian law.

Orestes looked more thoughtful than scandalized at what had befallen the queen and Adele was distantly relieved that his cool head might actually help her sort out this mess.

"Were there any witnesses to the fornication?" asked Orestes.

"Yes." Grotto nodded. "Me."

Adele felt her lip curl in disgust, but it rankled most deeply because it was true. Grotto had caught them together in Rainere's laboratory that one time.

"The queen was a very eager participant from what I could see," added Grotto nastily.

"Watch your tongue, Grottonski," warned General Ohrig before he was in turn shushed by the high magistrar.

Orestes turned to face Adelena and his gaze was cold. "If the act was consensual, the prince now has the right to marry you and take everything that is yours as his own, up to and including your throne and your children. It's Marchant law, Your Majesty, and just as binding here in the Golden Palace."

Adele thought of Ripenzo Shale, whom she had once accused of rape and then named an enemy of the crown. Her conscience was battered enough by her lies, and she would not claim victimhood again as a defense for her worst actions. The warm power within her growled its approval. "The act was consensual," she admitted and turned to Rainere, her chin raised as she held onto her dignity.

"Rainere, tell them I do not have to marry you. Please, I need you to make this right."

"*Prince* Rainere," corrected Grotto, sneering at Adele with triumphant spite. "He is your king and master now, Your Majesty."

Adele caught Rainere's gaze and searched inside the deep green glare for the man she remembered loving. Yet, all she could see was betrayal. In one single, gut wrenching moment, everything that Rainere had asked for - her hand in marriage and her crown - would be his. Everything he had wanted from her that had been denied him, was now laid out on the table ready for him to take. She saw the madness dancing in Rainere's eyes as he considered all of this. Then his lips quirked up at the side in a half-smile and the prince climbed to his feet. Adele heard Grotto hiss with excitement, and her hands tightened into a death-grip on the arms of her chair.

"I will address High Magistrar Orestes directly as I would like it on the official record that I, Prince Rainere of the Marchant family, did ask Queen Adelena to marry me. I believed that the queen was in love with me when she agreed to be my wife and accept my troth. I also believed that she was fully cognizant of all that her agreement entailed in my ruling by her side as the king of Unisia, and that I would act as a father to her children."

Adele let out a gasp of horror. Rainere flinched as if in pain. Raising his eyes to Adele's, Rainere leaned forward over the table, the intent and passion clear in his expression.

"But I betrayed the queen's trust, and it is an act I will regret for the rest of my life. I understand that because of it, she does not love me any longer. Therefore, I hereby accept Queen Adelena's withdrawal from my suit of marriage and I withdraw my legal right to insist on the marriage." A green tear slid down Rainere's cheek and his voice almost rasped away as he finished. "I know you will never forgive me, *cara mia*, but I need you to know I am so very sorry for what I did to you."

Adele choked back a dry sob at the same time as Grotto shrieked, "No, you can't! It's your crown she holds! That abomination has no right to what is yours master."

Rainere said nothing else but sat back down and rubbed the back of his hand against his cheek to erase the single tear that had fallen. He was finished. Adele remembered once more that day on Earth when her divorce had been finalized. She had been destroyed by her ex-husband's rejection of her, and their life together. *Am I treating Rainere any better than Justin treated me?* Adele wondered. *I know I was never so gracious in accepting Justin's decision to leave me, as Rainere is in accepting mine now.*

"If the prince wishes to forfeit his claim of betrothal," Orestes said, and looked to his brother, the relief clear in his expression. "Then there is no longer any reason why the queen should be forced to honor any promises made to him."

Grotto wasn't yet ready to concede defeat. Like some kind of human mantis, he leaned over Rainere's shoulder, his bony hands gripping the prince's arm, as he hissed in his ear. Rainere didn't respond except to shake his head and shrug off his manservant, much to Grotto's frustration. Rainere gazed across the table at Adele, his expression filled with the pain and the regret that consumed him, and his sadness rubbed against her own raw heart.

Adele's certainty of Rainere's wickedness was waning in the face of his efforts to help her. In the last two days, he had saved Stella's life by returning the Fire Orchid stamens, defied Unisian law by using dark magic in the Golden Palace, and now had sacrificed his only chance to marry her and claim her crown.

Could she honestly tell herself that if she had been in his position of power, she would have done the same? The image of Ripenzo Shale drifted across her mind again. Adele had also done wicked things in an effort to protect those she loved.

High Wizard Ohren had sat back in his seat, his face a calm mask, but Adele could see his hands tremble as he clasped them together on the table. Even without the prophecy, he had as much invested in her future as Adele did. Tension rolled off the high wizard in waves, and the golden magic in Adele seemed drawn to him.

"On behalf of the High Council of Wizards and the Court of the Golden Palace, we thank His Highness for his decision to…"

Adele would never have imagined anyone would be unwise enough to face down a wizard who was literally vibrating with power and anger, but Grotto did not look at all cowed by the company he addressed. In fact, the old manservant's expression had only become even grimmer and more determined. "You do not want to play this game with me, High Wizard Ohren," Grotto said, loudly interrupting. "I still have one more card up my sleeve, and you know it."

"Don't you dare try to threaten me, you filthy cretin," roared Ohren and was back on his feet, pointing a lethal finger at Grotto. "You have no place here, you're just a sick and twisted…"

Just as Grotto blurted, "Prince Rainere is Queen Adelena's elder half-brother!"

CHAPTER TWENTY-FIVE

"The Ties that Bind"

Grotto's pronouncement was choked off by Rainere's hand as it tightened around his throat. The prince had moved faster than the human eye could see, but the words still reached Adele's ears. A silence fell over the table, broken only by Ohren's hissed breath and Grotto's gasps.

"What?" Adele was stunned. "Rainere is my *what?*"

Adele looked around the table in confusion and hated that she was only one of the few who seemed shocked by this bombshell, she exchanged a troubled glance with General Ohrig. "Rainere, let him speak. I have to hear this," Adele ordered.

Rainere let go of Grotto's throat with a curse and sat back down again. Adele turned to her high wizard, as Ohren slumped into his chair and dropped his head in his hands. "You *knew* Rainere was my brother, Ohren?"

"Yes, I did." Ohren nodded and avoided her eye. "But I hadn't known you were sleeping with him before yesterday. You told me that the relationship was severed so I presumed that there was no reason for you to have to know. We needed you Adelena, even a bastard child of King Octavius and Princess Rainella was better than a commoner on the throne. It is all just so damned complicated, Your Majesty."

Ohren turned to Grotto ready to blame someone else for his lie. "Grottonski, you vowed you wouldn't disgrace the Marchant family name like this. I will see you dead before I let you…"

"You never told me you had an abomination waiting in the wings to steal my master's crown," sneered Grotto, his voice rusty after being squeezed by Rainere. "You broke your word, *High Wizard*, so I'm breaking mine. The crown on Adelena's head now belongs to her brother. She is only second in line by birth, and he takes precedence as the only adopted son of Princess Rainestra."

Grotto pulled himself tall and cast his scornful gaze over everyone at the table. "I have vowed to protect the honor of the Marchant family for the last three hundred years. Any secrets I reveal now are only to keep that vow. I will see a Marchant prince on the throne of Unisia in my lifetime, may the Goddess Lune bless me.

"As I stand here before you all, I will confirm on the Blood that the queen is a bastard born of mixed blood, the daughter of King Octavius III and the demon Princess Rainestra Marchant." Grotto's eyes gleamed with mad pleasure as he continued.

"This queen, Adelena, should have been killed at birth by the Marchant Elders but Prince Rainold had promised his wife Rainestra that he would see her bastard child safe. Prince Rainold knew that there was a chance that Rainestra might survive the Eldars when they came for her, and so he had the wizards of the High Council send her baby away alongside the newborn St Lucidis prince until the prophecy was ignited."

Ohren opened his mouth, but only a groan came out. He shook off his shock and Adele could see he was going to plead with her to forgive his lies. "Your Majesty, I had no choice. Olivia's baby son was as good as dead and I needed to hide you before the Eldars had a chance to kill you too."

Adele felt nauseous. Was this the reason behind her mysterious connection to Rainere, and why their attraction had always been so powerful, because they were - family? Adele's stomach roiled in disgust at the idea of incest. The Chime Voices sang a new song, something martial and strong, and the warm magic pulsed in response. Clarity reigned in her mind once more, and Adele found the questions she needed to ask as if someone was whispering them in her ear.

"If you both agree that Rainere and I share the same mother, then why was he adopted by Princess Rainestra?" Adele looked around the table until she caught Rainere's gaze. "It makes no sense for her to adopt her own son, does it? Ohren, I distinctly heard you call my mother Princess Rainella, not Rainestra. So someone is still lying to me."

Ohren also turned in confusion to the prince. "Your father, Prince Rainold didn't have two wives, did he?"

Grotto's natural malevolence took over and he could only spit at her. "*Your* mother really was the demon Rainestra, but Prince Rainere is a full-blooded Marchant, fathered by Prince Rainold on the late Princess Rainella of the last royal line of Marchant kings before the Exodus. You are the bastard filth of a St Lucidis king and an evil abomination."

"Could I just intercede with a point here?" asked Orestes and Adele marveled at the man's unflappable demeanor. "If this new information that Grottonski has given up proves correct, then the Queen Adelena, as the most recent natural child of the late Marchant princess, takes the place of the elder in the Marchant family, and she is in fact the princess Marchant herself now, and therefore the true custodian of the Grey Palace, and all Marchant properties."

"Absolutely not!" yelped Grotto. "The last child of the last living parent takes precedence over any adopted or bastard offspring."

"Adopted children like Prince Rainere, you mean?" answered Orestes, and Adele couldn't discern any emotion in his eyes or his expression.

"Of course. Rainestra isn't the last parent alive, Prince Rainold is," Grotto snapped, but his jaw twitched and he threw a furtive glance at Gorrik, where he sat by Ohren. Adele had forgotten about the old man, but a little smile was now hitching up the corners of his mouth.

"But you said Princess Rainestra was a demon," countered Orestes. "And then you admitted that she was taken to the Eyrie by the Eldars and not killed. So if her mother is still alive, then Queen Adelena takes precedence in the Marchant hierarchy."

"Well?" Orestes pressed his attack. "Is Queen Adelena the illegitimate child of the Marchant Princess Rainestra, or is she not?"

"She is, but, but-" stammered Grotto, and began looking wildly about as if for an exit. "But her mother only claimed to be a Marchant. If anything, your queen is just a wicked half-St Lucidis demon, not even Marchant at all."

"Yet, that is not what you said, boy." Gorrik had decided to pipe up now. "If the queen is the primary heir to the Marchant name then she also the custodian of the Grey Palace and whatever she did there she did on her own property. You've just lost your master his home with this argument."

Grotto shot an especially savage glare in Gorrik's direction, and almost choked on his vitriol. "My master, Prince Rainere is still the rightful heir, as the first born of his Marchant mother and father," insisted Grotto stubbornly. "Prince Rainold knows the truth, he will tell you that your queen is an abomination."

"Idiot," groaned Gorrik.

"Rainold is dead, sent by the Eldars to an Early Death," shouted Ohren, clearly beside himself now, but with fear or anger, it was hard to tell. "There is no coming back from the Eldars."

Yet Grotto had come too far to be thwarted now. "No, listen!" he shrieked. "I can tell you where Prince Rainold is. I can tell you where he hides." In a mad dash, he pulled away from Prince Rainere and tried to reach around the table to the queen, making the QG's leap to their feet in unison and pull their swords from scabbards. Captain Lucky pointed his sword at Grotto and warned him to stay back.

"*You* can take him to his father," Grotto shrieked and pointed at Adele, making the sword tip press into the flesh at his throat, not that it bothered him. "*You* can use your demon magic to take my Prince Rainere to the place of the Early Death."

"Why would I do that?" asked Adele, honestly curious.

Grotto's eyes narrowed and his expression became canny. "Because I heard through the door that you need a dragon." Grotto had the nerve to smirk in triumph. "And Prince Rainold knows where the last dragon in Unisia still lives."

CHAPTER TWENTY-SIX

"What Lies Behind Smiles"

"Mrs. Ollenby, why did they move Stella where we can't see her?" asked Natalie. She was sitting on the great Glass Bed in her mother's enormous bedroom. It has always struck Natalie that Mummy's bedroom in the Golden Palace was almost as big as their old house back on Earth. That's what she called it now: her 'old house back on Earth'. Natalie tried hard, but she couldn't remember the name of the city where they have lived, or even the name of their street that had led to the beach. It just seemed all too far away.

"I have already told you, my poppet." Mrs. Ollenby smoothed Natalie's hair behind her ears with a gentle hand, before returning to dressing the mannequin in Mummy's clothes for the fancy dinner tonight. "Your sister needed to be in a nice, quiet room where no one can bother her while she gets better with the medicine."

"The medicine that Prince Rainere gave her?" Natalie always noticed the pause that her favorite man's name gave everyone. Mrs. Ollenby paused too, but her eyes only looked curious and not angry.

"You know that Prince Rainere is a very powerful wizard, Natalie," said Mrs. Ollenby. "And we were all very lucky that he came to the Golden Palace to save your sister. I know that you didn't realize what a lot of trouble you would cause when you gave him those flower stamens. You were just being a sweet girl giving a nice man a gift, you mustn't feel bad about that."

Natalie, looked up from twisting her hands in her lap, and wondered for the umpteenth time if Mrs. Ollenby could see inside her head. "Mummy is angry with me for making Stella sick," Natalie whispered, and felt her heart almost burst under the sadness that pressed down on it.

There was a blur of movement, and then Natalie found her face pressed to Mrs. Ollenby's soft bosom and was enveloped by the smell of peaches.

"Child, you must never think that." Mrs. Ollenby's voice was strong and sure. "Your baby sister was born with no magic in her body, that's why she got sick with the Influenza. The prince gave the stamens back because he is a good man, and he helped save Stella's life, but now your mother has to find a way to make Stella properly healthy again." Mrs. Ollenby took Natalie's chin in her hand and forced the little girl to look into her lavender blue eyes. "You did a lovely thing for a friend, and it was not your fault Stella got sick, and your mother knows that. As soon as she has the time she will tell you herself." Mrs. Ollenby gave Natalie a kiss on the nose and one of her big smiles that made Natalie feel warm and safe. "Now tell me if you think these rubies go with this gorgeous organza gown?"

Natalie nodded. "I think it looks beautiful. Can I have a dress like that too?"

Mrs. Ollenby laughed her nice laugh but Natalie could still hear the 'no' in it. Before she had a chance to complain, the bedroom door flew open and Lady Olivia ran into the room as if she was being chased, it only took her an instant to calm herself when she saw she had company. Lady Olivia came to a stop in the middle of the room and regarded Mrs. Ollenby dressing the mannequin. Natalie caught Lady Olivia's flash of anger before she managed to plaster on an expression of pleased surprise.

"Why, Mrs. Ollenby! Here you are, with so much to do already and yet you still have time for my work too!" Lady Olivia swooped in to take the ruby necklace out of Mrs. Ollenby's hands and put it back on the velvet tray, almost bodily pushing the older lady out of her way. "I had decided to dress Her Majesty in the violet silk gown tonight. The neckline is so flattering for Her Majesty and she has remarked on it several times to me." Lady Olivia sounded almost apologetic for suggesting that Mrs. Ollenby didn't know the queen's taste as well as she did as she began to strip the mannequin. "I find that the queen likes to dress in a younger, bolder way when she is entertaining Prince Rainere." She gave Mrs. Ollenby a wide-eyed look that could have been innocence or well-masked spite. "Do you know how long he will be staying in the Golden Palace, or if will she be leaving to join him at the Grey Palace again?"

Mrs. Ollenby wasn't at all flustered by Lady Olivia's gossipy questions, but neither did she deign to answer the lady-in-waiting. Instead, Mrs. Ollenby collected Natalie from the bed, pulling her down onto her feet and helping put on her little leather slippers. "Princess Natalie and I shall leave you to your work, Lady Olivia," Mrs. Ollenby said and took Natalie's hand. "I do believe it is time for our tea and biscuits."

Lady Olivia laughed loudly, though no one had made a joke. "I honestly don't know how you do it, Mrs. Ollenby," she chortled.

Natalie waited until the she and Mrs. Ollenby made their way to the outside terrace before she decided to share a confidence.

"I hate Lady Olivia," she announced to Mrs. Ollenby. "She pretends to be nice but she is actually really mean."

"Oh, poppet, hate is such a strong word," said Mrs. Ollenby settling into her chair. "But it is clever of you to tell the difference between someone nice, and someone pretending to be nice. Perhaps you can tell me why you think Lady Olivia was only pretending?"

Natalie only shrugged. She just knew, and that's all there was to it. Mrs. Ollenby accepted the shrug and poured their tea.

Natalie watched Aaron playing tag with the three nannies, Siobahn, Seraphina and Caitlin. It was obvious that they were letting him win, but Natalie thought that was only fair, Aaron was still little and cried if he lost games. Also, she knew the nannies must be so bored without Stella to fuss over. Tra La-La had followed Natalie out onto the terrace and was sniffing under her chair, searching for biscuits crumbs that hadn't been dropped yet. Natalie loved her puppy, though Tra La-La was getting so big now Natalie almost couldn't carry her anymore. Tra La-La placed her heavy head on Natalie's knee and gazed up at her with adoring brown eyes, so Natalie kissed her.

"You are so good to your puppy," Mrs. Ollenby noted. "She loves you very much, I can tell."

Natalie ran her hands over Tra La-La's velvet ears and dug her fingers into the thick ruff of fur around her collar. "I wish she would talk to me though," said Natalie wistfully. "Aaron says that Hero Boy doesn't stop talking to him, and that my dog will talk too, but she never does with me."

Mrs. Ollenby coughed in her tea and had to dab at the corner of her mouth with a lace handkerchief. "Does Aaron talk to lots of animals?" she asked.

Natalie frowned and tried to recall. "I know he likes talking to the ponies when we have our riding lessons. Oh, and he talks to that little black cat too."

"Which little black cat? Gorrik's pet?" Mrs. Ollenby seemed to find that a bit surprising. The cat didn't come around very often, as it didn't like the children's three puppies, but sometimes it could be found sitting on top of the cupboards or tapping at the nursery window with its soft little paws.

Natalie shrugged again. "I don't know who owns him, but the cat told Aaron that he belongs to us. He is a very sweet cat," she added helpfully.

Mrs. Ollenby smiled at Natalie and gave the little girl another biscuit with her tea. "I'm sure he is, my poppet," she said. "But I might just have a little word with Gorrik, all the same."

Suddenly there was a loud 'boom' and the balcony shook. Everyone jumped in fright and the nannies collected Aaron and made their way to the couch where Natalie and Mrs. Ollenby were seated. The Household Guard looked about in consternation, searching for the source of the trouble.

"What was that?" yelped Natalie and climbed into the safety of Mrs. Ollenby's lap. She followed Mrs. Ollenby's gaze to a distant window of the palace, a few floors up. A cloud of gold sparks escaped and hovered outside the window before slowly drifting away and dissipating in the sun.

"That, my dearest child, is your mother putting her foot down, I believe," murmured Mrs. Ollenby and stroked Natalie's hair as she watched the window. "They *will* try her patience though, won't they?"

"They shouldn't make my mummy angry," agreed Natalie.

Mrs. Ollenby gave Natalie a squeeze and laughed lightly. "No, they shouldn't! Now let's get you out in the garden. Your favorite riding teacher is back from Belvoir. Benjamin, I'm told his name is."

Natalie heard the nannies giggling amongst themselves at Benjamin's name.

"Benjamin is very handsome, but I'm not going to marry him," Natalie told Mrs. Ollenby. "Come on Aaron, riding time."

She climbed down off Mrs. Ollenby's lap and everyone got up to follow her back inside, which always made Natalie nervous that she was going the wrong way, but being a princess meant everyone did what you said most of the time, and she was getting used to it.

CHAPTER TWENTY-SEVEN

"Where There is the Will"

Adele hadn't meant to blow up every particle of magic in the room.

After Grotto's shocking announcement that she must now find Prince Rainold if she wanted to find her dragon, the Chime Voices had returned in anger, and Adele had whispered their word of command like a curse. It was that command which had ignited the cloud of magic hovering over the table, surprising everyone with a green and gold fireball. A smell of burnt honey and hot metal lingered in the air.

So, I am a demon, Adelena thought in the silence that followed the loud, yet harmless, explosion. *I'm not even Marchant like I'd suspected. This must be why I have these two sides to my magic, but I still can't explain the Chime Voices.* Adele hadn't forgotten that after tasting her blood the Spider Empress had said that there was something darker than her Marchant heritage, something 'ancient'.

The Chime Voices sang quietly in the back of her mind, letting her work out the problem before her. Though the High Wizard had already lied to her about other things, Ohren had appeared genuinely surprised at Grotto's proclamation that Princess Rainestra had been a demon, and Adele felt certain that he had never known such a thing before.

Adele thought of her children and how she tried so hard to be a good person and a good mother to them. Like everything that seemed strange in Evendaar, perhaps being a demon wasn't as bad as she assumed. Yet, Adele couldn't escape the fact that almost every one of these powerful men around her looked just as confused as she felt right now, so it seemed logical to suppose that demons were uncommon here too.

Adele raised her eyes to Rainere who was quietly conducting a conversation with his manservant. She chewed her bottom lip and considered the bombshells which had left their fragile relationship with a new set of scars. Step-brother or not, Adele was relieved to have it confirmed that the two of them hadn't broken any of the laws of nature with their relationship.

It was clear to Adele that she had to face the impossible yet again. If her magic could help her travel to this Early Death to find Prince Rainold and have him tell her where a dragon lived, then that was what she would do. Adele almost smiled to think how slim the odds were, with so many 'what ifs' in the way, but she hadn't let that stop her before when she had needed to save Natalie and it wouldn't stop her when she needed to save Stella now.

Adele held up a hand and waited until the men about her fell silent. "We will hear from Grottonski how to find Prince Rainold in the Early Death." Adele let her gaze fall on the high wizard. "He will tell us everything he knows, and only then may he be questioned." Ohren nodded tightly at the warning in her tone.

Adele took her seat and Grotto stood tall behind Prince Rainere and directed his gaze to the window behind Adele, looking at a point above her head. It made a nice change from being the victim of his glare.

"What I am about to tell you breaks a code of silence maintained by the Elven Folk for over one thousand years," said Grotto, his voice clear and cold. "I had promised to guard this secret until my death, as many have done before me. What I do now, I do only for the good of my master, in the hope that it will help him regain the throne that was stolen from the Marchants by the St Lucidis family." Grotto closed his eyes, took a deep breath and then began.

"The Early Death is not death as a mortal would know it. It is actually a...cluster...of different dimensions, constructed by the Eldars in the days of old, shortly after the Goddess Serena had given them the gift of immortality. The most powerful immortal Marchants were experimenting with portals when they discovered the magic to create completely separate dimensions.

"These dimensions were created outside of space and time, and they were as fragile as they were dangerous. The first Eldars named the magic to create these dimensions the Early Death, after the fates of the unwary wizards who explored them. In time, the Marchant Eldars became able to harness this power, which they used to imprison immortal wizards who trespassed against Marchant law. The Early Death trapped these immortals in a separate dimension by keying the spell to the prisoner's blood."

"Keying the spell to the prisoner's blood?" asked Gorrik, "Grottonski, speak in clear terms for the non-wizards among us, eh?"

"Why would the Eldars keep these immortals imprisoned?" asked Adele. "Why not just kill them?"

Ohren spoke up, his brow deeply furrowed and his cheeks white. "Because Marchant immortals are extremely valuable creatures of magic. Every fiber in their bodies has absorbed a very powerful spell, and the very tissue itself can be used for all sorts of purposes. Immortal wizards are almost invincible, and it is why they can only be killed by other powerful God-given magics."

"Then tell me again why you were so afraid of the Spider Empress?" Adele asked Rainere. "If she couldn't kill you…"

Rainere visibly stiffened in his chair and his cheeks flamed with humiliation at her tactlessness, but Adele was too curious to be cautious.

"Because of the way the immortality spell works, Your Majesty," interjected Ohren. "With enough ancient magic of her own, a dark entity *can* destroy or eat the immortal body, ingesting the magic and then trap the soul that is still bound to the bones by the immortality spell. An immortal soul can then be re-used time and time again to fuel other spells."

"So for these immortals trapped in the Early Death dimension, are their bodies still alive, or is it just their souls that are trapped?" asked Adele.

"Their immortal bodies are preserved along with their souls," answered Grotto in clipped tones, almost rolling his eyes at her simple questions. "That is *why* their blood is needed to trap them in the Early Death."

"And is there just one singular Early Death dimension or are their multiple dimensions, one for each immortal?" continued Adele.

"Each immortal is trapped in their individual dimension," Grotto admitted, and sent Adele a baleful glare. "Prince Rainold cannot escape the Early Death but…"

Grotto paused, nearly choking on a wisp of magic that had appeared at his mouth. The glitter was almost black, and Adele didn't need anyone to tell her that this was dark magic puffing from Grotto's mouth like steam, surrounding the words that he was never meant to tell another living soul.

"…but there is a back door to the matrix of the dimension spell, found at its apex. The Eldars needed a way to retrieve the immortals if they ever decided to release them in the future, or in the event of the Goddess Serena's return to Evendaar."

"So even though Prince Rainold cannot escape, anyone with magic powerful enough to find his Early Death dimension *can* enter?" asked Ohren.

"Tell us how we find the dimension holding Prince Rainold," said Adele.

Grotto shrugged. "I do not know where they hid him, I only know where they didn't." He turned to Rainere. "Your father did not want you to remember him as a prisoner dragged away by the Eldars, so he left the Grey Palace before they came to get him. It was his last gift to you."

Rainere only nodded stiffly and gestured for Grotto to continue. "Explain the apex."

Grotto bit his lip, and a trickle of black blood stained his teeth. He visibly forced himself to continue speaking as the cloud of dark green magic floated up to become a halo around his sweating brow. "The weakest point of the dimension is the apex, and this is where you will be able to enter the spherical dimension."

"A spherical dimension?" Ohren was in awe. "Of course! A spherical dimension would be able to create pockets between the worlds…" Ohren paused to process this new magical revelation before his gaze re-focused on Grotto, sharp and cold. "But that means that the apex of Prince Rainold's dimension could be anywhere in Unisia." Ohren slumped back into his chair, deflated.

Grotto hadn't finished yet, and when Adele saw the cagey relief that flowed into his expression, something told her that Ohren wasn't asking Rainere's manservant the right questions. She let the warmth of her gold magic flow up to her head again and felt a sharp curiosity devoid of emotion.

"Why did you say that my magic could be used to pass through Prince Rainold's dimension?" Adele asked Grotto. "What is so different about me?"

Grotto sneered and showed his blackish teeth. "This is no simple portal magic that transfers an object from one point in this world to another. The magic required to cross a dimension and enter the Early Death must be able to contain and protect the body that is passing through. No mere light wizard, nor any single dark wizard, could live through the attempt. The demon magic you possess means only *you* are powerful enough to attack the spell at its apex. Only you can take Rainere to his father, and then finally hear the truth that Prince Rainere is the true heir to the Unisian throne."

CHAPTER TWENTY-EIGHT

"When Death is not the End"

High Wizard Ohren had gotten to his feet and begun to pace, pulling at his beard and muttering fiercely. "To create a vortex of such density that it could form its own dimension wouldn't require a large space, but it would have to be located somewhere structurally fragile. Maybe somewhere lots of portals had already been installed."

"Ohren." Orestes voice held a note of warning but his twin was already obsessed with solving this puzzle. Ohren turned to the only other person who might know such a thing, and better yet, would share that information.

"Gorrik, think man!" Ohren's cheeks were pink above his beard and the golden rings in his eyes glittered. "Where would the Eldars have taken Prince Rainold to find that combination of dense dark magic and environmental instability?"

Gorrik shrugged and petted his cat. "Who knows what those crazy Eldar Marchants got up to in their day."

"They could have used any dense concentration of power, couldn't they?" continued Ohren, too excited to stop. "But if the apex is not at the Grey Palace then where else would that many Marchant offspring gather together to create an enclave, even a hundred years ago, hmmm?"

Silence reigned until, "Oh!" QG Leith covered his exclamation with a cough, mortified at having interrupted the high wizard.

Ohren looked at the young guard with a mixture of irritation and exasperation. "Yes?"

Under Ohren's laser-like gaze, poor QG Leith could only shrug awkwardly, too embarrassed to speak.

Adele was just as surprised as anyone at Leith's interruption but if the young man could help she was ready to listen. "Have you thought of somewhere that a group of Marchants would have gathered, Leith?"

QG Leith shifted about in his seat as if he couldn't decide if he should stand to address the table or remain seated and face his queen.

"We are outside formality here, Leith," Adele promised her young guard. "Say what's on your mind."

"I don't know if it's any help, but, it's just that," stammered Leith. "I don't want to get anyone into any trouble if it doesn't mean anything." Leith sent Adele a nervous look. "Well, you see, there are these clubs in the LDC, I mean the Lower District of Concordis where people with Marchant ancestry tend to hang out together in clubs and bars. They actually perform in groups, using their power to create spectacles. I believe that they've been doing it ever since the Marchant Quarter was established, and I would think even a hundred years ago that a Marchant prince would certainly know about this area."

"That definitely sounds like something that could help us, Leith." Adele smiled at her QG, and then turned to see that Ohren was already shaking his head.

"QG Leith," Ohren began, "I know the area of the city that you have mentioned and I'm sure you also know that the St Lucidis family cleaned up that area decades ago, and there hasn't been a sighting of a Marchant congregation there since."

Leith chafed at the High Wizard's condescending tone and Adele saw the young man sit a little straighter in his chair, raising his chin to answer. "High Wizard, with all due respect, I have to ask how often any of the royal St Lucidis family have visited the Lower Districts recently?"

High Wizard Ohren frowned in response to the bold question.

"I know that Lord Orgustus visited the Guild Quarter this year to help with Influenza victims, but there was no word of his seeing to the sick people of the Lower Districts." Leith's voice had taken on a distinctly righteous edge that made Adele curious. "I might be St Lucidis, Sir, but I have family who live in the Lower Districts, and they aren't all immune to the influenza just because they have a bit of Marchant blood in their veins."

Silence reigned after Leith's little outburst and was only broken by Grottonski's snort of disgust. "Filthy bastards all of them." Adele could only guess Grotto was referring to the inhabitants of the Lower Districts and not their group at the table, though she wouldn't put it past him.

"My ancestors were known to be quite...prolific...in their appetites," said Rainere into the quiet. "I would imagine that the Lower Districts are simply crawling with Marchant descendants of varying strengths and weaknesses. At the very least, I think this would be a good place to start our search for the apex of Prince Rainold's prison dimension."

"Armed with this new knowledge," Ohren acquiesced frowning. "I suggest we first send Prince Rainere into this area of the Lower District of Concordis and let him determine if it could be the source of dense dark magic and gather what intelligence he can. I will lead a research team in the Accadaemia library, and then when Prince Rainere returns we can plan our assault on Prince Rainold's dimension."

"Actually, Ohren, I have decided what to do next." Adele raised her hand and stood up. Ohren's plan would simply take too much time. "I will lead a group to the Lower Districts, and the prince and I will determine if it could be the source of power to create the prison dimension. Grottonski you will tell us how to recognize this apex to Prince Rainold's dimension and then how it can be destroyed."

"When do we leave?" asked General Ohrig.

"Tonight," said Adele, and turned back to Ohren. "High Wizard, do you have any advice for how to deal with Prince Rainold if we should find him waiting for us?"

"Ah!" The High Wizard slumped back into his chair and rubbed a hand over his forehead. "That is when things are going to get really tricky."

CHAPTER TWENTY-NINE

"Fire and Light"

Adele stood in front of the beautifully-dressed mannequin in her bedroom and tried not to think about the important dinner she was missing tonight. Lord Orgustus was hosting and the discussion would center on how to commemorate the tragedy that had befallen Concordis with this year's Summer Influenza. Fortunately, the new infusion of tonics had slowed the death rate almost to a stop and the funeral pyres in the city squares were all but gone. Adele knew her absence would probably be remarked upon as a heartless show of contempt for her people in the city below the Golden Palace. These aristocrats could never know that she would instead be heading out to hunt down a wickedly dark spell to find a trapped Marchant prince, and begin the search for a dragon to cure her daughter's condition.

Adele's smile twisted with irony. Even in this fairy tale kingdom, the stories of her life here were just too incredible to be real.

"Your Majesty?" Mrs. Ollenby knocked quietly then entered. "The children have been put to bed with many songs and cuddles. Aaron is sleeping, but Natalie is still chatting with Seraphina."

"Thank you, Mrs. Ollenby." Adele appreciated the report. Bedtime with three little ones had always been tricky when she'd had to do it alone, so to have the support of other adults who adored her children made life that much easier. Though when she couldn't be there, Adele still needed to know each and every detail of their day before she could relax.

"They both ate so well at dinner," Adele said. "I'm glad I got to spend a little time with them today, even if it wasn't enough." Adele felt tears prick at the back of her eyes. "My poor little ones, I feel like I've deserted them just when they need me the most. Stella being so ill has made them both so sad, and now they can't even see her anymore, and I've had to spend so much time in these god-awful meetings all the time."

"The children miss you too, Your Majesty." Mrs. Ollenby came closer to place a gentle hand on Adele's arm. "But you are the queen as well as their mother, and Stella is depending on you to find her a cure. It's not an easy load you have to carry, but the children will understand that you only leave them because you have no other choice." Mrs. Ollenby gave Adele's arm a squeeze though she knew it was cold comfort she gave the queen. "Now, Your Majesty, you said that you have work to do tonight and you needed my help with something?"

Adele, wiped at her wet eyes, and pulled a piece of paper out of a pocket hidden in the stiff folds of her dress. "I need to wear something a little different than usual, and I cannot ask anyone else to get it for me." Adele fidgeted, a little chagrined at the list that Leith had drawn up for her of appropriate clothing for their expedition into the Lower Districts, not knowing what Mrs. Ollenby would think of it.

Mrs. Ollenby's eyebrows were sky high when she looked at the list, but her eyes twinkled with a glint of something that reminded Adele that Mrs. Ollenby had been young once. "I will do my best, Your Majesty, when will you need these items?"

"In just a few hours, I'm afraid," said Adele. "We leave before midnight."

Mrs. Ollenby gave Adele's shoulder a squeeze. "I won't ask where you are going but only that you come home safe tonight."

There was a knock on the door that led to the antechamber of her bedroom and Adele heard the High Wizard announce himself to the steward.

"Come in," called Adele, and waved to Mrs. Ollenby as the lady slipped out the side door to the sitting room.

Ohren was still wearing the same frown that he had been on his face when the meeting had finished just a few hours earlier. The frown told her he felt as unsettled as she did; that he knew next to nothing about what they were doing; that he thought the plan they had in place was ridiculously feeble, and that he was once again sending his queen into danger and he was powerless to help.

"Your Majesty, I apologize for intruding on you in your bedchamber, but I was just coming to check on the status of the Princess Stella," said Ohren. "No change, I imagine?"

Adele had only just been in to look on her baby and so she shook her head, swallowing down more tears. There wouldn't be any change for Stella until she could make it happen.

Despondent but not surprised, Ohren headed to a small lounge by the balcony doors to the terrace, and helped himself to a tiny glass of Firewhiskey, almost dropping the bottle on the marble table when his shaking hands tried to set it back down.

Adele moved to join him and curled up on the armchair opposite him. Now that she had him alone, Adele's mind was spinning with all the questions she wanted to ask the high wizard. She let him swig back his Firewhiskey before she started.

"Ohren, I know we don't have much time, but there are things I need to know," Adele began. She watched as Ohren poured them both a shot of the golden liquor. "Can you tell me what you know about demons?"

Ohren rubbed a hand over his face, pulling at his beard, and his expression remained grave. "My queen, there are too many tales to share them all, but the short history is this: demons are said to be created as the first servants and playthings of the gods before humans were brought into existence. It is thought that the demons left this world when the gods did and reside with them in their realm. I just don't know how it is possible that you could be a demon, as Grottonski claims." He stared at her intently, as if trying to read the truth in her eyes. "It could be just that he used the word as an insult to your mixed blood."

It was Adele's turn to frown. Her magic, and her temper were on a hair-trigger after the day she'd had and they swirled up inside her, growling and hissing together. "And we both know that's a lie, Ohren," she snapped. "So why don't you tell me what you really know."

Ohren slowly pulled himself up in his seat and his expression became icy. "My queen, if you had any idea of what it would mean if you were such a creature of dark magic, you would watch what you say to me." His eyes suddenly softened, though his mouth was still a hard line. "You don't know what I would be forced to do if such an accusation was proved to be true."

"But how can we know?" asked Adele, as her fear finally found its voice and she became desperate. "Ohren, if I am not a demon then what am I?"

"I don't know," said Ohren, shaking his head. "But that doesn't mean we can't hide whatever it is you are from the rest of the world." Ohren pulled a small ring from his pocket and held it out to Adele.

She took the ring and examined it. It was small, and pretty, a tiny grey crystal set in a heavily engraved, gold band. "What is this?" Adele saw a tiny flash of green within the grey crystal. She looked up at Ohren, suspicious. "Or should I already know?"

"This ring has been enchanted with an illusion charm," admitted the High Wizard. "It will disguise the silver in your eyes so that others will only see the gold when the rings turn. It is a relatively harmless charm, but very effective."

"Not as dangerous as the court finding out that I'm a demon, you mean," replied Adele dryly.

"No, not as dangerous as that," agreed Ohren and took the ring from Adele and slipped in onto the small finger of her right hand. "How does it feel?"

"I don't feel any different," said Adele but her voice started to wobble and she feel the tears burn in her eyes again. Her strength crumbled as she looked up into Ohren's electric blue gaze and prayed that he would have the answer to the one question that mattered. "Am I evil, Ohren?"

Ohren patted the couch next to himself. "Sit next to me, Adelena." His expression reflected her pain. "If you let me, I can try to see into your heart and maybe get the measure of your magic. You and I might at least get some idea of what you are."

Adele moved to sit next to the old wizard and noted that he smelled like Firewhiskey and warm honey. She checked the doors and windows for spying eyes before facing Ohren again. "Will it hurt?" she asked, wiping away the tears on her cheeks. Adele wasn't in the mood for pain right now.

Ohren turned himself to face her, their knees touching, and took her shoulders in his big hands. He gave her an apologetic smile. "It will feel very intimate, Your Majesty, and you may not enjoy the intrusion into your mind, but I will be as quick as I can, so stay very still and try to relax."

Adele looked into Ohren's bright blue eyes and marveled as she always did at just how deep they were. The blue in Ohren's eyes seemed to go on forever, and the golden rings which spun around his pupils blurred slightly as they shifted, and it was as if she was looking at two rings instead of just one. Almost as if there were two sets of eyes looking back at her.

Suddenly, the Chime Voices shrieked a word of warning and Adele felt Ohren's presence enter her mind. A thread of cold, gold wire prodded sharply at the edges of her consciousness where it didn't belong. Both the green, hissing magic, and the gold, growling power became alert to the intrusion. Ohren was right, his probing felt unsettling. Adele had to work hard not to protect herself and fling him out again.

Oddly, the Chime Voices accepted Ohren's intrusion and began whispering their little cajoling whispers, looking for fun. With a breathless command, they made Adele aware of the physical closeness of Ohren and let her see the power that lay within him.

Adele leaned in ever so slightly and continued to fall into the blue of Ohren's bottomless eyes. She tolerated another jab of the gold wire he was moving about in her head, and wondered what he was seeing in her, and what she might see in him in return, if she just only reached out a little more.

Adele released a tiny tendril of green magic into Ohren's chest and felt an enormous thrill that made her sigh and fling a few even finer strands of power out and around his heart. Instantly, her vision changed. All she could see was the ocean of Ohren's golden magic that welcomed her into its profound depths. She sank beneath the waves of magic within him, drinking in his power and sating the golden magic within herself. Adele only distantly heard Ohren's moans but it was enough to wake her from her daze and she instantly withdrew her power from Ohren so fast she almost had magical whiplash.

When she came back to herself, Adele was sitting on Ohren's lap with his hands in her hair and hers under his shirt, stroking his chest. They both recoiled from each other in mutual horror, Adele throwing herself away and back onto her armchair.

"Ohren, I'm so sorry!" Adele couldn't help the blush that burned her cheeks or forget the memory of Ohren's very human desire pushing against her leg quickly enough. "I hope I didn't hurt you."

Ohren was still trying to catch his breath and had pulled his robe to cover his lap. Leaning forward on his knees, he ran his hands through his hair. In the candlelight it looked blonder than before. "That was incredible," he gasped, and hugged his arms around his chest as though to hold himself together.

Adele couldn't help feeling ashamed of her power, and the strength of the hunger that made her act like a fool. She didn't want to ask, but she still needed to know. "Ohren, do you know what I am now?"

Ohren finally took a deep breath and he looked up, his eyes wide and his cheeks still pink, above his definitely blonder beard. "You are fiercely strong," he said and instead of anger, his voice was filled with awe. "You destroyed my probe and you were taking something from me but I wanted to give it to you so badly. I have never experienced anything like it, though perhaps…" Ohren drifted off and his eyes had a faraway look in them. "If you are a demon, then I want to be one too, Adelena. Such strength, such beauty, such music as I have never heard."

"The Chime Voices," said Adele in a small voice, not sure if that was good or bad.

"Yes, they chimed and sang. It was a song I'd never heard before, yet it was so familiar," mused Ohren and Adele could see he was still in his distant world, just like Rainere had always been after she had fed from him.

Wrong. Wrong. Wrong. I have to stop doing this, Adele berated herself. Though her body was now filled with jittering energy that made her want to jump and dance, she knew that it was Ohren's power rushing through her veins and she couldn't give it back. *That has to be wrong, doesn't it? To be a creature that takes and does not give in return?* Adele thought, more worried for Ohren than for herself.

Ohren was wearing a dreamy smile and his eyes remained glazed. Picking up her glass of Firewhiskey, Adele sat back and gave him a minute to come back to himself, which he soon did with a wrenching shake and a sharp expletive. Watching closely as Ohren took a moment to pat himself down, as if checking that all his pockets and belongings were in place, Adele imagined she saw his hair bleach itself grey again. Adele waited, dreading, to hear what Ohren would say now that he had sobered up.

High Wizard Ohren stood up, pulling himself to his full height and looked down on Adele. His blue eyes were hard and she felt like he would condemn her where she hunched before him in her little armchair, braced for his judgement.

"Adelena, I owe you an apology," said Ohren, and his voice still shook a little. "I should never have put you on the throne of Unisia. I should never have made you our queen, because as sure as I stand here before you, you are not human but actually a magical creature of the like I have never encountered before."

"Oh." The gasp escaped Adele as if she had been punched.

"But it is too late for all of us." Ohren's smile was as surprising as it was sad. "I made you our queen and you accepted the mantle of responsibility for Unisia. There is no going back on any of our promises, no matter what you really are."

"I'm an abomination," whispered Adele, miserable to have the truth confirmed.

"No." Ohren was suddenly fierce as he knelt down before Adele and grabbed her hands in the both of his. "You are mighty, Adelena! I felt both the light magic and the dark magic within you, living in harmony. You - I mean, we - transferred magic between us, I mean - I think we did. I could hear the voice of..." He shook his head. "Well, I don't know who, but I can tell you this Adelena, it was a light entity there, and it spoke through you. You are *mighty*!" he repeated.

Ohren let go of her hands and stood up. "We will need to learn as much as we can about Prince Rainere's mother Rainestra, because you certainly did not get that power from your St Lucidis father, King Octavius." Ohren gave a mirthless laugh. "That man didn't have a goddess-given bone in his body."

"Ohren?" Adele called out to the high wizard as he made his way to the door. "Thank you, for understanding, and for not, you know, being afraid of me."

Ohren gave Adele a wan smile. "You are welcome, my queen. Many in this world mistake great power for evil, but the magic itself isn't inherently dark, its dreadful reputation comes from the people who use it for wicked purposes."

Adele farewelled the wizard with a smile, and sat back in her chair again, staring into the tiny glass of Firewhiskey in her hands.

I'm a magical creature, she thought, testing the idea in her mind. *I've got light and dark magic, living in harmony within me, but which is which? I can use both of them to attack and hurt, and they both crave the power of others to fuel them. Still, it's a comfort to know that Ohren doesn't think that I'm evil after he felt what it is I can do. Magical or not, I couldn't make Stella well again, but maybe I really am mighty enough to break through the barrier to another dimension and find Prince Rainold.*

Adele freely admitted to herself, that taking Ohren's power had come at just the right time for her. Being awake day and night since arriving back at the Golden Palace, Adele had felt like she was coming to the end of her strength. Now after the deluge of fresh golden magic from Ohren, she once again felt well-rested and full of energy.

Adele allowed herself a small sigh of relief and sipped her Firewhiskey in celebration. After Stella was better she could take the time to find out more about her powers and what they meant, but right now she had work to do.

CHAPTER THIRTY

"The Slums"

The expedition party to the Lower Districts of Concordis had left the Golden Palace just before midnight and made its way through the city of Concordis in a nondescript carriage led by four chestnut mares of non-royal stock. QG's Owens and Bear drove the carriage along the quieter streets of the city, skirting the center and heading straight for the outer suburbs.

The cool night air did nothing to cure the stuffiness in the carriage where Adele had been wedged in with four of her guards. General Ohrig, Captain Lucky, and QG's Leith and Pepper were big men and took up most of the space on the padded benches, jamming her up against the window. Prince Rainere travelled alone, using old portals to test out the magic in the area.

The journey through the city to the Lower Districts of Concordis had been a very unpleasant education for Adele. She had never seen Concordis except from a distance. There wasn't much to see at midnight, but she couldn't fail to notice the scent of stale smoke in the air, the prevalent graffiti, or the anti-Queen Adelena posters plastered on the walls of common buildings and street lamps. In the wealthy suburbs of the Guild Quarter, Adele had been shocked to realize just how unpopular she was.

"Most people believe it is Lord Orgustus who leads the anti-monarchy charge here in Concordis, Your Majesty," General Ohrig told her. "And it's said that he is inciting the middle-class to protest your rule. He has always styled himself as a man of the people, and he has been using his former position as regent to his best advantage. Make no mistake, Lord Orgustus wants the throne back again, even if he never has a crown to wear on it."

"Do the people want a republic?" asked Adele and turned her troubled gaze to Ohrig.

"The people fear what they do not know, Your Majesty," said Ohrig. "In Unisia, those with magic tend to put themselves in power regardless of their education or competence as rulers. There are more people born every generation without magic, yet these commoners don't have any representation in the court of the Golden Palace, or in any law court of the kingdom. That makes people angry." He shrugged but Adele could hear the passion in General Ohrig's voice, and perhaps a trace of bitterness as well. "You don't need magic to use the brain in your head, which is something these wizards tend to forget."

"No wonder they don't like me," said Adele looking out the window again. "I was shoved on the throne with no concern for my education or competence. I'm sure that all these people see is that I've brought Unisia a nasty epidemic and taken a Marchant prince out of hiding. Hardly a ringing endorsement of my rule."

"Your Majesty, I apologize, I didn't mean…" Ohrig began, before Adele waved away his excuse. Ohrig didn't have a scrap of magic in his body, and he had no idea what it was like to be her, but Adele did know what it was to feel powerless.

Still, Adele couldn't help but be hurt by the posters where her image had been defaced, or the awful words written in place of her name. They called her a usurper, a child-killer and a Marchant whore. Lord Orgustus had really done his work, slandering her name and depicting her as a dancing idiot while the children of the city died of the Summer Influenza.

Adele stopped reading the posters and graffiti and let her anger replace the hurt. *These people don't know me. They have no idea about the world I've come from, and how little I want their precious throne. I've done nothing but fight for my life and the lives of my children since I got to Unisia, and these people think I owe them something?*

As they reached the poorer part of town, the posters became fewer and then disappeared altogether. Though Adele imagined that it was probably only due to the people's lack of interest in her at all. Down here they had bigger problems.

The Lower Districts of Concordis were on the very outskirts of the city, far from the King's Highway and the affluent marketplaces of the inner Guild Quarter. Here, the narrow streets displayed signs of poverty everywhere. The streets were dirty, the gutters choked with rubbish, and there were pawnshops and shady-looking money-lenders crowded onto almost every corner. Adele didn't see too many people out at this time of night, but those she did see made her duck her head back from the window. The carriage turned down a broad street whose lumpy paving stones and potholes rattled the passengers about as they passed rows of empty mansions with dark windows and hanging shutters.

"Marchant Avenue," murmured QG Leith by way of explanation. "This is where we should find most of the clubs that the Marchant kids organize."

Adele pulled the carriage curtain back. Here and there, she could spot Marchant dragon statues in the front yards behind rusted iron fences, and the occasional shiny black-lacquered door still sporting the pale green glow of ancient wards. She could smell the stink of decay and human waste, but it was the metallic bite of dark magic in the air that affected her most. Crowds of people milled about the streets, walking on the footpaths and in the road, heedless of the vehicles cruising up and down the bumpy street. Their carriage soon turned off the main thoroughfare out of the traffic and pulled into an alley between two old mansions.

"Well, I'm glad you couldn't find a worse spot to hide your club, Leith," remarked Ohrig as they all jumped down and assembled at the mouth of the dingy alley. The smell of cat urine fragranced the air and the entrance had already been decorated with a dose of vomit. Leith shrugged and stifled a grin.

Tonight everyone was dressed to suit their cover story, and Adele realized she had never seen the men of her Queen's Guard in civilian clothes before, and that now she could see more of their personalities in the way they wore their hair and held themselves. The older men, Ohrig, Bear and Owens were dressed in pieces of old Ordinary Army uniforms mixed with laborers' pants that looked like black jeans, as they were to be Adelena's mercenary guard - which wasn't too much of a stretch. The young men, on the other hand, had been dressed by Leith to act as the "hired company" to support Adele's cover of being a noble lady on a night out in the bad part of town. Leith assured Adele that it was quite usual to see aristocratic ladies out on the streets, wanting to indulge in a little wild life.

Adele shifted out of the light of the street lamp. Though a little uncomfortable about her own outfit, Adele had thought that Mrs. Ollenby had truly outdone herself with pulling it together at such short notice. The speechless reaction she had received from Leith when she had sought his approval was enough to bolster her feminine ego.

Adele smoothed her hands down the brass locks on the front of her bustier and patted at the spiked shoulder pads. She couldn't breathe too deeply, as the bustier had pushed her breasts up high on display but the leather frame was supple enough that she could still move. Her skintight leather pants had taken ten minutes and a handful of talcum powder to pour herself into, but they had molded to her form well, and her boots were sturdy, in case she had to run.

QG Leith had dressed himself and Pepper to show off their broad shoulders and well-muscled arms. Both were wearing tight black shirts with the sleeves ripped off, and black trousers that had been slashed through and roughly sewn closed again with heavy thread. The young men both had silver and black chains around their necks with several small amulets and pendants dangling from them. Leith had made a valiant effort to dye Pepper's bright, red hair black and the result was sort of a dark muddy brown that looked awful in the daylight but passable in the dark. Adele had to stifle a grin when she looked at Captain Lucky. Out of everyone, he was probably their weakest link. Captain Lucky looked exactly like Captain Lucky, except he was wearing neatly-pressed laborer's jeans and a black shirt instead of his usual immaculate uniform.

"Could you try and mess your hair up a bit, Lucky?" whispered Leith, exasperated. "You look like you are going to a church dance, not the slums of the LDC."

"We're not going into the slums, Leith," Lucky snapped back, clearly irritated with the younger QG's nagging. "We are going *around* them, so there is no need to be so concerned with…"

"Quiet," growled Ohrig. "Her Maj – I mean, ladyship, is going to give us instructions."

All the men looked at Adele. Before she could say a word, she felt a prickle of magic in the air and saw two figures step out of the shadows.

"Violet. Elodie. How're you doing?" Leith bowed politely as the figures pushed back their hoods, revealing themselves to be young women, probably no older than fourteen or fifteen. The young women didn't smile or say a word, instead they produced baskets full of coins from inside their cloaks and held them out.

"Of course," said Leith, answering for the group. "Her ladyship has something for the victims of the dread 'fluenza." Leith dropped a small but heavy bag of money into one of the baskets as Adele saw her QG's expression soften into a mask of grief. "I'm sorry about what happened to your mum, girls. Please let my mother know if there is anything else my family can do for you both."

The young women only nodded as they melted back into the shadows and moved off down the busy street.

"It was a shock when they lost their mum to the Influenza last week," said Leith to Adele when they got out of hearing distance. "No one knew that their mum had been a commoner because Violet and Elodie are both so powerful."

Adele's heart broke and she understood the doleful expressions of the two young sisters. "Who will look after the girls now?" she asked Leith. "Is their father around?"

"In the Lower Districts, the community helps its own," Leith answered. "They'll be looked after by whoever can take them in, and the money won't hurt their chances to find a foster family either."

Adele flinched. Life was tough out here on the streets. She wanted to ask about welfare organizations or shelters for the poor but there were other things to worry about tonight.

Adele pulled the device Ohren had given her from her pocket. The coin-shaped crystal swung it on its chain and glowed softly. Ohren had said that the crystal would light up like a beacon when it detected a dense concentration of power in the air needed for an apex. At least, that was what the he hoped would happen. The high wizard still thought finding an apex to another dimension somewhere in the underbelly of Concordis was a long shot, yet Adele had seen too many impossible things happen in the last few months to let his hesitation bother her too much.

"The plan, gentlemen," Adele said quietly. "Is to let Leith lead us through places he thinks might be meeting points for those of the Blood, and then we explore them. It sounds simple, but we will be surrounded by people looking for magic and we can't let on for a moment where we are from, or why we are here." She turned to Leith. "Leith, you know this part of town. You can do the talking if we meet anyone. Agreed?"

"Agreed, my lady. The slums are the worst part of the Lower Districts." Leith's chest puffed a little and Adele could see that her QG was proud of the role she'd given him. "We'll get there through a secret door behind one of these old mansions. If we don't find anything on the streets there, then I'll take us down into the old basement system where the gatherings and clubs are normally held. There is enough of us that we should scare anyone thinking about trouble away, but there might be a few who may want to challenge the Pr- I mean, *Rai-*, if they see him in our group so we should keep our distance when he shows up again."

Adele and Ohrig looked over their shoulders and saw the streets around them were bustling with dark figures, but no sign of Rainere. "I'm sure *Rai* can look after himself when he gets here," grunted Ohrig. "But we should start, my lady. The sooner we are in and out of these damned slums the better."

The group followed Leith down the urine-scented alleyway until Adele saw the hazy, green curtain of sparkles covering the end.

"It's not a portal but you do need a password," Leith whispered to Adele. "Tonight it's *mercurial.*" At Leith's quiet murmur the curtain of green magic immediately parted and Leith gestured for them to hurry through the narrow gap.

The other side of the curtain was another world. The narrow streets were lit by tall green lanterns and dotted along the pavements small groups of people could be seen huddled around fire pits. A gentle patter of raindrops touched Adele's cloak, making her look to the dark night sky.

"It rains here a lot in the slums," replied Leith to Adele's questioning expression. "Something to do with the magic, I think."

Adele pulled her hood further over her head and stepped in behind Leith, feeling the other Queen's Guard settle in around her, as they made their way through the sparse crowds. Adele couldn't see very much from deep inside her hood, but she didn't notice anyone stare at their group, or show any curiosity about them. Adele had been holding the device in her hand so hard that her fingers began to hurt. She loosened her grip and studied it, noticing its glow was still soft.

Adele pushed her hood back to talk to Ohrig behind her, and in doing so, caught the gaze of a figure standing in a nearby alleyway. The figure was tall and had a dark cloak thrown over his slim shoulders in a jaunty way, like one of the young courtiers from the Golden Palace court. The young man seemed out of place in this part of the city. Adele noticed his shoulder-length blonde hair seemed too clean, and that the dark scarf over his mouth and chin was made of silk. Like an elegant bandit, the figure raised his hand and gave Adele a little wave before disappearing deeper into the alley. The interaction couldn't have taken more than a few seconds, but it gave Adele a distinct case of the creeps.

"Let's move on," Adele murmured to Leith, trying to shake off the odd feeling that she had missed something important. Adele was almost irritated when Leith held out his arm to bar her way, and it wasn't until she looked up again that she saw that two men holding heavy clubs in their hands had come from around the corner. Forgetting the mysterious courtier, Adele assessed these new men and didn't need to be told that they were street thugs.

Adele felt a frisson of panic as her Queen's Guard pushed in about her in a defensive formation, and she was pleased to see that her guards were at least as big as the two cold-faced men in front of them. Then Adele heard a curse from Ohrig and looked around to see that the first two thugs had merely headed them off, and that another six men were circling around to surround their group. Adele felt her heart jump into her throat when she saw that three of the men surrounding them, had spheres of green sparkles coalescing in their hands. "Street magicians," hissed Ohren. "Your Majesty, stay behind me. This'll get ugly."

How's Ohrig going to defend me against magic? Adele thought, biting back a curse of exasperation. She tried to think calmly and suggested the easiest solution. "Leith, ask them what they want."

Leith, stepped forward, hands raised in peace, but before he could even speak one of the thugs with a bat stepped up to meet him. "Give us the woman and you can leave with your lives," the man growled. His accent was rough, and his face was even rougher. "Else we get to kill you too. Which, you know?" He shrugged a burly shoulder and gave a grin. "We'll prob'ly do anyway."

Adele felt an odd sensation as all the blood in her body rushed to heat her two magics. *No one is going to kill my men and then* joke *about it,* she thought with sudden fury. Adele shivered as the magic raced around her body, using her veins as conduits to reach every limb.

Adele looked at Ohrig, and Ohrig looked back at her. The general's eyes widened at what he saw in her expression and he shook his head, but it was too late, Adele was ready to fight for her men.

Adele pushed past her guards as if they were so many warm trees around her and felt the air at her back where Ohren had tried to grab her. She faced the enemy. Adele counted eight thugs altogether, mostly grouped in pairs and spread out evenly around them. Other than the three holding magic in their hands, none of the other thugs showed any hint of magic about them, so she decided to take the three magicians out first. Adele didn't yet know what she would do, but she had faith that the Chime Voices would let her know and felt them pick up the tempo of their chanting. Casting a quick glance about, Adele noted that the narrow street was now suspiciously empty.

"Gentlemen, none of my guard want to give me away." Adele kept her voice soft, and her eyes on the three men who were holding the fizzing green balls. "So it looks like you are going to have to come get me yourselves."

There was a burst of coarse laughter from the man, who was apparently their leader. "I was told you were feisty." He chuckled and his eyes narrowed with anticipation. "You're gonna make this fun. I can tell." His dark eyes flickered to the street. "Lads, you can take the rest, but this one's for me."

The Chime Voices sang a clanging note in Adele's head, and she spoke directly to them hoping that they were listening. *Chimes, tell me how to fight.*

CHAPTER THIRTY-ONE

"Prayers of a Boy"

Charlie lurched towards consciousness and opened his eyes. Instinct pulled him upright, but gravity pushed him straight back down again. His head felt like it was made of stone and his stomach roiled. It took him a moment to realize he was in motion. More cautiously, he sat up and looked around. It was dark, but he could make out the wooden walls of a wagon. The light of a half-moon shone through the barred window in the roof.

Charlie groaned and tried to gather his scattered thoughts but a noise in the corner of the wagon almost made him pee himself. Someone was in here with him.

"You awake then, Charlie?" It was the soft voice of Leafy, the girl he had tried to protect in a half-arsed attempt to be the hero he wasn't. Charlie didn't answer and felt at the back of his head where he had been struck, cursing at the amount of dry blood matting his hair. His head had copped a fair amount of abuse these last few days and this last knock was not helping the collection of bruises he had back there.

"I'm glad you're awake," Leafy said and her voice was thick with tears. "I thought that mean man had killed you."

"I wish he had," groaned Charlie and slumped himself against the closest wall, gingerly holding his head in his hands and trying not to throw up as the wagon jiggled and jerked with the pulling of the horses. "My head is killing me."

"I can't help you 'coz I don't have any healing magic," Leafy said. "But I do have some water I found. It only tastes a little bit like dirt."

"Bring it here then," ordered Charlie and then winced as the wagon bumped over a particularly large dip in the road.

He heard Leafy scrabbling over the wooden boards and then suddenly she was there in front of him. A wink of green glitter fluttered in his vision. "Why are you bothering to hide yourself like that when they already found you?" Charlie asked. "You should probably save your strength for when we get out of here."

Leafy squeezed herself in as close as she could to Charlie. At first, he tried to shy away from the contact but the little girl was warm and Charlie was shivering from cold and pain so he let her stay. He felt her shake her head against his shoulder. "My brother said to get rid of all my magic so when they saw me I'd be tired, and then they wouldn't think I was a Special," she said, her voice wobbling with tears again. "But when they took him I had to fight them, I don't know how my bite didn't work on them. Normally it makes people scream."

"What's your bite?"

Leafy held up a hand in front of herself. In the dark, Charlie could clearly see the fragments of magic coalesce in her hand. He felt his own magic light up and pull against him as if it wanted to join the ball of green flames that was forming in Leafy's palm. "See?" she said. "When I throw this, it bites and won't let go until I tell it to. My brother taught me that."

"Can it bite through wood?" asked Charlie. "Could you throw it at the wall and make a hole big enough to get us out of here?"

Leafy shook her head and let the magic wink out. "Can't you feel them, Charlie?" She leaned her little body against his and her words began to slur. "You should be able to see all those mean men out there, even through the wards. You're a Special like me, aren't you?" A moment later Charlie heard Leafy snoring, sound asleep.

Charlie found the water bottle in her hands and felt for the stopper, pulling it out he sniffed the water. It did smell like dirt, but then so did Skag. A little kid like Leafy wouldn't know the smell of Skag root so she must have helped herself. More disappointed than he could have thought possible, Charlie re-corked the clay bottle and let it drop, licking his dry lips with an even drier tongue. He straightened his legs with a groan of pain and Leafy fell into his lap, her drugged body lying across his thighs.

Charlie cursed the Goddess Serena that she would drop him into yet another pile of shit. His life had never been a picnic, and he knew working illegal magic for money, or living in the grace of the Boss, hardly meant he had an upstanding role in society. Ironically, this time, the trouble had come *because* he had tried to do right by the Goddess. This time he had been helping a queen who stood for everything that was noble and good in the world. She had asked for his help finding the Fire Orchid stamens, and she had relied on him to do the job he promised he could. Because he had let all that do-gooding go to his head, Charlie had fallen in with a dodgy priest, been kidnapped, and become responsible for a tiny child. Now he was even more vulnerable than he'd been before.

With nothing to be done about it, Charlie finally took Leafy's advice to enhance his senses, and try to establish where he was and count how many guards were surrounding him. The interior of the wagon became lighter as his eyes absorbed the threads of magic, and his ears could pick up the sound of horses, and the soft murmurs of at least four men in conversation. The sounds of the forest at night buzzed and whispered too, and the horses' hooves clopped on a packed dirt road and seemed to be heading in a straight line. Suddenly he heard the voice of Pere Raven pipe up.

"Now, Cedric, I wouldn't like to tell another man how to do his job, but I think you could have been gentler with the children back there." Pere Raven sounded cheerful, but Charlie heard the authority in his tone. "I will ask that next time, you do not bash them about so much. Charlie is a good kid and he did not deserve the pounding you gave him."

Cedric grunted, and Charlie could imagine the man's dead eyes as he responded to the priest. A tingle of exhaustion made Charlie pull his magic back. It was obvious that the priest was colluding with the villains. Charlie collapsed back against the wall of the wagon and without magic to dull it, the pain returned full force. Charlie whimpered, glad there was no one around to hear him. He gasped through clenched teeth until the pain abated enough to let him open his eyes once more.

There was nothing to stare at in the dark so Charlie's battered mind began to paint colors in the void before him. Charlie created an image of Queen Adelena's face and her smile warmed him a little. He added her shoulders and the round swell of her breasts above the green lace of the last dress he had seen her wear. Her expression turned soft and then sad. He remembered that her child was dying, and that it was going to break her heart. He knew what his queen looked like when someone broke her heart. All at once, a whirlwind of color brought Queen Adelena before him, tall and threatening as she screamed at the invisible people about her. Charlie knew that she would have gone into that Spider's Nest alone if she'd had too, and Queen Adelena would have killed every last one of them if it could have brought her daughter back. She was terrifying, as fierce as the Goddess Serena herself.

Charlie blinked away the tears that blurred his vision and concentrated on keeping the queen's face clear before him. Adelena would not allow a little thing like being kidnapped keep her from her family and those she loved, and neither would Charlie let himself be kept from her.

Determination burned hot in Charlie's chest and dispelled his lingering despair. The queen had powerful magic, but so did he. The queen had love for others, but now, so did Charlie. He would fight for her, and fight to get back to her. Queen Adelena needed him, not just as her spy, but as her friend. He would escape from this new hell and stand by her side again soon.

A soft sleep noise from Leafy made Charlie look down at his lap, and his determination skipped a beat. Leafy would be fine or she wouldn't, but he would do his best to see her right no matter where they ended up. Then, he would escape back to the Golden Palace and let the queen know about Pere Raven kidnapping children in the villages on Marchant land.

Resolute, Charlie conjured the image of Adelena wrapping her arms around him, grateful for his courage and loyalty. As a tiny smile danced across his lips, Charlie managed to drift off to sleep.

CHAPTER THIRTY-TWO

"Doors In Between Doors"

Chaos exploded on the street corner as a bright flash and a cloud of green swallowed the scene, followed by a blast of icy cold wind. Reflexively, Adele dropped into a crouch and tried to peer through the swirling smoke to see where the thugs had gone. Adele almost went flying when Ohrig knocked into her, shouting her name, his voice hoarse with fear.

"Ohrig, I'm here." Adele pushed the general off her foot.

"I've got her," Ohrig shouted as the smoke cleared and Adele could see the rest of her men gathering themselves together not more than a couple of yards away.

"Oh, sweet Christ," whispered Adele, and almost gagged on the sharp metallic odor in the air and her brain tried to understand what had just happened.

The dead bodies of the thugs lay strewn about them on the road and in the gutter. The three magicians lay in a pile, their wrists bleeding where their hands had been ripped from their arms. It looked as if the skin had been melted off their skulls. The bodies of the other five thugs had been thrown about like so many dolls, their limbs and heads twisted at strange angles, although there wasn't a drop of blood on them.

"Goddess forgive me," whispered QG Leith, looking as ill as Adele suddenly felt. "Who did this?"

Adele was all too sure that she knew. "Rainere."

The Marchant prince stepped out of the shadows across the road and Adele saw the excitement flicker in his expression before he could hide it. Whatever he had just done to these men, he had obviously enjoyed it.

Rainere stepped over the loose arm of a corpse as he made his way over to Adele. "I hope they weren't friends of yours, Leith?"

Leith swallowed heavily and shook his head.

"That was well done, Your Highness," Ohrig said to Prince Rainere, indicating the pile of bodies. To Adele, it sounded like he meant it. "The queen had jumped in front of us and I didn't know what she was going to do. I'm glad you could protect her from this ambush."

"Her Majesty was in danger. I disposed of the threat," answered Rainere, and the look he gave Ohrig was almost insulted. "I will always protect her."

Despite Ohrig's approval of the slaughter, and the fact that these thugs had been about to kill them all, they were still human beings and Adele felt a need to acknowledge their passing in some way. These bodies would need to be hidden to avoid the group calling attention to itself, and hopefully to confuse whoever had sent them to her. The Chime Voices urged Adele to sing an unfamiliar chant that sounded very much like a prayer.

Adele shook her head to clear it. "Ohrig, please have the QG's pull these bodies out of the gutter and put them in that alley over there." Adele gestured to the place where she had seen the young man.

"Adelena, we are wasting time." Rainere reached out and touched her hand, his cold fingers slipping into her palm. "The dead were just criminals and Marchant bastards, they don't deserve your pity."

"We will not leave them in the street, where anyone can find them." Adele tried to keep the hysterical note out of her voice, as the Chime Voices clouded her mind with their drone. "You will have to help me burn them." She turned back to General Ohrig who had already started the task.

Rainere watched slightly bemused as Adele helped her men heap the bodies together deep inside the alley. When they were finished their grisly work, Prince Rainere pulled two narrow rods from his pocket. Striking hard, Rainere showered sparks over the bodies and then whispered a few words that made the sparks swell and burst like tiny fireworks until a natural orange fire covered the pile of bodies.

As the fire took, Adelena intoned the words of the prayer that the Chime Voices gave her, and it finally rendered them quiet. Relishing the moment of blessed silence in her head, Adele let the fire warm her chilled hands for just a moment before she realized what she was doing and snatched them back again. Adele watched Leith tear strips off the bottom of his black shirt and tie them to nearby poles and drain-pipes. "To make people think it's an Influenza bonfire," he explained in answer to her curious expression.

"Your Majesty," murmured Ohrig, forgetting to call her my lady. Their cover had probably been blown anyhow. "We should keep going before any more trouble finds us."

"It was someone from the Golden Palace, Ohrig," said Adele, and turned her pale face to the general. "We have been betrayed by someone who knew we were in Concordis tonight."

"It could have been a chance encounter, Your Majesty," suggested Captain Lucky doubtfully. "Someone out seeking to kidnap and ransom anybody with wealth?"

Adele shook her head. "They were ready for us, Lucky, with magic and brute force."

"I wouldn't want to think it was the high wizard who did this," said Ohrig with a grimace. "But you, my lady, have a way of falling into mortal danger on the missions he sends you on."

The fire crackled and spat in the rain and Adele watched the bodies burn. "So many dead," she whispered, "all on my head."

"If the period of mourning for these dead cretins has passed?" interrupted Rainere, his tone cold as he gestured at the funeral pyre.

"Perhaps we should explore the old portal station that I have discovered and get on to finding the apex?"

"The prince is right," General Ohrig agreed, though he didn't sound happy about it. "If you're feeling up to it, Your Majesty, we should continue our mission."

Nodding, Adele collected her senses and looked to the dark skies, letting the rain fall into her eyes. It was now well after midnight and they had important work to do. The mystery of who was behind their attack would have to wait.

"Prince Rainere, lead the way," said Adele and ignored Rainere's stiff bow, before he strode off down the street, not waiting to see if they would follow.

The path to the portal station was winding and convoluted. Only Rainere was sure-footed as they made their way along narrow streets, climbing over walls of rubble and ducking under old archways that might have once been the doorways of great manor houses.

"How did 'Rai' get so far ahead of us to find this station anyway?" QG Bear grumbled as he tripped over a small retaining wall and stubbed his toe.

"It's not so long if you travel the High Way," answered Leith. "The prince seems to be taking us the long way to keep us undercover."

"Where's the highway?" asked Owens.

Leith pointed to the roof tops above them. "There are all sorts of bridges and paths up there, and it's a lot quicker to travel through the slums that way, but it's not as discreet or safe as down here."

A short way ahead of them, Rainere had stopped in the doorway of an old shop front. There was a line of greenly glowing street lamps along the pedestrian path. Adele could tell from the glass decorating the ground around it that the one closest to Rainere had recently been smashed. Ohrig went first, hugging the wall and staying in the shadows as he made his way cautiously to where the prince was waiting. After reaching the doorway, Ohrig signaled back, and one by one the rest of the group made their way along the street,

Rainere shoved the door of the shop open with his shoulder, and silently lead the group behind the counter and down a narrow passage into what looked like a storeroom. Adele studied the wooden boxes piled high on shelves and tried to work out what sort of shop it was, not that it mattered, of course. Rainere approached an open trapdoor in the corner of the room and immediately slid down the wooden ladder jutting out of the hole.

Adele made to follow after the prince but Ohrig hooked his hand around her elbow and stopped her. Adele turned in surprise to see Ohrig frowning at her.

"Are you sure about this, Your Majesty?" asked the general quietly, and frowned at the dark hole in the floor where Rainere had disappeared. "Anything could be down there, including a second trap."

Adele shook her head. "It wasn't Rainere who set us up, Ohrig," she said firmly and pulled the device out of the top of her bustier where it had fallen. It was glowing iridescent green, lit with a pulsing magic. "But he has found us a suitable source of power for an apex."

Adele put her hand on the ladder but Ohrig stopped her again. "Look, I know it wasn't the prince who sent those men but still, promise me you will think carefully before you follow him any further, Your Majesty." Ohrig gave Adele a worried glare, which was an expression that he seemed to save just for her. "Or if you do, then at least stay well behind the prince."

"Of course, Ohrig." Adele smiled despite her sarcastic tone. "But what could be dangerous about following a Marchant prince down a dark hole?"

Adele didn't hear what Ohrig muttered back to her as she slipped down the ladder, but she didn't need to.

Adele hopped off the bottom of the ladder onto the gritty floor of the basement, narrowly avoiding Ohrig jumping on her head as he slid down the ladder after her, and the rest of the Queen's Guard followed. Rainere held a small globe of blue light in his hand, which cast a weird bluish tinge on the old crates and dusty, broken furniture piled near the walls.

"It's just over here." Rainere's voice sounded close in the small underground room, and Adele resisted a shiver as the Chime Voices tinkled in her head, excited by his proximity. She followed Rainere over to the corner of the room, where he was intensely studying a dusty brick wall. There was a soft thudding sound coming through the walls, and Adele could hear the faint strains of music.

"Leith, where is that noise coming from?" asked Adele.

"We are very close to the underground clubs here, Your Majesty," said Leith, cocking his head to the side to listen. "There is a big fundraiser on tonight for the victims of the Summer Influenza. All the clubs are running and there will be music and magic shows until dawn."

"They missed a hell of a magic show outside," muttered QG Bear with a grimace. QG Owens grunted in agreement.

"That must be how the energy is accumulating," mused Rainere, ignoring the QG's comment and pulled the device from Adele's hand. He laid it against the old bricks. "Your Majesty, there is an ancient portal entrance directly behind this wall."

"How do you know that?" asked Adele, surprised that Rainere hadn't volunteered the information before.

"The slums used to be the Marchant Quarter," replied Rainere, slightly impatient that he must explain himself again. "Everything in this area once belonged to my family. Naturally, I'm familiar with the general layout. May I?" Rainere gestured at the wall so Adele nodded and stepped back.

The prince casually punched his fist through the wall, covering his arm in dust and masonry, and earning admiring comments from the men. Rainere kept knocking through the wall, easily pulling the bricks out, until there was a man-sized doorway before them.

Adele coughed on the dust and peered through the doorway, but all she could see was a long, dark tunnel.

"It couldn't be well-lit and carpeted, could it?" said Adele dryly. She nodded at the sinister looking darkness and gave Ohrig a look. "It'd be too much to expect that this could be easy."

Adele saw Ohrig's eyebrow twitch up in amusement before hunkering back down in a frown. "I don't think it'll ever be easy to deal with this sort of magic, Your Majesty, but at least we have brought light with us." He showed her a torch at his hip that lit up at his touch.

"I don't believe your Queen's Guard will be any help to you in the portal, Your Majesty. We will be confronting powerful magic that will be very dangerous to them," said Rainere angling himself in front of Adele's line of sight and covering her view of the general. "The only one with any magic in their group is Captain Lucky. Perhaps he could come in case we need a test subject, but it would be best to just leave the rest of them here to guard the entrance for us."

Adele sighed into the frosty silence that followed the prince's words. General Ohrig stepped out from behind the prince and gave her a sharp look. Prince Rainere was doing exactly what Ohrig had warned her he would. "He's right, Ohrig," Adele reluctantly admitted. "It's not smart to expose any of you to this sort of dark magic, and I might not be able to protect you all."

Adele took a step back as six pairs of blue eyes glared at her, their expressions uniformly affronted. Before Ohrig could protest she held up her hands. "Ohrig, there would be no point for me to find the apex only to walk into another trap back here." She gestured to the basement room. "You have to admit that this is the perfect spot for an ambush, with all of us down here in this basement and only one exit. Who knows if someone followed us here, or that whoever sent those thugs won't try to kill us again? I will need you and the men to guard this room so that I can get out safely again."

General Ohrig gripped the pommel of his sword so tightly his knuckles were white, but he nodded at the logic in her words. "If you order us to remain behind and hold this point we will, Your Majesty." Ohrig beetled his brows at her. "But you can't ask me to wait all night. If you aren't out by dawn then I will send Lucky in to find you."

Adele breathed a sigh of relief. "Agreed." She turned to Rainere but the prince had locked eyes with General Ohrig and they seemed to be having a silent debate that she had no hope of interpreting. It finished with Rainere nodding, though his expression remained cold. "I will not let her risk her life," he replied to the general's unspoken question.

Adele stood in front of the tunnel entrance, intent on examining it to avoid further patronizing conversations. "We don't have much time before dawn, Rainere. We should leave now."

Rainere stepped in beside her. "Let's begin."

"Your Majesty?" Ohrig called out, and Adele finally turned to her general.

"Yes, Ohrig, I'll be careful, I promise," she said, attempting to preempt his warning.

"Failing that, just come back alive," said Ohrig sternly, and then surprised Adele by giving her a crooked smile. "I really don't want to have to tell Lord Orgustus he will be our next queen."

Adele grinned. "We'll be back before dawn."

She turned back to Rainere and saw that he wasn't amused. Adele stepped forward and into the tunnel. It was time to work.

Chapter Thirty-Three

"Out of the Dark and Into the Depths"

Adele stepped out of the alcove and almost slipped on the shiny floor of the dark tunnel. The dim light of the device in her hand spread a soft glow to light their way but Adele still felt Rainere follow so closely behind her that his feet were almost kicking her heels. She was concentrating so hard on keeping her feelings under control that she almost missed the opening to her left. She stepped back, surprising Rainere. "Here's one!"

Side by side, Rainere and Adele studied the portal doorway. They couldn't see much until Rainere cast a ball of blue light into the doorway. The walls were of the same polished stone as the tunnel. When Rainere waved his hand no green sparks coalesced in front of him.

"This doorway is dead," Rainere pronounced, and they continued down the tunnel. The silence between them stretched into minutes before they found another portal doorway and tested it, then moved on again. The tunnel became narrower and Adele felt Rainere's arm brush her own, the sensation electrifying her. Rainere stopped walking and groaned loudly, "Stop doing that."

Adele couldn't play dumb. "I'm sorry, I can't help it," she said. Adele raised her eyes to his but Rainere was staring at the ceiling, his hands flexing into fists as he fought to control himself. "I'm not doing it on purpose. I don't want to react when you touch me. I just don't know how to stop." It was a lame excuse even if it was true, and Adele knew it.

"Adelena, I am not angry," rasped Rainere and moved so close that she could see his eyes flash in the dark. "But you must know that through the Mark, I can hear every time you think of me, and every slice of your desire stabs me just as deeply. We are still connected, you and I."

"We can't be together," Adele whispered, as much for her sake as for his. "What you did to Natalie is unforgivable." She almost choked on the word. "I am grateful for what you are doing for Stella, but please don't think that erases what happened. You broke everything apart because you wanted to control me, and now I can't trust you anymore."

"No, Adelena, you know it wasn't like that." Rainere grabbed her arms, forcing her to look up into his eyes, and in a single horrible instant she was taken back to the day he had stolen Natalie from her. He had pleaded with her to understand his insanity in giving away her little girl to monsters, and Adele had to become a monster herself to get her back. Rainere saw the coldness in Adele's expression, he let go of her and stepped away again.

"I will never stop trying to earn your forgiveness, *cara mia*," Rainere said. His voice was rough with the savage emotions that said more than his words did. "Even though you do not want me, I remain yours."

"No, *you* stop it, Rainere," snapped Adele, raising her hands to push him away. "I don't want your promises."

"Then what do you want?" shouted Rainere, and his voice thundered, filling her ears and bouncing off the walls to echo down the tunnel.

Rage filled Adelena's head pushing away the confusion. "I want you to never have taken Natalie away," she shrieked. "I want things to be how they were. I want to trust you and love you and throw myself into your arms and feel safe again. But you destroyed *everything*." Adele wiped the tears from her eyes with the back of her hand. "And there isn't one fucking thing I want in this world of Evendaar except to take my children back to Earth."

The green and the gold magics inside Adele struggled to be let loose to destroy the prince in retaliation for what he had done to her family, and to her heart, but Adele fought back with her own strength. *These magics belong to me*, she thought, *and they will do as they were told*. With a deep breath, Adele calmed herself and looked up at Rainere. His hand rested on his side, where the Mark lay under his shirt, and he was studying her with an odd blend of curiosity and desire lighting his gaze.

"It shall be as you wish, Adelena," said Rainere softly, and reached for her hand before stopping himself from taking it at the last minute. "We shall find my father in his prison dimension, and he will tell us where the last dragon in Evendaar lives and then we will find the dragon, and we *will* cure Stella."

Adele couldn't help but laugh. "Sweet Christ, that sounds so stupid," she sighed, her chuckle dying as suddenly as it had begun. "Dragons, and dead princes and magic curses."

"Evendaar may not be your world, Adelena," said Rainere softly. "But I will find the good in it for you, even if I have to kill everyone in our way to show you." The corner of his mouth twitched up into his gorgeous half-smile. "You're glowing, *cara mia.*"

"Rainere, please, stop it." But Adele felt herself softening towards him.

Rainere frowned. "No, I mean you're really glowing, Adelena, but I think the light is coming from the floor."

They both looked down and noticed that the floor in this part of the tunnel was black and shiny, like glass, but a greenish light lit Adele from below. Rainere knelt to examine it.

"This is obsidian," he said, mystified. "How in Evendaar did it get here?"

"Maybe we are deeper underground than we thought, if the bedrock is made by lava," mused Adele and experimented with stepping left and right to watch the light follow her. "I wonder why the light is only touching me and not you."

Rainere raised an eyebrow at her question. Adele grimaced. "I guess it only likes demons," she said.

"Let's see how far it will travel with you," suggested Rainere. "Perhaps it will lead us to its source?"

They both continued down the dark tunnel, now lit by Rainere's blue floating globe and Adele's pallid green glow. They hadn't gone very far when Adele heard the music. It was the same clashing strains of the music that had haunted her in the nest of the Spider People, and it made the hairs on the back of Adele's neck rise. She didn't bother to ask if Rainere heard it too. Tuning into the direction it was coming from, Adele followed the music to a glowing green door that had appeared to their left, inside an alcove.

"I think we've just found our source." Adele's heart started to hammer and her palms grew hot.

The portal door before Adele didn't just glow. It pulsed with life, sentient and malicious. It knew Adele was here, it knew she was an enemy, and it was preparing itself for a fight. Adele could already see the runes being retraced with acid green light as the spell strengthened itself. In the center of the spell was the apex. The apex looked like a rough grey crystal but it wasn't just a spell, inside it was a being – a being that didn't want to be destroyed. Adele felt the apex's animosity like sandpaper against her skin. Instinctively, she knew she could show no fear or hesitation against a spell like this. Raw power could overcome it but wouldn't help her if it got into her head with the whispering Chime Voices. This was pure black magic before her, and her body reacted instantly to protect itself.

With a growl and a hiss, Adele's two magics traced their way under her skin and through her veins. Suddenly, it was as if Adele wore the weight of her magic like armor on every one of her limbs. The Chime Voices chanted something martial and strong, and waited for Adele to catch up with them. She could almost taste the words of command they had for her, ready to whisper and shatter this nightmarish spell.

As Adele prepped herself for battle, pulling her hair into a rough ponytail and shaking off her cloak, she was shocked to see Rainere reach out to the door.

"Rainere, wait! Don't touch it!" Adele frowned at Rainere in surprise and pulled him back. "Can't you see what it is?"

Rainere took his hand away and studied the door intensely for a moment. "It appears to be an archway carved into bedrock and decorated with some rudimentary spells." He pointed and Adele sucked in a breath as he almost touched the stone again. "I see one mark here for 'silence', and one here for 'division of matter' but the runes are shallow and badly carved. Why, what do you see?"

Adele didn't know how much she should say aloud. The apex had started to pulse, and with a paranoid lurch, Adele thought she could almost feel it listening.

Thinking quickly, Adele decided to disguise her intentions. "Yes, of course you're right." Adele watched intently for the apex's reaction to her words. The green glow of the spell shivered, the glow reducing, as if it were calming itself. Adele slipped her hand around Rainere's elbow and signaled with her head that he should step back even further.

"I don't think this is the door we need," she said enunciating each word clearly. "The magic here is ancient, but not strong." Adele shook her head to disagree with her own words and gestured at the door with her eyes, hoping that Rainere would pick up on her clues.

Rainere looked down at his arm where Adelena's hand rested, and then looked up into her eyes. She saw the silver glitter of the rings spinning about his pupils. His mind was thinking of other things, and he didn't seem to understand her warning at all. "I will protect you, Adelena," he rasped and lowered his face to hers. "Always."

"I'm not scared for me," Adele snapped in frustration, and squeezed Rainere's arm to get his attention. "I'm prepared to meet our destiny, but are you? How will you defend yourself? I'm not even sure what I'm doing most of the time, Rainere, so I don't think you can trust me to protect you right now." Adele wiped the sweat out of her eyes. The glowing door was really throwing off a lot of heat and she was melting in her leather clothing. Rainere took off his coat and dropped it to the ground, as if he could feel it too.

"I think I should go alone. I think I have too," said Adele. She watched for a clue that Rainere understood, but he was unbuttoning his shirt and shrugging it off his shoulders.

"Rainere." Adele almost sobbed in frustration. "We really don't have time for you to be acting crazy right now. I'm talking about taking this journey by myself so you can't come. I'm ready."

Rainere gave Adele a wry smile and raised her hand to touch the Mark on his side. "And here is how you are going to protect me," he murmured, and then suddenly pulled Adele into his arms. He held her to his chest, his heartbeat thudding against her cheek. "I know I have given you no reason to trust me, Adelena," he said. Adele felt his voice rumble through her, his cold spicy scent enveloping her. "But I promise that together we can do this."

Rainere pulled away to look her in the eyes, and raised her chin with a finger, there was a sharp clarity there which told her he had understood her veiled message about the door. "I think that this will only work if we do it together. The Mark will bind us and you will take all the energy you need from me."

Adele stood on her tiptoes and tilted her head to whisper in Rainere's ear. "This is so much more dangerous than I thought it would be. I'm not sure we should go any further."

"Of course we should," said Rainere firmly. "I'm ready and you are ready. Adelena, no Golden Palace wizard can help us now, this is our world here, not theirs." He smiled again, and Adele could see that Rainere was desperately happy to be in this life-and-death moment with her. She couldn't decide how that made her feel, but she would worry about his emotional state later. Right now, she had to get them both past that apex.

There was only one thing she knew how to do that might be powerful enough to destroy the apex. The Chime Voices agreed and whispered an intense chant that would be the counter-spell she would need. Adele shivered just to hear it, and a bitter, metallic taste filled her mouth.

"Rainere, you are going to have to give me everything and I will hurt you." Adele felt the green magic in her rise and swell, ready to attack Rainere's magic. It would be the fuel for the fire she was about to light under this apex. "I'm sorry. It's the only thing I know how to do."

When Adele looked up at Rainere, his eyes were charged with lust and excitement. He nodded and licked his lips.

"Rainere," Adele whispered, and cast one last glance at the glowing, sentient apex. "Kiss me."

Rainere responded immediately, pressing his lips to hers and running his hands down to her behind and pulling her up to wrap her legs around his waist. The kiss stole the air from her lungs and every ounce of her good sense. To have Rainere all alone with her in this dark place filled with magic, Adele finally gave in to the shrieking of the Chime Voices and slipped her hand down to the Mark on his side. There was a curious sensation, as if the Mark was holding her hand fast to Rainere's skin. They were now joined by flesh as well as by magic.

Rainere groaned into her mouth, giving himself over to her. Adele dived headfirst into the swelling ocean of heady green magic inside of him. She drank recklessly, heedless of Rainere's pain, his moans only stoking her passion. When she felt completely charged with his power, Adele broke away from their kiss and let Rainere bury his face in her neck, as she raised the pulsing device in her hand.

"Hold onto me," she gasped and tightened her legs around his waist. "Never let me go."

Inspired by the High Wizard's exploration in her head, Adele pulled out a needle-thin thread of hot gold magic and connected it to the center of the device. With no time to realize what she was doing, Adele surprised the apex by nailing the device into the center of the door with her gold magic and hammering it there with the words of command that the Chime Voices fed her in a constant stream. The words boiled up and flowed out of her, riding the wave of Rainere's magic as they surrounded the apex and disintegrated the spell's hold on the doorway.

Adele and Rainere clung to each other, holding on for dear life, as Adele own magics destroyed the apex; snapping and squeezing it, biting and chewing at it until there was nothing left but floating green particles and a horrible, singed smell of acrid black magic in the air. Before them a wide gap in the stone wall shimmered darkly, a swirling portal waiting to take them into Prince Rainold Marchant's prison.

Adele uncurled her legs from Rainere's waist and slowly slid to the ground as Rainere swayed on his feet beside her. Both utterly drained, Adele looked up at her prince.

"Rainere, the door is open," she said triumphantly.

"We did it, *cara mia*." Rainere gave Adele a gorgeous half smile before his eyes rolled back in his head and he collapsed.

CHAPTER THIRTY-FOUR

"Behind Closed Eyes"

Grotto had been locked in one of the dungeons under the Golden Palace. Orestes had insisted, and Gorrik had agreed with him despite Ohren's objections. Without Prince Rainere to control him, no one wanted to find out what the crazy old elf could get up to.

"Nice shot, Grottonski." Gorrik actually managed a smile as he wiped the spittle from his cheek and shook his head. "But insulting me doesn't manage to answer the question as to why you would know so much about the Early Death when you are only a common manservant."

Grotto spat again and rattled his chains at the men, the heavy iron cuffs had already left deep welts on his wrists. "You High Elves always think you know so much, but we others have ears, we can listen, and we can understand even when you think us too lowly to comprehend your ways." Grotto's eyes were iridescent with fury. "I have always understood!" he shrieked.

Ohren grimaced against the noise and fervently wished that he could be back in his office. He was only here as a favor to Gorrik, and as distasteful as it was, Ohren owed him far too many favors to refuse.

"Grotto, just tell Gorrik what he needs to know," said Ohren. "I wouldn't like to have to give you incentive to talk, when it would be better if you just told us of your own volition."

Grotto sneered but Ohren didn't miss the nervous glance that he threw at Gorrik. "You can keep your nasty gold magic to yourself, High Wizard," Grotto snapped. "Gorrik is the worst kind of traitor. He betrayed his masters when he fell to the feet of the scum who call themselves St Lucidis kings. I could piss magic more powerful than this fool could ever conjure up." Grottonski raised his chin proudly. "There are few I fear in this world and I will only answer to them.

The Eldars will come for me after what I have done, and my death will be glorious."

"A lot of invective," noted Gorrik to Ohren, folding up the handkerchief that he had used to wipe off Grotto's spittle. "But not a lot of conviction." His expression still amiable, Gorrik turned back to Grottonski. "Look, son, I know you feel bad that you have broken the ancient code to protect the Eldar secrets, and I'm not really interested in how you find that glorious death of yours, but I am very curious as to how you came by the information. For a lowly manservant, you are privy to some pretty diabolical Eldar secrets. So until you tell me…" Gorrik pulled an amulet from beneath his shirt collar. The chain was burnished gold and the amulet appeared to be a grey crystal.

"Do you know what this is, Grottonski?" asked Gorrik as he showed Grotto the amulet. Gorrik approached Grotto who had pressed himself up against the wall and was now whimpering and shaking his head in fear.

Ohren had no taste for torture and Grottonski's obvious panic was making his stomach turn. "You know, Gorrik, I think he might have had enough, don't you?"

"This amulet," continued Gorrik blithely. "Has been enchanted to disguise the wearer from the sight of the Eldars." Gorrik smiled down at Grotto and his old face folded back in its strange concertina of skin. "So if you wear it, my dear boy, then they can't see you, can they?"

"No!" Grottonski's howl was feral as Gorrik slipped the amulet over the elf's head and let it drop to sit on his chest.

Grotto gazed down at it in horror. "You can't," he begged and looked up at Gorrik but seemed unable to touch the crystal himself. "The Eldars must come for me. I want to die for what I have done."

Gorrik patted Grottonski on the head. "Easy, kid," he said and his old voice was soothing. "You will pay for your crimes, just not in the way you hoped you would, and you can trust me on that."

Elf magic had always given Ohren the creeps and he hadn't understood one bit of what had just occurred between Gorrik and Grottonski just now. Ohren looked down at Grottonski on the floor, as pale green tears traced their way through the dust on his cheeks. Grottonski raised his eyes to Ohren's and the high wizard saw the madness in them, but madness tempered by something else, something selfless - like grief.

"Now, Ohren," Gorrik's old voice creaked in the quiet. "I just need you to pop a little golden stamp on that crystal for me if you would?"

"My personal Mark?" asked Ohren confused, looking at the crystal. "You want me to put my insignia on the crystal itself?"

"Yep, that's it." Gorrik nodded encouragingly. "Just pop your insignia in the crystal, and it will seal to its new owner."

A sharp shriek from Grottonski set Ohren's teeth on edge but the work itself only took a moment as Ohren jabbed at the crystal and watched as the thread of his golden magic stretched inside and wrote his insignia within the rock.

"And that's done." Gorrik was content and patted Ohren on the back. "Nice work, my boy. Time to leave I think." The two men made their way to the door of the prison cell, and only Ohren turned to look over his shoulder at the manservant, who had wrapped his arms around his knees and was hunched against the wall, sobbing his heart out.

"I thought that he would be less upset about the idea of dying," said Ohren, he was trying for nonchalant to match Gorrik's mood but the high wizard's voice wavered a little over the words. "You've hidden him from the eyes of the Eldars, and kept him safe, haven't you?"

Gorrik stepped out of the way for the guard to lock the door behind them. "Kept *him* safe, yes," smiled Gorrik but it didn't quite reach his eyes. "But when he disappears from their sight the Eldars will think he has died, and they will come looking for his master. Without Grotto to take the blame on himself, the Eldars will only see what the last Marchant prince has done in killing the Spider People and breaking the ancient pact between them *and* losing the Grey Palace to a St Lucidis half-breed. So we can trust they won't be happy." Gorrik's smile turned resolutely grim. "Then we will have one less Marchant prince about the place to worry about, won't we?"

"Oh, Gorrik, you could have told me." Ohren was shocked at his old teacher's machinations. "I don't think you understand quite how much Prince Rainere means to our queen."

But Gorrik only raised his hand and gave a loud "Pah!" as he shuffled off down the hallway. "This is not St Lucidis business, Ohren. This is elf business, and it's my responsibility to right the wrongs of my people."

Behind them, in his cell, Grottonski let out a piercing wail that made Ohren stumble a little on his feet. "Really, Gorrik?" he half-heartedly admonished his old friend.

"Let him cry, Ohren, he cries for his prince, and soon he will have no more reason to cry when the Eldars come. Then and only then, will I let Mr. Grottonski have his death." Gorrik gave his once-young student and beloved friend a dark look that told him to press no more.

Ohren thought of little Stella in her dark magic coma and wondered who could maintain its integrity if something should happen to Prince Rainere. At the bottom of the stairs, Ohren automatically reached out to take Gorrik's arm and help him ascend the long staircase back to the palace proper.

Deep in thought, he only felt Gorrik pat his hand and murmur softly. "It's alright, kid, that elf will get what's coming to him."

CHAPTER THIRTY-FIVE

"Where Time Stands Still"

Adele shook Rainere and gently slapped at his cheeks, but the prince was out cold.

"Come on, Rainere," groaned Adele through clenched teeth, as she tried to pull his shoulders off the stone floor and onto her lap. "You've got to get up. Please, I need you for this."

Adele was sitting close to the doorway and even without the apex protecting it, it still looked hideous. The stone had been chiseled with a map of lines and runes that she didn't understand at all, and green magic flashed from within the void in a weird pattern that could have be part of an entirely different protection spell.

To make matters worse, the Chime Voices had also returned, adding an eerie soundtrack to Adele's dreadful situation. Adele shuddered as the wail of violins and guitars entwined in a sinister rhythm that made her want to give into panic and hide.

Looking about the shadowy tunnel, Adele couldn't stop shivering. Tiny particles of what was left of the apex were still floating about her, and the obsidian floor beneath her was icy cold to sit on. She felt all the warmth in her body leaching out into the hard stone glass and tucked the skirt of her jacket under her behind. It helped, but it wouldn't last for long. The music increased its tempo and Adele had the awful feeling that she was being watched. She stroked Rainere's forehead and didn't like the cold sweat that drenched his bare head. The stubble of his once-thick black hair looked spiky but felt soft against her palm.

"Please, Rainere," Adele begged again. "Please wake up."

Finally, Rainere groaned and rolled his head on Adele's lap. She watched anxiously as his eyelids fluttered, and his lips twitched up in a smile. "Darling, hold me tight," he murmured and then fell into unconsciousness again.

The melody of shrill violins chittered in her head. Adele knew that something was about to happen, but not exactly what. The music was the only warning she would get.

"Goddamn it, Rainere, I'm going to wake you up before we both die," Adele cursed and slid her hand inside Rainere's tattered shirt front to rest on his heart. Through sheer force of will, she managed to focus her exhausted mind on her magic and called it. Adele didn't have any words of command. She had never needed any before because the Chime Voices had always been there to instruct her. Yet this time they were silent and Adele had to visualize the magic, the way it felt, and the way it tasted on her tongue when it flared up inside of her. She called on her two magics by naming the feelings they gave her – the serpent green magic, and the fierce leonine gold magic. There was a moment of desperate silence before Adele felt a shift from deep within.

The gold magic responded first. Leaping into her hand, Adele sent a thin stream of gold into Rainere's chest. She closed her eyes and saw in her mind's eye as the magic circled his heart and was absorbed through the heavy, red walls of Rainere's muscle. Adele could feel that she was giving her power to Rainere. The green magic hissed its disapproval and the Chime Voices finally spoke up, muttering in consternation. Adele was doing *something* and it felt good and it felt right.

Adele kept feeding the stream of gold magic into Rainere, pouring her strength into him, and knowing on a primal level that she was actually healing him. Deep in her trance, Adele yelped in fear when she felt a hand close over her wrist, and her eyes flew open.

"Adelena, my love." Rainere was smiling and it shone brighter than any light Adele could imagine in the dark of the tunnel. In that moment, the circle around his pupils glittered with gold magic and his skin was warmed by a radiant glow. Adelena could hardly breathe as love and pride closed her throat. Her magic had given Rainere strength and power, and it had changed him, bonding them even closer.

Letting go of her hand, Rainere pushed himself up to sitting and his smile faded, his mouth folding into a grimace. With a filthy curse, Rainere rolled away and began dry heaving against the wall. Adele pulled herself to her feet and knew that it was ridiculous to be disappointed that Rainere hadn't felt the moment of connection like she had.

"Okay, okay!" Adele didn't bother to hide the irritation in her voice at Rainere's loud heaving. "It was just a little gold magic to wake you up. You don't have to be such a baby about it."

Rainere wiped his mouth with the back of his hand. "It feels like you have filled my chest with excrement," he grimaced. "Fizzing, bubbling excrement."

"It's my gold magic, and it did the trick," replied Adele, snippily. "Maybe if you didn't faint quite so easily after I've been through you, I wouldn't have needed to revive you."

Rainere surprised Adele by laughing. The sound rippled through the air and for an instant, the sinister music in Adele's head stilled. "You love it," he said with a sultry snarl, and rubbed at his chest again. "It's not like you held back on me."

Adele helped pull Rainere to his feet and they both faced the portal, just as the music in her head began racing again.

"Rainere, I have a feeling that we are running out of time in this tunnel," Adele said, "And I feel like we are being watched."

Rainere joined her in studying the archway. "You are right about the time." He pointed to a particularly intricate knot in the pattern. "This spell etched here gives us a time limit to enter the doorway and return unscathed. I suppose the Eldars only ever wanted a quick way to access the prisoners if they needed to."

"If you still want to do this with me, then we should do it now," Adele said. Suddenly, a noise down the tunnel broke her concentration. "Okay, tell me you heard that! Rainere, we need to get out of here!"

Rainere didn't stop to respond. He had begun casting a complex, melodic spell that sounded like a poem being recited underwater. He touched several places on the door in successive order. Adele could see he was under a great deal of strain as Rainere was forced to yank out a piece of paper which Ohren had given him with the instructions for breaking a spell of this magnitude, but it only made the prince curse roundly.

"A cat could've written this better," he snarled in despair, and cast a look at Adele. "Do you want to try?"

"We could do it together?" suggested Adele. "I'll use my gold and you use your green magic. The combination might be stronger."

Rainere nodded and took Adele's hand. They stood side by side, and Adele felt a wild sense of vertigo as she purposely cast a thread of gold magic outwards and let it hover in the air before her. Rainere squeezed her hand and she saw a long, green strand of magic appear in front of him and entwine with her gold strand. Repeating the process as quickly as they could, Adele and Rainere managed to solidify a network of mixed magic in the air.

Gasping with the effort of keeping the magic working, Adele was distracted by a feeling of movement in the corner of her eye. Adele was sure she saw something shift in the shadows, and it was something with eyes that reflected the light. She tapped Rainere on the shoulder and jumped when he let out a happy shout. "There, I've done it. It will open now."

Rainere pulled at Adele's hand, and forced her to look at him. "Hold on to me," Rainere said and he smiled his beautiful half-smile. "Don't let me go."

Out of the corner of her eye, Adele saw the shadow leap just as the magic from the portal snatched them from one world and pressed them into another.

The journey through the walls of the dimension was unlike any other she had experienced before. As they passed through there was darkness and the sensation of enormous pressure closing in, pushing and squashing them together. Adele let out a cry as she tried to grip the power within herself. The Chime Voices whimpered and cried out in her head. *This was so wrong!* Panic suffused Adele. She had never heard that note of fear in the Chime Voices, their shrieks scratching like pins and needles against her organs. Adele felt a cold lurch of nausea, and then it was over.

Adele looked up, blinking, in the twilight of another dimension.

Rainere uncurled himself from her arm and straightened. "Well, that was foul," he croaked. He spat on the ground behind himself and Adele noticed she had a nasty taste in her mouth as well.

"It's Death," he said, at Adele's inquiring look. "A death spell, made with actual fragments of the dead. Disgusting magic, and it tastes awful." Rainere spat again and wiped his hands on his shirt. "I won't enjoy going back through there again."

Adele shuddered, and stepped away from Rainere to spit out the taste of death but her gaze was caught by the vision before her, and her mouth dropped open.

A new world was unfolding like a strange dream, and Adele and Rainere stood on a crease in the page. The ground beneath their feet appeared to ripple but they didn't move with it and once the soft, velvet green grass finished stretching out its wrinkles, it sat still again. Above them, the fuchsia sky was dotted with orange clouds as if lit by a tropical sunset. A darker azure rested on the horizon like a line of ink. The air was scented with raspberries and salt, and no breeze moved a single leaf on any of the tall trees, which stood in straight lines like a giant orchard about them. A vast savanna stretched far out to the east of the orderly forest, surprising, but existing all the same. Off into the distance, Adele could see what looked like a herd of giraffes slowly loping through the tall grasses silhouetted against the setting sun.

They had landed on a white brick path, which led to the gates of a large manor house. Stepping forward, Rainere pushed the heavy bronze gate open and entered before Adele, his desire to protect her over-ruling his gentlemanly habits. Adele gazed at the house. It was similar to the Grey Palace but much smaller, and with odd, cheerful additions. She could see a large candy-striped tent attached to one of the back corners of the house, surrounded by golden sand that glistened in the waning sunlight. Beside it was a lagoon surrounded by a string of palm trees, like a miniature recreation of Sandar. The opposite side of the house was covered by a vertical garden, trees and creepers mashed and knotted together like a great vegetal wall. Adele looked up at a bird call and watched as a flock of multi-colored parrots flew overhead, unlike any she had seen in Unisia but she had no time to wonder at it as Rainere continued walking towards the house as if in a daze.

Adele followed him to the bottom of the front steps, where he stopped and gazed up at the replica of his own home. Adele slipped her hand into Rainere's and squeezed. His was cold and clammy.

"Rainere, just remember..." But she blanked. What advice could Adele give Rainere when he was about to meet the father who had been forcibly imprisoned one hundred and forty-five years ago? "I'm here for you," she finished lamely.

"What if he doesn't even recognize me?" Rainere murmured and Adele heard the pain of that lost little boy in his voice and her heart bled for him. Who knew what they would find when they met his father, the ancient immortal, Prince Rainold Marchant? Adele needed to say something to comfort him so she pulled Rainere about to face her.

"Your father will be so happy to see you again," said Adele firmly. "And he will be lucky to know you." She reached up on her tiptoes, and Rainere's lips met hers in a tender touch. That was all Adele meant to do but Rainere didn't release her after the chaste kiss. Instead, he gripped her tight, and licked her tongue with his and slid a hand down to cup her behind, losing himself in familiar sensation. Adele didn't have the strength to deny him.

Adele and Rainere both started in surprise as a great clanging cacophony of clocks sounded from inside the house. Despite it being after midnight back in Evendaar, the clocks chimed twilight in this dimension. Adele caught her breath when she saw the front doors move inward, opening to reveal a single figure, standing shadowed inside. The figure stepped out to the top of the stone steps and flipped his short cape over one shoulder in a dramatic flourish. The man placed a hand on one hip and stared down at them, smiling.

"Hello, darling! Are you going to bring your sister inside, or are you going to just shag her there in the garden?"

CHAPTER THIRTY-SIX

"A Prince Among the Clouds"

Prince Rainold spread his arms wide and smiled beatifically. "Welcome, my children!"

Rainold Marchant didn't look any older than twenty-one. He was as tall as Rainere but slimmer in the shoulders. His shoulder-length hair fell in dark waves that complimented his long, narrow face. Though dressed in the traditional Marchant black and silver, the fabrics and cut of Rainold's clothes had an old-fashioned look about them. The trousers short and cut close to the knee, black silk stockings sheathed his calves, and black velvet slippers embroidered with golden bees adorned his feet. His coat was cropped to his slim waist, and the shoulder cape was black velvet lined with dark fur.

Rainere floated up the stairs, approaching the young prince as if hypnotized. "Father?"

Adele followed Rainere but hung back to allow the father and son to have a personal moment. They hadn't seen each other since Rainere was five years old and Adele had no idea of the emotions going through Rainere's head, let alone Rainold's. She could only imagine how she would feel, being reunited with her child who had thought her dead for over a century.

All at once, Rainold's smile melted, and his face crumpled into an expression of beautiful anguish as Rainere climbed to the top step.

"Oh, my sweet boy," whispered Rainold. "What have they done to you? That stupid elf let you get…old."

"Father," Rainere repeated. "I – I never thought…" His voice drifted off. It was only in that moment Adele could see that Rainere had not truly believed that his father really was alive, and so had no idea what to say to him.

"Come inside, little one." Rainold radiated sympathy as he stepped down to gather Rainere under his arm. "We can talk somewhere more comfortable, maybe have something to drink, hmmm? That death spell tastes awful, doesn't it?"

Rainold looked over his shoulder at where Adele was hovering a few steps below. "And you too, dear girl." He gave her a wink. "My, my, didn't you grow up to look like Mummy." Rainold laughed pleasantly and held out his hand for Adele to take. His skin was soft and smooth, his nails shiny and neat, and his grip firm.

The similarities to the Grey Palace ended as soon as Adele and Rainere passed through the front doors of Rainold's house. Inside it was more like a cozy manor house with colorful carpets on the floors, and dark wood paneling on the walls. Rainold brought the two of them through the entry hall, lined with a series of tall grandfather clocks, and into a large room off to the left. The room was filled with heavy, ornate furniture of exotic design, and the pale silk on the walls was decorated with images of cherry blossoms and horses. A multitude of lanterns and candles decorated every surface but remained unlit as the large bay windows flooded the room with bright sunshine.

"It's daylight in here," exclaimed Adele, and instantly felt foolish for having spoken. "It's just that it looks like late evening outside," she added, only compounding the feeling.

"Yes." Rainold nodded smiling, as if to encourage a child to be brave. "This is my *day* room, for the *daytime*. Please sit, both of you. I'll get us some refreshments."

Led to two puffy couches with a long, low table between them, Rainere and Adele automatically sat side by side on one. Rainold went over to a buffet and left them alone for a moment. Adele took the chance to squeeze Rainere's hand. He only had time to give her a bewildered glance before Rainold returned and set down a tray of tea and little cakes before them. The prince also had a bottle of Firewhiskey and three tiny crystal glasses, which he filled and handed to each of them with a smile.

"I think a toast is in order, don't you?" Rainold raised his glass and his finely-wrought face was pensive just for a moment. "To family!" He clinked his glass against each of theirs in turn and swigged his little drink down.

Adele only let the Firewhiskey touch her lips before putting her glass down and she was glad she did. This whiskey was as powerful as High Wizard Ohren's brew, less than a drop of it fizzing and bubbling on her top lip as if it had a life of its own. Rainere swallowed his in one draft, making Rainold grin.

"That's my boy!" he said approvingly. "You have to take it in one punch."

Silence reigned again as both Adele and Rainere sat staring at Rainold and he smiled at them, looking from one to the other.

"I'll start, shall I?" Rainold raised a perfect eyebrow and looked so incredibly and suddenly familiar that Adele couldn't help from blurting out: "How do I know you?"

Rainold's smile froze for a second. "Well, you have your mother's manners, that's for certain," he said. "She was always interrupting me too." He gave Adele a tolerant little frown that made her cringe in embarrassment. "Rainestra, you must learn to be quiet when your elders speak."

"My name is Adelena," corrected Adele, at the same time as Rainere said, "Her name is Adelena."

"What?" Rainold looked confused. "But your mother named you Rainestra, after herself. Why ever didn't you keep your name?" Rainold used his hands a lot when he spoke, and they looked like two white birds, elegantly parting and swirling the air about him.

Adele swallowed and had a strong wish not to disappoint Rainold again. "High Wizard Ohren gave me the name Olivia Adelena Serena when he sent me away to Earth the night I was born," she answered and Adele suddenly had a strange feeling of déjà vu. Even Rainold's voice was familiar to her.

"Well, isn't that just like Ohren, thinking he knows better than everyone else." Rainold sighed, looking deeply sad for just a moment before he shook off the emotion and his bright smile returned. "Well, never mind. It was after his sister I suppose, and the Goddess Serena only knew she was a feisty one, just like my dear departed wife."

"My mother," whispered Rainere hoarsely. He cleared his throat and started again. "There is some disagreement at the Golden Palace about my parentage, and it is said that Adelena and I have the same mother."

Rainold frowned in polite confusion. "I don't understand. Who thinks you have the same mother?"

"High Wizard Ohren believes that Princess Rainella was mother to both Adelena and I." Rainere said. "The high wizard had no idea that you had taken a second wife, the Princess Rainestra, who adopted me as her son. He didn't believe that you would allow your wife to have a bastard by a St Lucidis king."

Rainere's father laughed a genuine, full-chested laugh, his hands clapping in merriment. "You make me sound so sordid," he chuckled. "Well, I suppose it's true in a way." Rainold crossed his legs and leaned forward as if he was having a fine old conversation. "I did not tell High Wizard Ohren that I had taken a second wife because I didn't want him to know about her. You see, Rainestra wasn't what you'd call a politically astute match for me and she had her own reasons for wanting to keep our marriage quiet. But when she met your father, Adelena, she seemed determined to cover us in scandal before she died."

Rainold frowned at Adele, as if this had somehow been her fault. *There!* Adele thought, *the way his eyebrows knitted together over his green eyes like that.* But then he smiled again, and the memory slipped away.

"But after that," persisted Rainere. "During the civil uprising. Surely the high wizard would have found out that Rainestra wasn't in fact Rainella at all when she gave her baby to him."

"Rainestra never went near High Wizard Ohren as she hated him from the outset," replied Rainold with a shrug. "And Ohren never even wanted to acknowledge that I ever had a life outside of our work together. So after the baby - you dear girl – was born, it was I who carried her to the Golden Palace. I left Rainestra at the Grey Palace screaming curses and bleeding everywhere."

Rainold drifted off, lost in the blood-soaked memories of his past. A cloud passed over the sun, and the light in the room dimmed.

Then Rainold surprised both Adele and Rainere by coming to sit beside his son and folding him in a warm embrace. Rainere was far too shocked to return the hug and sat stiffly as Rainold rubbed his back in a familiar way. "My darling son, I'm so sorry that I ever made Rainestra your mother. She was really a terrible wife, and quite insane, you know." He *tsk*'ed sympathetically and lifted a hand to stroke Rainere's cheek. "You have Rainella's beautiful cheekbones though, don't you?"

Rainere flinched from the intimate touch. "Prince Rainold…"

Rainold's expression froze, and something flashed in his dark eyes as he took his hand away from Rainere's face and leaned back on the couch. "I'm sorry, my darling, perhaps I should have told Ohren the truth, or at least got that conniving Grotto to do it for me but I really didn't think it would matter at all. Now that I can see that it has, I'm sorry. Truly." He pouted and looked up at Rainere through long dark lashes. "Forgive your silly old Dad?"

Rainere was baffled and cast Adele a bewildered expression before replying. "If Rainella is my mother and you are my father…" Rainold leaned in and squeezed Rainere's knee, as if to say *of course I am* before Rainere continued, "then it should be clear that Adelena and I are only related by adoption."

Rainold poured the tea and offered cakes. "Why ever would you care about that?" he asked. "A sister is still a sister."

"Because I love Adelena and we have meant much to each other. And because Grotto seeks to have me take Adelena's crown as her older sibling, and I have refused to," replied Rainere with a defensive tilt of his chin.

Too shocked to say a word of her own, Adele just watched Rainold's reaction to his son's proclamation, but he did not seem phased in the slightest. "Well, of course you love her," Rainold smiled. "She is the daughter of an angel."

Rainere's father patted him on the shoulder before getting up to pull a framed picture down from the mantelpiece. He stared at it fondly, before handing it on to Rainere.

"This is you about a month before I left," he said and sat back down next to Rainere so close that their knees were touching. "You were such a grave little thing, just like you are now." He raised his hand to touch Rainere's face again but stopped just in time and placed it back in his lap.

Adele leaned in to look at the picture. A serious little boy stared out at her with an unmistakable Rainere-glare. His eyes were squinted up a little as if he was holding back tears and his bottom lip was thrust out in a pout.

"This is one of my favorites of you," smiled Rainold. "You were so angry when I wouldn't give you the camera that you stomped off to hide after I took this photo. We searched everywhere. Eventually I found you stuck under a bench in my laboratory, sound asleep. When I woke you up, I gave you the camera but you only threw it on the floor and looked at me like this again. That's when I understood: it wasn't the camera you wanted, it was that you wanted me to give it to you *when* you asked for it. You see? So, of course, my darling, if you want to love your half-sister-by-adoption then you have my blessing. Just please don't run off and hide, I would so love the chance to make you happy again. Will you do that? Will you give me that chance, *cara mia?*"

Rainere's mouth dropped open in shock. "Why do you call me that?"

"*Cara mia*, it means 'my beloved' in the old tongue," Rainold explained, then ran his hand over Rainere's cheek. "And you are my beloved - my beautiful son, Rainere Rainov Lucien Grey Marchant."

Chapter Thirty-Seven

"The Imaginary Dinner"

Rainere turned away from his father and Adele saw the overwhelming confusion in his eyes. This personable and affectionate young man was unbalancing his sense of the world. Rainere shifted on the couch so that he was as far from Rainold as he could be and pressed up hard against Adele. The movement wasn't lost on Rainold, who covered up his disappointment with a bright smile.

"Would you both like to stay for dinner?" Rainold asked and took the picture from Rainere's hands to replace it on the mantelpiece. Rainold stood at the fireplace, examining them both with his dark green eyes. Rainold frowned at their stunned silence and for the first time he looked like his son.

"But what is the time?" asked Rainere. "We came through just after midnight in Evendaar."

"It's any time I need it to be," replied Rainold breezily. "That is the benefit of making your own world. I find time so tiresome that normally I disregard it altogether. Everything you see in this world I made, you know. Before me there was nothing; no light, no land, no sky, no anything. I'm like a god in this world, just calling things into existence with my will. It's terribly invigorating, and supremely boring – so much work, you see, designing everything from dust alone. I now have so much sympathy for the gods of our realm."

Rainere and Adele sat silently before Prince Rainold, unsure how to respond.

"It was light that was the hardest to create," offered Rainold with a modest shrug. "You think you know how it should work, but it's a really tricky thing to actually conjure. I had to sit in the pitch dark for months before I got it right." He chuckled, almost self-conscious before his stunned audience.

"Anyway." Rainold waved his bird-like hands. "Come through to the dining room, it's so pretty with all its crystal and candles, it took me an age to build, you see. Or no time at all depending on how you look at it!" He said, laughing gaily.

Rainold guided his two guests out of the room and back into the corridor, which was now brightly lit with green flames. The walls glittered greenly for a moment but when Adele blinked, the sparkles disappeared and the walls were normal wood and plaster again. She tried not to think about the nothingness that existed before Rainold made this house, and how fragile his world made of magic really was.

Rainold ushered them down a wide hallway to the back of the house, where they made their way through a tiny manicured square of garden and entered the tent structure that Adele had seen from outside. It was a beautiful room, with a hundred crystal chandeliers dripping from the pink and black-striped satin ceiling. The floor was carpeted with vivid fuchsia and violet rugs laid over each other haphazardly. A long rosewood table had been set up in the center of the room and the chairs were gorgeous carvings of trees painted with gold and silver gilt, and the cushioned seat was the crown of the tree. The table had already been set for three, and each plate was surrounded by a plethora of glasses in all sizes.

Rainold set his guests to opposite sides of the table so they sat facing each other. Adele felt Rainold's hand on the small of her back as he pushed her forward to her chair. She caught a trace of his perfume and felt a rush of heat in response. Prince Rainold smelled like chocolate and wood smoke, violets and fresh water, with a lingering trace of masculine musk that caught her imagination.

Adele pulled in her chair and cautioned the giggling Chime Voices to shut up about Prince Rainold. She didn't need to be distracted by their attraction to the immortal wizard when she needed to concentrate. Dinner appeared on their plates as soon as Rainold seated himself at the head of the table, between them. The first course was a clear soup with delicate herbs and tiny flowers floating in it. Adele picked up her spoon and moved it through the bowl stirring the leaves and flowers together. The Chime Voices were whispering in the back of her mind, when an old children's tune swam to the front of her thoughts. Adele watched the soup drip slowly from the spoon as if it were slightly gelatinous, or something other than soup, or perhaps not even as real at that. *Fairy food*, the Chime Voices whispered the words over and over. Adele had read copiously as a lonely child and though she had always favored murder mysteries, any child could tell you that you don't eat fairy food in the Fairy Kingdom. If you did, you could never leave. Adele glanced over at Rainere and wondered if the same rules applied for immortal wizards, and how she could possibly warn him.

"So, tell me, my darling boy." Rainold beamed at Rainere and reached across the table as if he would touch him again. Rainere flinched. "How is it that you came to my little imaginary world? As far as I am aware, only the elves know the secret of the Early Death, and I would be surprised if that Grottonski told you about me. I would have thought he would be pleased to have me gone forever."

"Grotto, he…" Rainere began hesitantly, and utterly unlike himself. Rainold gestured for him to continue with an encouraging smile. "Grotto believes that the Prophecy of the End of the World has not ended. He still hopes for me to sit on the throne of Unisia and seeks to convince the Wizards Council to allow me to take the queen's hand in marriage or give the throne to me, as her older brother by marriage. Grotto revealed the secret of this prison dimension to the High Wizard and the Court of the Golden Palace in the hope that we could confirm that you were still alive."

Rainold sat back, his hands steepled in front of his lips, and looked thoughtful. "Has the world indeed ended?" he asked curiously.

Rainere shook his head. "No, of course not."

Rainold shrugged. "Grotto might have the right of it where the prophecy is concerned, but I feel like Rainest- Adelena, should have a say now." He turned to Adele and she froze in the intensity of his green-eyed gaze. "Do you want to marry Rainere?"

"Your Highness, there is more," interjected Rainere. "We are here in your world because of another issue. Adelena has a daughter who is gravely ill, and the only cure for the child is to find a Dragon Tear.

Grotto told the queen that you are the only person who would know where the last dragon lives, or if it still does."

"Wait. Tell me again: who is the queen of Unisia?" asked Rainold, with a raised eyebrow.

Rainere frowned at his father's confusion. "Adelena is the queen," he said clearly. "She is the queen of Unisia, and the Hidden Child of the End of the World Prophecy."

"Oh, is that so?" Rainere gave Adele an approving glance. "I was wondering why you would want her crown if she was just a princess. You know, I really didn't think Rainestra's plan to put you in that damned St Lucidis prophecy was going to work. You know, poor Rainestra was obsessed with it when I met her. I had always thought the prophecy was just another mad tale of a zealot king, but Rainestra she was sure it was real, and she was determined that it would help her daughter have the freedom she never had."

Rainere's frown deepened, and he refused to be distracted by the Prince Rainold's odd remarks. "But what about the dragon? Do you know where it lives?"

Rainold didn't answer the question but turned to Adele. "Why won't you give the throne to my son if it is really his?"

Adele returned his gaze, holding it for a long moment while the Chime Voices whispered in her ears. "It would be too dangerous for both Rainere and for Unisia if your son sat on the throne."

There was something deeply unsettling about Rainold, and not just because he looked so familiar, Adele now suspected it might be because he was completely mad. As if to confirm her suspicions, the soup before them disappeared and a pile of chocolate éclairs appeared on their plates, the cream pink and moussy, surrounded by a ring of shredded carrot. Adele couldn't hide her surprise quickly enough.

"I'm not a terribly good cook, you know," Rainold apologized, with attractive modesty. "I only make things that please me, and I just love eating sweet things like cakes, cookies and women." He laughed gaily again.

"Prince Rainold, I was brought to this world of Evendaar against my will." Adele was relieved that her voice was steady and strong. "I have encountered many different dangers since being here but the worst of these have happened to my three children. Stella, my little baby of two years, is in a coma after the Summer Influenza almost killed her. I have been told by the High Wizard Council and Grotto that only a Dragon Tear will save her, and I have been told that you are the only person who can help me."

"How did you manage to have a daughter with no magic?" asked Rainold, with no shared sense of Adele's urgency. "That was very careless of you. A woman of your strength should have at least shared a skerrick of your power with your own child, for goodness sake."

Adele shook her head, confused by his accusing tone. "My children were all born on Earth, and I had no power or magic there."

"Still, the other children have magic, do they not?" Rainold asked.

Adele nodded, and shrugged at the same time, thinking of how Aaron said he could talk to animals and Natalie being able to handle the magic of Rainere's spells.

"So why would you give it to them but not the little one?" Rainold's perfect brows knitted over his eyes. "Now, you expect Rainere to help you fix a problem that you yourself created." He looked back to his son. "You realize it's going to be like this all the time when you marry this woman? You having to clean up all her messes."

"I am not here to marry Prince Rainere," Adele blurted out, desperate to steer the conversation back to Stella. "My only priority is getting my daughter well again."

Rainold sat back in his chair, those frowning brows raised sharply at her tone. "Oh, I see. So if Rainere doesn't do what you say and help you find a dragon, then you won't marry him?"

Rainold raised his chin and looked down his nose at Adele. "You know, even though you are an angel, I think you might not be good enough for my beautiful boy."

"Father, enough!" Rainere's anger proved he was completely over his initial shock at meeting Rainold. Adele hoped he, too, realized that Rainold was insane. "I never thought that I would ever get the chance to see you again, and I am deeply moved to see you alive and well. But I made a vow to help Adelena find a cure for Stella's condition, and I would implore you to tell us anything you might be able to concerning this dragon."

Rainold crossed his arms and his gaze became stony. "I didn't raise you to speak to me like this, my son," he said imperiously.

Rainere gaped. "You didn't raise me at all!"

"Oh, you are going to bring that up again?" Rainold said, miffed. "Well, I'll thank you to accept that this was a two-way street. I have spent the last one hundred and forty-five years, eighty days and twelve hours, give or take a decade, trying to find a way out of this prison and back to you, my darling boy. I haven't heard how hard you've been trying to find *me*."

Adele saw the silver rings around Rainere's pupils flash and spin and knew he was getting angry now. "I was told it was impossible."

"Impossible is for fools!" cried Rainold as his hands flew into the air like white doves. "Impossible is the excuse given by every incompetent wizard and stupid child to fail. Impossible is not a word that applies to a Marchant prince. We hear that word and it is a joke to us." Rainold stood up and started pacing at the end of the table. "You know, they told me it was impossible to find the Eldars in their Eyrie, but I did. They told me it was impossible to find a dragon, but I did. They told me it was impossible to make a dragon cry, but *I did*. They told me it was impossible to tame an angel, *but I did all these things*. Do you see, my son? Do you see why that word annoys me so much?"

Rainere nodded, clearly disturbed by his father's insane passion. "Yes, Father."

Rainold shook his finger, his beautiful face scowling at his son. "Then never let me hear you say that word, 'impossible', again, Rainere," he said, and finally sat down.

Rainere stole a glance at Adele so she took the chance to give him a tiny, sympathetic smile. "I understand," Rainere answered the mad prince.

Rainold calmed himself and leaned over to pat Rainere's hand where it lay on the table. "Good. I am sorry I yelled at you, my darling boy. I have a short temper and no manners sometimes, but it is important that you learn as much as you can from me now that we are together again."

Rainere pursed his lips and Adele could see he was making a mighty effort not to shake off his father's touch. "I see that very clearly now, Father. May I ask: where did you find the dragon?"

Rainold sat back in his chair and waved his water glass about, the liquid threatened to spill over but never quite managed to. "Well, it was quite an adventure," he said with a laugh. "I went miles and miles and miles away. I went so far to the other side of Evendaar it would make your head spin, to a place where the magic in the air is so unstable that you have to walk everywhere." Rainold pantomimed exhaustion. "And then you have to talk to the dragon, which is an ordeal in itself."

"What could you say to a dragon to make it cry?" asked Adele, trying to follow the meandering conversation and only collect the pertinent points to Stella.

Rainold raised his green eyes to look into Adele's. She noticed that they were a brighter, clearer green than Rainere's, like the inside of an emerald. "You say anything you can to make a dragon cry, if you need its tears," said the prince softly. "Something sad, something cruel, something true…" the prince drifted off, staring into the distance.

"Can you tell me where to find the dragon?" asked Adele, not at all liking the description of the voyage that Rainold had taken.

"Yes, I could," smiled Rainold, and primly folded his napkin, laying it back on the table. Adele could sense he was watching her though his eyes rested on the plate of food in front of him. If this was his game, she had no interest in playing.

"*Will* you tell me where to find the last dragon?" asked Adele more bluntly.

Rainold looked from his son and back to Adele and gave her a mischievous grin. "If I do tell you, will you marry my beautiful boy?"

CHAPTER THIRTY-EIGHT

"Madness Is As Madness Does"

Adele's jaw dropped. "What?" she spluttered at the same time Rainere protested, "No, absolutely not!"

"Oh, so sweet," grinned Rainold. "Look at the way you two finish each other's sentences. That is really true love."

"I will not force Adelena to marry me to save her daughter," growled Rainere. "I made a vow never to make her to do anything against her will."

Rainold turned to Adele, his happy smile twisted at the edges. "Well, aren't you just the clever little minx," he said archly. "Look at all the promises you get my son to make to help you. Yet, I wonder what it is he gets in return, hmmm?"

Adele couldn't say a word. After what had happened at the Grey Palace, she had allowed Rainere to live, and that had felt good enough as recompense. Yet now, after everything she had gone through in the last few days, living without Rainere also seemed impossible. An image of Stella lying silent and immobile filled Adele's mind. Nothing mattered more than finding a cure for her baby girl. Adele remembered High Wizard Ohren's warning about Marchant princes and prepared herself for battle. Obviously, this mad Marchant was going to have to be forced to play ball with her.

"What if it was *your* son who needed the Dragon Tear to save his life?" Adele asked Rainold, "wouldn't you do everything in your power to make sure the person who could help you, did so? Tell me: what would you do to a man who stood in the way of a cure for your child's pain?"

Rainold was silent for a long moment, his gaze nailing Adele right between the eyes. Her heart beat faster.

"Are you threatening me?" Prince Rainold asked. His tone was curious but Adele felt an undercurrent of something dangerous.

Adele took a deep breath. She had faced down a Mage from Sandar, and an enormous Spider Empress, and they had both ended up dead by her own hand. Now this strange immortal wizard was staring at her as if he were the next challenger. Adele gripped her magic for strength and the Chime Voices hummed in anticipation of her needing them.

"I must find this dragon to save my baby girl," Adele said.

All of the light-hearted joy evaporated from their strange little party. The ancient-young-prince looked wounded as he gazed upon Adele, his long fingers entwined at his chest.

"So the reason that you two came looking for your old dad wasn't to help me escape my prison or reunite our family," said Rainold, eyes filled with wet green glitter. "But it was only to ask me to do something for you. Really?"

"It is Grottonski you should blame," said Adele boldly. "He is the one who kept the knowledge of this prison dimension a secret. I'm sure Rainere would have helped you escape before now if he'd known, but I must beg you to tell me where I can find that dragon, Prince Rainold."

"Unfortunately, for you," said Rainere and his look became canny. "You have eaten of my food and drunk of my drink. This means that I will hold you in thrall until I decide -"

"I haven't touched anything," replied Adele, too upset for diplomacy now.

"Well, more fool me," Rainold said, exasperated. He gave Adele a level look, all his mad humor dropping away. "What do you really want, Rainestra? You get the Dragon Tear, you heal your child, then what? You don't want to marry my son and you don't want to fulfill the prophecy. So tell me, what do you want to do in our world?"

Adele bit her lip and looked at Rainere. He was waiting for her answer, too. She shook her head. "It doesn't matter what I want," she said firmly. "All that matters to me is getting my daughter healed."

Rainold's stare never left Adele.

"She wants to go home." Rainere's voice was hoarse with sadness. "She wants to get back to Earth and get away from us all. She never wanted to be the queen of Unisia, and she never wanted…"

"Rainere, stop." Adele blinked at the sudden tears in her own eyes. "If you hadn't done what you'd done…"

"What did you do, son?" asked Rainold, his face rapt with instant curiosity.

"I stole her eldest child, Princess Natalie, and gave her to the Empress of the Spiders," said Rainere, sadly. "I did it to protect Adelena from the Empress. I had hoped that I could take the child back again but the Empress betrayed me and kept the child. Adelena led the rescue and killed the Spider Empress and her people, releasing me from my oath…"

"You took her child!" cried Rainold. "You silly boy, don't you know that is the worst thing you could ever do to a parent? You were lucky she didn't kill you, along with the Empress Ka-kik!" Rainold turned to Adele and placed his hand on his heart. "Rainestra, no, Adelena: nothing can fix what my son did to your family but maybe I, as his father, can be the one to offer reparations to repay the damage to your heart." Rainold leaned across the table and reached for her hand.

Adele's head was spinning with the whiplash effect of Rainold's moods and she flinched when he touched her.

"I have knowledge of a path that travels beyond the Black Mountains, through the tundra and into the Lands of the Snow People to where the only dragon left in Unisia lives. If I give you this knowledge, will you find it fitting to forgive my son his crimes against you?"

"Errr - yes," replied Adele, still poised to avoid a verbal trap with the mad prince.

Rainere opened his mouth to speak, but Rainold raised a hand to silence him. "You have done quite enough damage for one day, Rainere," he said firmly but then gave him a radiant smile. "But I forgive you, silly sweet boy. This is how we learn, isn't it, by making mistakes? I'm sure Adelena's children are exactly the same." Rainold stood up and clapped his hands happily. "Now, Rainere, I would like you to sleep."

Adele watched, horrified, as Prince Rainere gently lay his head down on the table, pillowing his cheek on his hands and fell straight to sleep. "Why did you do that?" she croaked.

Rainold ran a hand over Rainere's shorn head. "I had always thought he would have long hair like me," he said and laid a quick kiss on Rainere's cheek. "But he is so handsome anyway, isn't he?"

Rainold turned his attention to Adele and though his expression was calm she felt no desire to drop her guard. "I wanted to show you that map, my lovely. Do you want to see it?"

Adele could only nod.

"Then come with me into my laboratory, darling." Rainold gave her a wink, as if the order had been more like a lascivious suggestion. Helpless to do anything else, Adele followed the laughing Rainold out of the tented dining room.

CHAPTER THIRTY-NINE

"The Luck of a Thief"

The wagon came to a hard stop, and Charlie nudged Leafy up to sit. His head still pounded, but fear took priority as he held Leafy close and braced himself for what was going to come through those doors. Charlie didn't like what he was hearing through the walls of the wagon. They had not left the forest long ago but had already crossed at least two bridges over water before entering what sounded like a village. There was the scent of smoke and dust in the air. Charlie heard lots of shouting and the unmistakable rattle of metalwork.

The doors of the wagon were wrenched open and Charlie flinched when one of the unnamed Rangers leaped up onto the platform and glared down at the two of them. "Right, I'll take the little chit," he huffed, and reached to grab Leafy by the arm. The little girl started crying again and burrowed herself into Charlie's side, holding onto his jacket for dear life as she was dragged away.

Charlie felt his heart go into his throat as Leafy was thrown over the shoulder of the Ranger. He could only follow her out of the wagon, his coat sleeve still in her hands, as she shrieked his name and begged for the help he couldn't give her. As she was pulled out of his reach, Charlie was left standing on the last step of the wagon. He blinked in the early morning light and his jaw dropped. Before him, he could see that an entire mountain had been mined right down to its base. Its sides completely hollowed out in a gargantuan cone shape. The morning sun shone on the top of the grey rock walls, far above the small village at its base.

To call the collection of buildings a village was probably too generous. There was a handful of one-story homesteads set in a rough semi-circle on one side of the circular space, and on the other, a series of tall, heavy poles had been stuck into the ground, each with a different colored flag draped on top. A small podium was set at the bottom of each pole, and Charlie could see groups of people huddled around the poles as a guard stood on the podium and shouted orders at them. Everything was covered in a thin layer of fine grey dust, making it hard to judge the ages or nationalities of the people around him. Charlie had heard about the infamous child work camps in the country, and it didn't take a wizard to work out that's what this village was.

"Leafy! Leafy!" Charlie's head spun to the call and he saw a tall kid, probably no older than himself, fighting through a crowd of people to get over to the wagon. The kid pushed through until he lurched into the way of the Ranger who had the little girl. "Leafy, how come they got you? I told you to hide."

"Carl!" Leafy cried back. "Put me down, it's me bruvva, Carl." The Ranger only snorted and pushed Carl back out of his way.

"Tricky bit of chit, your sister, mate," said the Ranger, with a nasty chuckle and hooked a thumb in Charlie's direction. "She was hidden pretty good, but Charlie here got her out of the forest for us and handed her right over."

"What?" Carl was covered in dust and only wore a pair of rough work pants but when he turned to catch sight of Charlie still standing dumbfounded in the back of the wagon, he flexed his considerable bulk and his eyes narrowed in hate. Carl pointed at Charlie. "They got my sister because of you!"

Charlie shook his head and wanted nothing more than to piss himself in fear. This Carl kid was going to kill him, and he hadn't even gotten out of the wagon yet. "I never..." he protested just before Ranger Cedric appeared and all the kids dropped their heads and shuffled backwards, even the furious Carl.

"Out of the wagon, Charlie." Cedric's voice was cold and it seemed he didn't much care if Charlie followed his orders or not, but his air of menace and the fear of the other people surrounding them confirmed Charlie's worst suspicions. "The Key Master'll want to meet you."

Charlie jumped down from the back of the wagon and tried not to wobble on his weak legs as hunger made his head spin. He stumbled after Cedric as the Ranger strode through the crowd, heading for a little wooden hut in the middle of the large cleared area. Around him, Charlie noticed that everyone who wasn't a guard was wearing utilitarian grey, and had their hair cut very short. The only way Charlie could tell the males from the females was that the females wore square grey shirts with their work pants, whereas the boys wore only pants. Most of the people working here were kids not much older than him, and often much younger. He had lost track of Leafy in the crowd but he was horribly aware that Carl was following him along the sidelines.

Cedric stilled Charlie with a gesture a yard or so from the verandah of the tiny hut and mounted the two steps alone. He knocked on the door in a way that managed to make the sound seem sarcastic. After a long moment's wait, in which Cedric took the opportunity to spit on the doorknob, the door was yanked open to reveal a tall man wearing a sneer and a heavy leather belt covered with keys under his substantial gut.

"Well, if it isn't my best mate, the Ranger Cedric," said the man, but his accent was so thick even Charlie found it hard to follow. It sounded like he might have said "Wull, uff ut usn't me bes' mutt, tha Ranja Cedruc." The man's coffee-colored skin was covered in dust, but he still looked cleaner than everyone else in the camp. "Caught any little bunnies for me lately?"

Cedric sucked on his teeth and spat on the ground near the Key Master's boots. He hooked a thumb at Charlie and waited. The Key Master looked over Cedric's shoulder and caught sight of Charlie. Charlie felt the gaze fall over him like he'd stepped into a shadow. He shivered.

"That's it? (Thut's ut?)" The Key Master feigned shock, but Charlie could see he was planning to turn it to outrage soon. "I've got kids dying left and right on me every day. Now I've just found a new seam of crystal and you only bring me one bloody digger?"

Cedric turned his dead eyes on Charlie. "He's no digger, he's a Special, the priest said so," said the Ranger. "You might want to take better care of this one. These kids are a dying breed."

The Key Master leaned in and dropped his face to Cedric's so they were eye to eye. "Listen, you're giving me a cunt and trying to tell me it's a cock, mate," he snarled. "He's not a shaggin' Special, he's a bloody digger. I can spot one with both eyes closed. You've given me shit-all here." Charlie never saw his hand move but the Key Master felt the press of Cedric's knife against his balls before he had a chance to make another noise.

"Call him what you like, *mate.*" The Ranger's cold monotone had dropped a few more degrees. "I was told he's a Special by the priest, and now I'm telling you. You got a problem with it, have a word with the Church of Serena."

The Key Master raised himself up to his full height again. "I will tell the Church," he said, but his ego was bruised and both men knew it. "And I'll tell them you're a weak cunt who pulled a knife on me too."

Cedric bowed his head slightly and the corner of his mouth shifted, but not into a smile. "Please do," he said. "I live only to serve our Goddess Serena, and we are all but weak cunts before her mercy." With another shallow bow, Ranger Cedric turned away from the Key Master and made his way past Charlie without even a second glance, disappearing off into the shuffling crowd.

Charlie watched as the Key Master followed Cedric with his gaze, a snarl curling his lip and his meaty hands forming into fists by his side. Belatedly, the man remembered the reason for his fury and looked down at Charlie, quaking in the dust before him. The Key Master looked even angrier at having been made a fool of for the sake of such a pathetic figure as the kid before him. His eyes narrowed and he stomped down the two steps to tower over Charlie.

"Hear this, kid: you are a digger." He grabbed Charlie's shoulder in a vice-like grip. "And I am the Key Master, you'll do what I say or you'll die."

Charlie looked up into the man's small black eyes and didn't question his sincerity. The Key Master had a face that could scare the hair off a cat. His nose was a lumpy mess that had been knocked sideways a few too many times to heal right and the hairy black stubble on his face only served to highlight the scars that crisscrossed his cheeks. His breath was a foul combination of cheap liquor and rotten meat, and it almost made Charlie retch when he got a whiff of it. Charlie nodded.

"You run, you die," continued the Key Master and casually pointed to a body not five yards from Charlie, half propped on the verandah of the hut, its head twisted at an unnatural angle.

Charlie swallowed and his empty stomach turned sour.

"You hide...well, than't nowhere to hide," nodded the Key Master. "But if you try to, we'll find you and you'll die. You get me, boy?"

Charlie shuddered and hoped it would pass for a nod.

"You get lazy, than't good either," sneered the Key Master. "You work or you die." He shoved Charlie hard in the direction of a bonfire that was smoking by the side of the hut. "Now, go burn your clothes and get your work uniform."

Stumbling towards the fire, Charlie saw the small figure of Leafy stripping off her little leather tunic and raising her arms as her brother pulled a square, grey shirt down over her head. It fit her like a dress. Her old clothes smoldered on the fire.

Carl was hugging his sister but stood up when he spotted Charlie. Up close, Charlie could see that Carl was distraught and hiding it badly. "You're a dead man," Carl said, as he wiped away Leafy's tears. "Not today, but soon, you will die for what you did. Traitor." He spat on the ground for emphasis.

Charlie couldn't respond. He knew how the world looked from Carl's view, and he felt just sick about the part he had inadvertently played in Leafy's capture. No one knew he had just been trying to do the right shagging thing for once, no one except Charlie.

Anger started a slow burn in the bottom of his stomach. *No matter what I do, something always cocks it up,* he swore to himself. *Well, if they want trouble, then that's something I'm actually really good at.*

Not breaking eye contact with Carl, Charlie pulled his shirt over his head and threw it in the fire. He knew he was too skinny to be intimidating, but he had enough scars and muscle to show Carl he wasn't a pushover either. He was also wearing an amulet which, on the streets of Concordis, meant he had the protection of the Boss. *Surely that would mean something, even out here in the country?* Charlie pulled his pants down and pissed on the fire, the heavy stream drowning the embers by his feet. He felt something thrown at his back and looked down to see a pair of grey cotton trousers sitting in the dust. When he was finished he put them on and turned to find the Key Master watching him, clearly unimpressed by Charlie's machismo or Carl's death threats against him.

"Come with me," grunted the Key Master, and gestured for Charlie to follow.

Charlie remembered to wave at the little girl before he left. "Bye, Leafy," he said and gave her a grin, more to irritate Carl than to remind her that had once been friends.

"Bye, Charlie," replied Leafy before she was swung up into her brother's arms.

"You're working the green team today, digger-boy," said the Key Master. "See that pole over there with the green flag?" Charlie nodded. "That's where you go for orders. Listen, Charlie, before you go…"

Charlie should never have turned, he should have dodged or ducked, but he was too out of sorts to wonder why the Key Master had used his name, and he never saw the sledgehammer punch coming. When he could finally open his eyes again, he saw the face of the Key Master leering down at him. "Welcome to Paradise Mines, son." He cackled nastily and reached down, yanking off Charlie's precious amulet. "You're welcome!"

Shit. Life had just got about as screwed up as it could be, and as Charlie lay in the dirt he cursed the day his mother ever spat him out into the world. The only comfort he took from the moment was the long string of expletives shouted by the Key Master opening the door to his hut and finding a huge gob of spittle on it. Charlie pulled himself to his feet, made sure his jaw wasn't broken, and forced himself to smile at the watching crowd.

This time, Charlie would go looking for trouble before it found him.

CHAPTER FORTY

"A Deal with the Devil"

Adele followed Prince Rainold up a narrow wooden staircase that widened at the top into a long landing. Rainold walked quickly ahead of her and disappeared into the second door along to their left. Cautiously, Adele followed the prince inside and found that the room was an exact replica of Prince Rainere's laboratory back in the Grey Palace. Except here, the windows looked out over the savannah plains, which seemed, strangely, much closer to the house than they had outside.

Turning from the windows, Adele watched as Rainold fetched and set up four little globes on spindly stands and placed them in the corners of a long rectangular table.

"Is Rainere going to be alright?" asked Adele, trying to keep her tone conversational and not alert Rainold to her nervousness.

"My boy is fine," replied Rainold as he measured the distance between the four globes with a metal ruler. "He ate the meal I gave you both so he is in a deep thrall." Rainold beckoned her to come closer to the table. "I needed to speak to you alone anyway. You both have so many questions for me but they are not any of the ones I was expecting."

"I'm sorry, Your Highness," said Adele. "It must be such a shock to have us break into your world like this and demand so much from you. I really do wish that things could have been different, and that you and Rainere could have more time together."

Adele watched as Rainold conjured a miniature replica of Evendaar in the center of the table. Little mountains, rivers and fields appeared before her, all looking as real as the table itself. Adele couldn't help but be fascinated as she poked a finger into a little rushing river, temporarily damming it.

"Your map, my queen," said Rainold and his tone was curious enough to make her look up at him. "I take it you can memorize this and then be on your way before Rainere wakes up?"

Adele had been afraid that Rainold would attach a serious catch to his gift, but this was out of the question. "There is no way I can remember the map from looking at it only once," she answered firmly. "I am going to need a copy of this."

Rainold kept his eyes on Adele as he raised a hand and she watched a clear glass globe float across the room and land in his palm. He placed the globe in mid-air above the map as easily as if he had put it on a shelf. Adele could see the sparkles of green magic that trailed after his hand. At a word, all of the tiny little trees and boulders, streams of water and miniature ice-capped mountains were sucked into the ball of glass in a whirl of motion. There was a long moment of turmoil before everything settled down again and Adele could see the map trapped in the globe. She reached for it, but Rainold snatched it away at the last minute, holding it up high so she would have to reach across him to take it.

"Uh-uh, my lovely." Rainold gave her a flirtatious grin. "What do we say?"

Adele frowned. Rainold was going to try to play the oldest game in the book, she could feel it as sure as she knew the sun outside the window didn't really shine. "I could say, thank you," she offered, reaching out her hand again.

"Or you could suggest an exchange?" suggested Rainold with a bright smile, but Adele didn't miss the steel in his tone or the way his eyes travelled her body.

"Rainere is not mine to give," replied Adele, guessing the only other thing she could imagine Rainold would want. "Perhaps you should wake him up and ask him yourself."

"No, stop it!" Rainold shouted suddenly, his young face screwed up in rage. Adele could tell she had reached the edge of his fragile sanity. "I am Rainere's father, and I can see all the binds and bonds and promises that he has made to you wrapped around his heart like unbreakable chains. I cannot save him from any of that." Rainold took a breath and tried to calm himself, looking at the globe in his hand. "But I can save him from this."

Adele saw the determination in Rainold's expression and a father's fear in his eyes. "I will gift you this map in exchange for a promise that you will make to me now." Rainold held out the globe to Adele. "Promise me that you will not allow Rainere to accompany you on your journey to seek the dragon. It far too dangerous, and he will surely perish in the pursuit of saving your ungrateful arse at some juncture, sooner or later. You have a son too, so I know you will understand when I tell you that I will require you to make an oath in blood for this."

The prince's eyes were as clear and cold as deep water, and Adele shivered. She kept her gaze on the map as Rainold balanced the delicate globe in the tips of his fingers, the miniature Evendaaar sloshing about inside. She knew that Rainold would smash it if she didn't make her promise sincerely. There could be no lies here.

Adele took a small knife from her belt and pricked her thumb, offering the prince her hand. "Prince Rainold Marchant, if you let us leave this dimension then I promise on my life's blood that I will prevent your son, Prince Rainere, from accompanying me on the journey to find the dragon. He will instead remain at the Golden Palace."

Adele held out her hand to shake but Rainold only grasped it and pulled her in closer. Adele could see she had amused him, despite the severity of the prince's expression, and he raised her hand to his mouth, slowly sucking the blood she had spilled. Adele's body responded before her brain could tell her to be still. *Rainere help me,* she thought even as she saw the lust in Rainold's gaze and his face coming toward her.

Rainold's kiss was soft and his tongue was gentle, but he tasted like blood and Adele pulled away in disgust, quickly wiping the saliva off her lips with the back of her hand.

Rainold shrugged at her glare. "It's more traditional that way," he said sweetly, but Adele only felt like she had been tricked. The taste of blood had turned her mouth sour.

There was a shout from downstairs and Adelena heard the panic in Rainere's voice ringing through the house.

"Ah, that spell didn't last as long as I'd hoped," mused Rainold as he looked at Adele, his head tilted to the side. "My boy must be stronger than he looks."

"Rainere, I'm up here," Adele called out, and tried to struggle her way out of Rainold's hold. "In the laboratory."

"Oh, I don't think he'll find us," said Rainold with a grin. "Even I get lost here, sometimes."

However, Rainere's footsteps thundered closer, and Adele had no need to call out again before the door flew back on its hinges and crashed against the wall. Rainere filled the doorway, his black coat spread wide, like the wings of an avenging angel. He leapt to Adele's side and wrenched her out of Rainold's grip.

"Adelena, are you alright?" asked Rainere, looking her all over. "Did he hurt you?" Without waiting for an answer, Rainere turned in a fury on his father. "What did you do to her? I felt you do - something."

Adele tried to calm Rainere's fury before he acted on the rage she could see flaring in his dark eyes. "Rainere, I'm alright, I promise. Prince Rainold showed me the map," she said.

Rainere continued glaring at his father, pushing Adele behind him as he stepped up to Rainold. "Tell me what you did to her," he hissed through clenched teeth.

Rainold's eyes narrowed and moved over Rainere's face as if they were reading something there. "How did you know I did anything to her, my darling boy?" Rainold asked, his voice soft. "There is no way you should have been able to feel me touch her magic. Unless?"

Rainold's eyes widened in surprise and he gripped Rainere's shoulders.

Now it was Rainere's turn to step back and out of his father's touch. "I told her to put it on me," Rainere said and Adele heard the defensive note of protest as clearly as Rainold did.

Rainold's cheeks suddenly bloomed pink, and the silver rings around his pupils flashed dangerously. "What did you let her do to you, Rainere?"

Rainere raised his chin. "It is of no account…"

"It is of *every* account if a Marchant prince has been made a slave to a Unisian queen," shouted Rainold, and poked his son in the chest. "Show me the Mark she made on you. Now."

"No," growled Rainere menacingly, hitting his father's hand away. "I will not."

Adele needed to distract these wizards from the battle between them that she could feel coming, and she needed to get that map.

"Look, Prince Rainold," Adele interrupted the men and almost flinched when they both turned their intense gazes on her. She could see so much of the father in the son at that moment. "I have apologised to Rainere for Marking him with my insignia, and I will apologise to you too if it will help us get pass this. At the time I hadn't meant to…"

"Really? You apologised?" Rainold's eyebrows were sky high over his flashing eyes. "And how would you like it if I Marked your son, hmmm, Adelena? How would you like my *apology* after I went and made Aaron my personal *slave*?"

"How do you know my son's name," asked Adelena at exactly the same time that Rainere asked "How do you know she has a son?"

Rainold frowned, his elegant brows dropping into a deep furrow. "This is not so cute now that I know the reason you can finish each other's sentences," the prince said archly. "You probably called to him and that's why Rainere could shake off my sleep spell so soon, isn't it Adelena?"

"Tell me how you know my son's name," demanded Adelena and started to feel her pulse race in fear for another one of her children. Rainold was full of surprises and few of them had been pleasant so far. She didn't like that this mad prince could just drop Aaron's name so casually.

"I read the names of your children on your heart, Adelena," replied Rainold airily, waving the map-globe about. "Just as I read your name on Rainere's. It is a simple matter, if you know what to look for."

Rainere and Adele exchanged a glance and she could see that Rainere also found Rainold's answer just a little too glib to be believed.

"We are done here," Adele snapped, her patience and sympathy for the madman exhausted. She reached out and snatched the globe from Rainold's grasp. It was heavier than she expected, and she slipped it into the small bag she had at her waist, hoping the thin strap would hold. "It's time for us to go home."

Rainold nodded, looking from Adele to Rainere with a rueful smile. "A promise is a promise, Your Majesty," he agreed. "My boy is protected and yours will be too, in the end."

Adele frowned. She still had so many questions, but Rainold was already floating across the room, and out the door.

Chapter Forty-One

"The Trouble with Death"

Outside the house, the twilight had deepened and the breeze that ruffled Adele's hair was cooler now. Rainold pushed open the heavy wrought iron gates.

"This is as far as I go, children," Rainold said as he opened his arms wide to encompass them both. "You will have no idea what it means to me that you are both here, and that I got to see my beautiful son all grown up a man. And you, dear Adelena, I'm so glad you were worth destroying my family for." Rainold smiled sadly, as if he was unaware of the insult he had given her, and ran a hand through his shoulder length hair, looking so much the young man that he wasn't.

"Though I understand why you have to leave me, might we not exchange favors with each other, so that tomorrow when I do wake up alone I can look upon some small thing of yours and know it wasn't all just a dream? Something special that I couldn't possibly have invented to fool myself with." Rainold looked up at them both through his long dark lashes, and his bottom lip trembled, as if he was close to tears.

Rainere and Adele exchanged a glance, and Rainere nodded. "Take this." He thrust something at his father. It was the device, but the crystal was now smudged with soot, and the leather thong was charred and broken. "We used it to find you."

Rainold held the broken thing in his hands like it was a precious treasure, even giving it a kiss before he slipped it into a pocket. "And perhaps something from you, my sweet bastard-step-daughter-by-marriage?"

Adele hesitated. She really didn't want to mention the promise she had already given to Rainere's father, so instead she pulled a small bracelet from her wrist and offered it to him. Rainold slipped it over his own wrist and threw his arms around her for a hug. There was a brief moment of awkwardness when the bracelet got tangled in Adele's hair. Rainold laughed at his clumsiness and used the moment to squeeze her closer than was necessary, but she managed to pull away without yanking too much of her hair out. Then Rainold held Rainere in his arms for a long moment, pale tears glittering on his cheeks as the emotion became too much for him.

"I love you, darling, and I always have, please remember that," the prince smiled and clasped Rainere's hands in his own. "You'll come back and visit me again, won't you? If it's safe? I'll wait for you."

Rainere pale face didn't reflect his father's passion but neither did he avoid his touch this time. "I will do my best to free you from this prison, Father," he promised, and Adele saw a tiny flash of green spark up from their entwined hands, and the promise was made real. "Now that I know you are alive, I will not rest until you are brought back to Evendaar."

"That is all a father can ask of his son," said Rainold and ran a tender hand over Rainere's cheek. "Except perhaps, could you let your hair grow out, my handsome boy? I think it will suit you so much better than this crop."

Rainere nodded.

"Now, it is time for you to go!" Rainold announced theatrically, throwing his arms wide. "The entry to the portal is just over there where you came through the first time. Now a word of warning, when you wake Apex be very gentle..."

"I had to destroy the apex before we came through," interrupted Adele as she felt her stomach drop away. "I don't think it exists anymore."

Prince Rained looked genuinely surprised. "Apex is dead?"

"The apex, yes," agreed Adele cautiously.

"Well, isn't that something," said the prince and his smile stretched into a delighted laugh. "Then don't worry about my silly old advice at all. Apex is dead and you have a journey to make. Good luck with your daughter, my dear queen, and good luck with your queen my handsome prince." Prince Rainold stepped back and waved at them from a few feet away, as though they were boarding a cruise ship. "Bye, my lovelies. Good-bye."

Adele stepped out of the gate first and Rainere followed with a backward glance at his father. They saw the burnt line on the ground where they had landed the first time and stopped. She could see a very pale green haze above the line but had no clue as to go about forming a doorway. "Shall we just step over the line?" she asked Rainere.

Rainere took Adele's hand and she felt his calloused, cold skin against her own. "This time, maybe try to hold your breath," he suggested.

Adelena remembered how the magic that had flowed under her skin like armor and called on it to do this again. It rose to her command and she felt the weight of it flow down her body and slip across her hand to touch Rainere's.

"Hold on tight," she warned Rainere and took a deep breath. Reluctantly both Adele and Rainere stepped over the line and back through the death spell to be dumped sweating and spitting into the dark tunnel in Unisia. Adele, remembering the feeling of being watched by shadows, made sure they didn't waste any time hurrying out of the dark, and back to the basement room.

General Ohrig and Captain Lucky both started in surprise when Adele climbed out of the broken doorway and into the candle light. "Your Majesty, did you find anything?" asked Ohrig. "We don't have much night left so we'd better get going if you want to investigate anywhere else in the city."

In a flash, Adele understood that they had been to Rainold's Early Death dimension and back again, while no time at all had passed in the world of Evendaar. "It's done," she said and showed her men the globe Rainold had given her. "I've got the map to find a dragon."

Ohrig was silent but then a grim smile pulled up the corner of his mouth. "Of course you have," he said heavily, and exchanged a knowing look with Captain Lucky who only shook his head and rolled his eyes. "Why would you need all of us when you can just trip into another dimension and do everything by yourself?"

"I could never have done it without Prince Rainere," replied Adele and exchanged a loaded look with Rainere. They had needed each other.

"Now, we have what we came for we should return to the palace immediately," said Adele, and gestured for her men to gather. "There is no time to lose now that we know where the dragon is."

General Ohrig took the globe from Adele with her permission and slipped it into his jacket pocket to hide it from sight. He gestured for Adele to climb up the ladder in the basement room, and purposely stepped in front of Prince Rainere to be the one to help her up onto the first rung.

CHAPTER FORTY-TWO

"Magnanimity or Manipulation?"

The St Lucidis party started on their way back to the Golden Palace just as the sun was cresting the horizon, and Adele had a chance to see the city of Concordis waking up. The shops and markets were busily preparing themselves for a day of commerce and the scent of fresh, hot bread was in the air. There was a market set up in the huge town square, and when their carriage paused to pass the traffic of the stall-holders, Adele could watch, up close, as the ordinary folk of Unisia chatted and laughed amongst themselves as they worked. These people could have been from any city on Earth, and it struck Adele that even though they were aliens from another world, she looked like she could have belonged here.

Adele had been quiet the entire way back from the slums after she had given the general and the men a brief rundown of what had happened in Rainold's dimension. Rainere had decided to make his own way back to the Golden Palace.

As their carriage pulled up to the less conspicuous Stable Entrance of the Golden Palace, Adele pulled her cloak tight to cover her leather outfit and jumped down with a helping hand from Ohrig. The stable yards were always busy, but today there were at least two hundred Ordinary Army soldiers milling about in groups in the large courtyard, wearing their full military garb. Adele was alarmed, as she had never seen so many of them together before.

"Why are there so many soldiers here?" she asked the general. "Is something wrong?"

"It must be a training day," said Ohrig. "Every month, the Ordinary Army sends a battalion to train with the Royal Household Guard to keep their skills sharp, before they get too lazy from working inside a plush palace all day. They'll do weapons drills and basic fitness tests, that sort of thing."

"Does the Queen's Guard need to be a part of that too?"

"No," replied Ohrig and she could tell by his tone she had touched a nerve. "The Queen's Guard has never been considered as a real unit of the Household Guard or the Ordinary Army, so we train by ourselves."

"Damn right we do," huffed QG Bear behind her. "Those Army kittens couldn't keep up with us anyway, the general sees to that."

General Ohrig gave a proud nod. "We train much harder than anyone else," he agreed.

"Painfully so," added QG Leith with a grimace, and had his hair ruffled by QG Owens, who made a few snide comments about Leith's tendency to get injured and the whining that followed.

"Training once a month like this lot isn't going to get results, is it?" Ohrig sent Leith a stern frown, making the young QG duck his head, embarrassed. "We train for every situation, physically and mentally. No one thought we'd ever have a queen to defend though, so who's laughing now, eh lads?"

"Queen's Guard," shouted the Queen's Guard in unison and grinned at each other, and even Pepper smiled at the shout. Adele was reminded that he didn't do that so much of that any more, after the battle in the Spider's Nest. She told herself to make time for the young man as soon as things settled down. The thought reminded her of another young man.

"Lucky, could you please check up on Charlie's whereabouts?" Adele asked. "Hopefully, one of your sources has been able to find some trace of where he might be. I'll see if Rainere can ask Grotto, as well." She still couldn't believe that Charlie would have run away when he had seemed so keen to be a part of her world.

"Your Majesty." Lucky nodded and took his leave, dashing off down a corridor to do as she bid him. The rest of the men left too, heading for their barracks to get some sleep after a busy night. It was only General Ohrig who accompanied Adele back to the royal apartments.

Naturally, he had a reason for doing so. Ohrig didn't waste his own time lightly, and his determined expression meant that he had a few hard questions for his queen.

"Your Majesty, permission to speak frankly?" asked Ohrig just before they reached the door to the royal apartment. The steward, Hollis, was on duty and she waved him back when he spotted her coming down the hallway. She knew if Hollis opened that door, one of her children would dash out and the quiet moment with her general would be lost.

"Go ahead, Ohrig," said Adele. "But I know what you want to ask, and the answer is no, I did not agree marry Rainere or Prince Rainold in exchange for the map." She raised an eyebrow at her general and hoped he appreciated the joke. He did.

"And you didn't manage to kill anyone, did you?" Ohrig gave her a crooked smile, but his pale blue eyes were serious. "Forgive me, Your Majesty, but you do have a tendency to leave out important details like that when you recount your adventures to me."

The apex spell slipped into Adele's mind. Prince Rainold had called it 'Apex' like it was an actual being, and not *the* apex, and Adele had definitely felt for herself that the spell had possessed a malevolent energy. "The spell I destroyed protecting the prison dimension gave me the feeling that it was almost sentient," mused Adele.

Ohrig's frown deepened. "Do you think that might be a problem for us going forward?"

Adele laughed mirthlessly and patted Ohrig on the shoulder. *What a question.* "My guess is, I've totally screwed something else up in Evendaar and we won't know what that is until it's too late." Adele smiled but the sarcasm was tempered by the fact she was afraid it was true. "Go get some rest, Ohrig, and I'll promise not to cause any more chaos until I see you this afternoon."

Ohrig only nodded and took his worried frown away with him back to the barracks, made no lighter by her words.

With a deep sigh, Adele walked to the door of her apartment and was pleased to share a greeting with Hollis. For a man who only opened doors and ran messages all day, the steward had a permanently cheerful demeanor, and never asked anything uncomfortable of her at all.

Adele's little dawn-risers, Natalie and Aaron, were already awake when she entered the living room. The children were at the dining table with Mrs. Ollenby and their three nannies, eating breakfast and chatting away happily with them. It was such a sweet domestic scene but Adele's heart still tore at the corner as she couldn't help but see who was missing. Adele decided she would visit Stella after giving some precious time to her older children.

"Mummy!" The happy cry of Natalie and Aaron forced away her dark thoughts and Adele joined her little family for breakfast, letting Natalie butter her toast and Aaron spoon scrambled eggs on to her plate and a little onto her lap. Adele shrugged off her cape. She had completely forgotten about her tough-girl leather outfit until she heard a gasp from Siobahn.

"Your Majesty, you look amazing!" gasped the young brunette, and the other two nannies giggled in agreement.

"Ah, yes." Adele pulled her cape back over her shoulders, embarrassed. "I should probably get changed."

Mrs. Ollenby gave Adele a wink and a tinkly laugh. "I'm sure it was right for the occasion, Your Majesty, but perhaps something more comfortable would be better for the breakfast table."

As little as Adele wanted to leave her children, even for a minute, she knew Mrs. Ollenby made a good point, so she went into her bedroom and went to find something a little less constrictive.

Adele spotted the dressed mannequin immediately but was reluctant to put on the heavy gown with the lace train, as she'd never manage it on her own anyway. Instead, Adele went into the vast walk-in closet within her dressing room, to find one of the soft, floaty gowns that had been a gift from the Empress of Sandar on her visit there. Adele found them hanging right at the back and picked the pink one to wear. It took a few minutes to peel herself out of the tight pants and heavy boots but the relief to be out of leather was enough to make her sigh with pleasure. Adele hung the jacket and bodice up on a rail and slipped the pink layers of silk over her head and let them fall over her body… and then to the floor.

"Dammit," Adele swore, and pulled the dress back up to her shoulders, trying to find the ribbons at the back of her dress that kept it up.

There was a low cough behind her, and Adele spun to see Rainere leaning against one of the rails in her closet. Before Adele could protest his presence, Rainere gestured to the secret door that joined her closet to the small staircase that led to Stella's room. "I had wanted to check the princess, I hope that is alright?" he said.

Adele held bunches of fabric over her chest, trying to cover her nakedness but all thoughts went to her baby. "Of course it's fine, how is she?"

"No change," replied Rainere and stepped towards her. "And that is good news, Adelena. No change is exactly what we want for her." His eyes dropped to Adele's bare shoulders.

"I know you're right but it doesn't change the fact I'm still waiting for a miracle." Adele turned her back to Rainere and knew he would take it as a sign to approach her.

"Of course, a miracle would be preferable to a dangerous journey hunting dragons." Rainere was only a step behind her now and his hands reached for the ribbons on the back of her gown. With a murmured 'May I?' he did them up for her, but didn't take his hands away from her back. "Though after the attack in the Lower Districts, I can't really believe that the Golden Palace is any safer for you."

Adele thought of the promise she had made to Prince Rainold to leave Rainere behind when she journeyed to find the dragon. She wondered if perhaps it might not be the best thing after all. The journey might be far too long and dangerous to take Aaron and

Natalie with her, and with Stella in a stasis coma, there was no possible way to move her. However, with Rainere forced to remain at the Golden Palace, Adele would have one of the most powerful and canny wizards in the whole of Unisia to watch over her children while she was gone.

Adelena's thoughts were suddenly overshadowed by the accusation that Rainold had made when he said that she manipulated Rainere for her own ends, and that Rainere always suffered because of it. *Or was that just how I heard him say it?* she wondered, guilt laying heavy in the bottom of her stomach.

Adelena turned to face Prince Rainold. *It wouldn't be manipulation if I told Rainere everything, and gave him a choice though, would it?*

"Rainere, I haven't thanked you properly for saving us from those men in the slums," she said and looked up at the prince as they stood almost, but not quite, touching. Through a determined act of will Adele stepped back to give them both some space. "No one else would have been able to do what you did, not even Ohren."

"*Not even Ohren,*" Rainere mimicked her with a bitter twist on his lips. "Are you so convinced it wasn't the High Wizard who sent those men after you last night, Adelena?" Rainere caught a stray strand of her hair and pushed it behind her ear. "You must beware of Ohren. I don't think that he means to be stupid or closed-minded, but the man has lived with power and control for a very long time. Ohren honestly believes he is invincible and that his way is the only way to do things. You see that, don't you?"

Adele wondered if she were the only one here trying to emotionally manipulate the other. Of course Rainere would want her to question her trust in Ohren as all-powerful, because then she would believe she needed Rainere even more. Yet, despite her misgivings, she knew that Rainere spoke a kind of truth. To fulfill the prophecy he believed in, High Wizard Ohren would do whatever, sacrifice whomever, and say anything he had to.

Adele's head suddenly ached from the layers of complexity in her life.

"And who's to say it wasn't Grottonski who organized the attack?" she asked. "It's obvious to everyone that he wants me dead, and he knew you would never be harmed."

Rainere's cheeks heated and he retreated from her without even moving. His eyes going hard and flat, and his mouth became a straight line. "You think I am as easily confused as the High Wizard is, and that I can fooled by those about me without using my own reason and intelligence? Grotto couldn't use me like that, no matter how much I trusted him."

Adele resisted the impulse to touch Rainere's flaming cheeks. "What I'm saying, Rainere, is that all of us are caught up in our own little melodramas," she said. "Everybody is operating under their own rules, and as long as I can understand what the rules are, I don't have to like them, I just have to learn how to avoid being trapped by them. Do you know what I mean?"

Rainere tilted his head to the side and his gaze softened into something more intimate. "I know exactly what you mean." He smiled one of his gorgeous half-smiles. "I love you with every fiber of my being, Adelena, and nothing can keep me from protecting you and your family. That's the only set of rules I live by."

Adele shook her head and smiled ruefully. "And as long as all the players in this game know that about you, they will keep manipulating you by putting me in danger to prompt action from you. Rainere, please, you have to be careful with these people. They fear you, and all you can do, and they don't want you to have any influence over me. We can't let the court know just *how much* I trust you."

"Do you trust me?" Rainere dipped his face to hers, and the silver rings around his pupils lit up with excitement. "Adelena, what are you saying?"

Adele held her hands up between them. "I'm saying that I need you on my side, Rainere, but…"

"But not in your bed," Rainere finished.

Adele shook her head slowly but could not drop her gaze from Rainere's face as he struggled to control the storm of emotions that flickered in his eyes.

Rainere surprised her by leaning in and giving Adele a sudden and gentle kiss, before he stepped away again. "Your forgiveness is a gift I won't forget, Adelena," Rainere said, his voice only a rasp. "And I will not ask for more than that from you. Not yet."

Adele opened her mouth to tell Rainere he couldn't go with her to find the dragon, and to ask him to stay with her children but something held her silent. Was it guilt? Or was it a simple desire to hold this one perfect moment between them without wrecking it with her tactlessness?

Adele held out her hand to Rainere. "Come with me," she said. "We can have breakfast with the children before we go to see the high wizard."

CHAPTER FORTY-THREE

"Grinners Are Winners"

Charlie decided that this particular day was turning out to be the worst day of his life, and that was saying something for someone with luck as bad as his.

His head still pounded from the Key Master's generous punch, and his stomach cramped with hunger. At a word from the guard at the Green Team pole, Charlie had a pickaxe shoved into his hand and was made to follow behind a small group of four kids who took him to an opening on the edge of the mountain side. They stood in a row before another guard and were given complicated directions to the new seam they were to work on. Each kid took a lantern from a box at the mine entrance.

Charlie had never mined in his life. He was a city boy through and through, and his arms already ached just from carrying the heavy pickaxe as he followed his team, sweating his way down, down, down, deep into the side of the mountain. The tunnels were narrow and propped up by dodgy-looking, wooden supports that didn't appear strong enough to hold themselves up, never mind stop a cave-in.

Their team stopped at a juncture in the tunnels and consulted with a tall kid who was standing there to check the buckets of another group as they made their way back up the tunnel. Charlie's team shuffled to the side of the narrow space, their backs pushed up against dirt walls, as the other team passed them, buckets full of grey rock and their picks held over their shoulders. Charlie was shocked to see that the girl checking the buckets had bright green eyes, almost iridescent in the light. "Is that an elf down here?" he asked the little girl in the line in front of him but he didn't receive an answer.

The heat in the tunnel was starting to get unbearable, but only Charlie appeared to be uncomfortable when the group finally reached the source of the seam. The seam of crystal was in a natural chamber in the mountain bedrock. Spherical, like a geode, it had hundreds of sharp spikes of grey crystals pointing out from the circular walls. The roof was a few feet above their heads and maybe twenty feet across. Charlie watched as the rest of his team fetched buckets from a pile of them in the middle of the chamber, then started chipping away at the grey rock in between the jagged edges of crystal.

Charlie took a place and put his bucket down. There didn't seem to be a supervisor amongst his team, just four small, sad kids who had their eyes on the rock. Charlie judged the oldest was about his age, a skinny boy with ropey arms and rock powder dusting his short, black hair. The youngest was the little girl Charlie had tried to speak to before and couldn't have been more than ten or eleven. She wielded her pick like an expert, and it was only with the flash of green at her hands that Charlie realized these kids were using magic to give strength to their arms so they could hack away at the wall with more than natural force. He grimaced. No wonder they were all so dull, they were concentrating so hard on channeling their power they wouldn't have the energy for anything else. Charlie heard a noise at the entrance to the chamber and was surprised to see Leafy enter accompanied by the bucket-checker who looked like an elf.

Leafy's eyes were wide and she didn't greet Charlie aloud but managed to give him a little wave without the elf noticing.

"This is the new seam," said the tall elf-girl, pushing Leafy towards the spikes of crystal. "As a Special, it will be your job to pull the spikes from the wall and imbue them."

"What's imbue?" asked Leafy in her tiny voice.

The elf sighed and forced Leafy's hand onto one of the spikes. All at once, Leafy's eyes lit up, the silver rings spinning around her pupils and sparking with power. Charlie watched horrified as the crystal seemed to pulse into life, and green magic from Leafy's hand flowed into the smoky, grey depths. Leafy finally managed to wrench her hand away and cradled it to her chest, sobbing.

"It hurts less when the crystals are out of the mountain, and under the sun," said the elf, but not at all kindly. "You will be expected to imbue all the crystals that are brought out at the end of the day. This seam has yet to be properly cleared of false crystal, but when the work is finished you will come in here and pull the crystals with the other Special."

The elf-girl turned and left the chamber, expecting Leafy to follow. The little girl gave Charlie the tiniest of smiles through her tears before she left too, stumbling back into the dark tunnel. Charlie wished she hadn't, the gesture almost broke his heart. Poor Leafy was too young and too stupid to see there was no reason left in the world to smile.

Charlie turned back to his wall before anyone noticed he cared about Leafy and raised his pickaxe. The first strike jarred his arms enough to make him swear and drop the pick. The second strike only chipped away a tiny piece of the dull rock, or false crystal, barely making a dent. Charlie looked about at the others on his team and saw that even with the magic in their arms they weren't making much headway on clearing the rock from between the crystal spikes. He found a relatively clear place to lean on the wall and wiped his forehead, dust coming away with the sweat.

"You have to fill the bucket." The order had come from the older boy, his voice was thick and croaky. "Our team cannot leave until all our buckets are filled. The quicker we do that, the quicker we get out of here."

Charlie flicked his fringe off his forehead and appraised the boy. He hadn't detected any belligerence or attempt to bully him; the kid was just stating hard fact. "My name's Charlie," he told the boy. "How long've you been here?"

The boy snarled in response but his heart wasn't in it enough to be aggressive. He was far too beaten down and tired for that. His hollow cheeks and grey skin spoke of a long time in the mines. "I used to be Joel," he said and gave the wall in front of him a hard whack, chipping several small pieces off, and then bent down to put them in his bucket. "But now I'm just a digger. I've been here," - he whacked the wall again and a larger piece broke away, the rest of the team gave him a jealous glance then got back to work – "for two months, I think."

Two months, shit! I-Used-To-Be-Joel looked like an old man, and though the magic glittered greenly on his palms, the silver circles around his eyes were tarnished and slow as if they had been used to exhaustion. The kid wasn't going to last much longer like this. Charlie tried to quieten the panic in his mind that began shrieking warnings that soon he would look like I-Used-To-Be-Joel.

Charlie wanted to get out of this mine now. Without really thinking, he ran a tiny string of magic into his hands and when his pick hit the wall, there was the sound of a sharp crack, and the wall crumbled away from between the crystals, falling into a heap. When the wall stopped moving, Charlie had a large pile of rock in front of him, with several long crystals resting on the top. Not wanting to touch them, Charlie nudged them off the pile with his foot. He turned to face his team and was surprised to find them all staring at him, horror painted on their faces.

"There you go," said Charlie generously. "That's enough rock to fill everyone's buckets, isn't it?"

"No!" gasped I-Used-To-Be-Joel. "You can't do that, you're a digger. If they see you've dislodged the crystal they'll make you a Special. I have to tell the guard."

"Don't!" A girl stepped forward and brandished her pickaxe. At least Charlie thought it was a girl but the short hair and the dust made it hard to tell. "If you tell the guard then we'll lose another team mate, and we need him to finish our quota." She gave Charlie a look that was as canny as it was desperate. "Hide the crystals inside the hole in the wall. We'll wait for nightfall, and then take our buckets up like always. If we go up now, the guard will know something happened down here and they'll investigate. This way if we leave the fallen rock, when the guards do their morning check they will think that the wall collapsed naturally in the night.

I-Used-To-Be-Joel, and the other kids gazed covetously at Charlie's pile of rock. "So we just keep working?" asked Charlie. "Even though there is all this rock here? Surely, the guards wouldn't miss a bucket or two of it?"

"Don't touch it!" snapped the girl. "Maya will kill you in your sleep if you screw up the plan."

Charlie frowned. "Who's Maya?"

"I am," said the girl and resolutely turned her back on Charlie to begin chipping away at her part of the wall again.

These kids are so bloody weird, thought Charlie as he resigned himself to Maya's plan. He didn't think much of her threat to kill him. She was only a bag of bones with eyes, and he felt confident that he could take her. What he didn't like was the fear and madness that lit her expression, and the way the others had bowed to her plan. That meant they were either scared of her, or her plan actually made sense. He gingerly kicked the large crystals he had dislodged into a more scattered arrangement and piled a few rocks on top of them to look as if they had fallen that way naturally. With a deep sigh, Charlie moved to another part of the wall and began to chip again, this time without using any magic at all.

It was a long day. None of the kids spoke to one another in the chamber as they worked, and by a silent, general consent, the smallest girl slipped away at one point and came back carrying a handful of canteen straps in one hand and a leather sack in the other. The break was short, but Charlie hadn't eaten in over a day, so the hard bread and animal grease sandwich was welcome, even with the dust on his hands that added an unpleasant grit to each mouthful. The water in the canteen was warm and slightly sour, but Charlie couldn't detect any poison, and he was so thirsty most of it had gone before he had even thought to ask himself the question.

The only thing that got Charlie through the backbreaking labor was that the silence allowed him to continue his conversation with Queen Adelena. He wasn't stupid enough to project her image in the air, but he imagined her in his mind's eye as clear as day. The queen was a caring mother and she would be horrified to see the conditions of the children working here in the mine. He would bet his next meal that she didn't even know that this mine existed in Unisia, and the minute she did, she would lay waste to the Key Master and all the other shit-bags who ran the place.

Charlie concentrated on remembering every line and hair on Ranger Cedric's head. *He would be one of the first to go down when the queen was told about the work he did.* The priest, Pere Raven was a different story. He had clearly been working with the Rangers to round up all the kids with magic in the village, but he hadn't been on the wagon when Charlie had arrived. Whatever the story, he had a lot of questions to answer when Queen Adelena got ahold of him, and Charlie would be right by her side feeding them to her, when she did.

Though his daydreams didn't get romantic, Charlie was filled with pleasure as he mentally described to Queen Adelena all of the hardships he had suffered to get back to her and reveal the awful truth about the mines. He described the burning hunger and the pain of the blisters on his hands as they popped, raw and weeping, holding the pickaxe. He coughed as the dust started to build in his lungs, and he added that to the list of dreadful hardships that the queen would hear about. Charlie promised himself that if he managed to survive this work camp, then he would return to the Golden Palace a hero.

After spending so much undisturbed time in his own head, it was almost annoying when Maya announced sunset and Charlie was able to fill his bucket with the rock he had chipped, only surreptitiously borrowing a few from the fallen pile, and followed the others out of the mine and up to the surface of the camp. His team showed him where to dump the buckets of false crystal in a large open wagon, and the place to leave the pick axes and lanterns.

There was no time to wash before all the workers joined the long queue for the dinner meal. As he stood in the line feeling filthy and exhausted, Charlie couldn't help but look around to get the lay of the land. In his experience, Charlie knew there was a clear hierarchy between those with weapons and those without them, but he also knew that there were pecking orders within pecking orders too. Charlie straightaway noticed that there were a group of older kids who were wearing bulky blue jackets that looked padded and very warm in the chilly night air. They weren't lining up for food like the others but walked to the head of the line and had their bowls slopped full to the brim. Charlie cast a glance down the line of bedraggled kids in front of him and didn't see one of them complain. That meant something in itself. If you had a blue jacket, you had power.

Charlie poked the kid in front of him. "Oi, you," he whispered. "How do you get one of those blue jackets?"

But Charlie was stopped from asking again by a stinging sensation across his shoulders that was so intense it took a moment for his brain to properly register the pain. He spun to face his assailant and came face to face with the Key Master.

"No talkin' on line," said the Key Master. The look on his face was cold and bored, as if he didn't even remember Charlie from this morning, but the two Blue Jackets behind him were grinning like street-cats over a mouse. The Key Master moved on up the line, twirling his whip in his hands and leaving the two grinners behind him.

"New kid, has to be, innit?" said the grinner with the thick bull-neck, and small green eyes. His cheek sported an angry red welt that was infected and sore looking. Maybe in his early twenties and twice as heavy as Charlie, this grinner had the nasal drawl and dropped 'h's' of a town-dweller.

"Yep, new kid," agreed the second grinner. This guy was lanky but taller than the other one, with a crop of brown hair on his narrow head. His blue jacket was much too small for him, barely reaching to his bony wrists.

Charlie sized the pair up for weapons but all he could detect was the overblown confidence of bullies who felt themselves untouchable. And this — this he could work with.

"He's still got those soft pretty hands on him," said the Big Grinner. "Probably hasn't done a day's work in his life." He sniffed the air around Charlie. "I can almost smell the perfume on this princess."

Charlie doubted that he smelled anything like a princess after a day in the mines, but he decided to save his sarcasm for those with enough intellect to understand it. Instead, he got right to the point. "You boys couldn't show a fella where to get one of those blue jackets, could you? It's a mite chilly tonight." Charlie squared his shoulders but held himself lightly, one foot in front of the other.

The Skinny Grinner snorted. "Hear him! He wants a blue jacket now, after only a day in here!"

The Big Grinner's eyes narrowed. "You don't wanna be askin' for things on your first day, new boy. You gotta earn this jacket, or you gotta kill the kid who was wearing it first."

Charlie felt a spike of fear but pushed it back. Adrenalin was only good when it made his reflexes faster, not when it swamped his confidence.

The Big Grinner nudged his mate. "This kid thinks he can take me. Look at 'im!" He leaned towards Charlie, putting his hands on his knees to bend low as if Charlie was a child. "You think you can take me, new boy?"

Charlie licked his dry lips. Magic was hard enough to conjure when he was fit, and now he was dehydrated, hungry and exhausted. He tried to focus and held his hand out to the side forming a tight fist and moving slowly enough to ensure that the two goons followed his every move. Internally, he was scrambling to connect to the power that rested within him, deep in his chest, below his heart. He pulled a chunk of it out from the rest and drew it down to his other hand and pushed it out to coalesce in his palm. It felt like it took forever to do but it was the work of moments before Charlie held the power in his hand. It wasn't a perfect sphere, more of a rough, rock shape, but it was going to be hard and it was going to hurt.

When the Big Grinner pulled himself upright and saw Charlie with his hovering fist, he laughed. "Have a go, will ya?"

Charlie took his chance and with well-practiced aim, he lobbed the ball of magic right at his opponent's groin.

With a satisfying grunt, the older boy doubled over, clutching between his legs and gasping for air. Then before Charlie could turn his attention to the other one, he saw something fall out of the Big Grinner's shirtfront - it was his amulet. Desperate to have it back, Charlie leapt forward to snatch at the precious necklace and rip it from the bull neck of his enemy.

The move cost him dearly, however, as the Skinny Grinner was smarter than he looked and had slipped behind Charlie to pull his arms back sharply, putting his own around the front of Charlie's shoulders and then clamping his hands behind Charlie's head. With his arms locked tight, Charlie could only flail and kick his legs as the amulet dangling from his fingers was snatched away and the Big Grinner hauled himself up from his knees.

"You've just dropped yourself in the shit now, new boy," snarled the Big Grinner and Charlie tightened his gut in anticipation of the blows, desperately hoping his kicking legs would make contact before he was knocked out.

But it was worse than that.

Big Grinner stepped right inside Charlie's guard and slammed his meaty fist against Charlie's temple.

There was blackness. There were stars. There was pain, and there was a rolling, swishing nausea that let him know he was being moved. Charlie could see light as someone pulled one of his eyelids open. A primitive instinct for survival forced him to keep his focus on the light, just as a blurry face and two indigo blue eyes swam into his vision.

"Stay down, kid," the indigo eyes seemed to say. "I'll get you out of here." They were kind eyes, crinkled at the sides and edged in sandy brown lashes. So, for better or worse, Charlie let go of the light and the nauseating darkness claimed him once more.

CHAPTER FORTY-FOUR

"Map of The World"

Adelena had never been inside High Wizard Ohren's laboratory before. It was a large, square room, with a set of louvered windows on one side and three huge fireplaces on the other. The windows were opened to let in the breeze, which cooled the last of the afternoon heat, and brought in the sounds of insects from the terraced garden outside. The scent of warm herbs fragranced the air. Beneath her feet, the floorboards were speckled with stains and burns, and there were three long tables set up in a u-shape, with another counter facing them, as if ready for a science class. Glass bottles, various distillation paraphernalia, metal pots filled with different colored powders, tiny cauldrons, loose scrolls and sheets of paper decorated every surface of the tables and floor beneath them. Obviously, High Wizard Ohren preferred a messy work space.

Ohren was sitting at his counter writing on a scroll when Adele led the Queen's Guard and Prince Rainere into the room with a lot of noise and chatter, but High Wizard Ohren didn't even look up.

"Ohren, do you have a moment for us?" asked Adele, and didn't try to keep the acid out of her tone. "We've been waiting all day to show you the map that Prince Rainold gave us, and I also have another matter to discuss with you."

Ohren was pale and his blue eyes took a moment to focus on Adele before he looked over her shoulder and snapped, "Don't touch that!"

Captain Lucky was squatting inside one of the cold fireplaces and examining a dark stain in the coal tray. He stood up at the High Wizard's command.

"Was this stain made by the spider corpse we left here, High Wizard?" asked Lucky and stepped out of the fireplace. "Did you manage to examine it before it disintegrated?"

Ohren's eyes widened and he looked at Adelena. "Why was there a spider corpse in my laboratory?" he asked in a strangled voice.

Adele could barely remember the episode of finding the Spider, Oki, in her bedroom the night before she left for Sandar, so much had happened since to reduce it to only a minor trauma in her memory.

"I forgot to tell you that the Empress Ka-kik sent one of her sons to communicate with me before I left for Sandar." Adele shrugged at Ohren's horrified expression. "The creature appeared to me in its spider form in my bedroom and, naturally, I asked Lucky to kill it for me, which he did amazingly fast. You threw a knife at its head, didn't you, Captain?"

Lucky acknowledged the compliment with a modest nod. "I had never seen such a thing out of my Accadaemia text-books before, High Wizard, I thought to leave it in your laboratory in case you wanted to study it. I did leave you a note with a brief explanation but we left for Sandar the next day and there was no time for discussion."

"I didn't see any note." Ohren glared heavily at the young captain. "But I did find a huge, weeping mess of green gunk putrefying in a puddle on my floor. It took two days before it was properly destroyed, and I still haven't got the smell out of the walls." He turned back to Adele. "But that doesn't explain why you wanted it dead?"

"Even on my world spiders are dangerous, and this one was the size of a dog," replied Adele, affronted. "I didn't know at the time that it was a magical creature who wanted to talk to me and make an alliance between our people."

Ohren cocked an eyebrow. "And if you had?"

Adele hesitated, and frowned at the thought. *What would she have done if that hideous creature had introduced himself in human form first?*

"If you've quite finished making the queen question her judgement of past decisions, High Wizard?" Prince Rainere's voice cut through the tension like a knife. "Perhaps we should get to the matter at hand."

Adele tried to focus but a sudden clamoring of questions had swamped her head. *What if? What if? What if?* She barely felt it when General Ohrig touched her elbow. "Your Majesty?"

"Hmmm?" Adele looked up to see that her Queen's Guard had stepped in around her, concern and smiles on their faces. It felt like being surrounded by family.

"You did the right thing that night," said Ohrig firmly. "You should trust your instincts more, Your Majesty."

"Because we do," added QG Pepper, and Adele was deeply touched.

"Thank you, Pepper," said Adele and Pepper gave her a shy smile. ducking his head. "I wouldn't want to have any one else but my Queen's Guard to help me find this dragon."

"Hell, yes!" QG Bear and Owens exchanged a grin. "Hunting dragons sounds like a holiday in comparison to what we've just done anyway."

"As long as there aren't any dank, dark pits, I'll be happy," said QG Owens and made all the men check Pepper for his reaction to the joke, but Pepper only looked down at his feet, his cheeks flaming.

"I'm not sure about a pit but there will definitely be a dank, dark cave." High Wizard Ohren's voice carried from the other side of the room. He and the prince stood next to a long bench that had been cleared of its junk and the map sat trembling and beautiful on the surface of the table. Adele and the QG's moved to join the two wizards and marveled at the detailed world before them.

"It's an unusual way to present a map," said General Ohrig, answering Adele's first question. "How can we tell which is the exact path that Prince Rainold took to get to the cave of the dragon?"

"Here." Rainere pointed to the base of the tiny, perfectly formed Black Mountains Range. "This is the last point at which a portal can be formed. I have been there recently. We can only get so far with magic. We will have to pass through the Black Mountains by the old trade route through the valley."

"No other road exists?" asked the general.

Prince Rainere pointed to the little mountains. "These are sheer cliff faces here and all along here. There is a flatter path, but it travels into the Nation of Dos, then around the mountain range, and that would be far riskier."

"What are the dangers for us passing through the valley?" Adele asked, not liking the look of the shadows and dark places in the mountain range.

"It's hard to say, perhaps nothing lives there anymore," mused the High Wizard. "But knowing your luck, with these things we'll probably find nests of wasps lining the valley."

Adele looked alarmed. "You have wasps in Evendaar? I hate wasps."

"They are supposed to be extinct, Your Majesty," said Ohren. "Killed by the Goddess herself when she discovered that they had eaten most of the mountain tribespeople she'd created a thousand years ago."

"But you're not sure they're gone though?" Adele frowned. "Mind you wasps are nasty things on Earth but I'm sure yours change into human form and are able to be negotiated with, right?"

"Shadow Wasps were said to be as big as a pony, with sharp incisors that could bite a man in half and the ability to fly for days at a time. I don't think there was much to be negotiated with them as they were fairly mindless killers," explained Ohren.

"I believe they did have the ability to become invisible, hence their name," added Captain Lucky. "I did a project on dark entities for my Accadaemia portfolio one year, and I don't believe anyone has added to the research since then."

"Did that project include dragons?" asked Adele and was pleased when Lucky nodded.

"I'm sure High Wizard Ohren and His Highness know more than me but I have a basic knowledge of their habits and magical properties," Lucky said. Adele could tell that her captain was uncomfortable with being the center of attention, but he raised his chin and continued:

"Dragons share the same origins as the gods. They came from the same world and travelled together to Evendaar back when the doors between worlds were open. The dragons have often been described as the Steeds of the Gods, but this is inaccurate. The relationships between dragons and gods was more like a relationship between equals, and these relationships were both monogamous and inter-dependent - a dragon belonged to a god, and the god belonged to the dragon.

"In our world of Evendaar, the gods and dragons chose to take on physical forms. The gods favored the bodies of beautiful men and women, but the dragons' magic was too difficult to contain in such a small body, so they created the giant dragon form to more safely encompass their power. Despite retaining a physical body, they remain immortal and invincible creatures of magic. This is why all of their properties are able to heal the sick and even bring the dead back to life. Their magic is the most powerful in all Evendaar."

Lucky had slightly pink cheeks when he finished his speech but he held his formal stance and Adele thanked her handsome captain, as the questions tumbled through her mind.

"Are dragons kind as well as being powerful?" Adele asked, thinking back to the childhood fairy tales of Earth.

"Dragons are said to have different personalities and preferences, just like the gods do, Your Majesty," answered Lucky. "Some were considered evil, while others performed great deeds in Evendaar, giving all sorts of gifts to the human tribes that they favored.

"There is a tale of the dragon, Sighmere, the mate of the goddess Serena, who so loved the human tribes she created, that he went off to the frozen wastelands in the north of Evendaar to melt the ice and create more arable land for their settlements and villages. He had not returned from his mission when the war with the dark entities forced the Goddess Serena to leave Evendaar, closing the doorway behind her to stop any other dark entities traveling to Evendaar. It is said that Sighmere still sleeps under a mountain of ice, waiting for his goddess to rescue him from this world and bring him home to the Realm of the Gods."

"According to Marchant lore, Sighmere watches over the favored tribes of Serena, sharing his gifts with them, and ensuring their longevity in Evendaar," added Rainere. "But as there hasn't been a sighting in an eon, the lore has become myth."

"This is why Prince Rainold went to the Eeyrie to find the lost knowledge of the dragon's lair." Ohren pulled at his beard, deep in thought. "Of course he could have stolen all those dragon artifacts from the Eeyrie but I don't think so, he was gone for so long."

"But that is madness," Rainere said, confused. "Why would my father have gone to find the Eeyrie at all? What did he hope to do there?"

Ohren looked off out the window. "It was a dare, I believe," he said. "Some idiot dared him to find the Eeyrie and Prince Rainold took them up on it. Of course, he won."

"A dare?" Rainere narrowed his eyes at Ohren. "High Wizard, how well did you know my father?"

"This isn't helpful." Ohren abruptly turned back to the map. "Barring attacks from extinct wasps, we will travel through the valley of the Black Mountains until we reach the Barren Plains, and from there cross into the tundra, where we will come to the Ice Mountains. Hopefully, the people of the Ice Tribes will be welcoming and can lead us on a safe path to the mountain where the dragon rests. If it is indeed Sighmere like the legend suggests, he should be amenable to a request from a St Lucidis queen with dark magic in her hands."

"How long do we think this journey will take?" asked Adele, scanning the map, and seeing that the delightful tiny landforms would, in reality, be huge impediments to their journey. "If we travel by portal to the base of the Black Mountains, and then by horse through the mountains, and then on through the rest of it?"

The silence was strained as calculations were made. "Based on this map and the detailed terrain, I would venture to guess, perhaps a month, barring injury or death," suggested Prince Rainere, watching Adele closely for her reaction.

Adele felt the air leave her lungs. "It will be too dangerous to take the children on a trip like this, but an entire month away from them will be too long for me."

"I meant a month each way, Your Majesty," Rainere corrected her gently. "Two, in total."

Adele had to sit down as her knees buckled and she slumped onto a nearby stool. "What am I supposed to do?" she whispered to herself. "Stella will surely die if I don't go, but if I do go, I risk something awful happening to Aaron and Natalie without me here to protect them." She looked up at Rainere. To leave her children with him for a week or so would have been a risk she could take, but two months or more, and Adele was plagued by doubts again.

Rainere gave her the slightest of smiles. "While it is true that you do seem to be a magnet for dark entities, it is also true that you succeed whenever you are expected to fail. Having studied them extensively as a child, I will be able to guide us through the Dark Mountains unscathed. I would also hope that as soon as we get through the Dark Mountains then the magic in the atmosphere will become stable again and we can use the portals to travel, saving time."

Adele pulled herself to her feet and wondered about her decision to leave Rainere behind. *Would it make her journey faster to take him with all his knowledge and experience? Or should he remain behind to use his power to protect the children?* It seemed an impossible decision for Adelena. *Or is it that I am too stupid to find another answer?* She berated herself.

Gazing down at the map again, she noticed that there was a little golden light at the base of one of the peaks in the Ice Mountains. She pointed at it. "So this light marks the spot where the dragon is?" It was so far away from the tiny replica of the Golden Palace where it sat surrounded by its miniature manicured gardens.

All heads dropped to examine the map more closely. "Yes," confirmed Ohren. "Right on the border of the Known Lands."

Adele frowned at the fuzzy line where the Ice Mountains stopped. "That is where the world of Evendaar ends?" she asked. "Isn't your world a sphere, like Earth."

"No, our world is flat, 'like a platter amongst the stars' to quote a famous poem," said Ohren. "The sun revolves around the world, bringing day and night and the seasons, just like on Earth. Though in this dimension the Universe revolves around Evendaar."

Incredibly interesting as it was, this new information didn't solve a single one of Adelena's problems. She chewed her lip and tried to fight despair. Ohren had told her that he travelled across the stars to find her in her bedroom on Earth. *If his magic could do that, then how come it can't send me somewhere distant on the same world?* Adele thought of Rainold in his strange bubble dimension. Somehow, the Eldars had managed to slide an entire new world in-between the layers of time and space, trapping him there. At her call, the gold magic in Adele woke up and crept into her mind, covering her head in a light mantle. There was never an easy answer to the problems presented to her in this ridiculous world, but every time she killed a monster, her power grew and so did her strength. Adelena's mind whirled and visions of what she had seen in Rainold's world flooded her mind.

"It seems a little out of kilter to me that there is a Marchant spell to create an entirely new dimension," mused Adele. "but that no one has worked out a way of getting from one side of Evendaar to the other. Surely, we could just somehow just slide our way through the gaps left by these spherical dimensions. Then we wouldn't have to go very far at all, or at least the travelling wouldn't take up any time, and time is what I don't have a lot of right now."

High Wizard Ohren snorted at Adele's simplistic view of magic but Rainere caught on immediately and his face lit up at the idea. "Getting into the non-dimension between space and time could be possible and wouldn't require the airborne magic which is necessary to portals. Yet for such a large group to travel altogether, the spell would have to be devastatingly complex."

"But you can do it?" asked Adele, excited by Rainere's enthusiasm.

"I will return to the Grey Palace tonight to do some research in the Great Library, and see what I can find on transportation spells," Rainere answered with a nod.

"You have one night to do what you can," Adele said, then turned to the high wizard to ask for his help.

Ohren stared back, dismay clouding his expression, but at least he had the good sense not to argue with her. "When do you want to leave?" he asked.

"Tomorrow," said Adele and ignored the quiet protest of her general. "If we can get to this dragon through the fabric of time and space, then we can go there and back in no time at all. Isn't that right, Prince Rainere."

"While I appreciate your confidence in my talents, Your Majesty, it might not be as simple as all that," Rainere demurred. "To do the impossible is…"

"Impossible is not a word which applies to a Marchant prince," Adele repeated the words of his father and it had the desired effect on Rainere. She smiled sweetly at his irritation and clapped her hands. "The Queen's Guard and I will prepare our supplies, and High Wizard Ohren will make us a copy of this map if he would be so kind. And now gentlemen, you are dismissed."

Nobody moved.

Adele let out a huge sigh. "Alright, but at least let's take turns over who gets to tell me that this is a horrible plan which will never work. Prince Rainere, I will accompany you to the portal entrance to the Grey Palace and you can have your say." To his credit, Rainere only nodded and followed Adele to the door of Ohren's laboratory. As she made to leave, she threw her Queen's Guard another look, and caught General Ohrig's glower. "Ohrig you can go next. I'll see you at dinner tonight. You should have all your complaints ready by then."

Ohrig sent her one of his sardonic grins. "Oh, I'll be ready for you, Your Majesty," he said. "Don't you worry about that."

Adele resisted another sigh and followed Rainere out the door.

CHAPTER FORTY-FIVE

"That Which Is Given Freely..."

High Wizard Ohren's laboratory was in a quiet part of the Golden Palace, but the corridors were still busy with servants moving about in pairs and whispering behind their hands to see the queen and the Marchant prince walking together, unaccompanied.

"I presume you know where you are going?" Adele asked Rainere as he led the way through the hallways.

Rainere raised an eyebrow at her question. "Would you prefer to go the quiet way, or do you enjoy the gawping of the serving class?"

Adele raised her own eyebrow. "You know I love being gawped at," she joked drily. "But maybe quieter would be better."

Rainere turned suddenly at the next corner and took Adele to a non-descript door halfway along an empty hallway. Hidden behind a tapestry, the door opened with a push and swung back. "After you, Your Majesty."

Adele stepped into the dark passageway and could feel the sizzle of magic close in around her. Rainere slipped past Adele in the narrow space and took the lead again. Together they moved through the walls of the Golden Palace, the hundreds of passageways intersecting each other, once again delighting and terrifying Adelena, as she wondered *who else was using these secret paths in the palace?* After her time in the Lower Districts of Concordis, Adele now knew there were so many more of those born with Marchant blood in their veins, and that was all anyone needed to pass through these halls.

Rainere was counting under his breath when he stopped in front of a narrow door and Adele accidentally bumped into his back. Rainere's cold, spicy fragrance enveloped her and made her head swim for just a moment. Rainere placed a hand on the door and let out a soft sigh so she knew that he experienced the same sensation she did. Adele looked up into his forest green eyes, the silver circles spinning around his pupils, and her mouth went dry.

No. Don't do it, Adele told herself silently, and maybe he heard her thoughts because Rainere turned and quickly pushed open the door. They both stepped out of the darkness but came to a sudden stop in the doorway.

"This can't be right?" said Adele, as she looked about the tidy and richly appointed bedroom. There was a large four-poster bed against a wall, and lamps lit for the evening. A pair of men's slippers lay at the side of the bed, and a cloak and scarf had been thrown over the chair at the dressing table. A circular mirror with an engraved wood frame sat in a curious circular contraption beside the window, and it shimmered oddly in the candlelight.

"No, this definitely isn't right," said Rainere, and looked about the room with an annoyed frown. "This room shouldn't be here, the connection for the doors runs straight along a defined path, over to that bookshelf." He touched the cloak as he passed the dressing table. "There is magic here, but it's not what it should be."

There was the sound of running water, and Adele saw a doorway leading to a bathroom tucked into the corner of the room. She cautioned Rainere to be quiet and he led them quickly to the bookshelf, plunging them through the brick and plaster wall that wasn't really a brick and plaster wall. Adele relaxed when she saw they had got through in one piece. She smiled at Rainere's consternation, clear even in the darkness.

"It's alright, Rainere," she assured him. "Everyone makes mistakes, and you were taught the map of this palace over a hundred years ago, obviously there have been a few changes."

Rainere didn't answer her but only frowned more intensely at the doorway they had come through. On this side of the passage, a wooden door with a brass handle could clearly be seen, as it had only been camouflaged on the other side. They were now in the Golden Palace Portal Station.

Adele left Rainere to glare and poke at the offending door and wandered by herself out into the chamber. The walls were unadorned stone and torches flickered into life as she passed, making shadows lurk and jump from the corners. It was a spooky place, and Adele didn't like the weird, crackly energy in the air down here. The five portal doorways were lined up in a row of gaping, echoing archways, the names of their destinations engraved in the keystones above them. The lettering was unfamiliar, so Adele made an educated guess as to which one the Grey Palace was. The dust on the ground in front of the portal had been disturbed, and Adele guessed it had been by Charlie and Orestes when they had sent Charlie through to look for the Fire Orchid stamens.

"Rainere," Adele called to the prince and tried to keep her tone as nonchalant as possible. "I forgot to tell you that I sent Charlie through to the Grey Palace to steal back the Fire Orchid stamens for me a couple of days ago. He said he knew where you had kept them in the palace and could get them back for me. Clearly, this was before you knew what they were, but everyone was telling me that you would never give them back or that you would hold them hostage in return for..." Adele stopped herself from babbling anymore.

The curious door forgotten, Rainere made his way over to Adele in front of the portal. "You *forgot* to tell me you sent that cretinous boy to steal from me in my own home?"

Adele nodded. "I was panicking about Stella's illness. You must understand I was trying everything I could to get the stamens back to save her."

"And where is the little thief now?"

"That's the problem." Adele unconsciously reached out to take Rainere's hand. "Charlie never came back from the Grey Palace, and I'm worried about him, Rainere. I had thought that Charlie would return to me even without the stamens and now he hasn't I have a bad feeling about it all."

"Well, that's what you get when you hire street trash to do your dirty work," said Rainere archly. "Perhaps be more careful next time you chose an envoy."

"What?" Adele couldn't help but feel annoyed with Rainere tone. "You're the one who first sent him to me at the Belvoir Estate. He was in my room checking for magical protections, and if he hadn't had your magic sand, I would never have known he was from you. Charlie really is a terrible spy, you know, and he got me into so much trouble when I could have done without it."

Rainere's face went blank. "I never sent that boy to you, Adelena. The first time I had every laid eye on him was when he brought me your letter."

Adele felt her stomach drop away. *No, he couldn't be working for someone else. Charlie was such a sweet kid, surely he wouldn't have betrayed her like that?* "But he told me…"

"How did he even have Transposing Sand in his possession?" asked Rainere. "That is an extremely rare and expensive item, and not something that you would give a mere boy, no matter how strong the Blood in his veins. He must be working for someone very wealthy and dangerous." Rainere gave her a hard look. "And you sent him into my home again with only Grotto there to defend it."

"But?" Adele was confused, and it was taking her a moment to catch up to all the ramifications. "What would Charlie possibly have wanted from me?"

The queen and the prince stared at each other in the flickering light. Adele sighed. "Okay, I'm going to hope that is my last stupid question. Of course, he could have been trying to steal the stamens for a third party, or he could have been looking for information to prove a relationship between us. I guess I have no shortage of enemies here in the Golden Palace. For all I know, it was Ohren who sent him to me, knowing the exact day and time I would be at Belvoir when he told me to be there. That would explain why he never asked me to deliver them myself. I had wondered about that." Adele grimaced. "I know it sounds strange, Rainere, but nothing is ever what it seems in my life, and I feel like I have to trust that Charlie is a good person and genuinely wanted to help me."

"The boy earns your trust by offering to make a second attempt to steal the Fire Orchid stamens?" Rainere asked, his tone was heavy with sarcasm.

Adele opened her mouth but no protest came out. Charlie had, in fact, offered to get the stamens for her, risking his life and Rainere's anger at him. It had been a desperate plan, but if Charlie had been threatened, or coerced into getting those stamens maybe it had been worth the danger for him. Adele had only offered Charlie her gratitude for finding the stamens, perhaps someone else had promised him a proper reward.

Adele groaned and dropped her face in her hands. Every time she turned around she had managed to screw something else up. Adele only looked up when she felt Rainere's hands on her shoulders.

"*Cara m-* my queen." Rainere had gone from angry to soothing in the blink of an eye. "Please don't distress yourself. It ended well, didn't it? I brought the stamens to you when I discovered I had them in my possession and we managed to stop the course of the Summer Influenza. Stella is stable and all is well."

"But Charlie?"

"Charlie is gone, Adelena," said Rainere and didn't look upset about it. "I'm sure he left as soon as he discovered that I had taken the stamens away with me. No doubt, he has returned to his employer empty-handed, and paid the price for it. What should concern you is the extent that someone is willing to go to sabotage your rule. You have a powerful enemy here, and by using an inexperienced yet untraceable boy to do his bidding, your enemy has lost nothing by his failure. You know, it was very clever to use Transposing Sand to transport a spell to Belvoir. I wouldn't have thought it possible but the sand must have insulated the magic from the curse on Belvoir, keeping it alive long enough to use in your room."

"I'll be sure to pass on your compliments to the perpetrator as soon as I find out who it is." It was Adele's turn to be sarcastic. "Charlie appeared the morning after I got to the Belvoir Estate, so he must have been sent by someone with knowledge of Ohren's plan for me. Charlie is from Concordis, so he would have been recruited and sent out the moment I received the instructions to change course for Belvoir. The question is: who would have that kind of access to dark magic, and know how to find a boy to use it?"

"Someone in the palace, most likely," agreed Rainere. "But the choices are too many: Lord Orgustus, or any one of his courtier cronies, or Orestes of course…"

"Why Orestes?" asked Adele surprised. "He is working with Ohren to help me."

Rainere shrugged. "I don't like him."

Adele grimaced. "We'd have an easier time naming people you do like rather than not," she said. Feeling a sudden chill from the bad news and drafty chamber Adele wrapped her arms around herself. "But Rainere, now I feel like panicking again. Here, I have to leave my children at the Golden Palace while I go on this journey to find a dragon, and I have a desperate enemy lurking about in the shadows. I know it will be dangerous, but I will just have to take the children with me."

"No, Adelena, you cannot." Rainere looked down at the ground as if bracing himself, then shot a glance up at her. "But you can leave the children here, with *me*."

The silence stretched between them. "Rainere, I won't lie," Adele said softly. "I had considered asking you to stay behind at the Golden Palace with the children but this journey could take months. That is just too long to leave them."

"Adelena, I am the only person with the power to protect your children." Rainere looked down at Adele and she saw his sincerity. "The vow I once made to guard your life with my own can be transferred to your children, all three of them."

"My children are everything to me." Adele couldn't stop the tears pooling in her eyes as her fear came to the fore. "What if something terrible happens to me and I don't come back from this journey? The children will be left vulnerable to the horrible political games of the court. Lord Orgustus will tear them apart looking for political gain as Natalie is crowned queen and then Aaron is left as the next heir and Stella may be dead."

Adele broke off as she felt an awful breathlessness seize her chest. *How would her children live without her?* It was all too horrible to conceive of, yet she must prepare for it if she chose to leave them to find the cure to save Stella.

Rainere bent down over her, his face almost to hers. "None of that could happen while I guard the children," he promised her. "I will protect them with my immortal life and all the power that I have in my body. Let me do this for you, Adelena, to make up for the betrayal I wrought in stealing Natalie from you."

"The care of my children would not be a punishment, Rainere," whispered Adele. "They are not a burden to be borne. They are precious and fragile, and they need care and love as much as they need protection. You cannot just stick them in a room and hope they live through it. They need your time, they need to be hugged and kissed, and scolded if they don't eat their vegetables, they need to be taught right from wrong. Do you think you are even capable of giving that to my children? Honestly, most days I'm not even sure that I'm doing it well enough."

"I will learn, Adelena," promised Rainere. "*Cara mia*, please" - he closed his eyes as if in pain – "It is killing me to talk of not being by your side while you attempt the impossible but I know that the lives of your children are worth more to you than your own life. I understand that by protecting your children, I am protecting your heart."

I wanted this, Adele reminded herself. *So why does it feel so terrifying to hear Rainere say it aloud?*

Adele already knew how they were going to confirm their vows and the thought of it made her heartbeat ratchet up to panic pace. The two magics within Adele slithered and shuffled awake, and she felt them travel through her body, the Chime Voices began singing in a chorus of pleasure that they would get to touch Rainere again to do this.

Adele reached her hand down to Rainere's side and pulled up the shirt that was tucked into his trousers. She slipped her hand against his skin, finding the warm spot of the Mark she had left there all those miserable nights ago. She was only human if she loved the whisper of Rainere's breath, or when he stepped forward and dropped his forehead to hers, but it was the magic in Adele that released the tendril of power into Rainere to seek out the magic stored in his chest, just below his heart.

"*Cara mia,*" he begged, and pressed against her hand. "Please."

"Promise me," said Adelena and furiously thought of every last loophole she could close when Rainere made this vow to her children. She had to cover every eventuality of their lives in just this short moment.

"Promise me you will protect my children with your life, your heart, your mind and your soul. Promise me you will never think of me before you will think of them. That you will be there for them as a teacher and a guardian. Never, ever let them out of your care, Rainere," Adele whispered fiercely. "I release you from your oath to me and ask that you make this promise to protect my children."

The Chime Voices were excited to be inside Rainere again and wanted to dive fully into his magic. Adele held them back, keeping control of her magic, and the Chime Voices quietened beneath the strength of her will. A command was needed, and they gave her the word that would bind Rainere and never let him go, a command that would change everything. Adele considered the consequences of her actions. To bind Rainere to her children in a magical devotion wasn't ethical, but neither was anything else that happened in her crazy life here. She promised herself she would seek to redress the balance after the fact. Adele raised Rainere's face to hers with a finger under his chin.

"Make the vow," Adele whispered, her lips pressing lightly against his.

"This I vow, Adelena, my beloved." Rainere's eyes were closed. "In return for your forgiveness, I will take your children as my own and make my oath to protect them with my life."

Adele whispered the word of command before pressing her mouth against his. The command fizzed and hissed between them, pulling their tongues together and twining their lives tighter than ever before.

Adele felt Rainere's hands on her back, on her neck, and on her breasts as she ripped his shirt open. He pushed her back against the archway of the portal and she moaned into his mouth pulling him against her. He was hers again. Their bodies melted together as Rainere whispered the charm that loosened the ribbons and buttons on her gown. The green magic swirled and hissed, swollen and ready to invade Rainere and take what he offered up to her. Adele gasped for breath and opened her eyes. She ran her hands over the gorgeous hard planes of Rainere's chest and stomach and readied her magic but a hot roar sounded in her head, sending stars blinking across her vision.

It wasn't painful but it was horribly uncomfortable. Rainere pulled back, sensing her pause. "What is it, *cara mia?*"

"The magic, it doesn't want…" Adele took in a shuddering breath and the Chime Voices only whispered, chastened and quiet, at the back of her mind. "I feel odd. I don't think I can do this, Rainere."

"I know you said you would not take me to your bed again, *cara mia.*" Rainere ducked to kiss her neck. "But the magic requires a sacrifice of us all."

"No, Rainere, stop." Adele pushed him away gently. "That's the problem. It's the magic."

Rainere raised her chin and examined her eyes. "The rings in your eyes are shining gold, my love," he frowned and the glow of passion faded from his cheeks. "I haven't seen that before."

"I might be an abomination," said Adele. "But I'm still half St Lucidis and that part of me is fighting this relationship between us. Rainere, I'm sorry."

"So am I," whispered Rainere and looked so miserable that Adele almost changed her mind, but a low thrumming of power growled through her head, warning her not to continue. The horrible truth was that they *should* stop. Giving herself to Rainere now would only confuse things between them even more. Adele went up on her tiptoes, and kissed Rainere's pouting bottom lip before stepping back out of his arms and creating distance between them.

"Do you mind just helping me with this," she gestured to her heavy gown that was trying to slip to the floor with all the ribbons and buttons hanging loose.

With a dark mutter, Rainere did her dress up, the magic pulling the corset hard against her ribs and making her gasp. She frowned at Rainere. "It was never this tight," she said.

Rainere shrugged, an evil glint in his eye. "It looks better this way." They both stared at her squeezed breasts spilling over the velvet edge of her bodice, and Adele fought a smile. Rainere's desire for her always made her feel like a giggling fool, even when so much was at stake and danger swirled about them both.

"You should go," she sighed. "But I will wait for you to get back tomorrow before I tell the children that you will stay with them when I leave. I'm sure Natalie will be thrilled to have you all to herself, without me getting in the way all the time."

"I do not envy you your choices, *cara mia*," said Rainere, his expression solemn. "There are many in this world you cannot trust, but I will be loyal to you even if we are not destined to be man and wife."

Adele felt cold. She knew that it was for the best that Rainere understood they couldn't be lovers anymore but pushing him away was one thing. Having him accept it was another thing altogether. Adele swallowed the pain down and remembered she had to go and have dinner with her general now, and he wouldn't be nearly so accommodating as her Marchant prince.

"I will see you tomorrow, Rainere," Adele said and gave him a wan smile.

"Yes, you will." Rainere stepped through the portal to the Grey Palace and, in a flash of green sparks he was gone.

CHAPTER FORTY-SIX

"Friends in High Places"

Charlie was sure he had opened his eyes, but all he could see was black. He knew he was outside as he could feel a chill breeze blow over him, and his head was resting on the cold ground. Charlie allowed himself a low whimper of pain. His head ached and then pounded hideously, and his body shook with tremors that forced him to curl up in a fetal position.

Feeling stupidly vulnerable and hopeless, Charlie whimpered again and the fear that he had kept so tightly under control finally broke free of its chains and his tears dripped into the dirt as sobbing spasms held his body curled in misery. Charlie could feel himself slipping further away with every heaving sob. The magic crept through him, sensing his fatal misery, and loss of self-control. He felt the stinging vines edge slowly around his heart. The power in his body belonged to him but it also belonged to the Blood in his veins, and if he didn't keep it in check, it would consume him, eating him from the inside out as it absorbed the last of his strength.

Charlie was used to fighting for his life, and that struggle was one he knew well. Gasping air back into his lungs, Charlie stretched out his limbs and pushed himself to his knees. "Get back in your box, you catshit-munching whore, I'm not done in yet," he muttered to the encroaching magic, and the words gave him the strength to force himself up on his feet. He staggered a bit, but victory was still his and Charlie felt grimly satisfied.

Above him, Charlie saw a magnificent carpet of stars blanketing the velvet sky. The new moon appeared from behind a bank of cloud, and by its light Charlie could see into the enormous chasm that fell away not one yard in front of him. With a yelp, he leaped back and spun around to find himself standing on a wide ledge on the side of a cliff.

The rock platform stood out a good way from the wall of the cliff and was maybe fifty yards wide. There was a pile of boulders stacked against the base of the cliff but they were nowhere near high enough to reach the alcove he could see cut into the face of the rock above them. There was a sudden movement from the alcove, and Charlie blinked as he watched a rope ladder drop down and a figure scramble quickly down it. There was a tiny flash of gold light and the ladder fell down into the man's hands, before he shoved it behind the rock pile and turned to find Charlie standing and staring at him.

Charlie was too surprised to move when the stranger beckoned him forward and then took a seat in front of the boulders. "Come here, kid, I brought you food. Look." His voice was barely above a whisper but it carried clearly enough.

Two things made Charlie feel safe: the stranger's accent was city-bred and expensive, that spoke of education; and that he had brought Charlie food. Still maintaining his caution despite these things, Charlie edged over to the stranger and dropped to his knees beside the little feast spread out on a rough cloth. He grabbed the canteen of water, remembering to sniff it before drinking it down, then he attacked the hard bread and cheese slices.

"Easy, kid, the food's all for you, I promise," chuckled the stranger.

It took a few moments before Charlie had chewed and swallowed enough to re-focus on potential danger. He gave the stranger as shrewd an examination as he could in the darkness. "Who are you, and why are you helping me?" he croaked.

"I'm helping you because I saw a brave kid getting the stuffing kicked out of him and it tugged at my stupid heartstrings," replied the stranger with a smile in his voice.

Charlie heard the trace of mockery but there wasn't any overt aggression. He took another slice of cheese and shoved the whole thing in his mouth, chewing slowly as he considered this new information. The stranger hummed softly in the silence and Charlie didn't recognize the tune. He swallowed and sipped at the last of the water.

"I'm Charlie," said Charlie.

The man held out his hand and it was a sign of just how traumatized he was that Charlie flinched before cautiously reaching out to shake it with his own. The stranger's hand was warm and calloused, and his shake was firm.

"I'm Ripenzo, but you can call me Rip,"

Charlie stiffened. "Weird name."

Rip gave a low chuckle. "You're welcome," he said gesturing at the meal Charlie had just devoured.

Charlie belatedly remembered his manners "Thanks for the food, Rip. I don't know how you got your hands on it but it was worth it." He belched appreciatively. "Any idea where we are, though?"

Rip packed up the cloth napkin and rolled it into a bundle, carefully trapping any crumbs in its folds. "It'd be wise to keep your voice down," he suggested. "We are on one of the two Offering Tables on the other side of the mountain," - he pointed up at the hole he had climbed down from – "Paradise Mines is just through that tunnel up there."

Charlie rested his back against a boulder and hugged his knees for warmth. "And why are we here?"

Rip shuffled over close enough that their shoulders were pressed together. "*You* are here because you were causing trouble on the food line throwing your face at other people's fists, and the Key Master wants you dead. *I* am here because I knew you wouldn't last the night without a bit of help and pissing off the Key Master is one of my favorite things to do." Rip chuckled and nudged Charlie's shoulder. "Why does he hate you so much, anyway?"

"Why wouldn't I survive the night without you?" asked Charlie ignoring Rip's question.

"Because you have been volunteered to be an offering to the Marchant Eldars, my lovely lad," said Ripenzo. "Of course, I can't imagine you wanted to be eaten alive, so I'll do my best to hide you. I've never had to hide anyone as strong as you before though, so this'll be interesting."

"Marchant Eldars!" Charlie was horrified, and instinctively reached of his missing amulet. It had been his only protection from the Eldars who, it was said, could sniff out the Blood in the air from over a hundred miles away. "What do we do?"

"Well, we are going to stay calm and sit here really quietly until we hear the screaming," whispered Rip and his arm shifted to settle around Charlie's shoulders, pulling him in closer than before. Charlie fought the intimacy despite his fear. He didn't know what Rip wanted from him, but he would cut the man's balls off before he gave in to any of that shit.

"Calm down, Charlie," whispered Rip and Charlie heard the smile in his voice again. "I'm wrapping the spell around both of us. Get your mind off my cock and concentrate, then you can see the spell I'm weaving."

Charlie took a deep breath and paused before exhaling. He pulled strands of his magic up to the nerves behind his eyes, and with his altered perception, he could actually see the lightly shimmering net about them. "Can't the Eldars see this too?" he whispered.

"Not this kind of magic," replied Rip and the moonlight glinted off his straight, white teeth. "They only ever look for dark magic, that's the only kind they can eat."

Charlie shivered. "When will we know they are close?" His question was echoed by the sound of a distant scream, off and away to the left of their cliff ledge.

"That's how we know," whispered Rip, his lips on Charlie's ear. Rip's fingers dug into Charlie's arm as he pulled Charlie onto his lap, hugging him tightly. Charlie could feel the coarse fabric of Rip's shirt scratch against his cheek and hear the slow thudding of his heartbeat beneath it. Despite all his caution, Rip wasn't scared and that made Charlie feel strangely calm in this awkward embrace. Another scream rent the air, and then another. Charlie bit his lip to stop the whimper that wanted to escape.

"Close your eyes," Rip breathed into his hair. "Or they'll see the silver."

Charlie jammed his eyes closed tightly. He froze when a loud whooshing noise, like the flapping wings of a large bird, beating the air overhead. The Eldars had come. There was a thud and the vibrations shook the rock platform. A cold wind buffeted Charlie as he clung to Rip's chest, too scared to breath. He heard the sound of small rocks being scattered and the steps of a large creature moving about, first this way, then that. Something sniffed the air and the steps came closer, followed by a dragging sound. Charlie felt Rip's heartbeat ratchet up the pace and he held his breath.

A presence stood right in front of them but Charlie was too terrified to look at it. He felt a sudden cold, as if he had been doused in ice-water, and then sharp fingers scraped against Rip's net. After a few moments of scratching, a strong, buffeting wind blew over them as if a creature had taken off into the sky.

Suddenly a word of command tore through the air. The command was a hoarse and guttural call to join the Eldar, and it echoed through Charlie's head, pulling fiercely at his magic. Charlie couldn't resist the command that sang to the Blood in his veins and promised redemption and reward. He yanked at Rip's firm embrace and struggled to escape and go towards his destiny.

Then just as suddenly, the command was gone, cracking into pieces and drifting away on the night breeze, and it broke Charlie's heart. He sagged against Rip's chest and let the tears fall for the second time that night. Crying for something that never was going to be his — forgiveness and a home.

"It's okay, Charlie." Rip patted his back and tried to soothe him. "That command is brutal, hardly anyone can resist its call to the Blood. You did good, mate, you did good."

Charlie gulped back a sob and shuddered remembering the savage strength of the dark magic that had almost taken him.

"You can rest now," said Rip. "They won't come back, I promise. You get some sleep and everything will be alright in the morning."

Charlie figured it would be impossible to sleep after such a hideous experience but as Rip stroked his back and hummed his weird, haunting tune, Charlie began to feel warm and comfortable, and fell very slowly and deeply, to sleep.

CHAPTER FORTY-SEVEN

"Twin Alarm"

Ohren knocked on the door to his brother's chambers. He had gone to find Orestes to tell him what had been decided in the meeting with the queen in his laboratory this afternoon. He felt terrible about letting the queen go on such a journey but he felt worse about allowing her to go on a dangerous journey with a Marchant prince. Ohren knew better than anyone just what they were capable of.

"Hello, Orestes, you here?" Ohren hadn't waited for an answer to his knock but had walked straight in to find his brother at his desk surrounded by books and plates of biscuits, hard at work.

Ohren had always liked his twin's chambers, they were large and airy, not at all like his cramped attic space several floors up. What he didn't like was the accessibility to the public. He'd had to get rid of a line of waiting supplicants just to be able to have some privacy with his brother. Ohren threw himself into one of the plush armchairs in front of Orestes's desk and slung his leg over one side, slumping down and getting comfortable.

"So, I met with the queen," he began but Orestes had already held up a hand for him to stop.

"You realize she is going to bankrupt the kingdom with these trade concessions and the road she has committed to build to Sandar," Orestes blue eyes snapped with anger. "She has annoyed the entire Treasury committee and Lord Orgustus is making some not-so-quiet movements behind the scenes to have her held up on charges in front of the entire court."

"Charges of what?"

"Despotism." Orestes sat back in his chair and folded his hands in front of his chest. "I told you that little lion cub was going to be more dangerous than annoying one day. How do you think it's going to look for us when the queen is questioned?"

"No time for that." Ohren waved his twin's concerns away. "Adelena wants to lead an expedition to the Ice Mountains tomorrow. She intends to take her Queen's Guard and Prince Rainere with her. She has the Marchant prince working on a way to slip through the space-time continuum as we speak, to avoid a long journey across the surface of Evendaar. She wants to be back as fast as possible as she doesn't trust any of us to look after her children while she is gone, not even me."

Orestes leaned forward and placed his elbows on the table. He was holding his mouth in the funny way that he did when he had bad news. "Do you not think, dear brother, that maybe your experiment with our kingdom has perhaps come to a natural end? This false queen of yours has not only turned out to be an alleged demon, but she does seem to be leading us into the Days of Darkness of the prophecy, and not actually out of them. Our people have endured a catastrophic epidemic of the Influenza; the woman has been killing magical creatures whenever she encounters them, which can only bode ill for us; and she has fallen into the bed of one of the most dangerous men in Evendaar. Do I need to continue?"

Ohren shook his head and pulled at his beard. He stopped just short of telling Orestes what he had seen inside Adele's mind when he had examined her last night. Being a St Lucidis half-breed was bad enough, but if Ohren revealed that the queen was an actual creature of magic, he could be sure that Orestes wouldn't react well.

"Orestes, even if the queen is an abomination, or whatever you want to call her, that doesn't necessarily mean that she is from a race of dark entities. We didn't study anything on demons at the Accadaemia when I was there. You would think if demons were so dangerous, we would know more about them," said Ohren.

"Maybe it isn't in the Accadaemia library because the Marchant teachers in those times wanted to keep the knowledge a secret for some reason. Do you think that Prince Rainold knew that Rainestra was a demon when he married her?" asked Orestes

Ohren looked down at his lap. "I don't know, maybe? He was the most power-hungry wizard I have ever met in my life, and his greed wasn't tempered by good sense or ambition." Ohren's voice dropped even lower. "If he knew what Rainestra was, it was because he wanted to control her, or use her in some way. Prince Rainold and I weren't speaking so much after his son was born. I had never actually met Rainella, you know," Ohren said slightly defensively. "Rainold liked to keep secrets, even from me."

Ohren looked up at his brother and couldn't hide the pain his memories brought him. He hated talking about that time in his life, when as a passionate young man he had been working for his St Lucidis family, yet unknowingly betraying the nation he was trying to help. A pawn for his king and a fool in love. It seemed cruel to Ohren how so many of the mistakes of his youth kept coming back to haunt him.

"We will solve this too, Ohren," Orestes said, trying to be reassuring, but Ohren heard the sigh in his twin's voice and took it as judgement.

"I'm so sorry, Orestes." Ohren looked down at his hands again. "I'm so sorry I didn't listen to you so long ago. I never thought that things would go this badly."

Orestes grin was crooked when he threw a biscuit at Ohren's head, breaking the tension. "If I had a gold coin for every one of your apologies, Ohren," he said. "Maybe I could afford to build this road to Sandar. But we have no time for blame now. The queen is leaving on yet another journey, and as before, the timing couldn't be more perfect. We haven't found a way to properly disguise her heritage, and even I could see the silver glint in her eyes at the meeting table the other day. It will only be a matter of time before others notice. Maybe now that we know what she is we can change our research to something more specific, like how to contain a demon."

Ohren was shocked. "*Contain* a demon, Orestes? Surely you don't mean…"

Orestes had raised his hand. "You have already told me that Adelena has killed a man with her power and that she can control an immortal with just a touch. She is incredibly dangerous, Ohren. The best thing we can do for the kingdom is take her off the throne in the quietest and most careful way possible."

"No, Orestes," protested Ohren. "I think we should give her a chance to prove herself first. I mean, think about her children."

"The children will be tested, and if they are found to be clear of Adelena's demon magic, then we can let them live in the Golden Palace. It's obvious the baby has no magic in her at all, so you can keep the little one."

Ohren shook his head and this time he was firm. "No one shall lay a finger on those children, Orestes. They are innocent of the crimes of their mother. Almost as innocent as Adelena herself, who does everything out of natural ignorance. No, we just need more time to research her background."

"Very well," agreed Orestes slowly. "But if we do find out something else about the queen we should have a plan to eliminate her, just in case, Ohren. We don't want to put this kingdom in any more danger than we already have."

"Maybe Prince Rainere has the answers we need," said Ohren in a sudden brainwave. "If the old Marchant teachers didn't want anyone knowing about the demons, then they might have taken all the texts to their Great Library in the Grey Palace. If I asked him I'm sure the prince would allow me to enter the library to do some research on his beloved."

"It certainly wouldn't hurt to ask him," agreed Orestes.

Ohren felt better already. Talking with his brother had always helped him solve any problems he was dealing with. They were identical twins but their minds couldn't be more different. Orestes was perfectly suited to his chosen career as the High Magistrar of the Law Courts of the Crown. He had a brilliant mind, but he did best when he knew the parameters and rules of every situation. Ohren was the more creative and dynamic brother, and it was his personable nature that had won him the position of High Wizard of the High Wizards

Council. Of course, Ohren's longevity was an important factor in the position, but it was his personality that kept him there.

Or at least that's what the high wizard told himself. Although Ohren knew his power was well documented it was never his wish to rule by fear, but instead Ohren wanted the respect and love of the people of Unisia. Which is why he even kept the infuriating Lord Orgustus around. Having a human as the figurehead of the court was useful for more than one reason. Lord Orgustus's presence not only gave the people the feeling of having a voice, it was also nice to have someone on which to blame the troubles. Lord Orgustus might be an annoyance, but politically he was so desperate for recognition that he would take responsibility for all the issues of the kingdom as long as it gave him the spotlight that his enormous ego craved. Still, Lord Orgustus worked hard for the people of the kingdom, and he had been instrumental in helping the nation cope with this last strain of Influenza by representing the Crown and supporting the people of Concordis and the surrounding towns. Yes, it was high profile and increased his popularity with the common people, but it was damn useful too.

"How is the prisoner doing?" asked Ohren. Orestes had sanctioned Grottonski's continued incarceration at Gorrik's request and he'd had none of Ohren's qualms in doing so.

"Grotto is alive, and as well as can be expected," answered Orestes, and checked a scroll by his elbow. "It says here he is refusing food and water and has yet to sleep. His howls disturb the guards."

Ohren shuddered. "He is probably hoping to die before the Eldars come for him and Rainere."

"Well, you do realize that it won't affect us either way, Ohren." Orestes actually managed to smile. "The prince will follow his queen all the way to the Ice Mountains and the Eldars will probably get him when he is far, far away from our kingdom. But I think you should be prepared to accept that they might take your queen too."

"Goddess, I didn't think of that," gasped Ohren, and felt his cheeks blanch. "Travelling with the Marchant prince will be like putting a big target on Adelena's back. Orestes, I have to warn her."

"You'll do no such thing," cautioned Orestes and gave Ohren a deep frown. "Until we know just what a demon truly is, we don't know that we want one on our throne, brother. Let the queen journey with the prince to find the dragon, and if she makes it home, we will welcome her back with open arms. If she doesn't, then we will mourn her with a spectacular funeral fire and pass the crown down to the child who appears most free of Adelena's taint."

It was Ohren's turn to frown back at his brother. "Taint, Orestes, really? That word hasn't been used to refer to magic in an age, and I won't have you use it now. We might not understand Adelena's magic, but that doesn't mean it is dark, it just means we are ignorant."

Orestes shrugged. The world was very clear in the high magistrar's cold blue gaze.

Ohren chewed his bottom lip and ruminated on his twin's advice. It was harsh, yes, and hard to swallow but Orestes had made some good points. Too often Ohren had made mistakes because of his soft heart, and the fact that he genuinely liked Adelena, should not hold him back from making these tough choices now.

"I will go now and see if the Marchant prince has any answers for us concerning Princess Rainestra's pedigree," said Ohren as he got up out of his chair. "Or at least anything that he is willing to tell me."

"Be careful with Prince Rainere, Ohren," cautioned Orestes. "He might not be his father, but he is still very dangerous."

Stealing a biscuit off the tray, Ohren headed for the door without another word.

CHAPTER FORTY-EIGHT

"Family Dinners of a Sort"

Adele let out a loud shriek, and almost fell off her chair, making the three puppies bark and jump about the dinner table. The children were ecstatic and Aaron's cheeks were so red from laughter that Adele thought he might choke on his food. Adele giggled along with the children until their hysterics faded.

"And that's why you must eat broccoli," Adele finally said, and dropped a few more green florets on each plate. "Otherwise you will make me so upset that I won't be able to sing properly anymore, just howl like a crazy animal."

"Hero Boy said you smell good, Mummy." Aaron giggled and shoved a stalk of broccoli into his mouth. "He says you smell like good magic, and not metal like you sometimes do."

"Don't talk with your mouth full, darling." Adele smiled at Aaron but then turned her curious gaze to the puppy at her feet. Hero Boy was getting bigger every day, though he still had his too-long, puppy legs. The dog sat looking back at her, his mouth open, panting, and a happy air about him as if he was waiting for her to howl again. Adele reached down to stroke Hero Boy's velvet ears and ruffled the thick fur at his neck. Adele examined his pupils but didn't see any gold or silver rings, just a lot of doggy affection and a desire to play.

"Aaron, when you say Hero Boy talks to you, does he say his words out aloud or does he say them inside you head?" Adele asked her son, trying to keep her tone light. "Because he doesn't talk to me, you know."

Aaron shook his shaggy hair. *He would need a haircut soon*, Adele noted. "I don't know why only I can hear the animals talking, Benjamin says that it's because I listen so hard, and the horses like that." Aaron waved his fork about, a piece of carrot in danger of flying across the table. "But Gorrik's cat says that I'm special, and that he thinks I should be a king one day."

"Does he say anything about me?" asked Natalie hopefully. "Can I be queen?"

Aaron nodded and smiled in little-boy innocence. "I'd make you queen anyway, Natalie, when we get married."

"I'm not marrying you, Aaron," sniffed Natalie proudly. "You pick your nose all the time."

"Also brothers and sisters can't marry each other," added Adele, wanting to steer the conversation back to Aaron's apparent gift with animals. "You will need to find other people to love and marry, so that we can make our family even bigger and more wonderful."

Adele cut up a piece of chicken for Aaron and laid out the small squares for him. "Are the animals nice when they talk to you?"

"Yes, they are mostly nice to me," agreed Aaron. "But sometimes they say rude things to each other. The puppies don't like Gorrik's cat, and they say naughty things to him, and then the cat says swear words at them. Sometimes it's funny but mostly I walk away. Horses are nice though, they tell me stories about things. Titor is the best one at telling stories, all the horses go quiet and listen to him when he starts to talk about the Horse Gods and their magic, and the time before the Hoo-mums."

"He means humans," corrected Natalie. "Titor is Prince Rainere's horse, that's why he is the best one in the whole stables, you know."

Aaron nodded solemnly, his hazel eyes wide. "He is a prince too, just like Prince Rainere."

Adele felt a burst of pure love for her children that almost broke her heart into pieces. Natalie and Aaron were growing up so fast, and she never got to spend this quiet time with them anymore, not like in the old days on Earth.

Adele thought ruefully of how she had let misery rule that other life. The heart-rending divorce while caring for her young children after her unhappy marriage had always made her feel incompetent as a good mother. How different life was now, sitting here at this table, with a delicious meal cooked by a talented chef Adele had never met and having three nannies hover in the background waiting to step in and take care of the children for her. In Unisia Adele and her children wanted for nothing, and this was a paradise she had never expected.

But why did the cost of this ease have to be too much to bear? Their baby sister, Stella, was frozen in a living death, and their mother working every day at being queen, or out at night dealing with dark magic, but always away from them now.

"Who's left room for dessert?" Mrs. Ollenby trilled as she carried a huge cake on a silver tray over to the royal family. The children quickly shoved away their plates and cleared space for the enormous pile of confectionary. Covered in silver cachous, sugar flowers and sparkling, pink sugar-glass, the cake was a masterpiece of delectable art.

"What's the occasion?" asked Adele, slightly alarmed by the size of the cake and the idea of the children having sugar before bedtime.

Mrs. Ollenby set down the plates and forks for each of them. "Well, the chef accidentally made this horrible cake and before he threw it in the rubbish, I thought maybe we might eat it, Your Majesty, if that's alright with you?"

"Did the chef drop it on the floor?" asked Aaron hopefully.

"Maybe, he did," said Mrs. Ollenby but gave Natalie a wink to prevent the little girl's gasp of horror becoming a complaint. "Shall I cut it for us?"

Adele smiled up at Mrs. Ollenby and held out her plate. "I can't remember the last time we had cake altogether at the table after dinner, can you, Mrs. Ollenby?"

"You know, I really can't either." Mrs. Ollenby's twinkly blue eyes were always a window to her emotions, and tonight they were full of compassion. She gave Adele a warm smile. "I believe everyone deserves a bit of a treat with the ones they love now and again, Your Majesty."

It was only minutes after swallowing a few bites of fluffy vanilla cake before Adele's two children went mad with the sugar rush and raced about the apartment shrieking and jumping on the furniture. Adele gave chase, catching first Natalie then Aaron and tickling her little ones into hysterics, before letting them escape and chasing them again. Adele laughed until her sides ached, and the children included their young nannies in the game, before they could be finally corralled and taken out to the terrace before the inevitable crash and bedtime.

"Not my brightest idea," said Mrs. Ollenby with good humor as she picked at a few crumbs of cake from Aaron's plate. "But you looked like you could all do with a little boost of fun tonight. I hope I wasn't too out of line, Your Majesty?"

Adele winced as Aaron dashed back inside and crashed into a coffee table, sending a vase flying, before he lurched back out to the terrace. "It was sweet of you, Mrs. Ollenby," said Adele and meant it. "Is this because Ohren told you what I am planning to do tomorrow?"

Mrs. Ollenby nodded. "It is so brave of you to go traipsing off into the wilderness to search for a long-lost dragon, Your Majesty. But I have to share my concern over who will look after the children here while you are gone. I love our high wizard, he is a very bright and warm man, but he is a little too pragmatic to watch over the little ones like they need to be watched. Have you any thoughts on the matter, yourself?"

"I'm not sure how these things work within the hierarchy of the Golden Palace, Mrs. Ollenby, but I would want you to be in charge of the children and their nannies day to day while I am gone." Adele took a deep breath. She had no idea how Mrs. Ollenby would react to her next instruction. "But I am also aware that you do not have the authority to prevent those above you from interfering with the children if they should choose to, so I have asked Prince Rainere to remain behind at the Golden Palace and be the legal custodian of the children." She paused and waited for Mrs. Ollenby's horrified reaction.

"Why, Your Majesty, that is a brilliant idea!" Mrs. Ollenby lit up with excitement. "Prince Rainere is ranked higher than anyone else in the court bar none, and as you hold the Grey Palace he is entitled to accommodation within the court. The prince is also a formidable wizard, which will prevent anyone with power from challenging him outright, and the knowledge that he protects the royal children will mean that he will have a rank similar to regent, and that will work perfectly for me, as then he will be my next direct authority in matters of the children's welfare." Mrs. Ollenby's cheeks were pink with pleasure. "Oh, you are a clever one to think of all of that, Your Majesty!"

Adele shut her mouth with a snap. She had clearly underestimated Mrs. Ollenby. Yet, instead of being alarmed, Adele only felt relief at the realization that Mrs. Ollenby was already prepared to join the line between her children and those who would harm them.

"Actually, more lucky than clever," Adele had to admit with a rueful grimace. "I fear everyone and everything in this world, Mrs. Ollenby, but for so many reasons I don't fear you. I also know that the prince will burn this palace to the ground if he thought it would protect the children. I needed to know that he will stop at nothing to keep them safe, and he has proven that to me."

"The prince is a wonderful man with a big heart," smiled Mrs. Ollenby and Adele felt strange hearing someone compliment Rainere, and realized it wasn't something she had ever heard before. "For all the right reasons, he loves you and the children with an admirable passion. I'm very happy for you, Your Majesty, that amongst all the trouble we've caused you bringing you here to Evendaar, that you can have love in your life like the prince can give you."

Adele felt her mouth twist at the irony of Mrs. Ollenby's comment but she didn't want to contradict such a positive view point on her romance with Rainere. "I am a little nervous to tell General Ohrig about leaving the prince here, though," Adele said instead. "He doesn't have a very high opinion of the prince, as you probably know. He was at the Grey Palace with us when it happened…"

Mrs. Ollenby just waved away Adele's concerns with tinkly laugh. "Oh the general is a big puppy, Your Majesty," scoffed Mrs. Ollenby. "Just let him know that you listened to him, that you think his opinions are important and then do whatever it is you want to do. The general will stand by your side whether he agrees with you or not. Ohrig is nothing if not loyal."

To her surprise, Adele thought she might have detected a trace of bitterness in Mrs. Ollenby's words but before she could question the lady, the Queen's Guard announced their presence and it was time for Adele's dinner meeting with them. Mrs. Ollenby greeted every guard by name and the men bowed politely in return.

"Your Majesty, I will see an informal dinner served for you all on your private terrace, if you would prefer that to the dining room?" suggested Mrs. Ollenby and received Adele's grateful nod with a smile. She took her leave with a curtsy and Adele almost missed the quick hand Mrs. Ollenby laid on the general's arm, and the quiet word she gave him. The general didn't have time to respond before Mrs. Ollenby swished away, her tulle skirts brushing his feet, and only stared at the lady's back as the door closed behind her. Ohrig turned back to his queen a stern frown already bringing his brows low.

"Ah, Ohrig, remember how I said I wouldn't cause anymore chaos while you were off duty?" began Adele and ushered her Queen's Guard through to the private terrace of her bedroom chamber.

General Ohrig almost tripped on the carpet as he spun to face her. "What have you done, Your Majesty?" he groaned. "You know it's not even been a full day without me around."

"I only did what I had to, Ohrig," and Adele gave the general a sympathetic pat on the arm before gesturing back at Lucky. "Captain Lucky, can you please bring the cake with us? I think we are going to need it tonight."

CHAPTER FORTY-NINE

"I Knew Your Father Once"

Rainere looked up when he heard a knock on the door of the Great Library. He was on the other side of the room, deep within the stacks, but he dropped the book in his hands, and went to answer it, heedless of the book that dodged his legs and independently floated back to its place in the maze of shelves.

Since his return to the Grey Palace, Rainere had expected Grotto to show up at any minute with dinner on a tray and a bitter lecture on his lips, but his old manservant was nowhere to be seen. Instead, the prince was shocked to see High Wizard Ohren standing in the doorway.

The High Wizard looked chagrined as he skulked about the entrance to the Great Library, nudging at the door with his boot, but well aware he couldn't enter without the prince's permission. The Great Library of the Grey Palace was heavily protected from those without Marchant blood in their veins.

As he made his way to the door, Rainere tried but couldn't remember a time that the high wizard had ever been in the Grey Palace to see him, except under the greatest duress.

Rainere had had an unfortunate but highly necessary addiction to the Blue Tonic, and the high wizard had been his only source of the opiate as the recipe was a secret held tightly by the St Lucidis family for reasons known only to themselves. Rainere had always been in excruciating pain by the time he called on the high wizard for another fix of the opiate, so they'd never managed to form any sort of relationship with each other.

Rainere stared at Ohren through the half-opened doorway of the library. "Yes?"

Ohren's eyes flashed a little but he kept his composure. "May I come in? I believe that we have much to discuss with each other before tomorrow."

Rainere arched an eyebrow at the wizard's presumption, but his curiosity won out and Rainere held out his hand to help Ohren cross the threshold. The wards and runes on the door blazed alight and hissed angrily, but with Rainere's protection High Wizard Ohren managed to pass through unharmed. The two wizards stood holding hands for a moment as Rainere assessed the wards. When they had calmed enough, he dropped Ohren's hands and led him to a pair of ancient armchairs set by the cold fireplace. Rainere poured them both a snifter of Firewhiskey and settled himself into a chair to study the high wizard.

Ohren sat uncomfortably. Leaning back and then forward on his chair, clearly as awkward with asking for Rainere's hospitality as Rainere was with giving it. The high wizard turned to gaze out of the long sash windows. Ohren could see the clear night sky through one of the filthy windows that had been left open to catch the breeze. "It's not raining tonight," Ohren remarked. "Normally, it rains all the time here, doesn't it?"

"Yes." Rainere crossed his legs and steepled his hands in front of his chest, not breaking his stare.

"Queen Adelena is leaving tomorrow, and the journey before her will be incredibly dangerous, I think that's clear." Ohren paused and took a sip of his Firewhiskey. "You have more of an insight into her emotional state than I do. Is she frightened?"

"Yes," replied Rainere.

"Well, she should be," agreed Ohren. He set his Firewhiskey down on a rickety side table, and then picked it up again when the table started to sway under the weight of the fragile glass. "Have you managed to find any way of implementing her foolish plan to slip between the fabric of time and space to the tundra beyond the Black Mountains?"

"Yes." Rainere relaxed his hands and laid them on either arm of his chair, his long fingers playing with the broken threads of tassels.

"Oh!" Ohren looked surprised at the news, and Rainere thought he saw a flash of jealousy. "Well, that's wonderful. Could you explain it to me?"

"Yes."

"Oh, for the Goddess' sake!" Ohren exploded with impatience and almost lurched out of his armchair before remembering his manners and sitting down again. "This is no conversation if all you're going to say is: yes!"

Rainere stilled. "And this is no conversation if you come to my home and expect me to answer your questions like I am one of your craven lackeys. I owe you nothing, High Wizard, and you certainly have not led me to believe that I would like to be your ally. Rest assured, I will get the queen to where she wants to go tomorrow, and the logistics of the magic are my own concern."

"Your Highness," Ohren moderated his tone to a 'let's be friends' pitch, which grated against Rainere's nerves horribly. "I think it is very important that you and I come to some sort of an accord. The queen, may the Goddess Serena bless her, has managed to fall afoul of some very strange situations, and I cannot help but think that she needs her supporters to be united in trying to help her survive this."

"You speak, but you are saying nothing," snapped Rainere and uncrossing his legs, stood up. "If you do not want to be honest, then please leave, High Wizard. I have work to do." Rainere turned to walk away.

"Wait, Prince Rainere," said Ohren and sighed. "Alright. Let us speak together, honestly and with no etiquette to tie up our tongues. We have come this far, I suppose, it won't hurt to go a little further." The high wizard seemed resigned to having to treat Rainere as an equal, and not another pawn in one of his many games. Rainere found it condescending all the same.

Rainere stiffly sunk down into his chair again. "You are a hard man to trust," he said, testing the high wizard's new resolve.

"Yes." Ohren nodded and his mouth curled up into a smile. "I know I am, Prince Rainere *Marchant*."

Both men sat silent for a moment. The high wizard took another sip of Firewhiskey while Rainere wondered what Ohren really wanted from him.

"You look well," began Ohren. "What I mean is, you look better than you did the last time I was here. You've not asked for the Blue Tonic since the queen arrived."

"I have resorted to stronger means of recovery when time takes its toll on me," said Rainere evenly. "Though it has always been abhorrent to me, the Gift has its advantages when I need my strength."

"Does Queen Adelena know that you use the Gift to help you?" Ohren kept his eyes wide and innocent despite the intimacy of his questions. "Does she know what it is, and what goes into making it?"

It was Rainere's turn to gaze out the open window of the library at the stars beyond. "There is so much she doesn't know," he answered. "But I will tell her when the time is right. I can only imagine how appalled she will be when she learns the reason you and I can live so long comes at the cost of so many young lives in those hideous mines."

"No, I've never used it." Ohren shook his head. "My longevity is a natural consequence of other magic."

"Why do you choose to lie when there is no one but me here to hear it?" Rainere interrupted, and his glare was puzzled. "I do not care to join the audience for your long list of mythologies."

"It's not a lie," insisted Ohren and Rainere could tell the high wizard was not accustomed to being disagreed with. "You and I are different creatures, Prince Rainere. You live off the stolen magic of Marchant bastards, while I have created my own version of the Blue Tonic. It doesn't keep me looking young, but it works well enough."

"High Wizard, why have you come here?" asked Rainere, cutting off Ohren's irritating protests.

Ohren's electric blue eyes almost froze Rainere to his seat. The high wizard was getting angry now. "I was merely inquiring about your health, Your Highness. As a fellow immortal, I know how hard it can be to maintain your strength, especially when you have a demon invading your body and stealing your power every now and again."

Ah. So the high wizard knows about Adelena's dreadful and exquisite powers, thought Rainere. *Would she have trusted him with that knowledge? Or had he hurt her and learned of them when she defended herself from him?*

"What do you know about what Adelena can do?" Rainere didn't bother to disguise the threat in his soft voice.

Ohren took his Firewhiskey glass and made his way to lean against the mantelpiece, feigning nonchalance. He sent a shower of golden sparks into the cold hearth, and the logs stacked there blazed merrily within moments. "The queen is…" Ohren hesitated, and then returned to his chair. "She is very powerful, but it is not in any way I could have predicted. It is true that she has the gold magic of her St Lucidis father but she is stronger than he was. The green of her mother, Rainestra, is also there but it is tempered by something more - he shrugged helplessly- divine."

Rainere picked up his glass of Firewhiskey and swirled it, watching the firelight play on the golden liquid. *Now the high wizard is looking for more information on Adelena. Does he think that I would talk behind her back, when I have only just won her trust again? Perhaps Ohren is so accustomed to the politics and machinations of the Golden Palace court that he doesn't really believe in the strength of love any more, let alone between queens and princes.*

"How did you find out about the way her magic functions?" asked Rainere.

Ohren gave him a sharp glance. "I assume the same way you did - I let her seduce me."

Rainere's whiskey glass was smashed in the fire and his hands were around Ohren's throat before the wizard could say another word. Rainere's fingers flexed, mashing the wrinkled, white flesh of Ohren's neck between them. "Say that again," Rainere asked in a voice cold enough to freeze the blood in Ohren's veins.

To his credit, the high wizard only gave a strangled chuckle. "Get off, you fool. I'm lying, of course." Rainere let go and stood back, as Ohren rubbed at his neck. "Dammit, but you are just like your father sometimes."

Rainere returned to his seat as if nothing untoward had just happened, but his hands were trembling when he clasped them together in front of his chest. The high wizard had hit on just the nerve that Adelena had warned him about, and yet again he had fallen into the trap. The prince decided to change the subject.

"I've asked you before, but you never told me: how well did you know my father, High Wizard?" Rainere asked.

Ohren poured himself another Firewhiskey and swallowed it before sitting back down in his chair. "I knew your father for many years," he admitted. "Prince Rainold first came to me as a student at the Accadaemia. He was one of the few royal Marchants left in Evendaar, and he made it known it would be my honor to teach him anything he didn't already know." Ohren smiled down at his whiskey glass. "He was extraordinarily gifted, and thirsty for knowledge. He would keep me awake for hours through the night, asking question after question on whatever I had been lecturing about in class that day. He was tenacious when he wanted to solve any riddle or puzzle that perplexed him. I have never met another intellect like him."

"But even in my father's time the Accadaemia would have been hostile to having a Marchant student in their ranks," said Rainere, frowning at the high wizard. "How long did he stay there?"

Ohren shifted in his chair and his own expression darkened. "Not long enough," he replied. "I often came to the Grey Palace to tutor him after he was expelled. That is how he and I became better acquainted. He needed me, and so he was polite and very accommodating for a time, but the minute he didn't need me..."

Ohren cleared his throat. "Your father could be as callous as he was kind, and he could drive me to distraction with his moods and hysterics. There was only one thing that he truly loved, and that was his baby son, you. To be frank, Your Highness, your father talked about you so often, but he never spoke to me about his wife, or wives, I should say. Though he often seemed incapable of keeping other people's secrets, he was actually a very private and jealous man."

"Jealous?" Rainere thought it was an odd word to describe a protective father.

Ohren looked decidedly uncomfortable and smoothed his robe down over his lap, before turning back to the fire and pulling himself up tall in his chair. Rainere got the distinct impression that the high wizard was about to reveal an actual confidence to him, and he hadn't had much practice at it.

"Your father cherished his freedom and the mantle of Marchant prince was too heavy for him. Before I met Prince Rainold, I had thought that I was the only wizard challenging the dictums of magic but your father could take the laws of magic and turn them all on their head." Ohren began waving his arms about to emphasize the point, accidentally sloshing whiskey over himself.

"If he could have been allowed to continue his studies uninterrupted, he might have become the finest wizard of our age, maybe even in the history of Evendaar. But your grandfather, Prince Rainov, had other plans. He wanted Rainold married, with hundreds of children, and clawing his way back onto the Marchant throne." Ohren shuddered and fell silent.

"He is quite mad, you know," said Rainere quietly. "I think that the Early Death might have broken his mind. Rainold couldn't follow a train of thought through to the end or remember what he had just said even a moment ago. I don't know if the man you knew is there any more, Ohren."

"He always seems mad when he is thinking a hundred things at once," said Ohren with a smile, and even with all the lines around his electric blue eyes, he looked like a much younger man. "You can't listen to what he says, but you should watch what he does. He is quite the magician when there is something he wants. Imprisoned or not, Rainold is not to be underestimated."

"The prince asked for tokens from both of us, Adele and myself," said Rainere. "I had thought it harmless at the time, but it puzzled me later. What could he use them for in a dimension where his magic is completely contained?"

Ohren was puzzled too. "He wouldn't have asked without reason, you can be sure. If he had tokens containing your hair, or objects that had been in direct contact with your skin, he could use the magic in them to form the basis of a spell. Still, without a balance he wouldn't be able to direct the magic usefully. Maybe he is just lonely?"

Rainere considered this for a moment. "He spoke of Rainestra with great affection," Rainere said cautiously. "He mentioned several times that Adelena was just like her."

"What do you know about demons, Rainere?" asked Ohren taking abrupt advantage of Rainere's confidence. "I am embarrassed to say that no description of such a creature can be found in the Accadaemia library."

Rainere didn't know how much he wanted to say to Ohren, but he was desperate to discuss what he had discovered. He just prayed that what he revealed now would protect Adelena and make the high wizard much more cautious of ever betraying her.

"I have discovered that demons were indeed creatures of the gods," began Rainere. "Some texts have even described them as demi-gods. Other texts call them angels. But every document says that they are a race of eternal beings, and not dark entities."

"What was the role of these angels?" Ohren's cheeks had gone pale above his grey beard. "What did they do?"

"Angels were described as star-travelers and messengers of the gods," Rainere answered. "It was written that they would herald the arrival of the gods when they decided to return to Evendaar."

Ohren gasped. "The Goddess Serena will return to Evendaar?"

Rainere enjoyed shrugging off the high wizard's horror. He had already spent a sleepless night contemplating Adele's true heritage, and the shock had worn off a little. "I will be able to tell you more soon," said Rainere. "I'm not going to accompany Her Majesty on the journey to the Ice Mountains, as she has asked me to be the legal custodian of the royal children and watch over them in her absence."

Rainere's mouth twitched at the corner, amused by the look of naked fear on Ohren's face. "You didn't really think she trusted any of you St Lucidis bastards to do it, did you?"

CHAPTER FIFTY

"Give Me What's Mine"

Charlie was running hard, dodging the men who were always just behind him. His heart raced and he felt for his magic but it kept slipping out of his grasp. The Grey Palace appeared out of the mist and Charlie knew that she would be inside. His assailants were close behind, and the ravens flying overhead screamed. Charlie had to warn her what was coming. "Adelena!" His voice choked off into a whisper. "My Queen!" But it was no good, his breath had gone and as he approached the door Charlie felt the blaze against his face before he opened it. Fire burst forth and covered Charlie in licking orange flames, he was burning alive.

"Charlie, Charlie?" Queen Adelena stood at the top of the stairs, the baby held in her arms, and screamed his name. Charlie struggled through the flames but his legs were heavy, as if he waded through water. He would save her this time. He had too. "The Eldars are here!" The stairs crumbled beneath his weight and the charcoal became wet mud, sucking him down. "Adelena," he gasped but there was no sound in it. Adelena's beautiful face crumpled and she held out the little baby, letting her go, falling into the flames. "How could you, Charlie? How could you?"

"Adelena!" Charlie sat up and felt the air rush back into his lungs. He looked around wildly and fought off the hand that held his arm.

"Woah, kid." The voice was familiar. "That was some dream you were having. You almost punched my lights out."

Charlie saw that he was with Rip and sagged with relief. A crooked smile split Rip's tan face, but his indigo blue eyes were full of sympathy. "It's alright, mate, you're awake now. No monsters here until nightfall."

Charlie pulled his knees to his chest and wrapped his arms tightly around them to try to stop himself from trembling. The sun had begun to rise, and Charlie concentrated on his breathing as the light crept closer towards him. He reached inside and was thankful to feel his magic pulse back, strong and steady.

Rip stretched his legs and made theatrical noises while trying to get the blood back into them. "I'm glad you got some sleep, kid, but damn you've got a heavy head."

Charlie didn't like to think of himself sleeping on the lap of a man he barely knew. Instead, he concentrated on the line of light creeping closer towards him and tried to quiet the voices that plagued him. *"Charlie, how could you?"* The sound of Adelena's voice echoed through his head. *What if Princess Stella is already dead?* Charlie thought miserably. *Surely, not even the queen's daughter could survive the Influenza without the tonic?* Charlie rubbed his eyes to get rid of the image of the limp baby body falling into the flames.

"Who's Adelena?" asked Rip and flinched in feigned fear when Charlie glared at him. Rip raised his hands in a gesture of peace. "Come on, man, I had to listen to you whimpering her name all night. I got curious. Is she your girlfriend?"

Charlie climbed to his feet and started brushing off the dirt. "She is my queen," he replied shortly.

"Well, look at you." Rip's eyes had lost a little of their friendly sparkle. "So you're an agent of Queen Adelena, are you? What's she done this time then?"

"I'm not at liberty to say, it's Crown business," replied Charlie ending the conversation. He studied the wall where Rip's rope ladder had reached last night. "How do we get out of here?"

"You better watch that queen of yours, mate," continued Rip, regardless of Charlie's brush off, and leaned back against a boulder. "I have to tell you, there are better people for a smart kid like you to work for than that bitch."

Charlie whirled on Rip and raised his fists, his hands already glowing green. "She isn't a bitch," he snarled. "She is the Goddess-given queen of Unisia and she gave me a home and a job when no one else would've. I owe her."

Rip spread his arms and gestured around their mountain ledge, now bathed in sunlight, his expression full of derision. "And yet now you find yourself in Paradise Mines at her behest. Not much of a trade-off, kid."

Charlie dropped his fists when he could tell Rip had no intention of fighting him, but he stayed tense as the nightmare images flashed through his mind. "She didn't, and it's not her fault that I'm here," said Charlie. "I screwed up, again, when she deserved better from me."

Rip raised a sandy blonde brow at him. "Sounds like you're giving yourself a bit too much credit, mate," he said. "Your queen probably has a way of making you feel sorry for her." Rip pulled up his collar against the sun and shifted to turn his back to the hot rays. "Bet she just batted her big hazel eyes and got all teary, and you were just sure she would be grateful that you saved her neck. But she wasn't."

"What would you know about it?" asked Charlie defensively. "You've never met her."

"All queens are the same, mate," sniffed Rip. "You met one, you've met them all. Selfish, self-serving bitches, the lot of them."

"Why are you here anyway?" asked Charlie ready to change the subject. "You don't look like you have a scrap of Marchant blood in you."

Blonde, blue-eyed Rip didn't answer, but instead joined Charlie in gazing up at the hole in the wall. "They'll be peering over to see if there are any survivors soon. I'll hide myself, if it's all the same to you, and I'd see it as a gesture of true friendship if you don't mention it to any of the Blue Jackets that I helped you last night, Charlie. They don't take kindly to anyone breaking the rules in this camp."

Charlie nodded and watched Rip disappear behind the pile of boulders, tucking himself into a deep crack so that he couldn't be seen from above. "You'll be alright to get back up again, will you?" asked Charlie, just as a shower of sand and pebbles came from above.

"Ho, down there, any alive?" A bald head appeared, poking out of the hole.

Charlie raised a hand. "The Eldars sent me back with a message for your mum," he shouted. "They want her to stop offering herself."

Charlie heard Rip chuckle quietly from between the boulders. "Maybe get off the baking hot mountain ledge before you start dealing out shit, eh, Charlie?" he suggested.

Charlie grinned as the rope ladder dropped down and he kept grinning until he got the top of the ladder and got a clout across the ear. "Whad'you say about my mum?" asked Bald Head

"Nothing," grumbled Charlie and pulled himself off the ladder and struggled into the cool of the tunnel before he could be pushed back onto the ledge. He lay at the feet of the boy who had smacked him in the head. "Anything for breakfast?"

The boy had an oddly puffy face but his body was as skinny as the rest of the workers. His Blue Jacket was only really a vest, with the arms ripped off and the tattered fabric barely holding together at the seams. "Eh, you're the idiot who took on Riles and Shorn last night, on the food line, right?"

Charlie climbed to his feet, keeping his back to the wall in case this kid decided to help out his mates and finish Charlie off for them. "Maybe, I am."

"You're the stupidest cock I've ever seen," said the boy, and punched Charlie on the arm, but cheerfully this time. "So why aren't ya all beaten up then. Your face looks good for someone who just got properly done for."

Charlie felt his face, his hands checking for swollen bumps and bruises, but for the first time in several mornings he realized that his head wasn't pounding in pain and he felt good - hungry, sure - but good all the same. *Did Rip do that?* Charlie wondered and puffed his chest out proudly. "Those kittens couldn't punch the tits off a cat," he said and began making his way back down the tunnel towards the light at the other end. "They didn't bother me at all."

"But I saw you all bloody and knocked out," insisted the boy as he followed Charlie down the tunnel. "My name's Digger 1602, by the way, but all my crew is dead so you can just call me Tam. You gotta have your cock blessed by the goddess to survive the beatdown those two gave you. I promise, they see you looking this good today they are gonna be scared as all hell. Even the other Blue Jackets too."

Charlie had only been listening with half an ear to the babble of his new friend, but when they got to the end of the tunnel, he stopped. The path led down into the mining camp but travelled most of the way inside the circle of the hollowed out mountain before it reached the bottom. From this height, Charlie could see the piles of grey crystal left out in the sun behind the Key Master's hut. His shoulders ached just looking at it. It seemed like such a small gain for so much toil.

"Tim?" Charlie said.

"Tam," corrected Tam.

"How'd you get that fancy blue jacket of yours?"

Tam's puffy face screwed up a little and his mouth pursed like a cat's bum. "I killed a fella."

Charlie raised his eyebrows and gave Tam a long look down his nose.

"I took it off a dead kid," corrected Tam, and kicked the dust at his feet. "She didn't need it no more, did she?"

Charlie gave Tam a pat on the shoulder. "I'm sure she didn't." He gripped Tam's shoulder hard, his fingers digging into the bones, and watched Tam squirm a bit. "Would you mind if I borrowed it for a bit, mate?"

Tam shrugged off the tattered vest and handed it to Charlie. "Will you give it back, though?" he asked without much hope in his voice.

Charlie smiled. "Course I will Tam. I won't forget this, mate. Thanks."

Charlie was cautiously optimistic as he reentered the camp wearing his new garment and made his way to the front of the breakfast line to try and profit from it straight away. There weren't many kids left on the line this late in the morning but he stepped in front of a little kid and took the bowl that was offered to her. Charlie almost crowed at his success. Oh yes, this blue jacket was going to make his life a lot easier from now on, and that meant more time to come up with a plan to escape.

"Charlie?" Leafy was standing behind him, her hands still out to accept her bowl of watery porridge. Surprised, Charlie only looked down at the tin bowl in his own hands. He had just taken Leafy's breakfast.

"Leafy, just leave it." Carl was standing behind his sister and took her under his arm. "It's a Blue Jacket, we don't talk to them, okay." Carl's eyes were dark pools of hatred as he took in Charlie's ragged new clothes. "I'll share mine with you."

"Leafy, I'm sorry." Charlie tried to shove the bowl back into Leafy's hands but her brother had already pulled her away, and there was no way to make this right. Raising his eyes, Charlie caught a glimpse of Rip making his way over to the yellow team pole. After the kindness that had been shown him last night, Charlie had repaid the debt by stealing a little girl's breakfast. He couldn't help but think, *What would Queen Adelena say?*

Feeling like a piece of catshit, Charlie made his way to the green pole and couldn't even be pleased when he heard the news that there had been a cave in during the night and that only Specials would be working on the seam today. All he could think of was little Leafy's face, twisted in pain as the crystal drained the magic from her body.

CHAPTER FIFTY-ONE

"If These Walls Could Talk"

Adelena held out her arms for Lady Olivia to latch on the emerald bracelets. They matched the crystal beading on her white and gold gown. "I can do this myself you know," she said again, and this time Lady Olivia rolled her eyes and giggled.

"I know you prefer to dress yourself, Your Majesty," said Lady Olivia. "But these clasps are quite tricky, so please just hold still."

Adele forced herself to stand still, but it was difficult with the amount of adrenaline tearing through her veins. This morning she would tell the children that she was leaving them with Rainere and going on a journey to find a dragon, which may, or may not, still exist. There was no point in saying anything to the kids until she knew how long she would be away from them, and only Rainere would have the answer to that.

Adele twisted to expose the back of her neck when Lady Olivia put her necklace on. Adele knew that twenty-four hours hadn't been a lot of time to give Rainere but neither did she want to waste another minute with her daughter in a coma.

The dinner she had shared last night with her Queen's Guard had been long and volatile. Ohrig, predictably, had been against the idea of leaving Prince Rainere behind in the Golden Palace. The general in no way shared Adele's re-ignited trust in Rainere, and felt it was wiser to keep the unpredictable Marchant prince close with them, on the road. In the end, she had managed to get the general to concede that it would be better to travel fast and light, taking only the supplies they would need to survive. Adele argued hard against including anyone else in their party as she only trusted the men in her Queen's Guard, and the idea of others spreading rumors about the insanity of her trip into the Ice Mountains was too great a danger while her children remained behind at the Golden Palace with Rainere.

"There, now you are gorgeous!" Lady Olivia angled the full-length mirror so Adele could see herself. The dress was a triumph of white and gold brocade, the fabric of the skirts angled cleverly to appear full while still being light, and the boning in the bodice was only stiff at the top, holding its shape while still allowing Adele to breathe deeply without fear of cracking a rib. The sleeves were simple squares of white silk edged in gold thread, which sat lightly on her shoulders, fluttering in the breeze from the open balcony doors.

Adele stopped frowning and smiled at her image. "Lady Olivia, did you make this dress?"

"Why, yes, Your Majesty, I did." The young woman blushed prettily and curtsied. "I know you don't like many of those restrictive corsets and stuffy old designs Mrs. Ollenby had made for you, may the Goddess forgive me for saying so, so I wanted you to have something more modern and fluid to wear. I had designed this dress for one of the celebration dinners that Lord Orgustus is holding each night that the city remains free of the Influenza, but as you never attend any of them, I thought you should wear it today."

Adele grimaced. "How is Lord Orgustus these days? Still bad-mouthing me to the world?"

Lady Olivia began packing away all of the extra jewelry and shoes Adele had been trying on. "His Lordship does like the sound of his own voice," she laughed. "But wouldn't it do you good to get out to a party now and again, Your Majesty, instead of staying cooped up in your rooms all the time with the children, and all these boring meetings with your staff?"

Adele walked to the dressing table and automatically began setting things to rights, picking up powders and perfumes and replacing their lids. Lady Olivia stepped in and took the work out of her hands. Adele could see that the young woman had an expression of concern on her beautiful face.

"You know that you are strong enough to beat Lord Orgustus at his own game, Your Majesty," said Lady Olivia. "And it wouldn't hurt for the court to see you defy the rumors and dance amongst them a little. The courtiers are a fickle lot of braggarts and silly people but you could sway them with one flick of the wrist. Of course, I know the real you, but I would love for them to see you as I do, a wonderful queen and a great woman."

Adele smiled at Lady Olivia's flattery but the young woman saw through it to the denial already forming on Adele's lips.

"Please, just think about it, Your Majesty." Lady Olivia replaced a pin in Adele's hair, the touch soft. "You are far too young and beautiful and *unmarried* to be working all the time. Surely, even the queen of Unisia is allowed to have some fun?"

This time Adele laughed and pulled away from Lady Olivia, but an idea had occurred to her. "Does Lord Orgustus have a girlfriend or, you know, a boyfriend, or someone special in his life, Lady Olivia?"

Lady Olivia jiggled her eyebrows suggestively. "Why, Your Majesty! I had no idea you would be attracted to such a womanizer like Lord Orgustus."

Adele snorted at the very idea. "No, I mean, does he have anyone special in his life who perhaps I could *befriend,* in the interest of keeping tabs on him?"

"Oh!" Lady Olivia seemed a little shocked at Adele's question but she quickly recovered herself. "He loves all the ladies of the court, but it does help if you are young, blonde and have a pure St Lucidis pedigree. Lord Orgustus is an awful snob, you see. I know he is currently entertaining the attentions of a Lady Claudia St Lucidis of the Upper Hills district. She is a little older than his usual tastes, but she already has a four-year-old child and two marriages behind her, so I suppose she knows what she is doing."

"How old is Lady Claudia?" asked Adele, out of interest.

"Well, almost twenty-eight, Your Majesty, but she looks thirty if you ask me." Lady Olivia giggled before realizing what she had just said to her almost thirty-year-old queen. Adele waved away the fervent apologies.

"It's alright, Lady Olivia, I know you didn't mean anything by it."
Adele smiled ruefully. "But just so you know, having children ages
you terribly. Is this Lady Claudia anyone you could be friends with?"

Lady Olivia's eyes sparkled at the queen's request. "Well actually,
Your Majesty, the lady is already quite popular and she does share
Lord Orgustus's snobbery but the lord himself shouldn't be too hard
to approach. I am the Queen's Head Lady-in-Waiting, so that allows
me some rank in the court. I could get closer to one of his men-at-
arms quite easily." She clapped her hands in delight. "There is a very
handsome Lord Pine of Carparell, who is looking for a new belle
after being unceremoniously dumped by Lady Clarissa when she
went behind his back with his cousin, and now even the two mothers
are involved in the scandal..."

"I wouldn't want you to do anything that would hurt your reputation
in the court," said Adele, quickly interrupting the gossip. "I would
just like you to keep track of Lord Orgustus and report on what he
says about me at these little dinners of his. You wouldn't have to get
too involved with it, just listen and tell me later."

"Yes, Your Majesty, anything to be of service to my queen." Lady
Olivia smiled. "You can count on my discretion of course."

Adele smiled. She could tell that as a beautiful and competitive young
woman, Lady Olivia found it hard not to be considered important at
the palace. Adele was also sure that she already had another Head
Lady-in-Waiting, but she appreciated Lady Olivia's confidence that
she claimed the title for herself, and that she had enough courage to
offer to act as Adele's passive spy. Adele just wished she could trust
the young Lady Olivia with more than her wardrobe and a bit of light
gossip. Adele missed having female friends so much.

There was a knock at the door and Lady Olivia went to answer it,
opening the door to Captain Lucky who bounded into the room with
a low bow. "Your Majesty, the Marchant prince has arrived back
from the Grey Palace just now, and High Wizard Ohren has
requested your immediate presence for a meeting."

"Oh, the Marchant prince is back already!" Lady Olivia's eyes were wide and she turned to study her queen. "Were you expecting him, Your Majesty?"

Adele ignored the question as her anxiety came flooding back after the brief respite. She dreaded telling Ohren that Prince Rainere would be left behind to watch over the children. Adele had no idea what the high wizard's reaction would be but she was pretty sure that it wouldn't be good. Perhaps instead of meeting Ohren on his terms she should put the meeting in public so Ohren would be forced to control himself, and she definitely wanted her Queen's Guard close by.

"Captain, where are the QG's and Ohrig right now?"

"The Queen's Guard are training in the yards near the stables," Captain Lucky replied.

"Wonderful, my children are taking their riding lessons at the stables this morning and I promised them that I would come and watch." Adele felt grimly satisfied that she wouldn't have to disappoint her children just to take a meeting she didn't want to have. "Lucky, please tell High Wizard Ohren and Prince Rainere to meet me down at the corrals."

Captain Lucky bowed again and left, but not before he sent Lady Olivia a lingering look and a shy smile.

"Your Majesty, I had heard that High Wizard Ohren had thrown the Marchant prince out of the castle when he came to ask for your hand in marriage," Lady Olivia whispered, but there was a cheeky glint in her eye. "Shall I spread another rumor that the marriage might be back on?"

"Yes, of course," agreed Adele with a mock frown. "And tell them that I'm also pregnant with Ohren's baby and that Prince Rainere and I are really brother and sister. That should keep the gossips busy for a while."

Lady Olivia's laugh was loud and infectious, and Adele couldn't help but join in. "Ooh, that's a good one," she chortled. "Ohren's baby! Eeww, he's so old I can't even imagine it."

Still grinning, Adele gave her lady-in-waiting an affectionate hug and made to leave, but just before she reached the door, Lady Olivia called out to her.

"Your Majesty, I just have a tiny favor to ask you: I had heard that there is a little garret room just beyond your dressing room, Mrs. Ollenby told me it was for storage but I thought perhaps I might move in there." Lady Olivia curtsied again and gave an extra boost to her smile. "Just so that I can be closer to you, Your Majesty, should you have any need of me, day or night."

Adele thought of Stella in that little room and shuddered at anyone discovering her baby's whereabouts while Stella was so vulnerable. "I like my privacy, Lady Olivia, you know that," Adele answered, and forced herself to smile as if the question was just a trifle that didn't make her sweat. "Besides, I always have time to wait for my Head Lady-in-Waiting when I need her to make me look this pretty!"

Adele swept out of the room before she could be asked any more awkward questions but she hadn't missed the happiness her acknowledgment had given Lady Olivia. However, Rainere had returned and Adele's blood started racing again at the thought of discovering if he had any made any progress for the coming journey.

CHAPTER FIFTY-TWO

"A Man Promises What a Wizard Will Deliver"

It was only mid-morning, but the sun was already hot, and Adele had picked a spot under the roof of the stables to watch as Natalie and Aaron rode in careful circles on their little ponies, the leads held by two young squires as their teacher looked on, calling out directions.

"They're doing well," noted General Ohrig as he joined Adele at the corral. "Who's their instructor?"

Adele squinted. "I think that's Benjamin, that guard from Belvoir," she said, surprised. "I wonder why he is here?"

"What's that fool doing here?" QG Owens echoed Adele's question, as the rest of the Queen's Guard arrived and she was hit with an invisible wave of testosterone and male body odor as they crowded around her. The men were dressed in a tight white fabric, wrapped in a t-shirt style, underneath hard leather armor plates that covered their chest and abdomen, and dark canvas trousers. All of them were lathered in sweat, and red welts marked the bulging muscles on their arms and legs.

"I'm sorry to interrupt your training, gentlemen," said Adele, and tried to take a step down-wind of the men. "I'm going to be joined by High Wizard Ohren and Prince Rainere in a minute and I'd like to keep this meeting short, so we'll do it right here at the stables."

"So you haven't told the high wizard about your plan to leave Prince Rainere as a babysitter yet?" asked Ohrig and wiped the sweat off his forehead with the back of his forearm. Adele shook her head and Ohrig gave her a grim smile. "Well, good thing there are plenty of witnesses here."

"Oh, it's not going to be that dramatic," murmured Adele, unconvincingly. "I will simply explain why it must be done." Adele turned back to watch her children riding. Natalie and Aaron were both cantering now, and though Adele's heart thudded as Aaron wobbled about on the back of his pony, she called out encouragement and praise.

Soon Adele saw Captain Lucky leading the high wizard and Prince Rainere along the path from the palace to the stables. Adele took a moment to watch the High Wizard striding along next to the Marchant prince. Though they matched step in speed, their gaits were completely different. Rainere moved in a way that was half a leonine stalk, half an unhurried slope. Ohren almost raced along, leaning slightly forward as if he meant to break into a run at any moment. They both reached her at the same time.

"Your Majesty," High Wizard Ohren began. "I have to speak to you about the issue of Prince Rainere being left behind to guard the royal children, so to speak."

Adele threw Rainere a sharp glance. "You told him already?"

Rainere irritated Adele by shrugging a shoulder at her accusation. "He needed to know."

"*He* is standing right here," snapped Ohren, irritated with the both of them. "And if you'd bothered to ask me, I would have said that it's not a bad idea to leave Prince Rainere at the Golden Palace. At least now you won't have the chance for another lover's quarrel that could end the world as we know it."

"No, that was up to your prophecy, Ohren," Adele snapped back, her anger flaring too quickly to be helpful.

"Which you resolved for me, apparently." Ohren narrowed his eyes at Adele and she saw gold sparks shoot out from his fingertips. "But not how I had intended. The dark days seem inevitable now."

"You always knew I was a Marchant bastard," Adele replied and even Rainere raised an eyebrow at Adele's rough choice of word. "Don't play pretend with me now, Ohren. Everything that happens to Evendaar is because of what you did to me."

High Wizard Ohren looked like he would dearly like to answer Adele in kind but their conversation was interrupted by the children riding over to greet everyone.

"Ohren, watch me," yelled Natalie with a laugh, as she wheeled her pony around. "I can make her run now."

"You are doing very well, Natalie," replied Ohren and his face creased into a genuine smile at Natalie's shouts to keep watching her. "Remember to keep your heels down. That's it!"

After delivering a quick kiss to his mother, Aaron trotted off to follow his sister and the tense silence returned to the group.

Ohren gave Adele a sideways glance. "Natalie is getting really good, isn't she," he said, a little grudgingly. But Adele knew it was really an apology from the high wizard and she decided he deserved one from her too.

"The children have a wonderful life here at the Golden Palace," Adele admitted. "It's so much more than I ever could have given them on Earth."

Ohren accepted her unspoken apology with a slight nod, his shoulders dropping back down from his ears and the sparks disappeared from his hands. "Yet I don't suppose it will ever replace everything we took from them, including their father, Justin."

Adele started in surprise to hear High Wizard Ohren bring up her ex-husband, but she immediately saw that Ohren had directed his comment at Prince Rainere and by the death glare that he was receiving, Rainere was successfully needled by the high wizard. Adele sighed, wondering why everything had to be a game with Ohren.

"Rainere, did you manage to come up with a way for us to travel across the Black Mountains?" Adele said, changing the subject quickly.

Rainere turned to her and Adele saw that he wouldn't be easily distracted from his anger. "I have," he said in a clipped tone. "It's a spell from the old times, often used to move large war machines. I have found that if I condense the field and extrapolate the path, then I can send at least ten men and their horses through a great distance. I have no time to do any real testing so I have used my best estimations in the hypothetical experiments, and they have all been successful."

"That's wonderful news!" Adele was thrilled.

"Prince Rainere means that he has no idea if this spell will work or not, but he hopes it does," said Ohren drily. "That's what 'my best estimations' really means."

"I used the same spell to move myself and my horse from the Grey Palace to the Belvoir Estate," replied Rainere, glaring at Ohren. "At least the queen can trust that *I* would never put her life at risk to suit my own purposes." His accusation was clear.

Gold particles glittered from the top of Ohren's head, and his lip curled in anger. Before he could speak, Adele stepped between Ohren and Prince Rainere, and looked up at the high wizard. "Do you have a better plan for me, Ohren? Are there any mystical maps hidden away that shows me the whereabouts of a closer dragon? Any superior magic that can give Stella her health back?"

Ohren had the decency to shake his head and look away.

"Then know that I trust Prince Rainere, and his magic, and if he says that his best estimations are correct then I believe him." Adele stepped back and forced a smile for the benefit of her waving children. "I will stake my life on it."

"Fine." Ohren waved his hands as if he was willing to concede this one point to her. "But what would you like me to tell our scheming Lord Orgustus when he discovers that you have left the throne empty for, the goddess only knows, how long?"

"Tell him that I have gone on a journey to find a cure for the Summer Influenza and that I will be back in two weeks," said Adele firmly.

"And then another two weeks, and then yet another two weeks?" Ohren raised his eyebrows at Adele. "You could be gone months you know?"

"I *do* know, Ohren." Adele frowned. "But I think it would be best if Lord Orgustus never knew he had so much time to replace me. Also you should tell him that you are in constant contact with me, so he thinks I will know everything that he gets up to."

High Wizard Ohren didn't agree with her but neither did he disagree and that was worth something too, Adele thought.

Silence fell over the group again as the Queen's Guards fidgeted in the heat, keeping their thoughts to themselves. Adele threw a look at Ohrig but his expression was stony and didn't reveal anything of what was going on behind those pale blue eyes of his.

"That's all, gentlemen," Adele said, signaling that the meeting was over. "Let us prepare for the journey tomorrow."

"Prince Rainere, I suppose you can show me these estimations of yours," said Ohren reluctantly. "I would like to be assured that the queen's trust has a foundation with your spell."

"Actually, Ohren, I will need the prince just now," Adele said. "The only people who really matter still haven't been told that I am leaving them, and that they will have Prince Rainere to care for them." She looked towards her laughing children. "And God only knows how I'm supposed to say goodbye to them."

CHAPTER FIFTY-THREE

"With Friends like These"

The Queen's Guard left quickly, and even the high wizard managed to take his leave without handing out any more unwanted opinions. Finally alone with Adelena, Rainere felt supremely awkward leaning on the railing watching her children. There was so much to say, and so much that needed to be acknowledged between them, yet Adelena felt so distant from him as she watched Natalie and Aaron.

A childhood memory swam to the surface of his mind, and Rainere remembered the day his father had left him. Prince Rainold's eyes had been wide, and his smile had been so bright, as he waved and waved from the carriage that took him down the driveway and out of the front gates of the Grey Palace. Gone, forever. *Well, not anymore.*

Dragging himself back to the present, Rainere realized he was about to watch Adelena make the same sacrifice that his father had made for him. *Her children will suffer as I suffered without my father,* and the thought made Rainere feel hollow. *How can I be everything she is to them?*

Suddenly, Rainere heard a shrill and familiar whinny coming from deep inside the red-painted stables. There was a loud crash of hooves against wood.

"Titor?" Surprised, Rainere ducked inside the stables. Blinking in the dim light of the cool, straw-scented corridor, Rainere followed the sound of his horse until he found Titor down the far end of the stalls. Titor whinnied again when he saw Rainere.

"Hello, my boy!" Rainere soothed the excited horse as his own heart raced with joy. Titor looked so well, his mane brushed and his coat so glossy it almost shone. He was a little heavier on his legs but Rainere knew a week of good riding would fix that. Rainere opened the stall door and ignoring the stamping hooves, he pressed his face to Titor's neck, feeling all at once back home. Titor stilled and dropped his head to Rainere's shoulder, snuffling his jacket. "I missed you too, my beautiful boy."

Rainere ran his hands over Titor's shoulder and felt the muscle ripple under his hands. "Have you been happy here, my boy?" he asked and chuckled when the horse snickered and shook his mane. "I understand, it's not the Grey Palace, is it?"

"He really missed you, you know," said a small voice behind Rainere and he turned to see Aaron, dressed up in his little breeches and a velvet riding jacket, smiling up at him. "He talked about you all the time."

Rainere smiled at the child and impulsively lifted Aaron to sit on his hip, so that he could pat Titor's nose. "My poor horse must have thought I had forgotten him at the Belvoir Estate," said Rainere and scratched behind Titor's ears. "He would have been so lonely there."

"Not really," said Aaron with a little shrug. "He likes being out in the green fields, and he likes talking to other horses. He is a prince you know, and he needs to see his herd."

Rainere's eyebrows raised in surprise. "Where did you hear that?" he asked Aaron.

"Titor told me," replied Aaron. "He likes me, and he told me I was special." Aaron went quiet for a moment and grinned at Titor. "He tells me to say that he loves you and that he will be a father soon." Aaron threw back his head in a belly laugh that made Rainere smile. "He must have been kissing the girl horses."

"Indeed." Rainere leaned into Titor's neck squashing Aaron between them so he kept giggling. "Please tell Titor that I will be proud to see his children when they arrive."

Aaron was silent for just a moment. "He says he will have sons, and they will be princes like him, and he says, do you know where the apples are? I do, I'll get them!" Aaron struggled in the prince's arms so Rainere gently dropped him to his feet and watched as the child ran off to find the apple barrel.

So, Prince Aaron could talk to animals, an odd and curious skill. Well, that wasn't exactly from his Marchant blood, but neither was it from his St Lucidis side. Rainere was fascinated to discover how such a talent could have developed in him.

"Prince Rainere!" Natalie's shriek made Rainere spin just in time and catch the little girl as she flung herself at his legs. "Mummy said you came to see me ride today. You have to see my pony, her name is Unicorn and I love her so much, she loves me too and you should see her tongue when she licks the salt block in her stall, it's so cute! Why haven't you hugged me yet?"

Rainere dropped to his knees in the straw and dust and gave Princess Natalie the hug that her shiny green eyes pleaded for. He felt her little arms around his neck like matchsticks and smelled the scent of horse and a floral soap-scent in her hair. Natalie's face was still muffled in his shoulder but she began talking again, and her eagerness to fill him in on the day that they had been apart warmed his heart. If the children were always this happy to see him, then looking after them for a month or two should be the easiest part of this whole ordeal.

Rainere looked up when Adelena entered the stables with Benjamin, the children's horse instructor. Benjamin was watching Adelena from behind, as he prattled away at her. The cretin then had the audacity to smile and bow to Rainere and talk about Titor as if the horse was his. There was no doubt that Benjamin had the Blood in his veins for Titor to be able to tolerate him, but it didn't stop Rainere from wanting to disintegrate the young man where he stood.

"I will be sorry to see Titor go," Benjamin was saying. "I know he has taken a real shine to some of the fillies here, and there might even be a couple of his foals this time next year running about the stables." Benjamin gave Adelena a shit-eating grin that made Rainere want to raise a fist to it. "The mares just seem to come into heat whenever he is around. Another Marchant mystery, I suppose."

Adelena didn't deign to answer the filthy suggestion with a response except to roll her eyes. If he hadn't been holding Natalie in his arms, Rainere might have actually caused the bastard some serious damage, but instead he carried Princess Natalie out to the paddock so she could introduce him to her pony with the interesting name, Unicorn. Aaron chased them outside with his hands full of apple pieces to feed the ponies, and a couple of squires followed with brushes and combs in hand.

When the children had been led through the grooming and rubbing down of their animals, it was time for lunch, and the discussion that Rainere was dreading.

Mrs. Ollenby had been thoughtful enough to send down an enormous picnic to the quiet, wooded area beside the stables where an old tree trunk table and bench seating had been set up for just such a purpose. The benches were lined with velvet cushions, and the food was set out on china plates, but they were still eating outside and the children were more than happy to sit on the ground as they enjoyed the sandwiches and fruit tarts. After they had eaten, Adele took one of the tablecloths and spread it out like a blanket on the grass under a tree. The children and Adelena threw themselves down in a pile, but Rainere was unfamiliar with the protocol and sunk down on his heels to sit on the very edge of the cloth.

"Natalie and Aaron, I have got something really important to tell you," Adelena started, and Rainere felt his stomach clench. *What if the children screamed or cried, or were too terrified to be left with him?* Rainere held his breath, his gaze intent on the children as they listened to their mother.

"I have to go away on a long trip with General Ohrig and the Queen's Guard," said Adele and Rainere saw her face clench, as if she was trying not to cry. "But while I am away, I have asked Prince Rainere to stay at the Golden Palace with you. He is going to teach you lots of cool things, and you can teach him all your games," Adelena didn't stop talking though both the children had opened their mouths to speak. "Of course Ohren and Mrs. Ollenby will be here, and the nannies, but I thought it might be fun to have the prince here too."

"Where are you going?" asked Aaron, his hazel eyes wide and confused. "Why can't we come?"

"I have to go to the mountains, darling, far away from here." Adele smiled and stroked the hair off Aaron's forehead. "I need to find the medicine that will make Stella well again, and the only person who can help me is in those mountains, but I will be back to you as soon as I can be."

"If you are leaving us with Prince Rainere, does that mean we can go stay at the Grey Palace as well?" asked Natalie and her green eyes were shrewd as they examined her mother. "I mean, Mrs. Ollenby can come with us too, of course."

"I would prefer you to stay here at the Golden Palace, Natalie," Adelena said gently. "And Prince Rainere agrees with me."

"I would like a change," said Rainere, wanting to support Adelena. "I have lived in the Grey Palace my entire life and it will be nice to see more of Unisia."

"Do you want to sleep in my room?" asked Aaron.

"It's *our* room," added Natalie. "You would be too big for Stella's bed, but we can get you another one, if you like."

"I would like that, thank you, Princess Natalie." Rainere couldn't help but be touched by the little girl's regard for him.

"I don't want you to go, Mummy." Aaron climbed onto his mother's lap and snuggled into her chest. "I'm going to miss you too much."

"So will I," sighed Natalie, and climbed onto the other half of Adelena's lap, leaving Rainere to feel inexplicably lonely as the little family hugged each other in a tight bundle of love and slow tears. "Why can't we come with you, like we always do?"

"Because I have to move really fast so I can get back quickly," replied Adele and wiped at her tears with a serviette. "I can't take carriages and we'll have to sleep in tents with lots of bugs and beetles, so I don't think you'd like it much anyway. Besides, who is going to drive poor High Wizard Ohren crazy if you both aren't here to do it?"

"Will Stella be alright without you close by, Mummy?" Natalie's question made Adelena's eyes fill again, but she smiled regardless.

"That's why I want to leave Prince Rainere with you," said Adelena. "Because I know he can watch over Stella too. He has magic no one else does, not even High Wizard Ohren."

Natalie turned her bright green eyes to Rainere and he saw so much of her mother in that intense stare. "Because Prince Rainere is special," said Natalie but it was a statement and not a question.

Rainere caught Adelena's gaze over Natalie's dark head, and he saw the torment twisting in the shadows of her hazel eyes. He knew instinctively that Adelena didn't want to have to need him, and that she would give anything to stay with her children. Only desperation and courage could drive her so far away. Rainere felt the bond of his oath to guard Adelena's children sharpen its claws on his heart.

"Yes," agreed Adelena, finally. "Because Prince Rainere is special."

CHAPTER FIFTY-FOUR

"A Leaf in the Wind"

Charlie had followed his team of diggers around all day, but he'd kept his eyes wide open looking for a way out. The green team had been given the job of moving carts of the broken rock, and while it was tough work, at least it was outside in the fresh air and Charlie got to see more of the camp as he pushed the rocks from the entrance of the mine to one of three dump sites.

Charlie had to wait until lunchtime, when the sun was directly overhead and the workers had stopped to sit in clumps eating their dry bread and cold mush, before he got to see Rip again.

Rip was sitting in the middle of a group of young kids, playing a game and making them laugh. None of the kids could have been in the camp long enough if they still had the energy to laugh, or maybe Rip was just that funny.

Charlie sidled up to the little group under the pretext of fetching water from the barrel behind them. He hadn't realized he had gotten too close to the kids when one little girl looked up and caught his eye and the smile slid off her face. "Blue Jacket," she whispered and, in a flash, all of the kids had leapt up and run off in different directions.

"Do you often have that effect on children?" asked Rip pleasantly as he climbed to his feet and brushed the dust of his trousers. Rip nodded at Charlie's new vest and cocked his head to the side. "What'd you do to get that?"

Charlie shrugged. "Talked a kid into letting me borrow it for a while." He felt a little guilty under Rip's curious stare. "I'll give it back as soon as I find a way out of this dump."

"Good plan," Rip nodded. "And how're you going to do that, may I ask?"

Charlie looked about himself and frowned. "Maybe I'll get out through the forest. They have hardly any guards on the gate during the day."

"Because they don't need any guards." Rip rubbed the blonde bristles on his chin. "We are deep in the Dark Forest here, Charlie, and there are big, hungry creatures out there just waiting for a skinny meal such as yourself to come wandering in."

"You seen any with your own eyes?" Charlie asked, skeptical.

Rip pulled up the sleeve of his shirt to reveal four deep parallel scars running across his bicep. "Seen it, felt it, almost died."

Charlie winced in sympathy. "How'd you get away?"

"The Rangers were out hunting and I got caught in one of their traps. The creature only got my arm and then it couldn't jump high enough to finish the job." Rip grinned a hollow grin. "Getting put in this mine saved my life," Rip said, "yet now this mine is determined to work me to death. Life is ironic, isn't it?"

"Yeah, bloody ironic," said Charlie, not quite sure what that meant. "What are we even doing here, Rip? Why do they want us to dig up all this grey crystal for them?"

Rip cocked his head to the side as if surprised by Charlie's ignorance. "Grey crystal is a powerful conductor of dark magic and it can only be handled by those with Marchant blood in their veins. Once the crystals are dug up, they are imbued with magic by those with royal Marchant blood, they call them Specials. The grey crystal sucks the live magic right out of these Specials and stores it. Then the crystals are ground down and mixed in a solution to make it easier to inject into the body." Rip watched Charlie to see if he was catching on yet. When Charlie only stared silently back, Rip sighed. "It's all for the Gift of Life, Charlie. The immortal wizards need the Gift to help them stay strong, and when they are strong they stay in power."

Charlie was incredulous. "This whole camp is making this Gift for Prince Rainere Marchant?"

Rip smiled as if the comment was a joke. "Prince Rainere isn't the only immortal wizard in Evendaar, Charlie, and they *all* need the Gift. Every last one of them, Marchant and St Lucidis alike, but especially the Marchant Eldars. That's who the Church of the Goddess Serena is working for, and that's who protects this mine. It's been like that for the last thousand years, but soon there won't be any more Marchant bastards to bleed dry. It's the Church who started giving sacrifices to the Eldars too. Just to keep the particularly crazy ones happy and not hunting in the villages and towns like they used to. Causes too much chaos, you see?"

A loud bell rang out over the camp and all the workers began shuffling to their feet again.

"Am I going to be put out on the platform again tonight, Rip?" asked Charlie quickly, as he saw his group head over to the green flagpole and assemble for instructions.

"No, mate," said Rip confidently. "You're safe for tonight, unless someone tries to kill you for that shitty blue vest you're wearing." He ruffled Charlie's hair. "Just get through the afternoon, Charlie, one hour at a time. That's the only way to do it."

Charlie moved off when he heard his number called by the guard at the green flagpole. He followed Rip's advice and took the long afternoon one hour by the next, lifting heavy carts and shifting rocks as they were dumped out of the mine. He had so much to think about as he worked. The wicked work of the Church and the Gift, immortal wizards, and the evil behind it all – the dreaded Marchant Eldars. The queen needed to know it all and he had to get out of this shagging place alive to be able to tell her.

As the afternoon wore on into evening, Charlie's arms had reached breaking point and he stopped being able to think so clearly. On the very last cart, Charlie gave into fatigue and pushed a little green magic into his hands. The magic came thick and fast, stronger than he thought possible considering how tired and thirsty he was, and Charlie accidentally dumped over an entire wagon, when he'd only meant to tip it on its side. He quickly pulled his magic back inside but it was too late, a guard had seen the ruckus and come over to investigate.

"Stop where you are," the guard ordered and looked at the mess Charlie had made. The guard was tall and fit looking, but his face was old. The dust of the mine lined the wrinkles around his screwed-up eyes and his mouth was a hard line, but the look he gave Charlie was almost sympathetic. "No digger should have the magic to do that. You're a Special, in't cha?"

Charlie shook his head but a scream made them both turn around and watch as little Leafy was carried from behind the Key Master's hut on a crude stretcher. She was shrieking in agony and clutching her hands to her chest, sobbing. Carl burst out of the crowd and came running over to his sister, half-cradling her on her stretcher as she was dumped in front of the hut.

"What'll happen to her," asked Charlie, and looked for a shred of warmth or humanity from the adult guard.

"She'll be replaced," replied the guard. He turned back to Charlie. "But the good news is I've already found another one of ya."

"No," Charlie begged, suddenly panicked. "Don't do that, please, mate."

But the guard only looked tired and Charlie realized that any sympathy the man had was only for himself. "Have ta. You kids are all gonna die anyways, why d'you care which way you go?"

The sound of the end-of-day bell rang out over the camp and the workers slowly picked themselves up and headed off to return their tools and form a line for dinner. Without another word, the guard walked off in the direction of the Key Master's hut. Charlie stood as still as a statue. He already knew there was nowhere to run.

Chapter Fifty-Five

"A Prayer for The Condemned"

Not knowing what else to do, Charlie made for the dinner line. He hardly noticed as the other kids moved out of his way, so he had a clear view when the Key Master came out of his hut and descended the steps to where Leafy lay on her stretcher in the dust, her brother by her side, rubbing her back and talking non-stop. Mercifully, Leafy had stopped screaming but Charlie could still hear her whimpers, as she lay shivering and clasping her hands over and over again as if to stop them from flying away. *What the hell had those grey crystals done to such a strong little kid?* Charlie wondered.

The Key Master went down on one knee and grabbed Leafy by the chin, he held a short metal rod to her temple for a long moment, and then spat in disgust when the end only glowed green briefly.

"This one's used up," the Key Master shouted, and a group of Blue Jackets assembled close by to await his commands. "Take her to the first Offering Table."

"No!" Carl's shout was heart-breaking, and Charlie felt cold as if a bucket of water had been dumped over his head. "Please, she'll get better. Just give her time." Carl still held Leafy's hand as two Blue Jackets picked up the stretcher and carried her towards the path that led up to the offering tables outside the mine. Carl wouldn't let go, the tears streaming down his face as he begged for his little sister's life. The Key Master watched the drama unfold but only said something to the Blue Jacket next to him who noted it down on his slate board.

Charlie was starving but he had no appetite for the lumpy slop in his bowl. He didn't even have the heart to look for Rip, but instead sat on his own in the dirt then dragged himself to do his few small chores, washing his bowl and spoon, waiting for the moment that the

Key Master would call him forth and find him to be a Special, just like Pere Raven had said he was.

Charlie searched but he couldn't see the guard who had witnessed his magic anywhere. Sunk deep into his anxiety, Charlie jumped a mile when Rip caught him in a one-armed embrace. "Cheer up, Charlie, the work day's over. Let's head to the pub for a pint of cold."

Charlie couldn't even smile at the joke and his lips only trembled, betraying his fear. "They got me, Rip," he whispered. "One of the guards saw me tip over a heavy wagon, they think I'm a Special now."

Rip's face immediately lost all its humor and he frowned in concern. "Charlie, this is serious. What did you say to him? You had an excuse, right?"

Charlie shook his head. "I was too tired, I just used a little bit of magic and the whole thing went over. I couldn't help it, Rip. I just couldn't help it."

Rip gave Charlie's shoulders a squeeze. "Okay, alright, let's not panic," he said. "We can think of something, Charlie, I know we can."

There was a sudden shout from the Key Master and Charlie saw Carl being thrown to his knees in the dust before the Key Master. The boy's face was streaked with tears as he continued begging for his sister's life. A Blue Jacket held up a scroll and squinted at it before calling for silence. The entire camp went so quiet you could hear the creaking of the flagpoles in the wind.

"Offerings to the Eldar Marchants tonight will be as follows: Number 7109, Number 7226, Number 7227. May the Goddess bless you in her mercy. That is all."

Carl's head dropped and Charlie knew straight away that one of those numbers was his. Another girl stepped out from the crowd and stood next to the kneeling Carl. It was Maya, the girl from Charlie's work group. Her face was blank, and she quietly followed behind the Blue Jacket when he led her away.

This wasn't right! These kids were being slaughtered daily while the kingdom beyond the Dark Forest knew nothing about it. *This camp shouldn't even exist.* A fire kindled inside Charlie and burned away his fatigue. His magic hummed, giving him courage as he thought *what would Queen Adelena do right now?* Charlie already knew what she would do, and besides, he felt he owed Leafy for getting her captured. Leafy had trusted him, however stupidly, and he wanted to make good on his debt to her, even if he had to die to do it.

Charlie stepped forward and shook off Rip's warning hand on his arm. "Hey!" Charlie's shout got the attention of the Blue Jackets and the Key Master. "Leave Carl alone, ya cat-munchers, I'll go in his place."

The Blue Jackets all turned to the Key Master, who sucked on his teeth and spat. "Is that right, digger?" The Key Master's belly started shaking before Charlie could even tell that the braying noise he made was supposed to be laughter. "You wanna put your lily-arse out there again and give the old bastards another taste of ya?" The Blue Jackets began to chuckle sycophantically around their boss.

It gave Charlie the creeps to join in, but instead of fighting it he smiled too. "That's right, they've had enough of your old mum and wanted some fresh meat."

"Charlie, don't be an idiot." Rip's shocked whisper only reached Charlie's ears.

The Key Master stopped laughing. *That's done it,* thought Charlie with grim satisfaction.

"Put him on the first Offering Table with the little girl," the Key Master glowered at Charlie. "Let's see how clever you are when they come to take her away. I don't know how you got by them last night, but that girl will light you both up like a beacon."

Carl had been quiet up until now but at the mention of Leafy he leaped to his feet and started struggling against his guards. "No, don't take Leafy, I want to take her place," Carl shouted. "Send me and the digger out there."

"Leave 7226 and take 7228 instead," snarled the Key Master to the guards. "The big one'd only annoy them with his wailing, and I don't want the bastards coming down here to tell me how much, do I?"

Carl lunged at Charlie, surprising his guards for long enough that he broke free and managed to grab Charlie. "Don't let them put Leafy out there," Carl pleaded, desperate to save his sister. "She needs to be with me."

"I'll protect her, Carl," Charlie hissed back though Carl squeezed his shoulders painfully. "I'll get Leafy back to you."

Carl loosened his hold in surprise and the guards pulled him off Charlie. The two boys locked gazes and Carl's eyes were wide with fear and despair.

As Charlie was dragged away he tried to find Rip in the milling crowd, but instead he caught the eye of the guard who had caught him using magic. Charlie's bowels turned to water but the guard only shook his head and shrugged at him. Charlie had just proved the point that he didn't care which way he died, just as long as he died. The Blue Jackets wasted no time in taking him over and up the path to the tunnels leading to the Offering Platforms.

"Oh, and I was having such a bad day before you just pulled this stunt?" said one of the Blue Jackets, and Charlie looked up into the piggy eyes of the Big Grinner, who was carrying his left arm.

"Yep," replied the Skinny Grinner. "Couldn't happen to a nicer piece of catshit."

They both chuckled and Charlie stifled a groan. He had been feeling so righteous but now he knew he was going to get the stuffing beaten out of him before getting dumped out on the Offering Table.

The two grinning Blue Jackets let go of Charlie at the edge of the tunnel, and one watched him as the other dropped the rope ladder down to the platform. Charlie pushed himself to his feet warily, but the Big Grinner only nodded. "Give us your jacket and go then and be quick about it. We haven't had our dinner yet."

Charlie could hardly believe that these two weren't going to beat the crap out of him while he stripped off the threadbare vest and handed it over. Charlie could already hear Leafy weeping down on the ledge, and he overcame his caution of the Grinners enough to begin the climb down to the little girl. It was a different ledge to the one last night, and Charlie couldn't see any handy pile of boulders to hide behind. The evening sun was still bright out here in the open, even though it was already dark in the camp.

"Shake him off," suggested the skinny Blue Jacket. "We'll tell Rip he came to no harm before he died, but he's not really gonna know, is he?"

Charlie legged it down the rope ladder, skinning his shins before there was a powerful shake and he fell off onto the platform below. It was only a yard-high fall, but he hit his knee hard, and it didn't tickle. Charlie watched the rope ladder get pulled up again and heard the laughter of the two Blue Jackets. He waited until they were gone before he turned his attention to the small girl huddled on the ground by the edge.

At his touch, Leafy turned over. "Carl?"

"It's me, Leafy," said Charlie and tried to smile. "I saved Carl, and now we have to get you off this platform."

Leafy sniffed and sat up, curiosity overcoming her grief. "How we gonna do that?"

"We wait for, Rip," said Charlie with a surety he didn't really feel. "He'll come when the sun sets and hide us from the Eldars. He's got some special magic to do that."

"It's gold magic," sniffed Leafy. "I see it in him even when he tries to hide it. He's strong but I don't know why he's here, they don't need his magic for the mine."

"The Rangers brought him in," said Charlie. "Just like you and me." But he was puzzled too. Charlie hadn't even taken the time to wonder how Rip's gold magic could work in the mine.

"Look." Leafy pointed and Charlie followed her gaze. From here, they could see the other platform, and the figure of Maya standing on the edge.

"She's gonna jump," whispered Leafy. As soon as the words had left her mouth, they both watched the figure of Maya raise her arms to the sky and step off the ledge. Maya didn't make a sound as she fell and Charlie threw himself on his stomach and peered down into the valley, but the ground was so far below him, he couldn't see where she landed.

"That's one way out, I suppose," Charlie said dryly, but only because his brain was frozen in shock. He'd never seen anyone kill themselves before.

"Now there is only us left for the Eldars," said Leafy in a voice full of tears. "How we gonna hide now, Charlie?"

Charlie pulled the little girl into his arms and held her tight, feeling her heart pounding in her thin chest. "It's alright Leafy, Rip will be here soon. He'll get us out of here."

"Why?" mumbled Leafy, her face buried into his shoulder.

Charlie had seen too much of Rip's unprovoked kindness not to believe in it again. "He'll come," he said as he stroked Leafy's back. "He'll come, you'll see."

CHAPTER FIFTY-SIX

"Loyal to the Bitter End"

Grotto hunched in the corner of the bare cot, his knees high up under his chin and shivered. He fixed his gaze on the walls of his cell and watched the shadows gutter with the light of the green lamp he had been given. His eyes didn't need much light, but the lamp was a kind of company for him, and he let it rest.

Grotto looked to the ceiling of his cell. He could tell that twilight had fallen, as he felt it in the tides of magic that ran in his blood. The Goddess Lune would rise tonight, showing only half of her beautiful face to the world below, but he wouldn't get to see it.

Grotto hated being underground. The air felt stale and heavy here, and he was too far from the goddess who would listen to his prayers. The Moon Goddess, Lune, had always watched over her people. She wasn't strong like her sister Serena, the Goddess of Light, as she was only a servant to the other goddesses, but there was power in service, as Grotto well knew. A master depended on his servant to do what needed to be done, and to define his rule. In the end, a master couldn't live without a servant.

Grotto felt his ancient oath tighten around his heart like a metal band shrinking it. *No!* Grotto would not believe that he had failed Prince Rainere.

Grotto felt a wild howl of grief build in his chest, sucking in air and burning to be released. He rocked himself off the cot, his howl reverberating around his cell, over and over, bouncing off the walls and hurting his ears. Once started it wouldn't stop until the grief had worked itself out for another night.

The howl broke off into a weird high keening that scraped Grotto's throat as he collapsed back onto his cot. Pale green tears leaked out of his eyes and finally, his voice gave out and he was silent.

Grotto's screams had disturbed no one. The guards at his door were now hypnotized sentinels, and they wouldn't hear him. Gorrik had hidden him too well for anyone else to accidentally discover Grotto's presence in this deepest prison below the dungeons. Twilight had passed and night had fallen while he'd screamed. Grotto pulled his legs to his chest and shuffled back into the corner of his bare cot. *Maybe tonight the Eldars would come for Prince Rainere?* Grotto looked down at the amulet lying against his chest. He sent up a prayer to his Goddess Lune to watch over her fallen servant, and to watch over Prince Rainere Marchant, and roundly cursed the name of St Lucidis.

There was little else the loyal servant could do.

CHAPTER FIFTY-SEVEN

"Farewells"

Dawn was still a few hours away and Adele shivered in the dark of the mountain clearing. They stood at the bottom of a sheer cliff, surrounded by straggly trees, the ground littered with jagged boulders and rocks. The Queen's Guard had lit a few torches and had built a fire to ward off the chill but that only seemed to make the shadows about them dance more fiercely, and Adele felt very uneasy while she waited for Prince Rainere to create the portal for the journey through to the tundra.

Rainere had climbed up onto a high boulder and shucked off his cloak and jacket, his body outlined in a pale green glow as he sprinkled white and green powders on the ground while muttering a chant that made everyone's hair stand on end. Adele was always fascinated to watch Rainere at work and the Chime Voices in her head softly repeated the phrases he chanted, as if to memorize everything he said.

The portal was enormous. It stood twelve feet tall and was wide enough that they could ride three across on horseback. When it was dense enough to hold the familiar ellipse shape, Adele could see that the green magic Rainere was using was much darker than usual, and that green smoke gushed out of the bottom of the portal in clouds of smooth, billowing vapors. The metallic tang of dark magic filled the air and clung to the back of Adele's throat, reminding her of the danger of what they were doing here.

It was over an hour before Rainere had finished. Jumping down off his boulder, the prince wiped the sweat from his forehead with the back of his wrist and took a long slug of water. Though Rainere looked exhausted, he immediately began testing the seams of the portal for stability.

The men of her Queen's Guard had been keeping themselves busy preparing the horses and distributing the weight of their supplies as evenly as possible in preparation for their long, dangerous journey.

"All ready, Captain?" asked Adele as she made her way over and gave Captain Lucky a pat on his shoulder.

Captain Lucky turned and smiled at his queen. "We are as ready as we will ever be, Your Majesty." He ducked his head towards his horse. "Redfire will be happy to get some long strides in again. She got so used to the road to Sandar and back again, I think she misses it."

Adele laughed nervously. "Well, that makes one of us." She threw a sideways glance to make sure they could not be overheard. "And the men, are they ready for another journey, Lucky?"

"The men are prepared to serve their queen," said Lucky proudly, but then he dropped his chin and added in a low voice. "Bear and Owens are very eager to get on the road again, my queen, and they will help prop up Leith and Pepper's morale. The younger men are feeling a little nervous about what is ahead, but I'm sure they will overcome it."

General Ohrig approached Adele and Lucky where they whispered. The general's expression was grim. Gently, he laid a hand on Adele's shoulder. "Perhaps a few words for the men would be a good idea right now, Your Majesty."

Adele nodded and swallowed down on her dry throat as Ohrig called in the rest of the Queen's Guard, and they assembled around her. Prince Rainere stayed on the other side of the clearing, though he never took his eyes off Adelena.

"Men, I am glad that you spent last night with your loved ones," began Adele, and made sure to catch the gaze of each man. "I know you were not allowed to say your goodbyes because of the secrecy of our mission but let's now take a moment to pray to our gods to watch over us as we embark on this new journey. We have our strength and courage to guide us, but it won't hurt to ask for a little luck if the gods are listening."

The men formed a circle and linked arms with each other. Captain Lucky stood to one side of Adele and General Ohrig on the other so her arms were pulled a little awkwardly as they were both so much taller than her. Everyone bowed their heads and General Ohrig lead the prayer to the Goddess Serena asking that her might and mercy be granted to her loyal servants. The general was eloquent and Adele could feel the timbre in his words, as if it was an ancient sermon that had been repeated a thousand times before today. Her own prayer was to the God she knew on Earth, and was a much simpler *Ohplease-ohplease-ohplease, God, let me find the cure for Stella and help me come back to my babies alive. Ohplease-ohplease-ohplease.*

"In your light we live and into your Garden we shall fall. May the Goddess bless us all," Ohren finished and the last refrain was echoed by every man of her Queen's Guard.

Adele dropped her arms back to her sides and smiled. "May our gods have mercy on us all."

CHAPTER FIFTY-EIGHT

"His Heart's Blood"

Rainere was watching the men circle around Adelena, connected to her, as they prayed to the Goddess. She had her eyes closed, and he could see her hands perched on each shoulder of the two men next to her. Those delicate hands that he loved so much were touching other men. The sight of it made his blood simmer with a dark jealousy.

Rainere would never dare to tell Adelena what to do but he decided that his caution did not extend to the men of her guard. *How is Adelena supposed to see the error of her ways if she can find comfort in the arms of another man?* Rainere thought furiously. Adelena should be pining for him, as he did for her. This journey would be so long and they might be apart for weeks, or perhaps months. *Would Adelena, could she, replace his affections with one of the handsome men of her Queen's Guard?* Rainere knew how voracious Adelena's appetite was, and how keen her talents were.

The prince could only breathe again when he saw Adelena take her hands from General Ohrig and Captain Lucky's shoulders. He knew what he would do now, and the very moment presented itself when Adelena returned to her horse. Rainere approached the gathered group of Queen's Guards.

"Please remain a moment," said Rainere quietly, as the men automatically made to leave at his presence. Despite seeing his multitude of humiliations, and Adelena's public rejection of his love – still the men feared Rainere, and that pleased him.

"The road ahead of you all will be long and arduous and for that you have my sympathy, men of the Queen's Guard." Rainere kept his tone cold and quiet. "As you probably know, I would much prefer to be making this journey with you by the side of the queen, but that is not her wish, and so I will obediently remain behind."

Rainere examined the faces of the men around him, their expressions were frozen and gave away none of their emotions. "But I have my own request to make of you all, and I would like you to take it as seriously as any command from the queen herself. I would ask that none of you touch her. Ever. Queen Adelena and I share a fiercely powerful connection. If any of you lie with her, or touch your lips to her skin, or so much as hold her hand, I will know about it instantly, and you will have to answer to me on your return." Rainere let the rings of power dance and spin about his eyes as he glared at the men. To their credit, the guards' expressions hadn't changed one iota at hearing his threat.

"It is highly illegal to attempt to coerce the Queen's Guard to disobey her orders," intoned the general and Rainere almost admired Ohrig's spirit. "We will not disobey her in any case."

"I understand that, General," Rainere's voice grated over ice. "But I do not believe that she would order you to have sexual relations with her at any time, no? So your oath to her is not in question. What *I* am telling you is that: if you should voluntarily touch a hair on the queen's head, then I will know and I *will* gift you with a life worse than death on your return to Unisia. Do you understand?"

General Ohrig gave a stiff nod.

"Excellent," Rainere raised his voice to a normal level. "Then if the queen is ready, I shall open the portal to the Ice Mount—" But his words were cut off by the sound of an unholy scream far above them.

CHAPTER FIFTY-NINE

"Fly Away Home"

Leafy cuddled close to Charlie, and he was grateful for the warmth of her skinny, little body. It was freezing on the mountain ledge and both their teeth were chattering. Charlie was no judge of time, but he guessed by the way the moon was dropping that it was getting close to dawn.

Leafy was quiet now, but she had spent the early hours of the evening talking about the adventures she and her brother, Carl, had had in their tiny village. They were both orphans, and it sounded like they had lived at the mercy of anyone with the time and extra food to look after two lost kids. Leafy was happy as she was sure that Charlie had saved her brother's life today, and if she lost hers, then it was worth it. Before he had met Queen Adelena, Charlie wouldn't have been able to fathom that kind of love and loyalty, but it was as if a different room had opened up in his heart, and in that room was space for selflessness and hope.

Charlie ground his teeth to stop them chattering. *It's all very well to have an understanding of love and hope,* he thought to himself, bitterly. *It's just a damn shame it had to come just before I got eaten by an Eldar.* This was the voice in his head that Charlie normally listened to, but there was also the other voice, and this other voice was gobby and stupid, and Charlie supposed he could call it his conscience. It was this stupid voice that had him out on this ledge, on the edge of a mountain, waiting for the Eldars to arrive, if he didn't manage to freeze to death first.

Rip will come, the stupid voice assured him. *Rip will save you, and you will have saved Carl for Leafy. You aren't a saint but you did something right and that's got to count for something.*

Charlie studied the moon. She was only half a face and low in the sky. It would be dawn soon but not soon enough. Charlie sat in the dark and tried to count the stars to distract himself, but it was a fool's errand, and soon he was as cold as the ground he was sitting on.

It was almost a sick relief when, finally, a shriek rent the air and Charlie's head swiveled to watch the end of the valley where the call had travelled from. They were coming. The noise had sounded far away, but Charlie had no idea how quickly the Eldars could fly.

A sudden shower of tiny pebbles and dust on Charlie's head made him swear and flinch. His sudden movement woke Leafy, who got out of his lap, letting him get to his feet. Charlie watched as a dark figure made its way down the rope ladder. A puff of gold sparks was the dead giveaway that finally Rip had come to join them.

"Well, you took your bloody time," whispered Charlie angrily, as Rip made his way to the ground and pulled the rope ladder down after himself. "The Eldars are almost here. I heard them call."

Rip snorted, "That's gratitude!" he said. He made to pat Leafy on the head but she pulled away from his touch. "Hey there, darling, I'm not here to hurt you, I promise. I'm going to try to help, alright?"

"Get to it then," urged Charlie, and didn't bother to keep the panic out of his voice as another Eldar shriek echoed down the valley. "Do your magic net thing."

Rip's only answer was to put his hand on Charlie's shoulder and all at once Charlie understood. "You can only save one of us, right?"

"Mate, if you'd just kept your mouth shut and let Carl come out here with her, I would have saved Leafy for you anyway." In the dark, Rip sounded genuinely cut up about it. "But you are both too strong for me to cover with the net. There's no way I can do it."

"I wasn't trying to save Leafy, I knew you'd do that," Charlie said. "I wanted to save Carl for her. I owe Leafy 'coz I'm the bloody reason she was caught in the first place."

"Alright, I'll save her without you then," agreed Rip, a little heartlessly. "But stand away a bit would you, Charlie, your aura is going to send the magic crooked otherwise."

Charlie almost cursed his friend for being such a hard arse, but he went and stood on the edge of the mountain ledge. For one instant Charlie entertained the thought of stepping off and ending it all on his own terms, like Maya had. But he couldn't. Not just yet. Then another shriek echoed down the valley. It sounded closer this time but still, not too close. "Hey, Rip?"

"Give me a second, Charlie." Rip's voice sounded strained. "She's even stronger than she looks, I've got to adapt a bit here."

"Could you tell the queen I did my best, please?" asked Charlie. "Tell her Prince Rainere took her Fire Orchid stamens to the Eldars and tell her I'm - I'm sorry that I lied to her, and that I wanted to be a better man because of her. Can you tell her that, please?"

"As soon as I get my invitation to the Golden Palace, I promise I will deliver your message," replied Rip, his voice heavy with sarcasm. "Shut up, will you, Charlie?"

Charlie heard the distant sound of flapping and thought he could see a darker patch of shadow on the horizon. There was just one Eldar, but it was coming in fast. Charlie hoped his death wouldn't hurt too much as his bowels turned to water.

"Tell her I love her," whispered Charlie.

"Charlie, shut up." Rip's voice sounded muffled as if it came through a blanket.

The flapping was louder now, and Charlie could feel the breeze blowing back his long fringe. They had never cut his hair at the camp, and he wondered idly about that, as the Eldar came closer. He could already smell the cold metallic odor of dark magic that preceded the creature.

"Tell, her I was loyal to the end," whispered Charlie. "And that I died a hero. Please, Rip."

The Eldar landed on the far edge of the mountain ledge and its shriek solidified all the blood in Charlie's body. It stood tall, at least seven feet of well-dressed Marchant black. The Eldar looked like a man but it's face was like a mask, the luminous white skin stretched over sharply defined cheekbones and a long-pointed chin. The Eldar's eyes glowed silver in the dark and there was no other color, just the metallic pulse of magic and power.

Charlie stared at the creature as it stalked towards him. The cloak dragging heavily behind it, scraped at the rocks and dirt like it was made of something much stronger than fabric. The creature stretched out its long skeletal hands to Charlie and beckoned him closer, the eyes glowing brighter as its lips pulled up over long, sharp teeth.

Charlie hadn't been able to keep Princess Stella alive, but he could help Leafy. Charlie took strength from that and the freeze in his blood started to thaw. He thought of Adelena holding him up as he stood by her side facing down the Spider Empress Ka-kik. The queen had kept her cool and looked for opportunities when Charlie had only wanted to piss his pants and faint. The lesson remained. Charlie felt the fizz of magic in his hands and flexed his palms.

"No, I'm gonna help Charlie!" The little girl's shriek shocked the Eldar as Leafy barreled into Charlie from across the platform. She stood in front of him and bought both her hands up with two balls of green energy filling her palms. "You stay away from Charlie!" Leafy yelled at the Eldar and cast the two balls of light at its face. The balls of green magic hit the Eldar at the same time, and made it shriek and stagger under the impact.

Charlie held tight to Leafy's shoulders but he only had eyes for the Eldar as it wiped away the shreds of Leafy's magic harmlessly from its face.

"Ssssuch powerrrrr…" The Eldar's hiss was like a snake slithering over Charlie's skin.

Charlie heard Rip's swearing and out of the corner of his eye he saw a golden flash. Rip had destroyed his own invisible shield. Now they were three against one, and Charlie liked those odds. His pleasure made him snappy when Rip came into view again. "Seriously, Rip, you couldn't hold one little girl?" He risked a glance at his friend and saw Rip square up next to him.

"Fuck off, mate," murmured Rip. "You have put me in a very awkward position right now."

The Eldar turned from staring at Leafy at the sound of Rip's voice and its covetous glance became wide and confused. It hissed again, and Charlie realized it was talking. He felt Rip step right up behind him and risked asking him a question while keeping his eyes on the Eldar. "Rip, what's it saying?"

Rip sighed and Charlie didn't like the finality and sadness he heard in that simple sound. "Have you got a good grip on Leafy?" asked Rip, his voice low and his head bent down to Charlie's ears. "You have to hold her tight, alright, Charlie? And, you know what: say hi to your queen for me."

Charlie felt Rip's hands on his arms and almost jerked away from the heat he felt at the touch. "Rip, what are you…?"

"Good-bye, Charlie." With one almighty heave, Charlie was pulled off his feet and flung over the edge of the cliff, Leafy dangling in his hands.

Charlie felt as if they hung suspended in the air for a moment and he turned his head, horrified, to look at Rip. The Eldar shrieked as it lunged for Charlie, face contorted with anger, just as Rip threw himself in the way, taking out it's legs and landing with it on the ground. *Rip was trying to save them?* A surge of gratitude suffused Charlie just moments before gravity reached up and pulled him towards the ground.

CHAPTER SIXTY

"The Journey"

"What the hell was that?" Adele yelped, as her Queen's Guard formed a defensive circle around her. There was another soul-wrenching scream, and all eyes turned to the sky.

"I think it was an Eldar," whispered Rainere, his eyes wide with shock. A deep rumble of thunder echoed across the night sky.

"Where?" Adele felt a flash of fear that their journey would end here in the Dark Forest before it had even begun.

"Your Majesty, look!" shouted Captain Lucky and pointed to a glow high above them that was falling rapidly down the cliff face.

"Rainere, what is that?" Adele couldn't take her eyes off the glow as it became larger as it fell towards them. "Is it an Eldar?"

"No," said Rainere, mystified, "It's a body."

Adele looked up and felt the growl of her St Lucidis magic fire in her blood. Stepping in front of Rainere, Adele held out her hands and felt a rush of hot energy as the gold magic released a stream of sparks to catch the falling body. Adele felt the weight of the body as soon as her magic connected with it, and it was almost more than she could hold. Sweat sprung out on her forehead. "Sweet Christ, it's so heavy," Adele gasped and gritted her teeth. The Chime Voices sang their support but it felt to her like it was her gold magic itself that redoubled its strength and held the figure high above her in mid-air.

"Control your link, Adelena," Rainere cautioned her. "You've made it too strong, and you need to slowly lower it now."

Adele tried to do what Rainere suggested but the magic had a mind of its own, and once out in the air it was so hard to contain it again.

Her hands trembled and the sweat dripped into her eyes as Adele dropped the figure down to the ground in fits and starts.

Adele swayed on her feet as the gold magic detached from the dissipating cloud and whipped back into her body. She felt Rainere's arm curl around her shoulders and gratefully leaned into him, breathing hard.

"Adelena," said Rainere and gently shook her. "We should be far away from here if the Eldar comes looking for its prey." But Adelena wasn't listening to Rainere, instead she was staring in shock at the boy she had just saved.

"Charlie!" Adele threw herself down on her knees next to Charlie and grabbed his shoulders. She didn't want to believe that his blue lips and white face could mean that he was already dead. There was another little body by his side, but Adele couldn't tell if it was a boy or girl with its shorn head.

"Charlie, wake up!" Adele shouted and awkwardly pulled the boy onto her lap. "Charlie, come on, you have to wake up."

Charlie's lips moved slightly to emit a tiny moan, and his eyelids fluttered making her heart sing.

"Charlie, can you hear me?" Adele asked, relief creeping into her tone. "Sweet Christ, say something."

"Ya M'just-ee," mumbled Charlie and opened his eyes wide enough for her to see the muddy green of his irises bleeding into the whites of his eyes. "Ya cam fur me."

"Yes, Charlie." Adelena pulled Charlie to her chest and held him tight. His eyes had scared her. "I've come for you, and I'm taking you home now. Do you hear me, Charlie? I'm not losing you again."

Charlie closed his eyes again and sagged against Adele's leather jacket, "Knew ya would," he murmured, and then passed out cold.

"Rainere." Adele looked up at the prince as he stooped over her. "Charlie is burning up. Do you think it's the Summer Influenza?"

Rainere gave her a look she couldn't quite decipher. "No," he said. "He has the Waste, Adelena. It's an illness that consumes the body after performing advanced magic. You can see his pupils already dissolving without the silver rings to hold them together."

"What does he need?" asked Adele, and felt hot tears gather in her eyes. *No, not Charlie*, she wanted to scream. *Don't let this poor boy's death be on my head too.* "Tell me how we can make him better."

Rainere swallowed and looked pained. "The Gift will help him recover his physical strength, but his mind might already be too far gone to retrieve."

"We will try anyway," said Adele as she looked down onto Charlie's white face. "Take him back to the Golden Palace with you and look after him until my return. Give him this gift, or whatever it is." Adele's words were choked off by a sob as her tears dripped down onto Charlie's cheeks and sparkled there. "I cannot let Charlie die, Rainere. I promised him that I would look after him."

"Then perhaps you should stop making promises you cannot keep," suggested Rainere quietly, but the acid in his tone made her temper flare.

"I will not let this boy die when we both know that his death would be my fault," snapped Adele and struggled to her feet while still trying to hold onto Charlie. "He can answer to me for his lies when his life is safe again."

Rainere looked like he very much wanted to say something else but he held his tongue and the thunder growled again, closer this time.

"This other child is alive too, Your Majesty." Captain Lucky had taken the pulse and checked the eyes of the little figure lying on the ground next to Charlie. "I think it's a girl, and only very young, not much more than five or six, by my guess."

"Oh, the poor little thing," exclaimed Adele. "Let's get them both back to the Golden Palace, right now." She reached over and touched the little girl and felt a fizzle of energy against her palm, and an answering hiss of the magic in her own chest. Adele looked up at Rainere. "Rainere, I think this is another child like Charlie. I felt magic in her, and it's strong."

Rainere didn't answer but looked up the mountain wall to the sky. The wind whipped up in little eddies around the clearing. "Your Majesty, we should leave this place," he reminded her. "Now."

Captain Lucky and QG Owens picked up Charlie and the little girl and placed them on the back of Titor.

Adele followed Rainere to his horse. She didn't know when she would see him again, and she didn't want their last words to be an argument about Charlie.

"Rainere, I…" she began.

"Adelena, please if you don't go now you might not get another chance," said Rainere, cutting her off, and pointing at the enormous portal on the other side of the clearing. "I cannot promise you that the portal to the tundra will last much longer." He turned away, but Adelena put a hand on his arm.

"Thank you, Rainere." Adele squeezed his arm. "Thank you for everything you are doing for me, and everything that you've done. When I come back, perhaps we can talk again." She didn't need to say about what.

Rainere's lip curled. "If I do everything you ask, like a good little boy, then maybe I'll get you back in my arms again?" He looked down at her and Adele could see she had hurt his feelings. "I will do as you ask because my vow to care for your children is more powerful than any one of your promises to me, Adelena. So please don't try and bribe me with false hope, it insults us both."

"I'm sorry, Rainere," Adele's voice had dropped into a whisper. "But you have to understand that when I trust you to guard my children that makes you family, and Charlie and these men are my responsibility too."

"But you don't need to try so hard to prove you aren't a demon," said Rainere, his raspy voice sending chills over her skin. "It is enough just to be you, *cara mia*. Remember that."

Rainere gave Adele a sad little half smile before turning away and leaving through the smaller portal, taking Charlie and the little girl with him. Adelena stared into the swirling green magic as it faded and eventually disappeared, sucking into itself. Rainere was gone.

"Your Majesty?" Ohrig was at her shoulder. His gruff presence was a comfort after the confusion Rainere had stirred up inside her. Adele shook herself, wiping the drying tears from her eyes before she turned to her general.

The men of her Queen's Guard gathered around her and Adele could see the concern and anxiety on their faces as they readied themselves to face this new adventure by her side. Above them enormous clouds crashed and merged into each other, their insides lit by flashes of lightning.

"It's going to be a bad storm," she noted.

"It is," agreed General Ohrig, and gave Adele a grim smile, which she returned. "And it's going to be a hard ride ahead, Your Majesty."

Adele looked over at the mammoth swirling, portal that Rainere had constructed for them. Green sparks and flashes lit its dark depths and Adele almost laughed. "Isn't it always?"

Adele mounted up and turned her horse towards the portal and led her men forward, into the unknown.

TO BE CONTINUED…

BOOK FOUR – AN EXCERPT

"Sweet Deceit"

Lady Olivia gasped once more before she judged her ecstasy sufficiently faked. It did the trick, and Lord Orgustus finally rolled off her with a groan.

Orgustus lay onto his back, catching his breath, his cheeks still pink with his own climax, but already he was studying the ceiling with a look of distant concentration. Olivia was losing his attention as quickly as she'd had it.

Olivia pushed herself up on her elbow and pressed herself to the Lord's side. She ran her finger down the side of his face, adoring the curve of his cheeks and the strength of his square chin. She gazed at Orgustus's beautiful blue eyes, so bright and clear with the thinnest golden circle around the black pupil. His ancient magical heritage couldn't be more obvious. He was old blood and all the old money that went with it. Olivia sighed contentedly with her catch and leaned in to kiss his cheek.

Orgustus flinched from her touch. "Enough, Olivia," he commanded. "I told you I only had a little time for you tonight and now that time is done. I need you to leave me now, as I still have work to do."

Olivia pouted, but didn't give up so easily. "Why are you so grumpy tonight, Orgustus?" She loved the feel of his name in her mouth. It was so daringly familiar without the 'my Lord' in front of it, like it would be after they were married. Just the thought of Orgustus being well and truly hers made Olivia hot again. She pushed herself up to sit so he could get a better view of her chest and knew just what to say to capture his attention again.

"Queen Adelena doesn't need me until tomorrow morning." She smiled up at him from beneath her lashes. "I bet I could get you to forget your work for a little while longer."

Orgustus snarled, marring his good looks. "You know there is this little job called 'running the kingdom' and someone has to do it even though our queen seems too busy for the work. Where is she right now, do you know?"

Olivia ran her hand across his chest and played with the small patch of blonde hair there. She sighed inwardly and worked harder to put him in a better mood now that she had his attention again.

"I told you, she is at the Accadaemia with some history teacher researching cures for the Summer Influenza. I think her kids are with her too. Those little brats go everywhere with her." Olivia let her wandering hand move lower. "But not Stella of course, she is still locked in the hospital chamber. Only Mrs. Ollenby has the awful job of having to see to her."

"The baby hasn't died yet," mused Lord Orgustus curiously. "The babies in the city were dying left and right, and yet the queen's child clings to life. For some reason the queen tolerates the presence of the Marchant prince in the Golden Palace. Perhaps, he is helping her keep the child alive with his dark magic?"

"Well, you know what I think," said Olivia. "I think the queen and the prince are lovers. The way he looks at her, it is so obvious."

"But how do you know she returns his affections?" asked Orgustus sharply.

Olivia shrugged. "Because she changes the way she dresses when she knows he will be there, she wears perfume and she really cares what her make up looks like for once."

Olivia gave Orgustus a sidelong look before she delivered her final piece of information that she had been saving up for a special occasion. "And I saw them kissing at the Belvoir Estate. It was right after the ball for the prize winners, and it was dark but I saw them together, huddled in a tight corner. They kissed for ages and he clearly knew what to do with his hands, if you know what I mean." Olivia giggled but quietened at Orgustus's dark look. He liked his girls to be ladies.

"Did anyone else see them?" Orgustus asked.

Olivia shook her blonde tresses, curled just for Orgustus this evening. "Only me. I stayed until they stopped and the queen went back to her room."

"So she favors dark blood," mused Orgustus to himself. "Surely her Queen's Guard would know if there was a relationship there even if they are sworn to silence." He looked at Olivia with his eyebrow raised and a knowing smile on his lips. "I'm sure the good Captain Lucky would know everything about his precious queen."

Olivia wrinkled her nose at Orgustus's implication. "The captain is so boring," she whined. "All he ever wants to do is take walks in the garden and talk of his prospects in the Golden Palace, now that he has some actual hope for advancement with a queen to guard instead of just statues and hallways like before. He is too loyal to her and that general to be any help to us, Orgustus. Perhaps I should try with one of the other ones. Maybe QG Leith could be more help?"

But Orgustus was too clever for that, even though she kept her hand on his chest and her voice neutral.

His hand covered hers, gripping it. "Are you trying to make me jealous, my Lady?" He raised his eyes to her and gave Olivia the look she hated most. "Please use your brain, if you have one? What the hell would a lowly QG know that a Captain would not? Leith would be a waste of your time"- he eyed her breasts- "and your improving talents."

Olivia bit her lip. That last comment stung. She had never had a lover who had complained about her skills in bed before Orgustus. But Orgustus was a lord and ten years her senior, and he must have bedded hundreds of women so she would just have to work so much harder than all of the other women to keep him for herself.

"I didn't mean like that," Olivia said looking down, chastened. "I just meant that Leith is more susceptible to a little flirting and admiration. All the Queen's Guard's seem to be very tight. More often than not, all of the men are in the meetings with the queen, not just Lucky and the general, and they all seem to know what she is doing. Orgustus, if you had seen them coming back from the Grey Palace after the horse carnival you would know what I mean. The queen trusts them like she trusts no one else. I mean, I know she likes me but it's so hard to know what she is really thinking. And those eyes! Sometimes I think she can read my mind."

"*Sometimes you think she can read your mind!*" Orgustus's eyes widened and she didn't pick up he was making fun of her until he got out of bed, and backed away from her. "Goodness, Olivia, that is just so *spooky*. I wonder if this mind-reading-queen knows you are going to wear pink to the Court dinner tonight?"

Olivia fought not to roll her eyes. Orgustus really liked to labour a point when he had one but she didn't want to annoy him. Instead she pouted again and pushed her shoulders back to lift her best assets a little more.

"Orgustus, I only meant that the queen is very reserved. It's going to take a while to befriend her properly to get the sort of information you need."

Orgustus wrapped himself in a blue silk robe, an intricate golden lion embroidered on the back. It had been a gift from another lover and he knew that she knew it. "What I need, Olivia," he said, bringing her attention back to his point. "Is to have somebody on the inside of Queen Adelena's cortege and I thought that you were that someone. When you came to me, you said that you held the queen's confidence. Where is that confidence now, while half the kingdom dropped dead from the influenza and our queen is sneaking about the Palace with a Marchant prince?"

"I thought the Influenza was over now that the vaccines were given out," said Olivia quietly. She didn't want to make Orgustus any madder than he was but she did care about all the babies he constantly said were dying.

"They are, now!" He shouted. "But no thanks to *her*. I'm the one that saw their distribution to the city and into the villages. I'm the one who consoled the grieving families, and attended all the funerals. I'm the one who provided funding to our overrun hospices, out of my own pocket, using my own family funds. What has the queen done to help with the Influenza? Nothing, she hasn't even left the palace since she got back from Belvoir Estate and she cares for no one except her own child, who any fool could tell you is at death's door."

Orgustus's cheeks were flaming, and he stomped around the bedchamber, incensed by the trouble the queen was causing him. Olivia knew that her lord loved a silent audience for these little tantrums of his so she remained quiet and tried to look attentive to the drama, though she had already heard all of these complaints before.

Olivia sat up on her knees, naked, and clasped her hands in front of her chest, assuming what she hoped was a rapt expression. She waited for Orgustus to run himself out and catch sight of what she was offering him. Often his anger led to passion and Olivia wanted to please him with her body now that she had made him so frustrated with her lack of information for him. His eyes inevitably ran over her supple form and down to the blonde triangle of curls between her legs, and his complaints against the world petered out.

He approached the bed and stood in front of her, his robe open to show his broad chest and growing excitement. Pleased, Olivia, leaned forward to kiss her lord but he stepped back just in time. Only then did Olivia look up at his face and see the calculation turning his blue eyes to ice. He knew all her tricks already.

"Now, it's time for you to get your beautiful arse out of my bed, my Lady, I've got work to do." Orgustus gave her behind a sharp slap and moved away to dress.

Olivia bit her bottom lip as desire and disappointment clashed in an ugly mess in her gut. "Yes, my Lord, as you wish." She slid out of the bed, eyes downcast to hide her hurt, and collected her clothing strewn about the room. Orgustus left her there and went into the bathroom without another word.

Slipping the simple dress up over her shoulders, Olivia tied the laces as she left the room. Rushing along the candlelit corridors from Lord Orgustus palatial apartment and back to the servants dormitories, Lady Olivia almost made it to her room before the dry sob escaped her.

"Is that you, Livvie?" a sweet voice called from the bathing room, attached to the dormitory bedroom.

Olivia gulped down another sob and cleared her throat. "Yes, it's me," she answered in a voice passing for normal.

"We are in here braiding Petal's hair. Come in and tell us everything!" The demand was followed by the sound of giggling from her four dorm-mates. Olivia winced. Walking past the small mirror on the wall next to her bed she gave herself a cursory exam. Her lips were swollen from rough kisses and her eyes were still red from unshed tears. Olivia pinched her cheeks to put some colour in her wan complexion and plastered on her happiest smile. No one would notice if it didn't reach her eyes.

Entering the bathroom, she saw her roommates chatting and sharing a small slab of caramel fudge between them. Petal was the only one to give her a guilty look, and wiped her fingers on her nightdress. Olivia pinched off a sigh, if her chubby friend wanted to stay that way it was no skin off her nose. Petal was sitting on a small wooden stool as two of the other girls, Annelle and Daphne, braided her hair into intricate swirls on her head and another girl, Edith, pulled herself out of the bath.

"Well?" said Edith, the tallest and loudest, as she wrapped herself in a towel. "How is lover boy this evening?" The others giggled and looked on eagerly for the details.

Lady Olivia rolled her eyes and sighed hugely. "Well, you know... men."

"No," squealed Annelle. "We don't know any men. That's why we are asking you, Miss Lady Love."

"Well, he would like to be my lover." Olivia winked at her audience. "But I make it very clear every time that I will only kiss him. If he wants anything else from this lady then he will have to ask for my hand in marriage."

All the girls gasped in awe at their friend's dignity and confidence.

Olivia shrugged nonchalantly out of her dress and slipped into the still warm bath, letting the soapy water wash the masculine scent of Orgustus off her skin. *Not that any of these innocent, little rich girls would know what sex smelled like,* Olivia thought bitterly.

"You are so right, Livvie," agreed Annelle eyeing Olivia's well-formed, womanly body. "But how do you get him to ask your parents' permission and give you a ring?"

Olivia opened her eyes in pretend surprise. "How do I get him to stop trying is more the question, Annelle! I spent an hour alone trying to talk him out of writing to my parents this very night. I mean he is such a handsome man, a wonderful kisser "– this caused more excited giggling amongst her dorm mates- "and the Captain of the Queen's Guard at that, but I'm not sure I want to settle down right now. I'm only nineteen years old and the queen's closest friend. Who knows what gentlemen will present themselves before me in the next year or so. Of course, I want to be married by twenty-one at the latest, but there is plenty of time before I need to decide on who."

The four girls sighed with envy at Olivia's romantic life.

"If only I had your luck with men, Livvie," said Petal sadly. "I can't even get that Belvoir stablehand, Benjamin, to look at me, and he is said to have been with all the queen's nannies. And he isn't even a real catch like your Captain Lucky."

Lady Olivia smiled and stretched a long leg out of the bath just to look at how fine it was, her perfectly white skin and those long muscles, so much less defined now that she didn't have to work on the farm anymore.

"Not everyone can have a captain," she agreed condescendingly, but in her head she thought of Lord Orgustus. "But you know, girls, any boyfriend is hard work, whether he is a royal or a servant. You must always keep them wanting more of you, and let them make all the promises. As adorable as I think that Captain Lucky is, I would never put myself at his mercy without a heavy gold ring on this finger." She raised her left hand to illustrate the point.

Annelle giggled as she tied off another of Petal's braids. "I bet the wedding night will be some fun though!"

Olivia smiled and looked down as an honest flush crept up her cheeks as she remembered what she had just let Orgustus do to her not even an hour ago. It had almost hurt, and he hadn't even tried to make her feel good like the boys back home always had.

"Oooh, look at that blush!" smirked Edith. "I bet a girl would wake up pregnant the morning after a roll with Captain Lucky-pants!"

Edith's cackle stirred Olivia out of her reverie. Edith was getting slightly too big for her boots lately and needed to be taken down a peg. "Don't be so crude, Edith," Olivia snapped. "A lady doesn't think things like that."

Edith sniffed at the rebuke but Petal, Annelle and the shy Daphne, looked on in admiration.

"Well, I think it would be wonderful to have such a fine man in love with me," sighed Petal and reached for the block of fudge again.

"Yes," agreed Lady Olivia, suddenly too exhausted for words as she lay back in the water and watched the soap bubbles swirl and jostle each other. "Yes, I imagine it would."

ACKNOWLEDGEMENTS

This book is born.

Finally.

At times I didn't think it would ever be complete, but here it stands and for that I must thank a list of people. First and foremost, my dear beloved Reader, thank you. Without the support of your kind encouragement and cheerful words of praise, I might have lost heart so many times. You, the lovely people who follow my tiny wee FaceBook blog, and reply to me, or give me a little cheer every time I write you a letter – to all of you, I say thank you, a thousand times thank you. I have a delightful assortment of friends and family in my life who have supported the author if not the book, which I refused to show anyone until complete. For your forebearance and good humour, thank you so very much. I searched the world for editors for this fickle manuscript and had the very good fortune to be graced with the help of the wonderful Monica Hall yet again. Her intelligent critique and hard questions made this book be the story I wanted it to be. Thank you to the dear Mr D. Gorny, whose thorough and relentless examination of every word and phrase made this book a terror to revise, yet the challenge was welcome, and I have learnt so very much. If there are any errors to be discovered it will not be because of Mr D. Gorny, but the author's own fault. The delightful Anastasia Ward, who created the artwork for this third book in the series, an enormous and heart felt thank you. You are an incredible artist and I'm grateful as always to work with you. To my family, again and as always, you are my eternal font of inspiration and for that, I thank you.

To find out more about the author A.R. Winterstaar or the World of Evendaar please visit:

www.evendaar.com

A. R. Winterstaar on Facebook